Fat Kid Stuck in a Flume

By

Ian Edwards

&

Paul V

This book is dedicated to anyone who has made us laugh. And quite a few who haven't.

Table of Contents

Contents

Prologue 7

Chapter 1 11

Chapter 2 15

Chapter 3 18

Chapter 4 24

Chapter 5 27

Chapter 6 30

Chapter 7 37

Chapter 8 45

Chapter 9 47

Chapter 10 57

Chapter 11 65

Chapter 12 71

Chapter 13 75

Chapter 14 88

Chapter 15 93

Chapter 16 100

Chapter 17 112

Chapter 18 127

Chapter 19 133

Chapter 20 143

Chapter 21 160

Chapter 22 178

Chapter 23 193

Chapter 24..199

Chapter 25..209

Chapter 26..220

Chapter 27..242

Chapter 28..256

Chapter 29..267

Chapter 30..270

Chapter 31..291

Chapter 32..308

Chapter 33..326

Chapter 34..334

Chapter 35..349

Chapter 36..376

Chapter 37..382

Chapter 38..393

Chapter 39..401

Chapter 40..416

Epilogue..428

March 2nd 1982

The corridor was in chaos. Nobody knew what was happening. An ambulance crew marched through the stage door, pushing their way through the crowded mass of people and into the area where the dressing rooms were located.

The theatre manager, Trevor Ironhead stood at the doorway of the corridor that led to the changing rooms, only giving access to those he said were needed. He refused to answer any questions about what was happening and said simply that he would explain the situation as soon as he could.

In the absence of any evidence to the contrary, the human mind will fill in the gaps with anything even vaguely plausible and this was no exception. Theories circulating the crowd included; somebody had died; there had been an argument; a clash of two giant egos and someone had been hurt; a lighting rig had collapsed; or there had been an outbreak of food poisoning from a tray of suspicious looking quiche.

The only group of people who were untouched by the fever of speculation were those in the auditorium itself - the audience and the comedian on stage. They had no idea they were now united in a common bond. They were members of an exclusive club, a club that could genuinely say they were the last people to see Frankie Fortune perform.

The audience, blissfully unaware that they were all members of this exclusive club, briefly paused in their laughter when the Public Address system announced;

'Is there a Doctor in the house?'

The comedian on stage improvised a joke about hearing a TARDIS, and he was awarded with his biggest laugh of the night. The swiftness of the comedian's response was such that the audience were convinced that it was part of his routine.

By luck rather than design there had indeed been a Doctor in the house. As the audience had entered the theatre that evening they would have seen several men in six foot chicken costumes giving out flyers for a forthcoming play entitled 'Chicken Soup.' One of the chickens was by day (or night subject to shift) a Doctor and was quickly led down to the dressing rooms to the stricken performer, where he began to administer CPR.

On entering the dressing room, the ambulance crew were greeted by the sight of a man in a chicken suit straddling another man lying on the floor, apparently beating him to death.

'Is that chicken trying to hatch that man?' the first ambulance man said.

'Be careful where you step!' said the other ambulance man, 'there may be bits of broken shell around.'

The easy camaraderie between the ambulance men soon relaxed those in the dressing room. It was an act they had perfected over many years serving together and would eventually lead to a short-lived side career as a comedy double act after Trevor Ironhead booked them for a support slot on an open mic night.

Despite the presence of the ambulance men, it was the chicken, known by day as Dr Philip Weston, who declared the man was dead. The room fell into silence, the only sound being the rustling of artificial feathers as he stood up and stepped away from the body.

Trevor Ironhead pushed his way into the dressing room through the crowd of those who thought that they could help; theatre employees with a raft of skills from selling nuts, ice creams and programmes, to hanging coats on hooks and pouring drinks in the bar. He looked at the Doctor who shook his head. At least that was what Trevor assumed he had done as the chicken's head had fallen over his face and all that could be seen was a beak swaying slowly from side to side.

One of the barmen stepped forward and placed a towel over the man. Unfortunately it was a bar towel and it simply covered his face. Trevor made a mental note to dock the cost of the towel from the man's wages.

One of the ambulance men left the dressing room while the other sneezed. 'Sorry,' he apologised, 'it's the feathers. They make me sneeze,' he added blowing his nose into a handkerchief.

Trevor expected that the news would spread through the theatre like wild fire. By the time people started leaving the theatre they would know that Frankie Fortune was dead.

Frankie had died on a typically gloomy Tuesday night in March. He had died in a dressing room surrounded by two wisecracking ambulance men, one of whom had an allergy to the synthetic feathers worn by an off duty Doctor wearing a chicken costume, who had attempted to save his life by straddling him and hitting him on the chest. On being pronounced dead, Frankie Fortune was covered by an alcohol sodden bar towel that promised drinkers "Double Diamond works wonders."

Later, when asked, friends commented that it was what he would have wanted.

Chapter 1

'Thank you guys, you've been brilliant – see you soon.'

Polite applause accompanied Alan Rose as he walked off stage. The applause was courteous and thoughtful. This would have been perfect if he had been giving a talk on the advantages of plasticine adhesive over drawing pins to a convention of stationery buyers, but a bit disappointing for a stand-up comedian who has just delivered a twenty minute routine to a student union. Students should be loud and abusive, Alan thought. He had even tested them with a couple of comments about fallen 1970s celebrities, but even that had not provoked anything more than a solitary heckler. Maybe students have changed since his day. Perhaps, he thought, it's a reaction to an impending lifetime of debt associated with student loans.

As Alan left the stage he heard the host announce the main act. A comedian who had some panel show appearances to his name, and by working five nights a week could earn enough to live on for a year.

Alan made his way round to the back of the stage and was confronted by Sarah Gayle, the event manager, clipboard in one hand and mobile phone in the other. Sarah had shoulder length black hair framing an attractive face, soft olive skin and light brown eyes that hinted of the exotic and mysterious. Alan knew that a number of comedians would turn out to events that she organised simply because they fancied her.

'How did it go?' she asked.

'It was OK, could have gone better. I'm not sure that I hit the spot.'

'You got a better response than the guy who was here last week.'

That caught Alan's attention. 'Who was that?'

'I don't know,' Sarah replied helpfully.

'Oh... I'll tell my mum,' Alan replied, 'she's a massive fan of his.'

The comment washed over Sarah in a depressingly familiar way. Alan was constantly amazed at how often event managers at comedy clubs appeared to lack even a fundamental grasp of sarcasm.

'Are you sticking around for a drink?' Sarah asked.

'No, not tonight, I've got work in the morning. Big meeting about stationery. Though I don't expect any movement.' Alan smiled, hoping Sarah would acknowledge his weak pun. On not receiving any acknowledgement, Alan sighed and turned to leave.

'OK, in that case...' Sarah said, pulling a sheet of A4 paper from her clipboard and passing it to Alan. It was a flyer advertising:

'A 24 hour stand-up marathon fund raiser for the Merton Palace Theatre'

Sarah helpfully attempted to fill in the blanks. 'The idea is that comedians are performing all day from six at night through to 6pm the following day. People can buy tickets for the whole twenty four hours, or twelve hours or two hours, depending on what suits them. Do you know the Merton Palace Theatre?'

Alan looked into Sarah's eyes. She was clearly enthusiastic about the project and, if he was honest it seemed like a good idea. 'I know the Merton Palace Theatre,' he said, 'and yes, I'd like two tickets please.'

'No, no, I meant would you be interested in being one of the comedians?'

'Well I'm interested in being *a* comedian. It's kind of why I turn up to events like this. So I can earn enough money so I don't have to turn up to events like this anymore.'

Sarah's eyes widened and Alan thought he'd gone too far. 'Oh, I get it. Very good.'

'Thank you.' Alan replied. 'My jokes are so sophisticated it usually takes five or so minutes for them to sink in. Just listen to the laughter now.' Alan gestured to the stage. 'They've all just got my joke about celebrity perverts.'

'I think they might be laughing at the comedian on stage, Alan.' Sarah replied, innocently.

Alan sighed. This was pointless. 'Yeah, you could be right. Listen, email me the details of the event and I'll get back to you.'

'That'll be great, see you soon,' she replied.

Alan said goodbye and made his way to the dressing room. A room had been set aside for the performers. On the door was a note which simply said "Performers Dressing Room." Alan pushed the door open and walked in. Although described as a "dressing room," it was in reality a small stockroom with shelving on two walls and a table which had been pushed against a further wall to create an illusion of space.

Picking up his bag from the floor, Alan felt a slight chill across his shoulders. He looked around for an open window. Not seeing one he left the room. As the door closed behind him a breeze swept across the room blowing several sheets of paper off the table. The papers glided gently round the room before coming to rest face up on the floor;

24 HOUR STAND-UP COMEDY
MARATHON
IN AID OF THE MERTON PALACE
THEATRE RESTORATION FUND.

Chapter 2

Comedy doesn't pay, according to those who know. This included Alan's girlfriend Rosie, who doesn't actually know, but has an opinion that she is more than happy to share with Alan, or indeed anyone that will listen. At just under five foot five, Rosie Talbot was several inches smaller than Alan, though she more than made up for her lack of height with her quick temper and no-nonsense attitude.

'Comedy doesn't pay,' said Rosie, staring over the breakfast table at Alan, who was busy reading the back of a cereal packet.

'I think you mean crime. I got paid twenty five quid last night,' Alan replied, not looking up from the cereal box. 'It paid for this cereal. And the milk. And my bus fare home. Which was a bonus. I'd planned on walking.'

'For God's sake, you don't take anything seriously,' Rosie replied, running her hand through her brown hair.

'Exactly.' Alan said, putting aside the cereal box and scooping a large spoonful of cereal into his mouth.

'Alan, I don't want to be funny...'

'No danger there...'

'...shut up and listen to me. I can't carry on like this. You treat everything as a joke. Me, us, our relationship. Your career, my career.'

'Well excuse me if I find the idea of you taking pictures of things stuck up people's bottoms rather amusing.'

'I do NOT take pictures of people's bottoms. I'm a radiographer, not a photographer.'

'Like there's a difference...'

'Of course there's a difference...Look, Alan, you know I love you, but you need to start focusing on your real job. I just don't think you're cut out for a career in comedy. To be really successful you have to be...'

'What?'

'Well, you have to be funny.'

'You don't think I'm funny?' Alan replied, frowning at his girlfriend.

'Well, yes, I think you're funny. Just not comedian funny.'

'What does that mean? Not comedian funny?'

'Well, your jokes aren't...well...they're not funny.'

'Hang on, so all the times you've laughed at my routines, you been *faking it..?*'

'I just didn't want you to get upset.'

'Upset? You've basically told me you've been lying to me all this time. I mean, you can insult a man's driving, you can fake an orgasm, but tell a man he's not funny? That's a low blow. Like oral sex with a midget.'

Rosie frowned. 'This is exactly what I mean. I'm trying to have a serious conversation and all you can do is make jokes.'

'So you admit that's funny?' he asked, grinning.

'It's not funny, it's offensive, and you're doing it again. You're trying to not have a serious conversation.'

'OK. OK. I'm sorry. Now, which bit did you find offensive. Was it the blow job or the midget?'

'Oh, just go to work.' Rosie got up from the table and made her way over to the sink, her back turned to the room. 'Just don't expect me to be here when you get back.'

'OK. But that might be because you have your own flat.'

'Alan...just...just leave, will you?'

'I'm going, I'm going.' Alan said and moved toward Rosie, putting his arms around her, nuzzling the back of her neck. 'It was the midget, wasn't it?'

Alan sat at his desk pondering this morning's latest argument. It was a recurring theme. And one he was beginning to tire of, but he had no time to dwell on his fading relationship. Graham, his overbearing boss was heading his way.

Alan had taken a temporary job at the Civil Service five years ago and had accidently been made permanent two years later. It wasn't in the game plan. The plan had been to take a temporary job for a few months until he became a famous comedian. However, being a barely capable administrative officer in a Government Department had proved a lot easier than forging a successful comedy career. Not least because it appeared all you needed to be successful in the public sector was to talk a lot without actually saying anything. And to wear a tie.

Graham's tie this morning reflected his character; grey, stained and utterly uninspiring. As Graham leaned over, Alan had the urge to pull on the dangling tie and bash Graham's head onto the desk. He refrained. Not because he feared the sack, but because he couldn't be certain that Graham wasn't wearing a clip on tie for that very reason. It would be just like him to have prepared for every eventuality.

'Can I help?' asked Alan. It seemed the least offensive thing to say to someone hunched over his desk, encroaching on his personal space.

'Have you done that copying I asked you to do?'

Alan had indeed done the photocopying, but there was little fun to be had in simply saying so. 'Oh, what copying was this again?'

'The copying I asked you to do yesterday. For the meeting. With the Minister.'

'We're meeting the Minister?' asked Alan innocently.

'Not us, me. I'm meeting the Minister. And in about half an hour.'

'Blimey, you should get ready. It won't do to be under prepared.' Alan turned on his most charming smile. 'I'm sure the Right Honourable Bell End will want to discuss the latest figures.'

'What did you just say?' Graham asked, frowning, voice raised.

'The Right Honourable Bellem.' Alan replied innocently.

Herbert Bellem was the Secretary of State for Industry. An uninspiring career in the carpet industry had preceded an uninspiring political career in a safe seat that many thought could be won by placing a coloured rosette on a turd. Many more people thought this had actually happened, such was Bellem's lack of charisma. However, this lack of charisma, and, some would say, lack of talent, had led to his rapid rise up the political ladder. After all, a dullard with no skeletons in the closet is unlikely to cause the party embarrassment. Sadly, for Herbert Bellem, and his Party, his lack of personality and knack of saying the wrong thing at exactly the worst possible moment had led to one of the tabloids dubbing him 'Herbert Bell End.'

'Right. Yes. Well then...' Graham said. 'Have you done the copying or not?'

'Photocopying?' Alan answered.

'Yes. The photocopying.'

'Hang on. What's the copying for?' Alan could tell Graham was getting agitated, but this was too much fun.

Graham raised his voice again. 'Copying. For the Minister. My meeting with the Minister.'

'And that's this morning?' Alan replied. 'Blimey. You should have said.'

This was almost too much for Graham. 'I *f*...I did ask you. By email.'

'Oh, that.' Alan said 'I did that last night. It's on your desk.'

'It's most certainly not on my desk. If it was on my desk I wouldn't have asked you for it.'
'*We-ll*...' said Alan, leaning his head to the side to suggest he didn't necessarily agree.

'So, where is it?' Graham was almost shouting.

'I definitely left it on your desk.'

'Are you sure it was the right desk?' Graham's increasing anger was getting the better of him.

'I think so.' Alan replied. There was a photo of you and your dad on it.'

'My dad?' Graham looked confused for a moment before realising, 'that's my wife you...' Unable to contain his anger, Graham stood and strode purposefully back to his own desk.

'You shouldn't take the mickey like that,' said Sue, who sat next to Alan. 'You know he hasn't got a sense of humour.'

'Come on, Sue. Have you seen his missus? She looks like a chimpanzee. There's no way you could keep a straight face watching her lope down the aisle on all fours. I'm sure I've seen her on an advert for tea moving a piano up a flight of stairs.'

Sue let out an involuntary snort. 'You can't say that.'

'Oh come on Sue. You and I both know Graham's missus can peel bananas with her feet.'

*

Lunchtime. Management baiting aside, this was Alan's favourite part of the workday. A time to wander the streets of Victoria, mentally working through his routine to make it word perfect, thinking of the right moment to pause to let the successful jokes resonate with the audience, whilst removing those jokes that didn't work so well.

This was a major irritation to Alan. He had some jokes he thought were excellent but simply never got a laugh. All that time and effort carefully crafting a sentence to perfection. Nothing. Yet audiences seemed to laugh most at the stuff he had improvised his way through. Alan knew that improvising was a real art form in and of itself and not something most comedians could pull off, as much as they liked audiences to believe their carefully scripted gags were made up on the spot. Most great gags, Alan knew, grew out of a chance moment or saying which was then moulded to gain the best laugh.

Alan entered the local supermarket looking for a sandwich that would both fill a hole in his empty stomach and provide sufficient odour to annoy those working closest to him. It was, after all, the tiny little victories that made the day go that much faster.

The sandwich section was located at the end of an aisle. The choices were uninspiring to say the least, and vastly overpriced for what was effectively a bit of tinned tuna spread between two slices of bread.

Alan scoured the shelves for something, anything that was even slightly interesting, but being a creature of habit, he reached for the pre-packaged tuna sandwich. As he did so he felt a chill and the presence of someone standing next to him. Probably struggling with the same decisions, Alan thought.

'It's changed a lot since my day.'

Alan turned to his left to reply, but only the chill remained. That's odd, he thought. The guy must have wandered off. Alan turned full circle, looking for where the man might have gone, but it was impossible to tell who in the crowded supermarket had spoken to him. He's probably in a different aisle, looking for a better choice of lunch, Alan mused.

As Alan straightened up, he felt a slight breeze tickle the back of his neck. He turned full circle again. Still nobody there. I must be imagining it, he thought as he made his way to the self-service tills.

Alan always felt like a working class traitor when using the self service area. It was clearly a ploy to cut costs and reduce staff. What next, he thought, would people have to drive their own trains to work..? That's quite good, he thought. I could work that into the routine somewhere. Alan placed his tuna sandwich into a carrier bag whilst absent-mindedly creating a line about the least probable self service areas and wandered back to work.

Chapter 4

Despite Alan's assurance to Sarah that he knew the place, his knowledge of the Merton Palace Theatre was limited to knowing that it was a derelict eyesore round the back of the High Street which hadn't been used properly for years. As a result, once Alan had received the invitation, he relied on the internet to fill in the blank spots in his knowledge. According to the *History of Theatres* website;

The Merton Palace Theatre was built in 1910. It was modelled on the famous theatres of London's west end, only smaller. The designers wanting to offer the fast growing town of Wimbledon an alternative to journeying into the West End for live entertainment. In its early days it was considered a commercial success, and latterly, despite the dwindling interest in music hall acts, it became a popular venue for bands and comedians throughout the 1970s.

By the late 70s the building was in a poor state of repair, and once the accountants had worked out that it was not financially viable to keep the venue open it was closed down. The Merton Palace Theatre closed its doors for the last time on the 1st June 1983.

A group calling themselves the '"friends of the Palace Theatre" raised significant funds from other interested parties and reopened the theatre in 1989. It hosted occasional events but was predominately used for workshop theatre groups. It is understood that plans are underway to reopen the Theatre and restore it to its former state. A lottery grant has been sought and fund raising events are planned.

Alan opened his e-mail account and sent the Arts Group a quick e-mail confirming that he was available and happy to perform at the fund raiser.

'Is it safe?' Rosie asked.

Alan didn't bother looking around. He was used to Rosie moving around the house without making noise. She would suddenly appear at his side without any prior warning, and even creaking floorboards which would announce his return home in the early hours of the morning made no sound as she moved through the house. It was some comfort that in the event of impending financial doom Alan considered that he could persuade Rosie to become a cat burglar.

'Is what safe?' Alan replied.

'The Theatre. It hasn't been used for years, and when it was last used they wouldn't have had anything like health and safety,' Rosie frowned, looking over Alan's shoulder at the screen.

'No it's fine. The owners and the theatre group have been keeping the place maintained over the years. I think the capacity will probably be down, but it'll be safe, probably. Are you coming?'

'I might do, I'll see if Jayne's interested.'

Jayne was Rosie's older sister and had been a police officer for several years. She had a similar sense of humour to Rosie, which Alan defined as in fact having no sense of humour at all.

'Well, give it some thought and let me know so I can arrange some tickets,' Alan said.

'OK. I'll speak to Jayne and let you know,' Rosie said before moving quietly away.

Chapter 5

Alan opened his eyes and stared at the alarm clock. The green numbers glowing eerily in the darkness told him it was 3.55am. Another three hours sleep. Slightly more if he chose to avoid breakfast. He looked up at the ceiling, letting random thoughts run through his mind. He was alone in bed, Rosie was working a night shift at the hospital, so at least he wouldn't have to pretend to be interested in conversation when he got up.

He rolled over attempting sleep, but the familiar feeling of pressure in his bladder told him he needed the toilet. He considered for a moment whether he could sleep through it, but quickly decided that was not an option.

Alan slipped out from under the duvet and padded off the bathroom. As he passed the bedroom window something made him glance outside into the street below. Standing outside on the pavement, looking up at the house was a figure of a man. Alan stared, waiting for his eyes to adjust to the dark. As they did so, the figure slowly faded away. Alan instantly dismissed the experience as somebody else's problem and continued on to the toilet.

*

Alan gave his weird toilet experience no thought whatsoever during the day, and only mentioned it to Rosie in passing, when they were out for a meal that evening.

'A person? A man, a woman?' she asked.

'I don't know. I couldn't make them out. It was dark and I had to go the toilet, badly as it happened.'

'Well I think that's weird. I mean, who stands outside someone's house at three in the morning?'

'He could have been waiting for a bus,' Alan suggested.

'Alan, buses don't run down our road.'

'Maybe they realised that and walked off,' Alan said, hoping that his application of logic would end the conversation.

'How can you be so laid back about this? It's weird and a little bit scary,' Rosie said between mouthfuls.

'Maybe I've got a stalker.'

'What kind of person would want to stalk you? People can't be bothered to see your act, why on earth would they hang around outside your house at three in the morning?'

'A shy one?' Alan said.

'You really shouldn't joke about this. Some stalkers are quite dangerous.'

Alan's mind had already wandered. He had no desire to continue the conversation and he regretted telling her. His attention was drawn to a couple sitting behind Rosie who had spent the meal laughing together and sharing their food. If Rosie attempted to take any of his food he'd spear her with his fork.

'Shall I stay at yours tonight?' he asked. 'Just in case he comes back.'

'So you think it's a "he" now?' Rosie said.

'Good point. Might be a she.... I'll stay at mine.'

'No!' Rosie replied. 'You had better come back with me.'

*

Alan stood in Rosie's kitchen making coffee. Rosie in her usual stealthy way appeared in the doorway. 'The theatre gig. It's next Saturday?' she asked.

'Yep. Have you made up your mind about coming?'

'I think I will, and I'll bring Jayne.'

Alan sighed. That would mean at least two people who wouldn't laugh at anything he said. Rosie picked up on his reaction. 'Jayne's a police officer. She might come in useful if your stalker shows up.'

'She's the worst police officer ever,' Alan laughed. 'What use can she be, keeping a look out as I'm being axed to death?'

'I'm not listening. Can you get me two tickets or not?'

'OK, will do. You never know, you might even laugh.'

'I doubt it. You're really not that funny.'

Chapter 6

Clive Oneway walked into "The Post House" restaurant. Striding purposefully through the double entrance doors. He stopped at the podium and spoke to the concierge who came over to greet him.

Oneway felt at home in places like this. He looked around the restaurant, a dozen round tables capable of seating two people, and half a dozen larger tables which were suitable for larger groups. The décor was modern; polished chrome and white tablecloths. One side of the restaurant was dominated by large windows providing a view of the River Thames with Bishops Park in the background.

'I have booked a table in the name Oneway at 1.00pm,' he said.

The concierge made a show of looking at his watch. 'It's only 12.50. Would you like to wait a moment while I see if your table is available ...early,' he sneered, walking off pointedly into the half empty restaurant, and spoke to the waiter. Oneway guessed they were talking about him, as the waiter was looking over in his direction.

Oneway fought the urge to walk up behind the pair of them and administer a slap around the backs of their necks. Oneway himself had been on the receiving end of many such slaps or "neckbacks" at school and it never did him any harm. Well, nothing that many years of counselling couldn't put right.

The concierge walked slowly back to him. 'You are quite fortunate. We are able to squeeze you in early. Please follow me,' he said and without waiting for Oneway to follow, walked through a mass of empty tables to another empty table. The concierge showed Oneway to his chair.

'Would you like a drink, while you wait for your guest?' the concierge asked.

'Just a bottle of water,' Oneway replied. The concierge sniffed and set off to ask the waiter to get the drink.

Oneway had a simple approach to meetings. He arrived either ten minutes early or ten minutes late, but never on time. That way, he thought, he always held the upper hand.

Clive Oneway was a property developer. He lived for being a property developer. It was in his blood. From as long ago as he could remember he had stacked blocks on top of each other, forming towers, and used matchsticks to make small buildings in small towns.

After leaving university and starting work as a trainee architect, it all made sense to him. It wasn't so much the building he was addicted to, as much as the inability to accept open spaces. Any open spaces were anathema to him. He saw open spaces as an opportunity to build. He had spent several years building in back gardens, parks and on top of renovated buildings. He loathed the green belt and held a dream that he would be the man to turn this green and pleasant land into one gigantic shopping mall.

The restaurant doors opened, interrupting his thoughts, and a man walked in searching for a familiar face. He had sandy coloured hair and was wearing a dark blue suit. His slim build and six foot stature make him look younger than his forty two years.

David Crozier was a season Ticket holder at Fulham Football Club and member of Wimbledon Common Golf Club. However, none of this interested Oneway in the slightest. In fact there was only one facet of Crozier's life which he had the slightest interest in. David Crozier was the head of commercial planning at one of the local authorities whose jurisdiction covered the area where Oneway had made several planning applications. This was more than enough to keep his interest.

Oneway reached across the table and shook Crozier's hand. He would go through the charade of asking after his family and how the golf was going, despite having no idea or interest in it. He had worked out many years ago that if you asked two or three generic questions about golf, the golfer would then spend the next ten minutes telling you about his swing, his handicap and the increase in green fees without expecting anything more than a cursory nod of the head in a few strategic places. When Crozier had finished talking he would have convinced himself that he and Oneway had had an interesting conversation about golf and that everyone was happy.

Crozier looked across the table at Clive Oneway. He knew that Oneway had not taken anything in. He had been asked the same bland questions last time and the time before that. So much so that this time Crozier tested this theory with reference to a prumatical golf swing and a dringulating putting stroke, two references that he had clearly made up. Crozier then went on to express his disgust at the increasing number of "undesirables" who appeared to be taking up golf. Oneway nodded and said, 'Yes. That can be difficult.' By which point he knew for certain that Oneway hadn't listened to a word he'd said.

'Looking well Clive. Have you been away?' Crozier asked, changing the subject and himself not at all interested in the response. Oneway had never been on holiday for as long as he had known him, and he always looked the same. Short black hair cut smartly without any particular style, black framed glasses and a face that gave no clues as to his age. Crozier believed Oneway could get away with saying he was thirty, even though Crozier knew him to be in his mid-forties.

'No not this year. Nothing planned either. I've got some big deals coming up and I can't afford to be away.'

'Anything to you want to share with me?' Crozier asked.

Oneway grinned. 'Oh, yes!'

*

The waiter cleared their table and loomed over Oneway, one hand clutching a desert menu. Oneway looked up at the waiter and ordered two coffees without even checking with Crozier to see if that was his choice.

'Coffees' good.' Crozier said ironically.

Oneway either chose not to comment, or simply didn't hear him. Instead he reached into his inside jacket pocket and took out two sheets of A4 paper, passing them across the table to Crozier.

'This,' he said, pausing for effect, 'is the master plan. The biggest thing I have ever done. I could change an entire town with this,' he said, looking at Crozier expectantly.

Crozier read through the two pages. Once he finished he went back and read the first page again. Taking a deep breath he said, 'This is ambitious Clive, really ambitious. Even for you.'

Oneway sat back in his chair, laced his fingers together and grinned. 'I can do this,' he said, 'If I own that stretch of High Street, I can raze it to the ground and build the largest shopping mall south of the Thames.'

Crozier looked at the document again.

Oneway leaned across the table, thinking that the further forward he leaned, the more likely it would be that Crozier would accept his ideas.

'That stretch of the road is a dump, a slum. A collection of out dated retail units with pokey flats over them. It would cost the landlords more to refurbish them than they are worth. I'm offering them a way out at a decent price. I'm doing them a favour,' Oneway paused while the waiter placed two cups of coffee in front of them. He allowed the waiter to move out of earshot before he continued.

'There's some old theatre which has been deserted for years. I am going to have that and if anyone creates a fuss I'll tell them that I'm going to open an Arts Centre in the shopping centre where they can put on plays about lesbians and ethnics and any other drivel that takes their fancy.'

'Can I assume that won't actually happen?' Crozier asked, smirking.

'Of course not!' Oneway replied. 'It'll keep everyone happy for a while, and by the time they realise that they don't have anywhere to do mime classes it'll be too late.

This shopping centre will dominate South London. People will come for miles to spend their money. I might even name it after me… The Oneway To Shop Shopping Centre.'

Crozier noticed that a slight twitch had appeared on the side of Oneway's head. Crozier had not seen him this worked up since he arranged to have an old people's home bulldozed while the residents were on a day trip to the coast. A day trip that Oneway himself had paid for.

Crozier could see Oneway was becoming quite animated and, he thought, there was a very strong possibility that Oneway had wet himself. Crozier felt a certain amount of sympathy for the next person to sit in that chair.

Oneway continued. 'This has the potential to make millions. It dwarfs everything I have previously been involved with.'

Crozier thought he should try to calm Oneway down. A reality check was needed. 'I know this place. You'll have to purchase twenty one properties and get planning permission. There's a lot of things that need to be sorted out before you even get started on the build.'

Rather than calming him down, this actually excited Oneway even more. 'Well this is the thing. I have already signed contracts on twenty of those properties,' he said, whilst springing up and down in his chair, sweat beginning to appear up on his brow.

Crozier was now more convinced than ever that Oneway had wet himself. He picked up the pieces of paper. 'Which one don't you have?'

'The Merton Palace Theatre, and I'm going to need your help to get it.' Oneway said hopefully.

Crozier said nothing for a moment. He knew he had to get the response right. 'It'll be difficult….very difficult. There is talk of the theatre being refurbished, and I know that idea is attracting a lot of attention. If that plan is successful your scheme won't stand a chance.'

'But you have some influence,' Oneway whined. He had stopping jigging up and down in his seat, but the profuse sweating had, if anything, got worse.

'I do,' Crozier explained, 'but that influence may have to extend considerably further if you want all of this to go further than just a few run down shops.'

Oneway knew exactly what Crozier implied. So often in this game it was what was not said that smoothed the way and sealed deals. 'That's not going to be a problem,' he said.

Crozier passed the papers back to Oneway. 'Leave it with me,' he said. 'I'll make some enquiries and get back to you.'

Oneway folded the papers and put them back in his pocket, finished his coffee and stood up. The wet patch on the front of his trousers could not be missed. Crozier stood up and the two men shook hands. 'I'll look forward to hearing from you soon,' Oneway said as he left the restaurant.

Crozier didn't immediately follow Oneway out of the building. Instead he needed some time to think over Oneway's plan. He turned back to the table and sat down, realising immediately that he was sitting in Oneway's vacant chair – his damp vacant chair.

Chapter 7

Alan had arranged to meet James in the Cloven Hoof at eight o'clock. True to form, Alan was a good ten minutes late, which he counted as being early, and most certainly within the bounds of acceptability.

The Cloven Hoof public house was an oasis of real ale in a sea of glass and chrome identikit bars. The clientele ranged from inebriated old men shuffling to and from the bookies, and extremely drunk old men sitting at the bar telling war stories to anyone who would listen. Occasionally a young fresh faced couple would wander in, order a bottle of wine and try (and fail) to blend in.

Alan pushed through the doors and looked around the half empty bar. James was sitting at a table in the corner. There was a free chair facing James which had been reserved for him by the approved Anglo German method of putting a bag on it and scowling at anyone who looked even vaguely interested in claiming it for themselves.

Alan pulled the chair out, lifting the bag from it and tucking it under the table. He dropped into the chair and gestured to the fuller of the two pints. 'This mine?' he asked, pulling the glass towards himself without waiting for a response. He got one anyway.

'All yours, mate.' James replied. 'The top half and the bottom half,' he added.

'I'll be sure to enjoy both halves equally.' Alan grinned and lifted the glass to his mouth, savouring the sharp, bitter taste of the beer.

'So...how's things?' James asked.

Alan finished drinking and looked across at his friend. 'The usual, you?'

James shrugged. 'OK.'

Friends since primary school, and very much comfortable in each other's company, Alan and James needed nothing more than a brief acknowledgement whenever they met. In the event that years passed between seeing each other, the greeting would invariably still be limited to a nod of the head and a brief, 'you alright?'

James was also known as "The Captain". He wasn't really a Captain. He had no history of service in the armed forces and no record of collecting for the Salvation Army. He had never excelled at sport and been entrusted with captaincy of the team, nor had he ever been referred to as a 'captain of industry'. However at the age of twelve he had been in the sea cadets for two weeks which had led to Alan naming him Captain Pugwash, which for convenience had been shortened to "The Captain" and it had stuck with him ever since. It also helped enormously that the Captain's real name was James Cook. Only three people called James by his real name; his wife Amy, his mother, and Rosie, who thought the nickname silly and childish.

James took a drink, relaxed back into his chair and asked: 'So, any gigs planned?'

Alan jumped at the opportunity to talk about his stand up career. 'Actually, I'm doing a fund raiser for the Merton Palace Theatre. You know the old theatre on Merton Road? It's being refurbished and there's a few fund raising events being organised. I'm doing a twenty four hour comedy extravaganza.'

'Twenty four hours? Won't you be knackered?'

'Smart arse.' Alan grinned. 'You know what I mean. Anyway, I'm on the bill.'

'Yeah, I know the place. I thought it had been condemned years ago?' said James, sipping from his beer.

'It was closed, but the local arts group reopened it a few years ago. They've been having small plays there and drama workshops, but they want it to open properly and put on plays and comedy.'

'Quality. We need a proper venue round here. I get tired sitting on a tube all over the place to watch you perform in front of half a dozen sneering undergraduates. It'll be cool to watch you get sneered at by some local South Londoners for a change. When is it? I'll bring Amy.'

'Next week.' Alan replied, ignoring his friend. 'But I didn't think Amy found my material funny.'

'Mate, she doesn't. But I'm sure there will be other acts she will think are funny.'

Alan ignored the comment. It was the nature of their friendship; never take things seriously. In fact, Alan had a whole five minutes routine on it, suggesting that male friendships were like catheters; always taking the piss. He felt that James's wife, like Rosie and her sister, simply lacked the intelligence to appreciate his humour.

James continued, 'Are you still doing that routine about the fat kid and the water park?'

'Pretty much, but I'm adding a few new bits to it.'

'I guess it still upsets a few people?'

Alan sighed and raised his hands in mock surrender. 'Occasionally. How was I to know that someone in the

39

audience had a fat kid who had been stuck in a flume for three hours while they waited to be cut out? I didn't build the thing and I didn't feed a kid a diet of doughnuts and coke. Something I pointed out to her at the time. She wasn't amused.'

'They never are, mate' James laughed. 'But at least you got a reaction.'

'Yeah, but I seem to be getting the wrong reaction from too many people at the moment.'

James guessed this had nothing to do with obese children. 'Rosie still think that you're wasting your time with the comedy?'

Alan nodded while swallowing the rest of his pint.

James continued, 'She thinks you should give it up and concentrate on a proper job?'

'In a nutshell. The thing is, I *have* a proper job. And it's shit. I hate it. Rosie's my girlfriend. Surely she wants me to be happy? To follow my dream? I encourage her all the time.'

'No, mate. You take the piss all the time. There's a difference. And anyway, Rosie's dream is to settle down and start a family. You've been together what? Three, four years?' James asked.

Alan shrugged. 'Nearly five.'

'Can you really blame her, though? You don't even live together.'

'Well, not officially. But we spend practically every night with each other.' Alan replied.

'Face it, you do have a bit of a phobia about commitment,' James said, goading him.

'Rubbish, I can be very committed.'

'Oh come on,' James said, 'You won't even have a store loyalty card because you don't want to be tied down.'

Alan laughed. 'Can I use that one?'

'Of course.' James paused before responding further. It was the type of pause that a patient parent would leave before answering their slow witted child. 'Mate, she needs more than that. If you can't give more, you might want to call it a day. Though be careful, there isn't exactly a queue of women lining up for you.'

Alan sat back in his chair, laced his fingers behind his head and said, 'I know. I'll get this theatre gig out of the way first, then I'll give it some thought. Anyway,' he continued, 'Rosie Rose would be a ridiculous name.'

James sighed resignedly, looked Alan in the eyes and said 'I bet you don't.'

Alan laughed. 'No. Probably not.' Both men laughed. It wasn't that Alan was afraid of commitment. He loved Rosie. It was just that he struggled with serious conversation. The more serious a conversation became, the more Alan looked for a way out, and jokes offered him that escape.

Several drinks later the two friends had put the world to rights. James had been throwing Alan lines and ideas for material. Alan had been rejecting them out of hand whilst championing the use of wasps in crowd control. 'Genetically engineer the fuckers to the size of hummingbirds. It's the only way.'

James had heard this before, and had serious concerns that the size of the nests would be a problem. He stood up and made his way to the bar using his six foot frame to push his way through the now busy pub.

Alan knew that his friend would make his presence felt at the bar and he would be back in no time at all. Hunching over the table, grasping his empty pint glass with both hands, he decided to talk to Rosie. Maybe it was time to move in together.

An icy chill ran down the back of Alan's neck, as if somebody had left the door open. He turned around to see if he could ask someone to shut the door, but it was closed. Turning back he suddenly became aware of someone sitting in James's chair.

'Sorry mate someone's sitting there.' he said, but the chair was empty. Alan looked around, thinking someone must have sat down and quickly got up again, but there was no evidence that anyone had even been near the table.

Alan felt, rather than heard, someone whisper; 'Hello? Hello? I need to get the hang of this...' as a slight gust of wind brushed his shoulder. Startled, Alan jumped slightly, squeaked *'What the..?'* and looked around the bar again. No one was paying him any attention at all. James was still at the bar chatting to someone in a football shirt. *Well, that's weird.* Alan thought. *I must be pissed if I'm hearing voices.*

James came back from the bar with two pints, said; 'That bloke at the bar reckons England will win next weekend. I had to put him straight. You alright? You look like you've seen a ghost.'

'I think I did.' Alan joked. 'That or I've had too much to drink.'

'That's always been your problem, mate.' James said 'Never could handle the ale.'

After finishing their drinks, Alan and James made their way out of the bar and walked towards the station and bus stop.

'So where are you tonight, yours or Rosie's?' asked James mischievously.

'I'm at mine. Rosie will be there...she's made a spreadsheet so we know where are staying each night....'

James chuckled. 'You are *kidding*, right?'

'I wish I was. It's coloured coded and everything.'

'Blimey. There's nothing like spontaneity in a relationship. And that's *nothing* like spontaneity. She should work for South West Trains.'

'What, and have people actually turn up to the right place at the right time? They'd never go for it. Besides, her decision to do a spreadsheet *was* spontaneous.'

They reached the station and said their goodbyes. James continued walking up the high street while Alan walked towards the bus stop for the short journey home. As he did so, his thoughts turned to the weird moment in the pub. He must have imagined the whole thing. The breeze, the voice. It was the only rational explanation.

As he waited for the bus to arrive, Alan begun to feel a slight chill, followed closely by a strange feeling that someone was watching him. He looked around but saw no one. The only movement was the flickering broken light of the bus stop.

The bus, when it came, was virtually empty. Even though he was only travelling a few stops, Alan climbed the stairs to the sanctuary of the top deck and sat down. He shivered to himself again. As much from the cold as from his weird experience.

Gazing out the window, Alan turned his thoughts towards the Merton Palace Theatre gig and his routine. He would definitely do his fat kid routine. After all, he thought, it's not like fat kids could chase him down the road.

As the bus turned the corner, Alan felt another gentle breeze across his shoulders and looked around to see which of the windows were open. They were all closed. The hair on the back of Alan's neck raised, sending shivers up and down his spine. Too nervous to look round, but more afraid not to, Alan turned his head slowly to his left.

Nothing.

Breathing a sigh of relief, Alan turned his head back to the window. It was nearly his stop so he got up to walk downstairs. As he turned round, he felt another slight breeze and a faint whisper 'Hello? Hello? Can you hear me?'

It was the same voice he had heard in the pub.

Chapter 8

Alan moved around the small kitchen, a bowl of cereal balanced in one hand and a cup of tea in the other. He sat himself down at the table and started eating while the radio blasted out an unnaturally cheerful song about people smiling more when the sun shined.

'Do you remember when you used to get free gifts in boxes of cereal?' he asked.

Rosie was spreading a healthy alternative to butter on a slice of toast and had no desire to enter into Alan's reminisces about cereal in days gone by. 'No I don't,' she replied automatically, whilst she focused on both eating toast, drinking coffee and clearing away her breakfast.

Alan continued, 'They used to put proper toys in cereal boxes in the old days. I got all manner of cartoon characters, Daleks and badges all from boxes of cereal when I was a kid. Those toys would have been tastier than the excuses for cereal we buy these days. I think there's a cartoon feline that would be furious if the poachers hadn't got him.'

The wave of disinterest from Rosie almost swept Alan off of his feet, and in an effort to have what could be classed as a conversation before they left for work he changed the subject. 'James is bringing Amy to the theatre gig, is your sister coming? Only I'll need to get the tickets.'

'I'll call her and find out. It'll be good to see Amy again, and James. Her voice faded away as she left the kitchen and went into the bathroom, the door shutting behind her.

Alan stood up from table, wandered across the kitchen and put his cereal bowl in the sink. It was the same every morning. Rosie was an efficient machine capable to performing several tasks at once in order to prepare for work in the quickest possible time, whilst Alan was slow and easily distracted. He reached across and retuned the radio to Radio 4 just in time for the shipping forecast.

'What are you listening to that for?' Rosie said as she silently re-entered the kitchen.

Alan adopted a look of shock. 'It's important to know what's going to happen in the Shetlands. I'd feel guilty if I was wearing the correct clothing in Victoria whilst knowing that fisherman in the North Sea are cold and wet.'

Rosie stared back at him and shook her head. 'I'll see you tonight,' she said walking out of the kitchen. Before Alan could move she reappeared in the doorway, and with look of indifference on her face added, 'I suggest you put some clothes on or it won't just be the fishermen of the Shetlands who are inappropriately dressed.'

It was 3.15pm. Alan had tried to make an effort. He had spent several hours going over data and spread sheets, trying to prepare a briefing paper for a forthcoming meeting. Despite his best intentions, he was no further forward than he had been before he started. Let's be honest, he thought, he was just could not care less. He couldn't give a monkeys about this data, he didn't care what it meant, what it could mean or how it can be dressed up. He just wasn't interested.

Alan looked around the office for somebody who he could have a chat with. There were lots of empty desks today. People were either in meetings or on leave, and those that were left made his database and spread sheets appear a more attractive option. He picked up his mobile phone and sent James a text;

'YOU LAZY BASTARD'

This was one of Alan's regular games. James was a teacher, and it amused Alan no end to send James a text message as the schools were closing. A teachers working hours were a constant source of material for Alan.

He didn't expect a reply. James didn't normally respond to this type of message. Instead he would bide his time and then on the first day of the long summer holiday he would send Alan a text message which said;

'DAY 1 OF THE SUMMER HOLIDAY ONLY 5 WEEKS AND 6 DAYS LEFT'

Alan never responded to that that sort of message either.

Alan's mobile buzzed, indicating that he had received a text. Excellent, he thought to himself, I have finally goaded James in to a response as he checked the screen. Sadly, it was a text from Rosie. The message read;

'JAYNE WANTS A TICKET FOR THE THEATER HUB SEE YOU TONIGHT MY PLANS'

Alan shook his head in disbelief. Not only did Rosie not understand predictive text, she didn't know that she could turn it off. Alan imagined that the code breakers at Bletchley sixty years ago would have been in very much the same position as he was when he received a text from Rosie, but at least they had the Enigma machine.

Alan's inbuilt Enigma machine translated that message into; *Jayne wants a ticket for the theatre gig and that he was due at Rosie's tonight.* He sent a quick text message back telling her that he'd collect the tickets on the way home and he would see her tonight at her place.

*

Alan had never been to the Arts Centre before, although he knew it involved getting off the tube two stops earlier. The local Arts Group were partly funded by local authority grants, partly funded by the national lottery, and partly from donations. The council had provided premises based on the "out of sight out of mind" mentality, and as such the Arts centre was situated in a narrow side street across from the medical centre.

The centre was a two storey building, the first floor consisting of offices while the ground floor was given over to two studios. Alan emerged directly from the street into a reception area via a set of double doors. A desk was directly in front of the doors which was manned by an attractive black haired girl. To the left of the room was a door which had the words "Studio 1" above it and to the right an identical door which was helpfully called "Studio 2"

On closer inspection, Alan recognised the attractive woman as Sarah, the regular event organiser who he had met at many events and gigs over the last few months. Sarah looked up at Alan, two brown eyes peering out through her fringe.

'Alan. Hi,' she said, 'How are you?' Before Alan could reply Sarah added, 'There's been a change in the running order for the theatre show. Are you ok with that?'

Alan stared at Sarah, resisting the urge to brush the fringe away from her eyes and simply said, 'I don't know what the change is yet.'

Sarah laughed nervously. Oh yes. Sorry. I'm all over the place at the moment,' she flicked through a sheath of A4 papers on her desk. 'Here it is...the revised running order for the 9.00pm – 1.00am slot. Ned Kendall the hedge trimmer juggler is in hospital so I've moved you into his place thirty minutes earlier - is that ok?'

Alan had no difficulty in placing the unfortunate Ned Kendall. After all, there weren't many people who could tell bland, unfunny jokes while throwing hedge trimmers into the air. 'Poor old Ned. One hedge trimmer too many again was it?'

'No, he's got appendicitis.'

Alan inwardly mourned the loss of opportunity for some hedge trimming puns and some banter before responding. 'I'm fine to be moved around in any slot that suits you, but I'm actually here to get some tickets for the event. Four if you can.'

'Yes, I can do that. Wait here a minute I'll go and get them.'

Alan watched as Sarah stepped out from behind the desk and walked across the room, long skirt flowing behind her as she climbed the staircase to the left hand side.

Alan took the opportunity to look around the room. There were posters of famous comedians and entertainment shows on the walls, together with posters advertising productions put out by the Arts Group. His attention was suddenly drawn away by shouting and yelling coming from Studio 1.

Intrigued by the noise, Alan gradually made his way closer to the door, where he hoped he could hear more clearly. However, as he neared the door, the yelling stopped. No longer interested, he turned back towards the desk, where he saw Sarah appeared coming down the stairs in a whirl of skirt.

'What's going on in there?' Alan asked.

'Oh, that's the mime group,' Sarah replied.

Alan looked puzzled. 'Mime as in silent performance?'

'That's the beginners group,' Sarah responded, as if that would answer any questions that he had. Here's your tickets,' she said and placed them on the desk.

Alan handed over the money for the tickets and said goodbye. 'I'll see you at the theatre. Let me know if there are any other changes.'

Sarah smiled back at him, her eyes peering out through her fringe. 'Thanks for filling my slot.'

Alan bit his lip and walked out of the Arts Centre before breaking in to a huge grin.

*

Alan returned to the underground station to resume his journey home. Or, he thought, more specifically to Rosie's. It was after all allocated as a night at Rosie's based on her spreadsheet.

Thankfully, there were few people on the southbound platform at this time of the evening, so Alan found himself an empty bench and sat down to wait for the train.

The indicator board told him that there were four minutes until the next southbound train. Could be worse, he thought, and took the four tickets out of his pocket, mindlessly flicking through them. The tickets were not too far back from the stage, but far enough so that Alan would not have to see the girl's blank faces staring back at him whilst he was delivering fantastically witty observations.

Alan shuddered as the temperature suddenly dropped several degrees. He slipped the tickets back into his pocket and stretched his legs out. The indicator board now showing the next train as arriving in two minutes.

From the far end of the platform, a drunk launched into a rendition of what Alan thought might be a current popular song. However, he thought, it could have been any number of songs, such was the level of shouting involved. Alan chanced a look towards the end of the platform, where, perhaps unsurprisingly the drunk was now shouting the chorus through the narrow end of a traffic cone.

Eventually the drunk finished singing, much to the relief of the few commuters standing on the platform. Alan glanced again at the indicator board. One minute until the train was due.

'Frankie!!!'

Alan almost jumped out of his skin. The drunk was standing directly in front of his bench, the traffic cone now abandoned and replaced by a large plastic bottle of cider.

The drunk staggered slightly, making Alan momentarily think the drunk was addressing him. However, Alan quickly realised the drunk was in fact talking to the empty space next to him.

'Frankie!!!' the drunk shouted again.

Alan weighed up his options; move away from the bench leaving the drunk to shout at the empty space, or engage him in conversation.

'Frankie. You're brilliant,' the drunk slurred, this time in a much quieter voice.

Alan was spared having to make a decision, as a breeze blew out of the tunnel and the train appeared. Alan got up and moved to the platforms edge, mentally crossing his fingers that the drunk wouldn't get on the train with him, but the drunk didn't appear to notice Alan at all.

Alan just had time to hear the drunk say, 'Frankie, where have you gone?' before the train doors closed.

Alan took a seat facing the platform. The drunk was now slumped on the bench drinking from his bottle of cider.

Poor guy, Alan thought, pissed out of his mind and seeing things. Alan hoped he never ended up like that as the train passed into the tunnel.

*

James slouched on a large three seater sofa, a laptop open on his right and a pile of exercise books on his left. Mundane early evening TV played out in front of him on large flat screen.

He was simultaneously managing to keep an eye on the quiz show, groaning with despair as the contestant failed in his third attempt to identify Canada on a map of the world, whilst a compilation of goals from England's world cup campaigns was showing on the laptop beside him, drawing his attention away from the Year Eight homework he was supposed to be marking.

He heard the front door open and looked up as a strikingly attractive woman entered the room. A fraction under six feet tall, with shoulder length fair hair and a ready wit, Amy had been James's wife for the last three years.

She put her bag on a chair and wandered over to the sofa. 'Are you actually multi-tasking here?' she asked, 'or failing to do three things properly?' she added while stepping out of her shoes.

'To be honest it's not taking much effort. The idiot family,' he pointed at the TV 'are having trouble picking out the planet Earth from an aerial photograph of the planet Earth,' and this, he gestured at the laptop, 'is keeping me entertained whilst I try and make sense of Year Eight's homework.' He paused before continuing. 'To be honest, I don't know why I bother trying to teach the intricacies and nuances of music to thirteen year old morons whose limit of musical knowledge is a drug fuelled adolescent in trousers that don't fit shouting over a pre-programmed bass line.'

'Bad day at work?' Amy asked innocently.

'No more than usual.'

'So, they don't appreciate you giving up your time to turn them into little Mozarts?' Amy asked playfully.

'No, the ungrateful shits, and not one of them,' he picked up one of the exercise books, 'can tell the difference between rhythm and quavers.'

'I know that one,' Amy quipped. 'One is a tasty cheesy potato snack, like crisps.'

'And rhythm?' James asked.

'Is a dancer!' Amy dropped back into her chair with a smug grin on her face.

James laughed. 'Good shot. How was your day? The dribblies OK?'

Amy was a special needs teacher, and did not share her husband's disillusionment with teaching. 'The *children,*' she emphasised the point, 'were great today. A real pleasure to be with.' Standing, she asked, 'Tea?'

'Please.' James replied.

He watched Amy leave the room before turning back to the TV. The idiot family appeared to be struggling to identify the capital of France from a choice of Paris, London or the Moon. James picked up the remote and turned the TV off.

*

James walked back into the kitchen, mobile phone pressed to the side of his head. 'OK mate, thanks for that. I'll see you later.'

He ended the call and put the phone down on the table. Amy picked at a bowl of pasta and looked up. 'Alan?' she asked.

'Yep. The tickets are sorted for the theatre night. We'll meet them in the foyer at 8.30ish.'

Amy put her fork down. A conversation, even about Alan and comedy, had the edge on her bland pasta. 'Do you know who else is appearing?'

'He hasn't mentioned anything, though to be fair he probably doesn't know himself. These events tend to be adding acts right up until the start.'

'I hope that the hedge trimmer juggler is there. He's really funny.'

'Funnier than Alan?' James questioned, rather indignantly. 'The man juggles hedge trimmers. He may be brave, he's definitely stupid, but he is not funny.'

'I'm just saying that Alan isn't necessarily going to be the funniest guy at the gig.'

'He went down well at our wedding, everyone was laughing.'

Amy raised an eyebrow. 'Were you at the same wedding as me? Other than you, the only people who laughed at his speech were my dad - who had mixed alcohol with his medication - and my aunt who is deaf and only laughed because my dad did.'

James shrugged and offered a conciliatory, 'Well, I think he's really good and it'll be a decent night out.'

Jayne eased the Nissan Juke through the Saturday evening traffic. Alan sat in the back of the car, running his set through his head for what felt like the hundredth time that day. He had decided that rather than try out anything new, he would stick with twenty minutes of his usual routine. He wouldn't go out of his way to be controversial, it was a charity event after all. There would be better nights to tell the world what he thought of van drivers and those idiots who pretended to be statues at shopping centres. He was booked for a night in one of his regular comedy circuit pubs the following week and he would try that material out then.

In the front, Jayne and Rosie were discussing recent developments in a TV show where contestants made cakes for judges who would publically ridicule them if they weren't perfect. From the occasional snatches of conversation that Alan caught from the front of the car somebody called Brad had criticised somebody called Rachel who had put a cherry on the wrong side of a cake. Rachel was reduced to tears, and according to Jayne, the public had all come down on the side of Rachel. 'This will affect the show's ratings,' Jayne decreed.

Yes, they'll probably treble, Alan thought.

'What's the difference,' Alan asked from the back of the car, 'between watching that show or standing outside our local bakers and watching the simple girl with a squint try to ice buns?'

There was a sigh from the front, though Alan couldn't quite work out who it had come from. Rosie was the favourite though Jayne still had the polite air that familiarity destroyed.

'So you're not a fan?' Jayne asked.

'The trouble with most TV at the moment is that it is so one dimensional. The only one that isn't is probably the game show The Cube.' Alan let that hang in the air, but was unsurprised that the two women in the front of the car did not acknowledge it.

Alan settled back and looked out of the window. People were walking along the streets, heading out for Saturday evening. No doubt some were heading out on dates, some were meeting friends for a night in the pub or in a restaurant, and some may even have been on their way to the Merton Palace Theatre hoping for a night of comedy and entertainment.

Alan listened to the sisters continuing their conversation about celebrity reality shows. He spent very little time watching that type of show, and didn't feel like he had missed out at all. He imagined it was similar to being the only one of your friends not to have had a lobotomy.

'That's it,' Jayne announced as the theatre appeared to their right. It looked unimpressive. The front doors and posters adorning the walls either side of the doors were illuminated, hiding the poor state of the exterior of the theatre. Alan could see some people entering the theatre while others stood outside. It was much busier than Alan expected and he could imagine how impressive the theatre would have been in its heyday, playing host to any number of famous music hall acts from the past.

'Take the first left. There'll be plenty of places to park down there,' Alan said.

Jayne drove down the suggested road. The houses all had their own drives, so she pulled up outside a house, taking care not to let her large car obstruct any of the driveways.

Alan was first out, door open and stepping out onto the pavement, while the sisters looked at the themselves in little mirrors produced from bags which, Alan thought, may have resembled what an 18th century tin miner's lunchbox would have looked like and, probably cost more than he would expect to earn from a couple of months' worth of comedy.

Alan walked around to the front of the car and stared in through the windscreen. In his opinion both sisters were very attractive. Rosie had brown hair cut in a bob, while Jayne's fair hair was cut short, a habit she had got into when she joined the police. Rosie was a little taller of the sisters, while Jayne was slightly the heavier set of the two. Alan had met their mother after having been with Rosie for six months, and in his opinion, that was where the sisters had got their looks from. When Rosie would stare blankly at things he found hilarious he would comfort himself with the expectation that if women grew to look like their mothers, in thirty years' time he would be the luckiest guy in the warden controlled flats. Putting up with Rosie's humour free zone was, he thought, simply like paying in to pension, though in this case it was more carnal than fiscal. He lifted his right arm and made a show of tapping on his watch. 'Can we get a move on,' he pleaded with them.

*

Rosie and Jayne followed Alan through the theatre doors and into the foyer. Even in its current state of disrepair, it was obvious to see that in its prime the theatre would have been an impressive sight. To the left was the ticket office, and to the right the entrance to the bar. Straight ahead was a staircase leading down to the stalls or up to the dress-circle. There were a number of people queuing at the ticket office which Alan took to be a good sign.

Alan turned to Rosie. 'The bar. We'll wait in the bar for the others,' he said striding across the foyer. He opened the door to be met by a hum of conversation and laughter. James and Amy were already there, and were standing in the corner drinking from bottles of beer. Alan and James exchanged looks and Alan pointed to the bar.

'They're over there,' Alan said, pointing to a corner of the room. 'I'll get the drinks. The usual?' he asked, and without waiting for an answer, he weaved his way through the crowd.

James was also making his way to the bar from a different direction, although whilst Alan was squeezing past people and offering a succession of "excuse me's" and apologies, James had an unimpeded walk as people simply moved aside for him. Alan could never understand how that happened.

'What are you doing tonight, anything new?' James asked.

'Nothing you haven't heard before. Thought I'd keep it safe tonight.'

James pulled a surprised face. 'Not even the fat kid stuck in the flume?'

'Oh yes. I'm doing that one. How could that possibly upset anyone?'

James laughed as Alan paid for the drinks, and between them they carried five bottles of over-priced lager back where their partners were now huddled together.

As they reached the girls, Amy turned to Alan and asked, 'Alan, is the hedge trimmer juggler here tonight?'

'No, sorry, he's not... He's ill apparently. I think he just lost his nerve. That happens when you're genuinely not funny. It's the fear of being found out.'

'But you're still here and getting away with it! 'Rosie grinned, adding, 'It's a shame, I always thought he was really funny.'

'Well he's not here, so you're have to put up with me.'

Amy sighed, 'Shame, he was funny.'

James rolled his eyes and turned to Alan. 'Sorry mate, nothing I can do. Maybe it's the danger that turns them on.'

Alan laughed. 'OK, I'm off. Rosie has the tickets. I'll see you back in here after the session finishes. I think it'll be about 10.30.'

'Good luck mate.' James said as Alan left the bar.

*

Alan walked across the foyer to the ticket office. After explaining to the vacant looking girl at the counter that he was one of the performers, he was directed to a large room behind the stage which was described as the "Event

61

Control Centre." A sign on the door confirmed to Alan this was indeed the place, although the fact that it was written in marker pen on a sheet of A4 paper and stuck on the door with sticky tape made him think it was a fairly rushed job.

Typically for a comedy venue, specifically one in desperate need of repair, the room was basically a slightly larger than normal store room. Two desks had been pushed together and several sheets of A4 paper listing the running order had been laid out on them.

Sarah was in conversation with a man and woman who he recognised as a double act but could not recall their names. He studied the running order. He was due on at 9.00pm, in thirty minutes time. The act before him would introduce Alan and it would be Alan's responsibility to introduce the comedian following him. The timetable said that he would be followed onto the stage by someone called "Fletch." Alan knew him quite well. Fletch had spent some time in prison when he was younger, and his act focused on the many implausible, but Alan understood, all too true stories of Fletch's five year incarceration.

Sarah finished with the couple, who Alan still could not place, and turned to him.

'Alan, hi. Everything OK? Do you know what you're doing? You're on at nine and you're down for thirty minutes,' she said without taking a breath.

Alan laughed. 'Calm down, everything's fine. I'll go and wait in the wings to be introduced and I'll introduce Fletch when I'm done.'

Sarah launched into an account of the day's events so far, but Alan had little or no interest in any of it. His job was to turn up and make people laugh. However, he gathered that some performers had not turned up, whilst some had turned up on the wrong time slot, and one of the comedians in the designated family session had entertained the audience which consisted of 50% children with a "Where are they now" piece about 70s celebrities. Sarah was concerned that the parents who stayed would have had to answer a few difficult questions on the journey home.

'And don't forget you can use the downstairs bar afterwards,' Sarah added, almost as an after-thought, flashing Alan a smile.

Alan wasn't sure if it was the word "bar" or the smile that secured his attention but it worked. 'What bar?'

'There's a bar downstairs. It's the original staff bar, it used to be used by the performers after their acts. We've managed to get it open for tonight although there's no beer plumbed in.'

Alan liked the sound of that. He could wait in there for a while before meeting up again with the others. 'I'm up for that. See you there?'

Sarah nodded and was about to say something when a man appeared at her shoulder. She introduced him as Stevie and explained he was responsible for the acts. He would take Alan down to the stage and direct the departing act to the downstairs bar or back to the room.

Alan accompanied Stevie through a number of tiny corridors until they came out at the side of the stage. Alan could hear the comedian currently on stage thanking the audience and asking them to give the next act, Alan Rose a big hand.

With a gentle push on his back from Stevie, Alan walked out on to the stage to a smattering of applause and a half empty audience.

The theatre was not empty, nor was it full. In fact as numbers go it wasn't a bad crowd for Alan. Numbering at around one hundred and fifty, nearly half the seats were taken, but the problem was that the audience were widely spread out so any laughter or applause would be thin. Alan's eyes adjusted to the light and he could see that the first four rows were empty. In fact the first people he could see were Rosie, Amy, Jayne and James. Rosie was chewing the ends of her hair, Amy and Jayne were chatting to each other and only James seemed interested, leaning forward, almost as if he was afraid that he might miss something.

OK, Alan thought to himself, *Show Time.*

Chapter 11

'...So, I'm standing at the top of the water slide and I'm thinking to myself, there's no way this fat little sod is going to make it all the way down the chute...'

Alan paused for a moment to let the audience visualise the scene. Sadly, there was only muted giggles in the sparsely populated room. He had really liked this story, but perhaps Rosie and Amy had a point. *No.* He thought. *This is good.*

'You're not funny,' someone from the audience shouted out. *'You're supposed to make us laugh.'*

'I guess you *were* the fat kid on the water slide. I can see the resemblance. One. Big. Fat. Arse.'

This got more of a positive reaction so Alan went for the jugular. 'I'm sorry I didn't recognise you without your ill-fitting swimming trunks and acne ridden back. But I can see it's you now. Did it take them long to cut you out of that chute?'

More audience laughter. Probably just glad he wasn't picking on *them,* Alan thought. Still, like all good comics, he took his laughter where he could find it. Strangely, the heckler had gone quiet. Shame really, Alan fancied a bit of banter. Sensing it was better to get back on script, Alan returned to his set.

'Where was I? Oh yes, matey over there was just about to get stuck in a fifty foot water chute.' Alan found he couldn't help himself, but he didn't care. What was it with hecklers? They paid good money to go and shout at a comedian. It wouldn't happen in other industries, he thought. There wasn't a procession of drunken idiots hurling abuse at checkout girls. In hindsight, in Merton, there probably was. Especially if they had been barred from The Cloven Hoof.

'You see, its simple physics. Round chute. Fat kid. If the kid is fatter than the chute, you don't let him slide down it. It's not going to end well. And it didn't. This kid was *huge*. I mean, seriously huge. He looked like, well, you know. All fat kids look the same. Like melted cabbage patch dolls. And the poor firemen; they had to lift this kid out. The crane was wilting under the pressure.'

This got a few nervous laughs, as though the crowd realised they should be offended but couldn't help laughing. The heckler was almost conspicuous by his silence.

Alan looked across the stage to check how long he had left with Stevie. However, someone else was standing by the curtains. Alan thought it must be another comedian as he seemed vaguely familiar. Turning back to the audience, Alan finished off the fat kid story.

'It took the fire service three hours to cut the kid out. Naturally I had to stay and watch. But, ladies and gentlemen, after they'd cut the fat kid out, his mother told him he had been a brave boy and deserved an ice cream. To which one of the fireman replied *"Madam, don't you think it was all the fucking ice creams that got him stuck in the first place..?"* Seriously, you couldn't make it up.'

This got a better than usual response from the crowd. Except for the disgruntled heckler who had spent the last few minutes staring down at his shoes after being told off by the woman sitting next to him.

*

Alan sat in the downstairs bar, nursing his pint. Unlike a lot of comedians, he tended not to stick around to watch the comedians after his own slot, preferring to analyse his own performance instead.

All things considered, it had gone OK. Strangely, the fat heckler had helped squeeze an extra laugh or two from his routine. A fact that made Alan silently grateful for comedy nights in pubs. Granted, drunken crowds could quickly become too rowdy, turning a gig into a bear pit, but there were as many happy drunks as there were idiots. And sometimes the idiots actually helped with the laughs. Though never in the way they hoped. If indeed hecklers hoped for anything above making an arse of themselves.

At the far end of the bar something, or more accurately someone caught Alan's attention. Staring straight at him was the man who had previously been standing at the side of the stage during Alan's set.

He certainly looked familiar, but Alan couldn't place him. He seemed to know Alan though, as he stood waving his arms in Alan's direction. For a second Alan wondered if the strange bloke was waving at someone else, but there was no one else. Alan had his back to the wall.

As the man approached, Alan could see the man had a shock of wavy blonde hair and wore a slightly faded bottle green velvet jacket with a ruffled shirt that put Alan in mind of the TV playboys of the 1970s. But there was something else, something vaguely familiar about the man who was now making his way towards Alan's table.

67

Suddenly the chair beside Alan was pulled back and a bag deposited on it. He instinctively turned to his right and saw Sarah standing there. 'Well done. Stevie says that you went down really well. Better than the fat kid on the water slide anyway,' she said smiling while pulling out the chair opposite him and sitting herself down.

Alan, momentarily distracted by Sarah's arrival, looked back to where the man had been approaching, but he had gone. He looked quickly around the room but the man was nowhere to be seen. Sarah meanwhile took out a packet of peanuts from her bag and attempted to open them.

'Who's the guy with the green velvet jacket and the frilly shirt? Older than us. Probably mid-fifties,' Alan asked.

Sarah looked up at Alan and put the bag of peanuts on the table. 'Not sure we've got anyone like that – in fact I don't think there's a comic on this set who's older than forty. There were a couple of older guys on during the first session, but neither was wearing anything like that. Why?'

'I saw this guy standing off stage during my set, and just now over there,' he gestured towards the far side of the bar. 'He looks familiar but I can't place him. I assumed he was one of the comics.'

Sarah went back to her peanuts, still struggling to open the packet. 'No one I know. Why are these things so difficult to open?' she said, as suddenly the bag split open, showering them both with nuts.

Alan laughed at Sarah's embarrassment. 'Sorry,' she said.

'I was expecting to have things thrown at me tonight, it was just a bit later than expected.'

Sarah swept a handful of peanuts from the table into the palm of her hand. 'I'll just dump these,' she said and walked away from the table.

Alan looked at his watch. The session would be coming to an end shortly and he would have to meet the others in the main bar. Sarah sat back down placing two bottles of an obscure beer on the table. 'Thought you might like this,' she said.

Alan looked at the unfamiliar label. Did that say Albania? 'Thanks,' he said, looking suspiciously at the bottle.

Sarah put her drink down. 'You know, if we can get this place up and running there will be a need for regular comedians.' She looked at Alan and reached a hand towards his face. Alan's heart quickened as Sarah placed her hand on the side of his face and ran it up and down below his ear.

'Sorry. There were bits of peanut stuck there,' she said.

Sarah's touch ignited something in Alan that he wasn't comfortable thinking too deeply about, but he couldn't work out if it was the prospect of regular work, the fact that she was actually quite attractive or the effects of the Albanian beer. Whatever the reason, Alan knew it would be a good time to leave.

'Thanks for the drink and the peanut clean up, but I've got to be making a move now. I hope the rest of the event goes OK.'

Sarah didn't seem to be put out by Alan's sudden departure. 'Thanks for coming along and giving up your time, I'm really grateful.'

69

Alan smiled and got up to leave. As he did so he heard Sarah call his name. He turned around and Sarah said, 'If I see the guy in the green jacket do you want me to ask him anything?'

'Yes,' Alan replied, 'can you ask him what the hell he wants?'

David Crozier liked his office. It was an office befitting an executive, a man admired by his peers and a man at the top of his profession. The name plate on the door read:

David Crozier – Head of Commercial Planning Decisions

In the age of corporate speak job descriptions Crozier's job title did exactly what it said on the door. He had, for six months, held the post of head of commercial planning decisions. This meant he was the man responsible for ensuring that commercial planning applications were treated appropriately and placed before the planning committee in an impartial manner and with all the procedural points set out correctly.

Whilst it was publically perceived that the planning committee had the final say on the approval of both commercial and residential planning applications, changes in planning laws over recent years had seen more central Government interference in decisions and appeals. There had also been a significant increase in residential planning applications. Concerned that commercial applications were being pushed aside in favour of local applications such as house extensions, including, Crozier recalled, a ludicrous application for a conservatory for a first floor flat, the local authority restructured its departments, appointing one person to consider all commercial applications. Consequently the role of Head of Planning Decisions was created. David Crozier was this man, and he took his responsibilities very seriously.

Sitting behind his executive desk, Crozier logged onto his PC and, after entering several different passwords, he accessed the database of outstanding planning applications. His position entitled him to far greater access rights than anyone else working in the planning department, and he could monitor the progress of every application.

Crozier considered himself to be a powerful man. Planning applications would stand or fall based largely on his opinion. He also considered himself to be a pragmatist and was more than happy to facilitate the successful completion of certain developments. To say Crozier was in bed with developers was a massive understatement. It would be more accurate to say that he was nicely tucked up in a sky blue onesie enjoying a warm milky drink with developers.

Crozier sighed as he cast his eye over the outstanding applications, scrolling down the screen until he reached the applications he was interested in; several applications pertaining to a number of retail units on Merton Road. A number of applications had been made, all conditional upon the sale of the adjacent units and all dependent upon the sale of Merton Palace Theatre. He accessed another database and typed the theatre details into its search engine. Within seconds he had established the names of those who owned the Theatre, together with details of all existing covenants and restrictions. Conscious not to leave any electronic trails, he took a pad and pen from his desk drawer and began copying the information from the screen onto paper.

*

Crozier finished copying out the relevant information, so that he could deliver it personally to Oneway when they met in a couple of days' time.

The telephone on Crozier's desk rang, disturbing him from his thoughts. It was a single ring, indicating an internal call. The phone's display screen gave an extension number that he didn't recognise, but he picked up the handset regardless.

'David Crozier speaking,' he stated.

The caller was female, but he did not recognise the voice. 'Hello David, its Jenny from planning secretariat. Is Alison with you?' she asked. 'Only, I need to run through the agenda for the next planning committee with her.'

Alison was David's secretary, and one of her responsibilities was to manage the planning committee meetings.

'I'm sorry,' Crozier replied, 'she's a bit tied up at the moment, but I'll get her to call you when she's free,' he said, and put the phone down without waiting for a response. He stood up to stretch his legs and straighten his aching back. After several seconds he walked across the office, towards a large metal cupboard.

Crozier took a key from his trouser pocket and unlocked the doors. Standing in the corner, tied up with rope, blindfolded and gagged was an attractive blonde woman. She was little over five feet tall and fitted comfortably into the space provided. Crozier pulled the blindfold and gag off of her.

'Can you call Jenny? It's something about a planning meeting,' he said.

Alison cleared her throat. 'Yes of course, I'll do it as soon as I'm finished here.'

Crozier untied a knot that was tightly wound on her left hip and let the rope fall to the ground. He stepped back from the cupboard, yawned and walked back to his desk. Alison stepped out of the cupboard, smoothed her clothes down and put her shoes on.

'Is there anything I can get you first?' she asked.

Crozier turned to face her. 'Tea, and please remember it's just the one sugar.'

Alison left the office, closing the door behind her while Crozier went back to his computer. You just can't get the staff these days, he thought to himself.

Chapter 13

Rosie pushed hard as she began her climb through the Alps. Jayne was beside her, gently tapping out a steady rhythm on the pedals. The climb ramped up and both Rosie and Jayne increased their effort. Rosie looked at the small screen on the handlebars of her bike and realised that her pace was slowing, so she got out of the saddle and forced the pedals round. Jayne followed suit, standing on her own pedals, face reddening with concentration.

They reached the summit of the climb at the same time, faces glistening with the effort of the last thirty minutes. Next they faced a 5km descent into an Alpine village.

Jayne adjusted the setting on the control pad attached to the handlebars and sat up, pedalling at a far more sedate rate. Rosie followed suit and the sisters began their descent.

As they cycled into the small Alpine village, the words "Congratulations Workout Completed" flashed across their handlebar screens.

Rosie looked at her sister. 'That was a tough one. Next week I think we're doing the cycling tour of Holland program.'

Jayne nodded and wiped her face with a towel. 'It would have been easier to have cycled the actual Alps than that,' she said, grinning, 'and at least we could have stopped in the actual village for tea and cakes.'

The cool down program on their exercise bikes kicked in and the pace dropped, allowing heart rates to return to normal and the chatting to start in earnest. Rosie took a drink from her water bottle and turned to her sister. 'So how was the blind date?'

Jayne slowed her pedalling to a virtual standstill and said, 'It was an embarrassing mess. It couldn't have gone much worse. For a start he was at least six inches shorter than me and ten years younger, but he actually looked about thirteen.'

'A toy boy, then!' Rosie smirked.

'More like an actual toy. It was awful, the restaurant chairs were quite tall and his feet didn't reach the floor. They just swung back and forth for the entire time we were there, and just when I thought that it couldn't get any worse the waiter gave me the desert menu and asked me if my son would like an ice cream.'

Rosie put a hand over her mouth in an attempt to stifle a laugh, but failed.

'It is not funny. It was horrible, just cringe worthy, and then, just to put an end to an already embarrassing evening, as we were leaving he grabbed my hand and led me out of the restaurant in front of everyone.'

Rosie was still laughing. 'So, are you seeing him again?'

Jayne threw her towel at Rosie and climbed off the bike, unimpressed by her sisters' lack of sympathy.

The weekly gym session provided the sisters with an opportunity to spend time together and to get some regular exercise. Rosie always looked forward to her time with Jayne at the gym, despite Alan's constant ribbing that the sisters only sat in the sauna moaning about men.

As Rosie and Jayne left the Cardio section of the gym, they saw a woman walking in the opposite direction.

Jayne waved to her and wandered over, leaving Rosie to refill her water bottle.

'Alison, Hi. We've just done the Alps bike run. You did well to give that one a miss.' Jayne said.

'Not through choice though,' Alison replied, 'I was tied up and couldn't get away from work. Are you going to the bar?'

'We're on our way there now, after a shower. We'll wait for you.'

Alison said goodbye and wandered off to the treadmills, passing Rosie on the way. 'I'll see you in the bar after this,' she said.

'Great. You can ask Jayne about her blind date,' Rosie said mischievously, grinning as she left.

*

Seriously. What's the point of wasps?

It doesn't matter who you ask. Even biologists can't give you a reasoned argument. You can ask the about spiders and you'll be told they are useful in that they eat flies and bugs.

Bees help pollinate crops, and at least they have the common decency to die if they sting you, as they leave half their backsides hanging out of your arm. I mean, that's bizarre in itself right? Why would any self-respecting bee want to sting you knowing it was going to leave half its' arse behind? Perhaps that's why they're called BUMble bees.

Alan stopped typing and straightened his back. He wondered if that was a good enough joke, knowing the only way to find out for sure was to test it on an audience. He continued typing. *I suppose the humble bumblebee is driven by a complex guilt system, whereas the wasp is driven simply by the desire to sit on food or fizzy drinks and generally wind you up on a picnic.*

Alan stopped typing again and looked at what he had written. It's moving in the right direction, he thought, but I still need a rhythm. More of a hook. Standing up, he wandered over to the fridge and took out a bottle of water.

Looking back at the table he could see the power cable from the laptop was wrapped around the table leg and stretched taut across the kitchen floor to the wall socket.

Alan made a mental note to make sure that the cables were tidied away, or at the very least safe before Rosie got back after the gym. Having worked all her life in a hospital, Rosie knew exactly how people ended up there, and it normally involved carelessness at home. He went back to the table, carefully stepping over the cable and sat back in front of the laptop.

OK, he thought to himself, where was I? Oh yes, *so what use is there for wasps? Well you remember the riots a couple of years ago? There was all that fuss afterwards about water cannons. Should we use them? Are they humane? Is it the only way some of the rioters would ever get a proper wash?*

Well let me tell you that there is nothing inhumane about firing a fast moving jet of water at a fifteen year old scrote who's climbing out of the window of an electrical store with a forty two inch Flat screen HD ready TV under his arm.

So I got to thinking. Why don't we find a use for all the fucking wasps? You build a giant wasp's nest at Scotland Yard, fill it up with wasps and keep them starved of sweeties. Once the riots start, the police hose the rioters down with fizzy pop and then let the wasps out of cannons. Let's see how brave the rioters are then – screaming for their mums and waving their arms in the air. At least they'll leave electrical stores alone. Though they may have to break into the chemist instead to nick some anti-histamines.

Alan cricked his neck and realised he was getting cold. Very cold in fact. It wasn't a cold night, certainly not cold enough to put the heating on. In fact if anything, the room was getting colder by the minute. He could see his breath misting on the laptop screen and his fingers were going numb. Alan blew on his hands in an effort to warm them up, whilst reading what he had written. Not bad, he thought but by Christ it was getting cold.

He reached for his sweat shirt, conveniently thrown over the back of the sofa, and slipped it over his head. That's better, he thought, and looked at the screen whilst he waited for his fingers to warm up.

'What do I need now?' he said out loud, 'Come on Alan, what do I need?'

'You need to put a joke in!' a male voice whispered.

The human brain is capable of millions of calculations every second and it took less than that for Alan to hear the voice and his mind to assess it. The voice was quiet yet non-threatening. It only took Alan another second to jolt back to reality and form a suitable response.

'What the fuck was that?' he squealed, shooting to his feet and knocking his chair over. As he turned to face the kitchen, he saw a figure standing in the doorway. It was a familiar figure, leaning on the door frame with his arms folded across his chest. The man was wearing a velvet looking green jacket and a white frilly shirt.

Alan had no time to gather himself before the figure slowly disappeared in front of his eyes. Alan's mouth hung open in disbelief. *This can't be real,* he said to himself, *I must be having some kind of seizure. Perhaps I need an ambulance.*

In an effort to understand what had just happened, Alan moved towards the kitchen. However, his left foot tangled itself in the still untidied laptop cable and he fell forward, instinctively putting his hands out to protect his head.

Unfortunately, his hands failed him and Alan's head caught the edge of the table and everything went black.

*

Alan sat on a bench outside the A&E department, a towel and a bag of ice cubes pressed to the side of his throbbing head.

There were several people - presumably patients - standing outside, dressed in pyjamas and dressing gowns, smoking. Despite the pounding headache Alan could still see the irony of people being treated for illnesses and then standing outside doing something which may well be the reason that they were in hospital in the first place.

Alan made a mental note to himself to look at whether he could shoe horn this in to a routine.

Lost in thought, Alan glanced to his left, to the person who sharing his bench. A large lady with tight curly brown hair was eating chips from a polystyrene tray with her fingers. After every couple of chips, she would lick her fingers to make sure nothing was going to waste. She was wearing a vest top which did nothing to hide her large figure.

'I can smell your chips,' Alan said to the woman.

As she turned to face him, Alan thought she could be the mother of the fat kid stuck in a flume.

'You can't have them,' she mumbled through a mouthful of chips, 'they're mine,' and to emphasise the point, she wedged another couple of chips into her already full mouth.

'I don't want one,' Alan replied, 'I'm just saying I can smell them. Anyway your need is greater than mine,' he added, letting the comment hang in the air before continuing. 'Haven't we met before? Do you go to the water theme park?'

The woman stared back at him. 'No. I don't like swimming.'

'No. Really? That's a surprise,' Alan said as he watched the group of smokers being replaced by another.

'Are you a patient or do you work here?' he asked her.

The woman had finished her chips and was licking the crumbs out of the tray. 'No. I live over there,' she pointed through the gate at a row of terraced houses facing the hospital. 'I come in here 'cos I like the chips,' she said, pointing again, this time at the mobile fast food van across the car park.

Alan looked to where she had pointed, through the hospital gate at the houses beyond. 'I suppose the walk over here does you good?'

The woman opened a can of diet cola and took a mouthful. 'So why are you here? Are you hurt?'

Alan took the towel away from the side of his head, revealing an egg shaped lump, the bruise already starting to show. 'I have a stomach ache,' he said.

'You should get them to take a look at the bump on the side of your head while you're in there.'

Alan smiled and put his thumping head in his hands. 'Thanks. I might just do that.'

'Why are you sitting out here anyway, you should be in there where the doctors are.'

Alan moved his head slightly, which only made the pounding worse. 'I was in there. They know I'm out here, and they'll come and get me when they want me. My girlfriend works in there. She's in there now talking to people.'

The woman drained her drink. 'What does she do ... in there?'

Alan looked around and moved closer to the woman and said 'She sticks cameras up people's bottoms.'

'Well I never...' the woman said. 'I'm off, but I'll be back tomorrow. For the chips.'

Rosie was perched on the corner of the desk in the nurse's office on the A&E Unit talking to a nurse called Linda.

'I got home from the gym and found him laid out on the sofa with a bag of peas on his head.'

'It says on the notes that he banged his head on a table – how did he manage that?' Linda asked.

'He says he tripped, though I'm not sure how. There wasn't anything to trip over, but I thought he should come in anyway. Best not take a chance with head injuries, and that's one almighty bruise he's got.'

'You're right, it's always best just to check there's no concussion.' The nurse looked at the notes again. 'He says that he didn't suffer any loss of consciousness, so he should be OK. Did he appear confused at all when you found him, not making any sense?'

'No more than usual,' Rosie admitted with a sly grin.

Linda laughed. 'There shouldn't be too long a wait now.'

*

Alan had lost track of time. He had been sitting outside the A&E unit for what seemed like hours. The chip woman had wandered off ages ago and Alan had spent his time people watching. Without warning, Rosie suddenly appeared at his side startling him, and making his head throb.

'Will you please stop doing that? One shock a night is more than enough.'

'What does that mean?' she asked.

Alan put his hands back on his head. 'My head hurts,' he groaned, ignoring Rosie's question.

'Well I've come to get you. The doctor can see you now.'

Alan stood up, one hand keeping the towel and ice cubes pressed to his head. He leaned against Rosie and whispered into her ear. 'Will you have to stick a camera up my bottom?'

Rosie didn't react, instead she led Alan slowly towards the entrance. 'You'll have to ask nicer than that,' she said.

*

After another couple of hours of examinations and observations, Alan was surprisingly diagnosed with a head injury. He was given a helpful leaflet to read about what to do when you had suffered a head injury, one of which was not to operate heavy machinery. 'There goes tomorrow's go on the combine harvester,' he had said to the nurse. He had been given a prescription for pain killers and sent home with clear instructions to return to the A&E unit if he felt worse.

Alan sat in silence as Rosie drove them home. Stopping at a red light she turned to her left and said, 'You're very quiet. The pain killers should be kicking in very soon.'

Alan looked blankly at her. He removed the towel from his head and inspected the shiny bruise on his forehead in the rear view mirror.

'Do you know what the weird thing is? Just before I fell over, I'm sure that there was a person, a man standing in the kitchen.'

'An intruder? Christ did he hit you?'

'I'm not sure, but I can remember this person standing in the kitchen doorway looking at me just before I fell.'

'Did somebody else hit you, an accomplice, perhaps?'

'No. I'm pretty sure that I slipped and hit my head on the table. Look...' he pointed at his head. 'Bruise to the front. I would have seen someone hit me there.'

Rosie slowed the car to turn into their road. 'What happened to this intruder? There was no one there when I got back. Should we call the police?'

Alan paused. This was awkward. If he told Rosie that the person had simply vanished in front of his eyes, she would surely take him back to A&E and they'd keep him in for observation. He'd better be careful what he said next.

'You know, the more I think about it, it's far more likely that it's my mind playing tricks on me. You know, reacting to the trauma.'

This seemed to placate Rosie. 'Well we're going to have to keep an eye on you for a few days, and you should probably take a few days off work.'

Alan grinned. 'OK, two days minimum. You can't take a chance with head injuries.'

It was after 2am by the time they got home. Alan paused as he walked past the kitchen. There had definitely been someone there, he thought, and I've seen him before. There's no way I could have been hallucinating.

*

Alan woke up at 7am after a few hours' sleep. His head throbbed and his body ached. He could hear Rosie moving around downstairs getting ready for work, and he eased himself out of bed, gingerly walking downstairs.

'You should stay in bed,' Rosie said, whilst pouring milk into a mug. 'I've made you some tea. Take it back to bed with you, and if your head still hurts take the pain killers.'

She gently turned Alan's head so that she could get a better view of the bruise. 'I think the swelling has started to go down already.'

'Still hurts a bit,' he replied, taking the tea and returning to the bedroom before Rosie could suggest he might consider going to work.

Alan lay in bed, the mug of tea balanced on his chest. What would he do today? He wasn't properly ill. Properly Ill meant the flu, sickness or an upset stomach where you spent all day on the toilet. He regarded himself as injured, not ill, but it was probably not a good idea to do anything too strenuous, and there were plenty of DVD box sets he hadn't watched yet.

Rosie called out to say that she was leaving for work and that if he wanted anything he should call her. He called out a feeble goodbye and heard the door shut. As he lay in bed he played the weird events of this previous evening through his head.

A knock on the door jolted him back to reality. His first thought was that it was Rosie, but he knew she had her own keys and wasn't the type to lose them.

Alan settled down, hoping that whoever it was would give up and go away. However, the knocking started up again. Alan pushed his head under the pillow, the sudden movement making his head throb. He forced himself out of bed and plodded down the stairs and opened the door.

'I can't believe you forgot your keys...'

Alan stopped in his tracks. Standing opposite him was not Rosie, but a man, arms folded across his chest. He wore a green velvet jacket over a white frilly shirt. It was the same man who had appeared in his flat. The man ran his fingers through his white hair, smiling.

'We need to talk!' the man said.

Chapter 14

Alan stared at the strange man on his doorstep who, over the last few days had appeared and disappeared in front of his very eyes. Alan had so many questions he wanted to ask the man. Who was he? What was he doing here? How did he get in to Alan's house, but most important of all, Alan wanted to ask if this man had nothing better to do than ring on his doorbell at 7am on a weekday morning. Didn't he know that normal people had jobs to go to? Maybe he did, Alan thought momentarily, and maybe the man is actually from his Department's HR team, coming to coerce him in to the office.

But before Alan had a chance to say anything, the man said, 'What happened to you? You look like you've taken a right hiding.'

Hang on, Alan thought, I should be the one asking the questions. This wasn't right at all. This strange man was standing at his front door quizzing him as though it was the most natural thing in the world.

Alan wasn't going to stand for this nonsense. He was going to demand answers. Instead he said, 'I fell over and hit my head, just after you vanished out of my kitchen.'

The man scratched his nose with his thumb. 'I'm sorry. I haven't really got the hang of this at the moment. Sorry if I startled you.'

'What do you mean *"haven't got the hang of it?"* Haven't got the hang of what?' Alan demanded, at last feeling in control of the conversation.

The man thrust his hands into his pockets. 'The whole coming back from the dead thing. I thought it would easy, but to be honest it's a bit like travelling on British Rail, you know you're going somewhere but you're never quite sure where, or even when you'll arrive.'

Ignoring the comments about the state of the nations' railway network, Alan said, 'What do you mean dead?'

'Oh, I'm dead. I think I died a few years ago, but I can't really be sure. Time moves differently on the other side,' the man replied and then, almost as an afterthought he asked, 'What year is it?'

Suddenly all the questions Alan had wanted and needed to ask this strange man seemed rather irrelevant. 'It's 2015. I'm sorry, how can you be dead. You don't look dead. You look old but not dead.'

The man winced. '2015, that's weird. I thought I may have been dead a while, but I didn't think it was that long. That's a lot of years.'

Alan stood on his doorstep staring back at the man, desperately trying to rationalise the whole scenario. Perhaps he was an escaped lunatic. Perhaps Alan was still concussed and was hallucinating. No, Alan thought, it has to be something more obvious.

'Did The Captain put you up to this?' he asked. 'Is he round the corner, filming this for a laugh?'

Alan moved to one side and looked over the man's shoulder to the end of the path. He called out, 'OK, you can come out now – good joke. Now take the old man back to the home and get yourself off to school before there's a crisis with the xylophones.'

The man turned to where Alan was shouting, then, turning round to face him said, 'I've got no idea what you're talking about. As I said, I'm not too sure myself what's going on but this is no joke. Anyway, who's the Captain? Are you in the army?'

Alan felt his headache take hold again. 'Of course I'm not in the army. Why would you think I'm in the army?'

'Well, I thought this Captain fellow was maybe playing a joke on you.'

Alan was rapidly losing his patience. 'No, he's not in the army. He's a friend.'

'Oh. OK. So why is he called the Captain? Is that his name?'

'Kind of,' Alan replied. He was not going to go into the history of James' nickname, but instead asked the question that he had wanted to ask the moment he had first seen the man standing at the side of the stage at the comedy gala.

'Who are you?'

'I'm Frankie,' he said. 'Frankie Fortune.' As if this would be enough of an explanation.

'Sounds like the name of a Las Vegas entertainer from the sixties,' Alan said.

Frankie grinned, 'Nothing so glamorous, I'm afraid.'

*

90

Despite having lived in the flat for several years, Alan had not really made an effort to get to know his neighbours. He would nod a pleasant greeting to the lady downstairs when their paths occasionally crossed, he would smile politely at the couples who lived either side of him, and try not to make any eye contact at all with the family who lived in the house directly opposite him. In the event that one day Alan cracked and went on a killing spree, he was sure his neighbours would simply say that he was a quiet man who kept himself to himself.

Mr and Mrs Brevitt lived in the house directly opposite. Mornings were normally chaotic affairs with children to get to school and adults to get to work. However on this particular morning everything had come to a halt. Both children were peering out of their bedroom window at the sight of their "quiet" neighbour standing on his doorstep appearing to talk to himself.

'Mummy, he's doing it again. He's talking to himself,' Sophie, the youngest called out.

Mrs Brevitt joined her children at the window, watching fascinated as their "quiet" neighbour appeared to be conducting a heated conversation to no one in particular.

*

Alan looked at Frankie. 'OK, let's just say for argument's sake that you are dead. Can anyone else see you, or is it just me?' he asked.

'I don't know. I suppose I could jump out on someone and we could find out. Why do you ask?'

'Well it strikes me,' Alan said, 'that if I'm the only one who can see you, I'm not much of an audience. I mean it's just me, and I'm not really buying into all this *"I'm dead"* rubbish.'

'There's never been an audience that I couldn't tame. Throwing a line to the punters, watching them digest it, take it, holding them in suspense, waiting for the punchline and then the delivery. Got them.'

'I really don't know what's going on here.' Alan conceded.

'Listen son, it's not exactly plain sailing for me either. You're not having to deal with being dead, so just consider yourself lucky.'

Alan looked to the heavens. 'Will you please just go away!' he shouted, and to emphasise the point he leaned forward and poked Frankie firmly in the chest.

However as Alan tried to push Frankie away, Frankie vanished into thin air and Alan fell forward onto the path.

*

In the house directly opposite, Sophie called out, 'Mummy, he's fallen over.'

Mrs Brevitt came back into the room and looked out of the window. She could see Alan laying on the path outside his front door.

'Come on Sophie, let's get ready for school. Leave the man alone, he's probably had too much to drink.

Chapter 15

Alan sat at the kitchen table trying to find a way to explain away the previous twenty minutes. In fact, the more he thought about it the more there was to try and explain. The man at his front door calling himself Frankie Fortune was definitely the same man who had appeared then disappeared in his kitchen. He was also, Alan thought, the same man he had seen twice at the Merton Palace Theatre.

Strangely, Alan was not in the least bit scared by someone claiming to be a ghost standing on his doorstep. In fact, he was more annoyed and angry that he had been disturbed from his lie in.

There had been nothing sinister about the man calling himself Frankie. If anything, Frankie reminded Alan of his slightly eccentric uncle who would embarrass himself at weddings after drinking too much scotch.

Alan took two of the painkillers that the hospital had prescribed, and washed them down with a glass of water in an effort to take the edge off his throbbing headache, and the pain down his left side from where he had just fallen.

Alan's normal response to situations that he was unfamiliar with was to file them away at the back of his mind, only revisiting them if he thought that he could get them into a stand-up routine. This was different. He wasn't ready to file this one away just yet. Alan was a man who could pass off anything that he did not want to think about as someone else's problem, but something was stopping him adopting that approach now and he found it rather disconcerting.

He picked up the remote from the table and switched on the CD player, hoping that music would divert his mind away from recent events. On reflection, he turned the volume down. The last thing that he wanted was the neighbours complaining about the noise. He had had enough unwelcome knocks on the door today and it wasn't even 9.00am.

Alan made himself another mug of tea and took it through to the bedroom. He climbed into bed, leaning back on a couple of pillows, the mug of tea warming his hands and considered his options. He could pretend that nothing had happened, forget about it and carry on as normal. Or he could wait to see if this Frankie person reappeared, and then try to have a more rational conversation and attempt to work out what on earth was going on.

Alan finished his tea. There was a third option, he thought to himself. He could speak to someone. It was time to seek advice from The Captain.

*

Someone had taken his mug. It was deliberate act. They all knew it was his mug as it was marked with the words, "The Captain's Mug."

James looked around the staff room, groups of people sitting in worn out chairs, having worn out quiet conversations. He could see the science teachers in their huddle, sitting around their usual table which they had nicknamed "the periodic table" much to their, and

James's amusement. James thought they were probably making jokes about litmus paper and Bunsen burners.

Then he saw it, sitting on the table in front of the inappropriately named Diane Shakespeare. Despite her literary name, Diane did not teach English. She did, however, teach Chemistry, hence her presence at "the periodic table."

James strode purposefully over to where Ms Shakespeare was seated. 'Will...' he said, knowing that using her nickname would annoy her, 'Is that my mug?'

Diane Shakespeare looked up at him and then down at the mug on the table. 'Sorry James, I think it is. Don't worry, I'll wash it before you use it next. Mine's over there in the cupboard. You can use that one if you like.'

James hesitated before replying. She had not reacted to him calling her Will, and had addressed him as James. This was clearly a cunning science teacher way of getting back at him. She had his mug and was showing no remorse whatsoever. She had even offered her own mug in return. This simply was not on. There was no way he could use her mug, it had *"Scientists Do It Periodically"* written on it. James considered that there was clearly one joke that satisfied all the many scientific principles that he could never be bothered to learn.

It annoyed James when he was spoiling for an argument and people were simply nice in return. He paused before responding, hoping to give the effect that he was accepting the offer of her mug as an apology. 'OK, thanks Will,' he said, and sloped off back to the kitchen section of the staff room.

James stood in front of the cupboard and looked at all the mugs that were precariously stacked on top of each

95

other. Most were bland, chipped and offered no clue as to the identity of the owner. Two were apparently awarded to the "dad of the year", which made James wonder if there had been a real contest, and another was suggesting that Crystal Palace were the pride of London. There was no way that he was drinking from that. Not in a million years. He would sooner share a mug with Mr French, the perfectly named French teacher who always looked like he was suffering from some kind of mouth infection.

At the back of the cupboard was a large glass beaker, which looked like it was once the property of the science department. 'That'll do nicely,' he said, and removed it from the cupboard.

*

Five minutes later James was sitting in a worn chair alongside his normal break time companions' from the PE Department, Tony Finch and Mary Mitten.

'Why are you drinking out of that glass bowl?' Mary asked.

'The science freaks took my mug.'

'Did they hold you down and take it off you? Did they all sit on you while Will prised it out of your hand one finger at a time?' Tony asked innocently.

'You,' James said to Tony, 'can fuck off. I could take that lot with one hand tied behind my back. They got down here early and took it, while the rest of us,' he looked at the two PE teachers and corrected himself, '...while I am using the whole period to try and get the kids to unlock their hidden Beethoven. The science freaks simply boil some water, ask the kids to write down what's happening and finish the class ten minutes early.'

Mary laughed. 'I've had a tough morning teaching Year 8 the finer points of Basketball. Some of them can actually run and dribble the ball at the same time now.'

'….and the others?' James asked.

'Still tripping themselves up with their feet. I just leave them on the ground and play round them.'

'Year 8 are an example why England will never be a world force in sport ever again,' Tony said with some authority. 'I should be coaching a premiership football team with my qualifications and experience.'

'I can't argue with that. You've done such a good job with the school team this season. Don't you still hold the County record?' James said sitting back and draining the rest of his tea from the giant beaker.

Tony looked puzzled, a frown crossing his brow.

'The nine second record?' James added helpfully.

'Still not with you,' Tony replied.

Mary smiled, she knew exactly what James meant. 'That game against St Klum's,' she said. 'One down after nine seconds …… and you kicked off.'

James grinned. 'There you go, the record. You still hold it.'

'That was not our fault. The opposition tricked us by being really good and,' Tony said, struggling to justify managing the worst football team in County history, 'there was a really steep slope on that pitch. The ball kind of got away from us.'

'There's no need to get all defensive,' James said laughing. 'Anyway, it's probably a bit late for that now!'

Tony laughed and stood up. 'Time to get back, I'll see you at lunch.'

Mary rose from her chair and pointed at the beaker in front of James. 'I'd fill that and get it to the lab before lunch if you want the results by tomorrow.'

James sighed and looked at the beaker. If he was honest, he quite liked it, and wondered if it was possible to have his name put on the side.

As he stood up his trouser pocket buzzed and trembled. He reached and took out his mobile. The flashing red light on the top indicated that he had received a text. Scrolling through the menu he found a text from Alan which simply said;

EGM – Cloven Hoof @8

An EGM was the childish code that he and Alan had used for years, or at least since they had had mobiles. It meant that there was something urgent that had to be discussed and could not wait. The fact that EGMs only took place in their favourite pub was merely coincidental.

James knew he had nothing on that evening. Not that it would have made a difference. That was the point of the EGM. It was urgent business and could not wait. The last time an EGM had been called was when Alan had been convinced that a girl he saw on the bus journey to work every day fancied him.

The action points from that particular EGM were for James to accompany Alan on his bus ride. Unfortunately, the girl on the bus also took the journey with someone else. A rather large man who looked like he played rugby who couldn't keep his hands off her. Alan later admitted that he might well have misread a signal or two.

James replied to the text confirming his attendance. Maybe they should have a code for that too, he thought. It could be something to mention later at the EGM. He made a mental note to include this in the "any other business" part of the evening.

Placing his mobile back in his pocket, James wandered off to his classroom, stopping only to put his new tea mug in the dishwasher.

Chapter 16

Crozier sat in his Mercedes and watched the rain fall in steady rivulets down his windshield. He had given up using the demister ten minutes earlier. The steady hum having got on his nerves. He was parked on a driveway, boxed in by a couple of hundred feet of grey painted plywood hoardings to his left and right, with a gate stretched across the width of the drive directly in front of him.

Crozier switched on the windscreen wipers and watched them rub across the windscreen a couple of times before turning them off. He was left with a clear view of the gate for a few seconds before the continuing rain reduced the visibility once again.

The inside of the car lit up as a Land Rover pulled onto the drive and came to a stop next to his vehicle. The headlights of the bigger car cutting through the gloom. He would have recognised Oneway's distinctive blue Land Rover even before he saw the personalised registration number plate '1 Way.'

The Land Rover's headlights blinked off and Crozier heard a car door shut. Oneway walked up to the gate, took a key from his pocket and unlocked a large padlock. He pushed the gate open, turned round and beckoned Crozier through the gap. Crozier started the car and eased through the other side of the gate and, within seconds the passenger door opened and a very soggy Clive Oneway got in.

Without looking across Crozier asked, 'Raining is it?'

'No. I've been for swim!'

Crozier laughed. 'Well next time try taking your clothes off. It'll make it easier. Unless you are doing a proficiency badge,' he said as he pulled away and, as directed, followed a driveway which lead to an open space riddled with pot holes, which he assumed had once been a car park. He continued through the car park, bouncing along an uneven concrete path, which was by now more puddles and pot holes than actual path.

As the car bumped and bounced over the uneven surface, Crozier asked, 'What is this place? It looks like an old school.'

'It is. Or rather was,' Oneway replied. 'My old school in fact. When the Council closed it down I bought the site.'

'Why did you buy your old school? Did you like it that much?'

'No, I hated it. Hated every single second I was here. Hated every single brick, every single step I took, and every single person who was here.'

'Sorry for asking what is probably an obvious question then, but why buy something that evokes such awful memories?'

Oneway sighed and looked out of the window at the rain and the two storey buildings in front of them.

'Look at it now,' he said. 'It's such a dull grey featureless building. It looks like it's completely suited to the rain, as if it wouldn't have existed on days when the sun was shining, but here's the thing; I can't remember it ever raining when I was here. I'm sure it did, but in all my memories the sun is shining.'

'And you bought it because..?'

'I needed to. It's just over here.'

Crozier was directed to park under a covered walkway which provided some shelter from the rain, but not from the wind, which blew into their faces the moment they left the safety of the car. At either end of the walkway there were entrance doors leading to the buildings. Oneway took a bunch of keys from his pocket and unlocked the door, leading Crozier into the building.

'Cloak and dagger enough for you?' Oneway asked.

'You know the way it is. No e-mails or anything with my handwriting on, no post that can be traced back to me, and I don't pass this information on in public places.'

'I think you're safe here then. This hasn't been a public place for ten years.'

Crozier looked around the gloomy damp corridor. 'How long have you had this place?'

'Six years near enough.'

'You bought this what, six years ago? I thought you would have pulled it down by now and put something modern in its place. Something with smooth lines and smoked glass.'

Oneway smirked, 'All in good time David, all in good time.'

The long corridor had a series of doors on both sides that Crozier presumed had once been classrooms. Oneway led Crozier through a door to his left and into a cold and damp classroom. The windows were surprisingly intact, but were filthy and made worse by the rain. There were no desks, as these had been sold when the school had closed down.

Crozier took an envelope from his inside jacket pocket and passed it to Oneway. 'There are no restrictive covenants on the land. There is nothing to stop the owner knocking the theatre down and applying for planning permission to build a shopping centre on the site,' he said.

'So I simply have to get the planning permission?' Oneway asked.

'In theory yes, but as we both know, it's never that easy. You'll have to convince the owners to sell in the first place, and that could potentially pose some difficulties. The local arts council have been managing the place, and are committed to restoring it to its previous state. A couple of weeks ago they held a fund raising comedy night which attracted a lot of interest. If you're going to do this, you should move quickly.'

Oneway opened the envelope and started reading the documents. 'Who has ultimate responsibility? Who has the power to accept my offer; the arts council? The Council?' He asked.

Crozier leaned against the wall, enjoying the feeling of power over this horrid man. 'The Trustees who own the building on behalf the original family are a firm of solicitors. Their details are in there,' Crozier gestured at the documents that Oneway was holding, 'If your offer is good enough, I'm sure they will accept it. You know how it is, no one will turn away a generous offer.'

'And the council. I assume that planning permission will be granted without any problems?'

Crozier smiled. 'That shouldn't pose any problems. But I think you've got to keep the arts council onside. The last thing you want is them making waves.'

Oneway folded the papers and put them back in the envelope.

'What's your time frame?' Crozier asked.

'I'll start putting feelers out with the trustees and the arts council, get an idea of how an offer would be received.'

'I suggest that you take it easy. You don't want to draw attention to yourself, or let anyone get wind of your plans.'

Oneway walked towards the door. 'I have a couple of ideas, I'll keep you informed.'

As Crozier drove back through the car park he saw a weather beaten sign which read;

YOU ARE NOW LEAVING BUGGERLY MOUNT SCHOOL

PLEASE LOOK BOTH WAYS BEFORE PULLING OUT

He turned to Oneway. 'Hell of a name for a school.'

Oneway continued to stare out of the window and without turning to face Crozier he said, 'It was a hell of a school.'

*

Amy stood by the classroom door as the children slowly filtered out. Each one said *"Goodbye Mrs Cook"* as they passed. Amy nodded and smiled at them in turn.
After the last child left, she closed the door, went over to her desk and opened the drawer, taking out a bundle of papers. She carefully flicked through them until she found what she was looking for. She removed the papers she wanted and placed the remaining bundle back in her drawer before leaving the room.

Amy taught a special needs class in a primary school across town from where James struggled to teach music to secondary school children. Amy's school was a typical Victorian building with high ceilinged classrooms, complete with tall windows and a large concrete staircase which ran through the centre of the building.

Amy bounded the two flights of stairs that separated her first floor classroom from the headmaster's office. The headmaster, Stretton La Mon, had been a controversial appointment two years earlier. Amy recalled her conversation with James at the time;

'He was a banker for twenty years. He knows nothing about teaching! Four years, he's only been a teacher for four bloody years,' she had told James when Stretton had been appointed.

'Fast tracked was he?' James had replied helpfully. *'They do that a lot now, it's the Government's retraining programme.'*

When Stretton had addressed the staff for the first time, Amy had not been impressed and she made sure that James knew.

'He kept referring to the skills that he had learnt in twenty years of banking. Skills! He and people like him lost millions of pounds of other people's money. That's why we had a recession. People like him were playing roulette with other people's livelihoods.'

After he had been in place for one week, an irate Amy had called James. *'....he says that his office isn't suitable for a man in his position. Apparently it's not big enough for him to govern the school from. He wants to shift Freda out of her office next door and knock them through to make one big office.'*

'Freda? His secretary. Where's she going?' James had asked.

'She's going in the stationery cupboard.'

'What, with the stationery?'

'No, he wants the stationery moved.'

'Where?' James asked suddenly becoming concerned.

'The staffroom.'

James had paused for a moment before asking, 'Will you still be able to get me those A4 pads? We don't have them here.'

'Do you not get it? What he's doing? He's messing the school up to satisfy his own ego,' Amy was on the verge of tears.

James shrugged on the other end of the line.

'Did you just shrug?' Amy asked.

'What? No, of course not. How could you think I was shrugging at a time like this? Anyway, shrugging is silent,' James said, valiantly attempting to defend himself.

'I know when you shrug. You do it when you don't answer my question straight away. I know you're shrugging, even when you don't know you're doing it.'

'I didn't shrug, I..... sneezed. I covered the phone so as not to sneeze in your ear.'

'I also know when you're lying,' Amy continued. 'Aren't you interested in what this idiot is doing to the school?'

'To be honest Ames, not really. I .....' James didn't get to finish his sentence as Amy had ended the call.

Amy was brought back to the present as she poked her head round the door of the one- time stationery cupboard. 'Freda,' she said. 'Is he in?'

Freda Newhouse, secretary to the last three headmasters, looked up from the desk she shared with three boxes of printer paper, her thin face almost hidden by a mop of curly brown hair and large glasses.

'I don't know Amy, he never tells me anything.' Freda stood and lifted the boxes of paper off her desk. 'If you bear with me, I'll check his diary.'

Amy watched while Freda pulled out an A4 desk diary and flicked through it, coming to a stop, Amy assumed on the correct date.

'According to the diary, he hasn't anything scheduled today, so he should be in his room. Although as I said, he doesn't tell me anything.'

Amy said her thanks, turned and left Freda alone in the one-time stationery cupboard.

Neither Amy, nor her colleagues liked the headmaster. It may have been because they resented his accelerated progression through the teaching ranks, or it may have been because they simply did not like "banker types." They had never really explored the issue in any depth. They simply knew that they did not like him.

Amy also knew that Stretton La Mon fancied her. He had asked her out within two days of starting at the school, and although Amy had politely turned him down, this did not seem to have made the slightest difference, and he had continued to ask her out for drinks, meals, shows, and even once a weekend break, despite being fully aware of her marital status. Whilst Amy had no intention of ever accepting his invitations, she knew that his attraction to her would give her an advantage when asking him for a favour.

Pausing outside the office door, Amy checked her reflection in her compact mirror. Happy with what she saw, she knocked and within seconds a green light above the door flashed signalling that she may enter.

Stretton La Mon had never lost the banker look, Amy thought. In his crisp white shirt and yellow tie, he still looked more a banker than the headmaster of a London primary school. The office itself offered the same pretence. Its design and content would not have looked out of place in the Square Mile, but in the context of a primary school, looked like a gigantic naughty step for posh kids, perfectly emphasised, Amy thought, by the extra space taken from Freda's office, which was now occupied by a large conference table and eight chairs.

Stretton La Mon stood with his back to the door looking out of the window, whilst rocking gently on the balls of his feet. 'It's a great sight. Makes it all worthwhile,' he said.

'What, the children on their way home, playing outside? It certainly does,' Amy agreed.

Stretton turned to face her. 'Oh no, I don't mean them, I'm talking about my new BMW. Take a look. It's in the car park, all new and shiny. I was thinking of letting the Year 4 children wash it for me.'

'Stretton, can I talk to you about something?' Amy asked, changing the subject.

Stretton turned away from the window and sat down, gesturing that Amy may take a seat on the other side of his desk.

'What can I do for you?' he asked.

Amy unfolded the sheet of paper she was holding and placed it on the desk, so that Stretton could read it. 'I saw this advert,' she said. 'The local arts council are holding these learning through drama workshops.'

'And ...' Stretton asked.

'...and this would be a fantastic opportunity for the children in my class. They would get a chance to perform on a stage in a theatre with a professionally trained actor. It would build their confidence and get them used to talking in front of people.'

'This actually takes place at a proper theatre, not here at the school?' Stretton asked, looking up from the sheet of paper that Amy had placed in front of him.

'Yes, the Merton Palace Theatre. Do you know it?'

'No.' Stretton answered immediately, without appearing to give the question any consideration at all.

'It's an old theatre that the Arts Council are trying to renovate. They had a fund raising event there a couple of weeks ago. I went. A friend of mine's a comedian and he performed there.'

'Is he funny?'

'Not really,' Amy answered honestly.

'How much will this cost?'

'It's all there,' Amy said, standing up and leaning over the desk. She pointed to the prices, making sure that her chest was in his line of vision for a few seconds more than was entirely necessary.

Amy sat back in her chair and smiled innocently. This was taking longer than she had thought, and now wished she had worn a skirt that morning instead of trousers. That, she thought, would have sealed the deal.

Stretton sat back in his chair and laced his fingers behind his head. 'Fair enough Amy. Take your class to this workshop, we are after all investing in their future.'

'That's great, thank you Stretton,' Amy said standing up.

As she opened the door she heard him say, 'Let me know when it is, I may well come along.'

Amy's heart sank.

Chapter 17

'You're not going out!' Rosie said.

Alan inwardly groaned. He knew this was a mistake. Why didn't he tell Rosie that he was going to stay at his own flat this evening? He should have told her that he was resting up and hoping to return to work the next day. Instead he had made life difficult for himself. He had arrived at Rosie's as arranged, but then told her he was going out for the evening.

'Why not?' Alan asked naively.

'Why not!' Rosie snapped back at him, 'Where do you want me to start?'

She stood before him, hands on hips, still in her work uniform which, as far as Alan was concerned gave her disapproving tone of voice a greater sense of authority.

'Twenty four hours ago you knocked yourself out. You spent the evening in A&E being checked out for concussion, you have a lump the size of a golf ball on your head which, by your own admission, only stopped aching a couple of hours ago, and you've been taking painkillers which shouldn't be mixed with alcohol.'

There was a brief moment of silence. Alan wasn't sure if Rosie had finished or was just catching her breath. He decided to take a chance and reply. 'I won't be drinking,' he said truthfully.

'OK, fine, but why do you want to go out anyway?' Rosie asked.

'Football,' Alan lied, 'It's a big champions' league night.'

'I don't care if it's the World Cup final, you're still not well enough to go out to the pub.'

'The World Cup is every four years. The next one is three years away,' Alan said helpfully.

Rosie ignored this comment, not in the slightest interested in football schedules.

'Why can't you watch it here?' she asked.

'It's on a special channel that only pubs get.' Even Alan couldn't believe he'd said that. There's no way Rosie is going to buy this, he thought to himself.

Rosie wandered through to the kitchen. 'Are you eating before you go?'

Alan let out a sigh of relief. Unbelievably, the battle had been won. There would be other battles, and he would undoubtedly lose most of those, but for tonight at least he could enjoy the spoils.

'Just tea,' he replied. 'I had something before I came over.'

Rosie took the kettle over to the sink and filled it from the tap. Without turning round she said, 'Are you around in a couple of weeks' to spend the weekend at my parents?'

Alan suddenly realised this was why Rosie had stopped her opposition to his plans for the evening. She wanted him to do something with her. If he was honest, Alan had no objection to a weekend at Rosie's parents' cottage in the Sussex countryside, but guessed he should not seem too eager.

'That should be fine. I'm pretty sure I don't have a gig.'

Rosie filled two cups with boiling water. 'That's great, I'll tell mum that we'll be there.'

*

Alan hated lying to Rosie. Generally he hated lying to anyone, not through any devout belief in honesty to all men, but more because he was likely to forget what he said and to whom. It was, he decided after a particularly awkward moment at a family wedding, best to just be honest and deal with the fall out. This was different however. Telling the truth was not an option.

Attempting to explain to Rosie that the reason for the EGM was that he thought he was being haunted would have been a mistake. She would have put it down to hallucinations from the head injury and rushed him back to the hospital citing concussion and possible brain damage. Alan therefore decided that this deception was merely a series of small, tiny, inconsequential little untruths, rather than a bare-faced lie.

Alan had declined Rosie's offer of a lift, just in case she noticed that there was no football advertised outside the pub. Instead he said that he would prefer to take a bus and get some fresh air after being indoors all day.

*

The two men were silent, in stark contrast to the noise of the bar. James sat across the table from Alan, eyeing him up and down, saying nothing.

The purple bruise on the side of Alan's head had spread round his face and almost joined the shiny black bruise under his eye. He looked, James thought, like a paint chart for different shades of purple.

James had gone straight to the bar when he walked in, expecting Alan would arrive fashionably late. It was only after he had paid for his pint that he turned and saw Alan sitting in the corner, head down over what looked like a pint of fizzy pop.

'You look different,' James finally said. 'Have you had a haircut?'

Alan laughed.

'So why are we here? Have you seen the face of Keith Chegwin in a Pot Noodle again? No that can't be it, by the looks of it were you been attacked by a jealous husband?'

Alan took a sip of his drink. On another day he would have enjoyed holding James in suspense, letting the anticipation build, as though he were playing to an audience, waiting for the moment to deliver the punchline. But this was not that day.

'OK. Let me finish before saying anything.'

James nodded and took another mouthful of Warty Toad.

'I think I'm being haunted!' Alan said.

'Can a person be haunted?' James asked. 'Normally its houses or castles. People are normally possessed and sometimes sexually interfered with. Remember that film, *"The Entity"* when we were kids?'

Alan stared at his friend. 'What? What are you talking about,' he said angrily.

'Nothing. Sorry mate. Carry on. I'm listening.'

115

Alan took his time and told James about the strange man he had first seen whilst on stage and then again in the bar, followed by the events in his kitchen and finally on his doorstep that morning.

'Look,' Alan said, holding out his right hand palm up so that the grazes could be seen. 'That's when I fell this morning.'

'When he disappeared in front of you?'

'For the second time,' Alan confirmed.

James finished his Warty Toad. 'What does Rosie say?'

'Haven't told her. She'd think I was seeing things and have me straight back in the hospital. I told her we were watching football tonight.'

James grinned. 'She'd have you sectioned, mate.'

'Too be honest, when I think about it, there's been a few odd things happening over the last few months. I didn't give it much thought at the time, but this guy Frankie, he said that he'd been trying to get through to me for a while.'

'OK, what are we going to do about it?' James asked.

'You believe me then?'

James sat back in his chair. 'Well, it's more likely than seeing Cheggers in your Pot Noodle. In any case, you've got enough rubbish in your life without going to the trouble of making weird stuff up. Though, to be fair, this is pretty weird. Even for you.'

'I don't know what to do. Should I just wait and see what happens next or be proactive?'

'You don't normally do "proactive" though, do you?'

'Can't even spell it,' Alan grinned in between sips of his fizzy pop. 'Tell me, what would you do if you were me?' he asked.

'Stop buying Pot Noodles.'

'I'm serious. What would you do?'

'First we need to find out who this Frankie person is,' James said. 'Have you looked on the internet?'

'No...I haven't. To be honest, I hadn't even thought of that,' Alan confessed.

'But you think he was a comedian?'

'That was the impression I got. He said something like he knows what it's like to make people laugh. It was like he was saying that we had a connection.'

'You know your comedy history, did he look familiar?'

Alan shook his head. 'No I didn't recognise him at all,' finishing his drink, he pointed at James's empty glass. 'Another Warty Toad?'

James nodded and looked at Alan's empty glass. 'Is that what I think it is?'

'Afraid so,' he replied, and added as if by explanation, 'I'm on tablets.'

As Alan ambled off to the bar, James reached into his pocket for his mobile phone. Staring and jabbing away at the screen, he swore several times as his thumbs proved far too big to hit the right keys.

'Who you calling?' Alan's question brought James' attention back from his phone.

'Ghostbusters. Who else?' James replied smiling. 'I'm trying to access the internet with this piece of shit,' he gestured at the mobile on the table in front of him. 'But it's as good as useless. Stupid little buttons, I've no idea if I've accessed the internet, made a phone call or turned the poxy thing off.'

Alan placed the dark brown drink in front of James and sat down. 'What are you trying to do anyway?'

'Thought I'd make a start and search the web for your new friend Frankie.'

'Good luck with that,' Alan replied. 'The signals' a bit rubbish in here and the Wi-Fi is non-existent. I'll try later.'

James took a long mouthful of his Warty Toad, looking disappointed. 'Aren't you eager to know if this bloke's real. I know I am.'

'It'll have to wait until later, probably tomorrow. I'm at Rosie's tonight and I'd sooner not do it there. She'll ask me questions and I'll have to lie to her, and she'll find out eventually. It's not worth the grief.'

'No time like the present then. Drink up we'll go back to mine.'

'Are you sure?'

'Definitely. Anyway,' he pointed at the blank TV on the wall, 'there's not much happening in the football tonight.'

*

James lived a fifteen minute walk from the Cloven Hoof in a newly built estate of three and four bedroom houses. As they walked up the path to James' front door, Alan could see that the house was in darkness.

'Amy not in?' he asked.

'Volleyball tonight. Probably not back until after ten.'

James opened the door and led Alan into the hall. He flicked on the light which revealed the neutral coloured walls and framed prints.

'The Den?' Alan asked.

'Go up. I'll get some beers. Or do you still want a soft drink?'

'Beer. I only promised Rosie that I wouldn't be drinking in the pub.'

Alan walked up the stairs and along the hall to the third bedroom, which James had taken occupation of and christened it his "Den." Alan and James had spent many hours in there arguing over music, football and playing computer games.

Alan opened the door and switched on the light. The room was small, with shelves lining two walls. The shelves were filled with CDs, books and DVDs. A desk under the window held a laptop, a 19 inch TV and games console. Alongside the desk stood James's pride and joy - his most treasured possession - an electric guitar on a stand.

Alan pulled out a chair from under the desk and sat himself down. There was a CD case on the desk which Alan noted was The Beatles' Red Album.

The door opened and James strode in armed with two open bottles of German lager.

'Have you got anything by the Monkees?' Alan asked and put the CD case back on the desk.

'I'll pretend I didn't hear that and if you mention them again I'll beat you to death with the guitar.'

Without looking at James, Alan said, 'At least you'll get some use out of it.'

James ignored Alan's attempts to goad him and put the beers on the desk. He pulled the laptop across the desk closer to him and turned it on. 'Right,' he said, 'Let's get this sorted. Frankie Fortune?' James asked.

'That's what he said,' Alan confirmed.

James typed the two words into his search engine. Almost instantaneously the page refreshed and from his position Alan could see a number of entries. James clicked on the first entry and a page opened in front of them. At the top of the page was a black and white photograph.

James moved the laptop along the desk towards Alan. 'Is that him?' he asked.

Alan looked at the screen. It was a shot of a man in his early fifties with white hair and a fairly large nose.

'Bloody hell, that's him!' Alan exclaimed. 'He looked older when I saw him, but it's definitely him.'

Taking the laptop back, James began to scroll down the page. 'It's only a small entry,' he said.

'That's what Amy says about your wedding night.' Alan commented.

Ignoring Alan's attempt to wind him up, James read from the page. 'Says here he was born in 1919. He served in the Second World War, there's no details about what he did though. But it says that he started performing in Music Halls in the fifties and was a regular on the comedy circuit during the sixties and seventies.'

James read a little more. 'He made a few appearances on a TV show called *"Stand Ups"* during the 1970s.'

'I've heard of that,' Alan said, 'I think it was clips of comedians telling a few jokes. I suppose it did for them then what the internet does now.'

James continued on. 'There's not much else other than he died in 1982 …..' he paused.

'What?' Alan asked.

'You are not going to believe this!'

'What?' Alan asked again.

'You are really not going to believe this.' James swallowed and read what was on the screen again, this time out loud. 'Frankie Fortune died on 2 March 1982 after appearing on stage. It says here that he suffered a heart attack in his dressing room following an appearance at the …. Merton Palace Theatre!'

Alan reached over and pulled the laptop towards him. He read the entry and looked at James.

'Well that's fucking weird,' he said.

*

James pressed play and waited for the clip to start. The picture on screen was not great, but as Alan pointed out, full HD was fifty years away. In fact they should be grateful that there was a clip of any description to view.

The clip began. Looking a little younger than when he appeared in Alan's kitchen, but wearing the same green velvet jacket and frilly shirt, Frankie Fortune began his routine.

'Sorry I'm a bit late tonight. I was stuck in traffic on my way here. A lorry load of fabric conditioner was stolen from a truck on the motorway. The police were on the scene, but said the villains made a clean getaway!'

The audience applauded.

'It's the wife's birthday tomorrow. I said to her what do you want, she said "something to make the wrinkles go away" so I bought her an iron!'

The audience applauded, some whistled.

'I'm not saying the wife's ugly, but wasps close their eyes before they sting her!'

The audience applauded and whistled again.

'Don't get the wrong idea. I love my wife, and her mother is a lovely person. In fact I have a soft spot for the wife's mother – the quicksand on Morecambe Bay!'

The audience applauded again.

Alan looked across at James. 'Are you laughing?'

'Well it is a bit funny. Don't you find it funny?'

'Not really, he's just insulting his wife and mother in law. Not really clever is it?'

'Unlike your attack on that fat kid who got stuck in the water flume.'

'That's different,' Alan replied, leaning over and pausing the clip.

'OK,' James said, 'What now?'

*

Alan and James sat slouched in their chairs, half empty bottles of beer in their laps.

'Three hours ago,' James said, 'all I was thinking about was whether I could persuade Amy to go to a fancy dress party as a French Maid. Now my head's full of ghosts and weird shit.'

Alan drained the remainder of his beer and put the bottle on the floor. 'You should have said something. I would have asked Frankie to delay haunting me until you'd sorted out your sexual fantasies.'

James looked at Alan. 'You'll have to get an exorcist. You can't be haunted, you hate ghosts. Remember when we went to see the Blair Witch Project? You were terrified and had to sleep in your parent's room for a week.'

'It was a bloody scary film and in any case, it was only two nights,' Alan replied. 'Anyway where do you suggest I find an Exorcist? Shall I look at the wanted ads on the board outside the church or look in the yellow pages?'

'Neither,' James responded smugly. 'We know an exorcist.'

Alan stared at James. 'Fuck off we do. Really. Who?'

'You know Geoff? Arsenal fan drinks down the Hoof.'

Alan sometimes wondered just how James managed to collect so many oddballs as friends. 'Geoff? He's a plumber, right? He fixes leaks and pipes. He doesn't do exorcisms.'

'That's where you are wrong, my friend. By day he's a plumber, but at night he does exorcisms.'

'Aren't they supposed to be special priests or something?'

'That's what I thought, but Geoff saw an advert for an on line course in exorcism and thought he'd give it a go. He really liked the film and thought it would be a bit of a lark. Anyway, he did really well, he's recently gone from a Grade one to a Grade two exorcist.'

'Grade two?' Alan asked. This conversation was losing him fast. Maybe this was what it was like for Rosie when she was listening to him.

'Yes. A Grade two means that he can exorcise goblins and little demons and your basic non-malevolent entity. I suppose like your man Frankie.'

'What did he have to do to qualify as a grade two?'

'Pay another tenner.'

Alan sighed. 'I think I'll pass on Geoff, thanks all the same. None of the films I have seen featuring an exorcist ever end well. The exorcist always aggravates the spirit and I have no faith in Geoff's abilities to help out on this one,' Alan continued, suddenly thinking of something else. 'Didn't Geoff plumb your washing machine in?'

'Yes.'

'And didn't it flood, causing a grand's worth of damage?'

'Yes.'

'And didn't Amy say that if she saw him anywhere near the house again she'd slice his nuts off?'

'Yes, she did say that,' James admitted.

'So you can forgive me if I'd sooner not have Geoff the failed plumber dabble with the powers of darkness in my house. Knowing him, by the time he left, the house would be full of moaning wailing spirits clanking chains and opening the gateway to hell while I'm trying to watch Football Focus.'

James put his hands up in mock surrender. 'OK, calm down. Just trying to help.'

Alan slumped back in the chair. 'I don't know what I'm going to do. To be honest I'm more annoyed than scared.'

'OK, if not an exorcist, what about a medium?' James asked helpfully.

'Let me guess, a friend of yours happens to be a bricklayer by day and a medium at night? For a small donation of £20 they'll put me in touch with any number of dead people who may or may not bear a vague resemblance to one of my dead relatives. And anyway, I've already had a conversation with him. I'm not sure what a medium could do for me.'

'Yes, but you told me he keeps vanishing. That's got to make talking difficult.'

Alan shifted in his seat. 'Maybe he'll stick around longer next time.'

'I'm serious, what about a medium?' James said.

Short of a more intelligent solution, Alan conceded, 'Oh for heaven's sake, go on then.'

'As it happens I know a medium. My mum used one to talk to my dad.'

Alan frowned. 'Your dad's still alive.'

'Yes, but when he split up from my mum, he lived next door to a medium. He and my mum weren't speaking at the time so my mum used to send messages to my dad via the medium. Mrs Slocombe I think her name was.'

'And Mrs Slocombe can speak to the dead?'

'I have no idea, but she's still practising. I've seen her advert in the local paper.'

Alan sighed. 'OK, let's go and see her. What have I got lose?'

'That's the spirit,' James grinned.

Chapter 18

'I can't see there being any problem whatsoever,' Crozier said into the telephone, while doodling aimlessly on the pad in front of him, emphasizing his lack of interest in the conversation. After a pause he continued, 'I'll be recommending that the planning committee approve the development plans.'

Crozier paused again while listening to the concerned voice on the other end of the telephone. 'No I really don't see there being any problems. Yes, I know how much you have riding on this, and its money well spent. You really have to trust me.'

Crozier paused again before adding, 'I briefed the committee yesterday on the objections, and advised them of our response to them.' He shifted in his seat and transferred the telephone from his right to his left ear.

'Well for a start your plans are only in respect of seven hundred dwellings. You've got some affordable properties there and that'll help the council meet their targets, so they're on your side already.'

He listened to the response before replying, 'No, No, I understand the objection about insufficient GP resources but the committee accept that there is an adequate A&E unit eighteen miles away. If people are sick then they can travel to the hospital. That's what hospitals are for - healing sick people.'

He laughed at the response. 'No, it's not being shut down or being down-graded. Not in this financial year anyway.'

Crozier studied the document in front of him. Taking a pen in his right hand he underlined the second line several times for emphasis.

'And the issue over the lack of school space won't stand up either. The council have given the local primary school permission to install two portakabins which they can use as class rooms. It might be a bit hot in summer, but they'll be installed in winter and no one will actually realise that until it's too late.'

Crozier turned a page and a smile crossed his face.

'The objections raised by the users of the children's playground will be thrown out. I explained to the committee that there had been several instances of needles being found in the playground, and that it was considered a hazard by the local community.' Crozier smiled again, 'I assume that you did as I suggested and got someone to actually leave needles around the playground?'

He tilted his head to the left, squeezing the phone between his ear and shoulder and put the document into a folder.

'Yes, I was quite pleased with that myself. I've used it a few times before and it's normally successful, and anyway there's a soft play area and a ball pit at the local leisure centre, that's more than enough to cater for the needs of the local community.'

Crozier leaned back in his chair, looking to bring an end to the conversation.

'So there's nothing to worry about. Why don't you relax and wait for the committee to approve your application? You can fill time by lining up your bulldozers and waiting for the green light.'

Crozier paused and listened, 'Lunch next week? Tuesday? I think that should be ok I'll check.'

Crozier looked across the desk to where Alison sat bound to the swivel chair opposite. Unable to speak through the red rubber ball gag, she nodded to indicate Tuesday was fine, her blonde hair falling over across her face.

'My secretary just confirmed that Tuesday's good. I'm looking forward to it. Let me know when and where, and I'll be there.' As an afterthought he added, 'I'm sure we'll have something to celebrate. Goodbye.'

Crozier put the phone down on the desk.

'Damien's getting nervy about the planning meeting tomorrow,' he explained. 'You heard me try to tell him that it would be OK. I don't know why he keeps worrying.'

Alison blinked.

Crozier stood up, put his hands in his pockets and slowly walked around the desk. He stopped behind Alison's chair and slowly turned it round on its swivel until she was facing him.

'I haven't heard from Clive since we met at that weird old school of his. Are you sure that he hasn't called?'

Alison shook her head.

'He was supposed to have made an approach to the owners by now. I thought he was going to keep me updated.'

Alison stared back. 'Mmmmm,' she mumbled from behind the gag.

'Sorry, what was that?' Crozier asked.

'Mmmmm,' Alison mumbled again.

Crozier bent down and untied the gag.

'Do you mind if I leave a bit earlier tonight? I have to collect some dry cleaning,' she asked.

Crozier wasn't expecting that. 'Er, yes... just make the time up will you? Tomorrow if you can.'

'I will. Thank you.'

Crozier replaced the gag. He stepped back as he casually pushed her chair, spinning it round as he continued talking.

'He also said that he was looking to get into the theatre, have a look round and get a feel for the place. I don't know why he wants to do that if he's planning to knock it down. It's not like he's popping round to measure the place for curtains.'

'Urghh,' Alison said.

Crozier stopped spinning the chair round and looked at Alison. 'Sorry, I got carried away. Hang on,' he said, bending down to remove the gag.

'Dizzy,' she said, 'Feel sick.'

Crozier watched her normally pale face take on a green hue.

'Don't worry, I can fix that,' he said and began to spin her round in the opposite direction.

The chair completed another half a dozen revolutions before she groaned again.

'Urghhhh.'

'What was that? 'Crozier asked. 'Do you want me to stop?'

'Pleeeaaaase!'

'OK,' Crozier stopped spinning the chair and looked down at her. 'Is that better?' he asked, and began to untie her.

'Feel a bit sick,' she said weakly. 'Need some fresh air.'

Crozier untied the last of the knots. 'There you go.'

Alison gingerly got to her feet, taking three steps before collapsing on the floor. Crozier stood leaning against the desk, making no effort to assist her up.

'Are you feeling better now?' he asked.

'Yes. Thank you,' she replied groggily. 'Can I stay here for a bit? At least until the room stops spinning round.'

Crozier had moved back behind the desk and sat back in his chair. Without looking back at the figure lying face down on the floor he said, 'OK, take a few minutes.'

Crozier turned to his PC. There were a number of e-mails that had arrived during his conversation with the nervy Damien, none of which required his attention. He knew that he should be preparing for his meeting with the planning committee the following day, and there were more than just Damien's application to consider, but he had no financial incentives to support any other applications.

'Alison,' he called out.

'Yes David,' she replied, still lying on the floor.

'Any chance of a coffee?'

Clive Oneway chewed the end of his pencil thoughtfully while looking over the picture of the Spinning Jenny. What on Earth is that? *He thought to himself.* How can it be anything?

He took his pencil and began to sketch the Spinning Jenny onto a blank page in his exercise book. He heard the cry "Neckback!" a second before he felt the slap on the back of his neck. His head shot forward with the force of the blow, and he dropped his pencil on the floor. He heard the laughter from the rest of the class behind him and tried not to react.

The offender, Neville, walked round to the front of Oneway's desk. 'Arggggh Stumpy!!' he screamed into Oneway's face.

'Neville! Will you please go back to your desk and sit down!' Mr Knave, the class teacher called out, showing Neville, Oneway thought, far more respect than he deserved.

Oneway picked his pencil from the floor and attempted to continue his drawing of the Spinning Jenny. He could hear Neville laughing behind him. Oneway was sure that he was the subject of the joke. He forced himself not to turn round and instead chose to look out of the window at the rain.

*

Standing in the cold damp classroom, Oneway stared out of the window at the rain. It was different rain, obviously, but it was the same window in the same classroom. Just thirty years later. The view had hardly changed. Maybe the concrete walkway was a little more cracked, and some of the windows in the classrooms opposite were missing, but it was still essentially the same bland, soul destroying view that Oneway had stared at so often on his school days.

The classroom was empty. The building had been gutted of all furniture and fixtures that had a resale value. Oneway had no interest in anything inside the school. All he wanted was the building.

*

The light hurt Oneway's eyes. He had been in the locker for the entire lunch period, propelled there by the toe of Neville's monkey boot. Oneway had let his guard drop briefly, turning his back on the corridor just as Neville and his gang came marauding past. Later, much later, Oneway would almost admire the swift seamless action that Neville had adopted, briefly pausing to flick him into his locker with his right foot before slamming and locking the door behind him.

Oneway half stepped, half fell out of the now open locker, landing at the feet of the teacher who had become his rescuer.

'What were you doing in there Oneway?' the teacher asked.

'I tripped and fell in, Sir,' Oneway replied unconvincingly, while trying to straighten out his body.

'And the door slammed shut and locked itself behind you did it? Do you think I'm stupid?'

'That's what happened, Sir.'

The teacher rolled his eyes. 'Detention. One hour after school tonight,' he said and walked away.

Oneway was actually relieved. He regarded an hour in the detention class as a lucky break. He would get his homework completed and would avoid Neville and his idiot friends on the way home.

Oneway knew he could easily have said Neville had kicked him in the locker but he knew he would then be considered a grass and however bad his life was at the moment, Neville could quite easily make it a hell of a lot worse.

*

Oneway walked down the corridor on his way out of the building. The lockers were long gone, although the darker shade of purple on the wall indicated were they had been.

From his first year to the day he had finished at Buggerly Mount School, Oneway's life had been a misery. Picked on by the other pupils and treated with contempt by the teachers, he had escaped into books, records and television. He had told himself that he was living out a modern version of Tom Brown's Schooldays, with himself as the principal character, and Neville as the notorious school bully Flashman. Something which, if Neville had ever found out, would have pleased him no end.

Being small didn't help. He had been the smallest child in the school for the first three years he was there, giving him the nickname "Stumpy." Unfortunately, by the time he eventually started growing, the nickname stuck.

*

Oneway crashed in through the front door and was heading up the stairs to his room when his father came out of the dining room.

'Clive, it's considered good manners to at least say hello when you get home.'

Oneway stopped and turned round, walking back down the stairs until his father could see him.

'Oh my god! What happened to you?'

Oneway stopped on the stairs. His hair and forehead were bright blue.

'Well. What happened?' his father asked again.

Oneway sniffed. 'They held my head in the toilet and poured stuff on it. Blue stuff.'

'I can see its blue, but who did it? Who poured the stuff on you?'

'The big kids,' he replied.

'Clive, half the school is bigger than you, please be more specific?'

Even his own father would mock him.

*

Oneway smiled to himself as the memories slowly seeped back. This was not unusual. Since he had bought the school, he had walked around the building several times, experiencing a mixed range of emotions ranging from bad to terrible, and depressing to suicidal. He found he would often feel the need to perform this masochistic ritual after having had a successful period at work, and as he got closer to the biggest deal of his life, the desire to walk the now deserted and derelict corridors was stronger than ever. This action, he had decided after a few drinks and a long period of self-analysis, was his way of sticking two fingers up at scene of such misery.

'Look at me now. Look what I've done!' he shouted to himself in the empty room that used to be a workshop.

Unsurprisingly, the workshops had been cleared of anything with a resale value long before Oneway had purchased the school. As he looked around the damp room, his thoughts were of chisels, screwdrivers and hammers, rather than dove tailed joints and lathes.

*

'Oi Stumpy!' The cry filled the corridor. *Oneway, for a brief moment thought he would run. He was sure he could make it to the end of the corridor and be through the double doors before Neville could reach him, and that might, if he was lucky, put off the encounter for a couple of hours. Unfortunately his hesitation cost him the opportunity of escape, and he felt a hand on his shoulder and Neville's voice in his ear.*

'Didn't you hear me you deaf sod? I was calling you.'

'S...S...Sorry Neville. I didn't hear you, he said apologetically.

Ignoring him, Neville continued, 'You coming tonight?' It sounded more like a statement of fact than an invitation, and he feared the answer to his question.

'What's happening?'

'It's that Kier Hardie mob. They've been pushing their luck again.'

Oneway knew what this meant. A fight with another school. Kier Hardie Comprehensive was the nearest boy's school, and the usual targets when Buggerly Mount's self-appointed guardians of justice got bored.

'What have they done?' he asked.

You know Rudder in the fifth year?'

He nodded. Rudder, or to give him his proper name, Gary Layton, had a club foot and had been renamed Rudder by the wits of the school.

'A car load of Kier Hardie fuckers came past and were calling him spaz,' Neville said.

Oneway stared up at Neville and thought about all the times he had heard him call him spaz too, but decided it was wise to keep quiet on that point.

'Come on Stumpy. You have to be there. The honour of the school is at stake.'

Neville referred to "honour" as if he had been accused of cheating at cards in a 17th Century Gentleman's club, and was preparing for a duel at dawn. Whereas in reality,

138

Oneway doubted that Neville could even spell "honour" and would willingly burn the school down with all the pupils and staff still inside simply to get an afternoon off.

'I don't know, I can't fight,' he mumbled.

'For God's sake Stumpy, sort your life out. Be outside after school.'

Oneway nodded and wandered off down the corridor, listening as Neville pressganged other kids into defending the honour of the school.

It was no surprise that a school fight was looming. Over the last few days, those that attended the woodwork or metal work classes would have noticed that the number of tools was reducing; hammers, chisels, screwdrivers and a lathe had gone missing. All likely weapons for the school fight that afternoon. The experienced teachers knew that this meant that something was up, and decided to stay locked in the staffroom for a couple of hours. The experienced pupils, who also guessed something was up, left school and headed straight to the likely scene of the fight, keen to secure a good vantage point.

Oneway had no intention of being beaten up in a school fight, and as soon as school finished that afternoon, he slipped away, exiting via Buggerly Mount's rarely used back entrance. His plan was to take the long way home, thus avoiding the roads and parks that lay between Buggerly Mount and Kier Hardie Comprehensive. Oneway was confident that the likely blows that Neville would take to his head during the fight would lead to him forget that Oneway was supposed to be there.

Oneway would often look back at that decision as being one of the worst that he ever made.

He left school as planned, avoiding Neville and the rest of the tooled up idiots who were gathering at the school entrance. Being generally anonymous, it was relatively easy to slip away unnoticed. However, his detour took him across Fitzhugh Common, and it was as he left the overgrown woodland area and joined a foot path the he saw the four girls walking towards him. They were wearing the dark brown uniform of the Holy Cross Convent School, the nearest girl's school to Buggerly Mount.

He moved off the path to allow the girls to walk past him. As he moved however, the girls spread out blocking his route.

'Look what we've got here,' the girl directly in front of him said. 'A little first year from the Mount.'

He looked up at the girl, his eyes drawn to the stud in her nose. 'Actually, I'm a fourth year,' he said defiantly.

'You look like a first year. You're tiny,' one of the other girls said, laughing at him.
He made to walk to round the girls, but as he did he felt his bag pulled back.
'What's in here?' the girl with the stud in her nose asked.
'It's mine,' he said and pulled the bag back towards him.
'I want a look!' the girl said again, this time with far more menace in her voice.
Not wanting to be mugged by some Convent School girls, he sprinted away. Breathing hard, chest burning, he

allowed himself a quick glance behind to see if the girls were following him, and at that moment ran into a tree.

He had never told anyone that the black eye and cut nose that he had sported at school for several days after the school fight, had actually occurred when he ran into a tree whilst being chased by four schoolgirls. His story that he had been set upon by an advanced party from Kier Hardie was accepted by everyone who asked after his wounds.

One person who was missing from school following the fight was Neville. Oneway later learnt that Neville had been arrested by the police when he was caught assaulting a Kier Hardie pupil with a hammer, and no one was quite sure when he would be returning.

*

Oneway locked the main school gates and got back in to his car, his tour of the site complete for the moment. A private security firm was responsible for the site overnight which often struck him as an unnecessary expense. Who would be so stupid as to break in to this hell hole, he thought. In his experience, anyone who ever spent any time at Buggerly Mount had spent most of that time devising ways of getting out.

Before starting the engine, he picked up his mobile and chose one of the saved numbers. 'Hello,' he said, 'Its Clive Oneway. I was wondering if Tatiana was available tonight. She is? Excellent, I'll meet her at the usual place.'

Clive Oneway smiled, put the mobile on the passenger seat and drove back to work.

Chapter 20

Amy stood in the playground and watched as the children boarded the luxury coach for the thirty minute journey to the Merton Palace Theatre. Whilst she accepted that the term "luxury" could mean many different things to many people, this was stretching the definition to its very limits.

The coach may have been cutting edge in passenger transport in 1975, it was however, falling short in the luxury aspect forty years later. Amy conceded that its burgundy and cream bodywork was shiny and clean, and even the coach company's logo "Runaway Coaches" caught the eye. However there was no getting away from the fact that it was a forty year old coach.

Amy watched the last child, lunch bag slung over his shoulder, climb the steps and board the coach. She looked around the playground making sure that no one had been left behind and then boarded the coach herself.

Predictably the children had started filling the coach from the back. Her heart sank when she saw the headmaster, Stretton La Mon sitting in one of the seats directly behind the driver. He smiled at her and patted the empty seat next to him in an avuncular manner.

There being no alternative, Amy reluctantly dropped into the seat alongside her headmaster.

'I saved the seat for you!' Stretton said.

Amy doubted that the children had been fighting amongst themselves to grab the empty seat next to him, but graciously sat down as invited, once Stretton had moved his hand from the suspiciously stained seat.

'Thanks,' she said.

Stretton leaned forward and tapped the driver on the shoulder. He turned around and Amy could see that he appeared to be in his late fifties or perhaps early sixties. She imagined that he was old enough to have seen the coach set off on its maiden journey. He wore a blue jacket with a name tag over his chest pocket which simply said, "Harris."

'Harris,' Stretton said, as if he was addressing an old family retainer.

'Who's Harris?' The driver wheezed with a voice that suggested the effects of breathing in leaded fuel fumes for a very long time.

Stretton stared at the driver before saying, 'You are. It says so on your jacket.'

The driver pulled the badge out and looked down at it. 'My name's Harrison. They couldn't fit it in, Harris is all that fits.'

Knowing he was beaten Stretton continued, 'Merton Palace Theatre. Do you know where that is? I have the postcode if you want to put that into the sat nav.'

The driver glanced over at the dashboard. Amongst the switches and knobs was a radio which Amy thought was probably the original, and would at best only receive long wave and short wave. It was wildly ambitious to assume this museum piece would have a sat nav.

'I know where it is,' the driver wheezed.

'Ok then Harris,' said Stratton. 'Ready when you are.' He sat back in his seat and leaned across to Amy. 'Right,' he said, 'that's all sorted now. Next stop the theatre.'

Without warning, the coach began to shake and splutter. The driver kept his foot down and turned the key in the ignition. After a few more seconds, the engine roared into life. The windows shook and the roaring of the engine got louder. Amy gripped the arm rests as Stretton looked over.

'Take off is always the most dangerous part!' he said and laughed.

Amy turned away from him and thought, *'Knob.'*

The noise gradually subsided and the coach eased out of the school playground, joining the traffic. Amy looked across at Stretton. 'What happened to our usual coach company?' she asked.

Stretton put down the newspaper that he had been attempting to read. 'Cuts Amy. The budgets have been squeezed. We've practically run out of funds, so I had to cancel the contract with the normal company. Fortunately these guys - Runaway Coaches - were able to step in and help us out. They are far more affordable and offer a full refund in the event of the coach crashing or breaking down.'

'Oh what a result. Haven't we done well?' Amy replied with her tongue firmly in her cheek.

'We've had a lot of expense recently,' Stretton continued. 'The Governors box at the Albert Hall needed to be paid for, and there has been a fair amount of decorating and building work that needed doing.'

Yeah, that was your office. Amy thought.

'And not forgetting that we had to have new gates on the school entrance.'

Because you were worried about scratching your car on the old one, Amy thought again.

Stretton's fiscal concerns were interrupted by a cry from the back of the coach.

'Mrs Cook, Harry's not well.'

Amy stood up and heard the sound of retching followed by a splash.

'OK, I'm coming,' she said. 'Can I ask you to use the bags in the netting in the back of the seat in front of you if you are feeling ill?'

Amy heard the driver's wheezing croaky voice behind her, 'We haven't got any.'

Great, she thought and glared at Stretton as she walked to the back of the coach.

Stretton turned his attention back to his paper. He could hear the sound of retching and decided to keep his head down and his feet off the ground.

*

The coach made slow progress. It appeared to hit every red traffic light on its route, every speed bump required two attempts to get over, and Stretton could not decide if the gasping noise he heard was the coach or its driver.

Amy eventually reappeared. She was carefully holding a bulging carrier bag. Stretton had no desire to know what was in there. Instead he looked at Amy. He thought she was extremely attractive. He liked the way that she

146

had tied her hair back in a ponytail, and she had very long legs, which was normally enough to keep him distracted whenever she spoke.

Amy deposited the bulging carrier bag in the bin by the door and then took her seat next to Stretton. He thrust the newspaper that he had been reading at her.

'Have you seen this?' he asked, pointing at the lead item on the page. 'It's predicted that in ten years, eighty percent of children will be obese. There's going to be a point when the kids won't be able to get their podgy little hands around their games console controllers. Think of the design issues that that will cause.'

Amy was wiping little pieces of carrot off of her boots and replied to Stretton without looking at him, 'I would imagine that there are more long term problems than being able to handle a controller comfortably.'

'I think we should do something about this. I think as a school we have to be seen to be doing more than just paying lip service to the problem.' Stretton delivered his opinion as if he was running for public office. He continued, 'I think we should increase the number of hours that the children have for exercise and games, offer more extra-curricular sports, and make sure that we offer the healthiest choices at mealtime.'

Amy was impressed. 'That's an impressive statement. What about the budget problems where...' she was prevented from finishing her sentence by the sudden laughter and shouting from the back of the coach.

Stretton stood up and walked into the aisle. 'Children,' he called out, 'Mrs Cook and I are discussing important school business. If you can please keep quiet for the rest of the journey, I will buy you all chips from the chip shop on the way back.'

This news was greeted by a massive cheer from the children, whilst Amy looked to the heavens and slumped back into her seat.

*

The theatre had no designated parking spaces, so the coach stopped outside the theatre, blocking the traffic.

The noise and shuddering of the coach took a couple of minutes to subside once the engine had been turned off, much to the amusement of the children, and to the frustration of the drivers of cars trying to get past. When the engine finally came to a stop, the door opened and Amy stepped out.

The children filtered out of the coach in single file, looking paler than they had when they entered. Amy directed them to stand outside the theatre's doors in an orderly manner. When the last child left the coach, Amy did a head count. Thankfully, it tallied with the number on her clipboard. Ready to move on she looked into the coach. Stretton was talking to the driver.

'Harris,' he said, 'you know to be here at 3.00pm sharp to collect us and return us back to the school?'

The driver pointed a sheaf of papers which were pushed down between his seat and the floor. 'That's what it says there.'

'OK. We'll see you then,' Stretton replied before turning and walking down the steps to the door. Before leaving the coach he paused, turned round and called out.

'Is there any possibility that you can do something about the smell of the kid sick before you pick us up?'

'I'll get the boys back at the garage onto it,' the driver replied with contempt.

'Good man,' Stretton said and exited the coach.

The driver leaned forward in his seat resting both forearms on the steering wheel. 'Tosser,' he said.

*

Amy led the children into the theatre. The foyer was as imposing as she remembered from the fund raising night. Without the crowds of people milling around, she was able to appreciate the architecture.

A folding table, looking out of place amongst such ornate surroundings, was positioned to the left of the foyer. Two large cardboard boxes were stacked on the table behind which stood a man. He wore a denim jacket and Amy thought he looked no older than twenty five. Smiling, he extended his arm to shake her hand.

'Mrs Cook?' he asked.

On closer inspection Amy reassessed his age to be nearer eighteen.

'Hi,' she said, and shook his hand.

'I'm Nav,' he announced. 'I'll be your host for today.'

'Hi Nav, I'm Amy.'

'If it's OK with you, I'll speak to the children now and tell them what we've got planned for today,' Nav said.

'That's fine. Please do. They're quite excited. A lot of them have never been in a theatre before,' Amy said.

Nav smiled and was about to start his introductory speech when another person appeared between him and Amy. He looked at Nav and said, 'Stretton La Mon. I'm the headmaster. Who are you?'

'This is Nav,' Amy said. 'He's our host for today. He's just about to speak to the children, explain what they're going to be doing all day.'

'Excellent. Carry on. Pretend I'm not here,' Stretton said.

Wishing that was possible, Amy stepped aside so that all the children could see Nav. He coughed nervously and said, 'Hello and welcome to the Merton Palace Theatre. Today you're going to spend some time working with some actors, who will teach you some theatre skills, and then help you put on a play for your teachers here,' Nav smiled at Amy. 'Mrs Cook and Mr Lemon...'

Amy stifled a giggle and Stretton said loudly, 'It's La Mon.'

Nav raised his hand in apology and continued. 'Putting on a play for your teachers Mrs Cook and Mr La Mon,' Nav gave a quick glance in Stretton's direction. Stretton nodded and Nav continued. 'But first I'm going to give you all a pack that contains information about the theatre, and gives you more information about what you are going to be doing today. After that, I'm going to take you on a tour of the theatre. Would you like that?'

The children shouted that they would indeed like that and Nav turned to Amy.

'Mrs Cook could you help me give out the packs?'

'Of course,' she said 'and it's Amy, not Mrs Cook. Every time I hear that, I expect my mother-in-law to appear round the corner.'

Nav smiled and reached into one of the cardboard boxes. He took out several plastic envelopes and passed them to Amy. 'These are the packs. Can you pass them around to the children?' he asked.

Amy took the plastic packs and began handing them out. Nav turned to Stretton.

'Mr La Mon, would you like to help distribute these?' he asked.

'Most certainly not! I'm the headmaster. You do it. I'll stand here and keep an eye on things,' he said.

Nav wondered what things needed an eye kept on them, but took one of the cardboard boxes and began to distribute the packs himself.

*

Even Stretton had to accept that Nav put together a fascinating tour of the theatre. Both he and Amy found themselves as captivated as Nav walked them through the corridors and passages which ran around the theatre like a spider's web. He showed them the dressing rooms, the storage rooms, and the space under the stage, explaining how the magicians and music hall acts had originally used it.

'I was here a few weeks ago,' Amy said to Nav while they watched the children looking into the trap door. 'A comedy fund raising night.'

Oh yes, that's all part of the theatre restoration project. Did you enjoy it?' Nav asked.

'A friend of mine is a comedian. He was performing. It was quite good actually.'

'Good. I'm glad you enjoyed it. Do I know him, your friend? Is your friend funny?'

Amy sighed. 'His name's Alan Rose, and no, not really.'

'Oh. OK,' Nav replied. 'Never heard of him. Anyway, the plan is to refurbish the theatre in its entirety and put it back to its original condition.'

'How's the appeal going?' Amy asked.

'Not bad. It's still early days, but we've got plans and we're hoping to attract contributions from local businesses as well as a lottery grant. It's an exciting time.'

The conversation was cut short by the appearance at Amy's side of one of the children.

'Mrs Cook, Mr La Mon is stuck in the trap door!'

*

Clive Oneway had lied all his life. He had lied his way through his school days, although he would argue that was predominately for self-preservation. He lied through his university days, and he lied in business. Indeed it was questionable whether he could actually distinguish between truth and fiction anymore.

152

Oneway stood in the foyer of the Merton Palace Theatre as a result of another lie, and like all good lies it held an element of truth in it. Thanks to Crozier's efforts, he had established who the owners were and that the local arts council were responsible for its day to day running. Contacting the local arts council, he introduced himself as a local business man. That was at least truthful - who was keen to make a contribution to the theatre restoration fund, and would welcome the opportunity of having a look round when it was convenient.

Unsurprisingly, the arts council had proved to be more than accommodating, and they had arranged for him to visit at the same time as a school visit. Now here he was, listening as a young boy named Nav told him all about the theatre's history. At least that was what Oneway assumed he was being told. He had switched off some time ago, as he considered architecture and building history as even more boring than Crozier recounting his golf stories.

His desire to see the building was based on nothing more than idle curiosity. He had looked round all the neighbouring units, although not under any pretence. The owners having already gratefully accepted the financial offer he had made. No, he simply liked to get a feel for the site, and visualise how it would be replaced with something else. Something profitable.

Unlike the school party that stood in the foyer two hours earlier, he was completely unimpressed. The grandness did nothing for him. In fact all he could see was chipped stonework and cracked tiles. To Oneway, the building was cold, empty and smelled funny.

He was suddenly aware that Nav was quiet. 'Sorry. What was that? I was just looking around. It's an impressive place. It must been very grand in its day.'

'It certainly is, Nav said. 'I was just saying that I understand you want to make a contribution to the theatre restoration fund.'

'Yes, that's right.'

'That's very generous of you.'

Oneway was constantly amazed at how gullible people were. They were usually desperate to believe what he said, so had no problem accepting his words at face value.

'I just think it's my opportunity to put something back into the community,' Oneway lied while fighting to urge to add *by pulling this slum down and putting up a nice new shopping centre.*

'I'm sure that you won't be disappointed with your investment,' Nav said.

'Oh, I'm sure I won't,' Oneway grinned in return.

'OK I'm going to walk you through the theatre now, give you a chance to see everything that you're investing in.'

Oneway followed Nav into the heart of the theatre.

*

Oneway quickly decided that Nav's tour of the theatre was one of the dullest things that he had ever endured. They had marched along endless corridors, looked into damp store rooms, and peeked into deserted former dressing rooms. He really did not care about the golden age of music hall, or the magic of theatre. All he cared about was how fast the damn place could be pulled down, be put in skips and dumped somewhere up north. For the sake of his act however, he kept nodding and making encouraging remarks whenever Nav paused in his monologue. It reminded Oneway of those dreadful family gatherings that his mother (before he had her put in a home) used to drag him to. Long forgotten relatives telling him dull and tedious stories about things that he had no interest in. He would then, as now simply nod and smile.

After climbing a flight of stairs, Oneway noticed that one door had red striped hazard tape across the doorway, and a sign stuck to it which said;

DANGER – DO NOT ENTER

'What's through here?' Oneway asked as he tried the door handle.

'That's' the loft space,' Nav said. 'I'm afraid it's not safe. No one is allowed up there until we can make it safe, and that's not going to happen until we have the funds in place. The door stays locked until then.

Oneway shrugged. 'Where next?'

'Just the auditorium left now. If you like what you've just seen you're going to love this,' he said, explaining about the capacity of the auditorium.

'Fascinating,' said Oneway and followed Nav back down the stairs.

Nav and Oneway stood at the back of the auditorium. Rows of empty seats separated them from the stage. On stage there appeared to be a number of children making a lot of noise and running around.

'We cater for school groups,' said Nav by way of explanation. 'They come in, get a tour of the theatre, similar to the one you've just had, and then spend some time with some actors and then they put on a small play.'

Oneway could see that there were two men and a woman on stage directing a group of children to dance in rhythm.

'Come with me, I'll introduce you to the actors,' Nav said, walking towards the stage and the front row of seats. Oneway noticed a woman sitting in the first seat.

'Mrs Cook,' Nav said, 'I'd like you to meet Mr Oneway. He has expressed an interest to contributing to the restoration fund and I'm just showing him round.'

The woman, who had been watching the stage turned to face Nav and politely stood up. As far as Oneway was concerned she was beautiful, stunning even. She was several inches taller than him and seemed to glow against the lighting of the stage.

Oneway reached over to shake her hand. 'Please, call me Clive. Nice to meet you Mrs Cook.'

Amy smiled as she took his hand. 'Nice to meet you too. It's Amy. It's very generous of you to contribute to the theatre fund. Are you fan of the theatre?'

'I love it. It's in my blood. My mother was an actress, and I spent most of my childhood in theatres. I can't get enough of them, bit of a weakness I'm afraid.' Oneway lied with such conviction that he surprised even himself.

'Are you with the school party?' he asked.

'Yes. I'm their teacher, I'm sorry if they're making too much noise up there,' Amy pointed onto the stage.

'Not at all,' Oneway replied, continuing to construct the fantasy life that he was now living in. 'The important thing is that they enjoy the experience and get something out of it.'

Amy smiled again. 'Would you like to watch the play that the children are going to put on?' Amy asked.

'I'd love to,' he replied and took the seat next to Amy.

*

The play was terrible. An awful mess of noise and laughter, children running without purpose around the stage whilst talking unintelligible drivel. Oneway however pretended to love it. He laughed and applauded at the same time as Amy, and even when little Des messed himself, he offered to help Amy clear it up. An offer which in hindsight he was relieved was turned down.

Whenever he could, Oneway would glance across at Amy. He noticed the wedding ring on her finger, but didn't pay too much attention to it. After all, he thought, one in three marriages ended in divorce.

When the play finished, he joined Amy in a bout of over enthusiastic applause.

When she finished clapping, Amy turned to Oneway. 'The children loved this. It's so good to get away from the classroom and have the opportunity of doing something else. It's these little things that really help develop their confidence.'

'I'm sure that you play no small part in their development either,' Oneway said, in an attempt at flattery.

Amy smiled again. 'I'll have to go now,' she said. 'I need to help them clear up and get the children back to school.'

Oneway felt a pang of disappointment. 'Do you need any help?' he asked.

'No. It's OK, thank you. The headmaster is around...somewhere,' she said, standing up and looking around the auditorium.

'It's been nice to meet you Clive.'

Oneway put his hand into his inside jacket pocket and produced a business card, giving it to Amy.

'If you fancy a drink sometime give me a call. I'm sure that we would have lots to talk about,' he said.

'I'm really flattered,' Amy said awkwardly, 'but I'm married. I don't think it would be appropriate.'

Oneway had expected this, but experience taught him exactly how to respond.

'I'm sorry, I wasn't suggesting anything untoward. I just feel we got on and could spend some time talking about the theatre and the opportunities it could offer the children. I expect to have some influence once I make a donation to the restoration fund,' he paused for a moment then added, 'give it some thought and give me a call. My number is on the card.'

Without giving Amy an opportunity to respond, he said goodbye and left the auditorium.

Amy turned the card over in her hand and looked at it;

ONEWAY PROPERTY DEVELOPERS

Managing Director Clive Oneway

As Oneway had said there was a mobile telephone number on the back of the card. Amy looked at the card for a moment or two before slipping it into the back pocket of her jeans, before setting off to find Stretton and getting the children back to the school.

*

After thanking Nav for his time, Oneway made his way out of the theatre. He thought again about Amy, obviously everything that he had told her about the theatre was complete rubbish. All he was interested in was having the chance to take her out and impress her with his luxury flat, his cars and his lifestyle. She was just a teacher, after all, with a teacher's salary. How could she not find him attractive? And after all, if that didn't work he still had the Rohypnol.

Chapter 21

James turned the SUV left into Goddard Road, complaining all the while about the number of other cars in his way. 'I just don't see what they're doing at this time of day,' he moaned, glancing briefly at Alan who was looking pensively out of the passenger window. 'I mean,' he continued, 'shouldn't they be at the football or IKEA or something..? Hello...Hello...earth to Alan.'

'I'm sorry, what?' Alan asked, distracted, turning to face his friend.

'I'm just saying there are too many cars about. I can barely squeeze down the road.'

'That's because your car is the size of a small flat. Why did you even buy this thing? It's far too big and is giving kids asthma as we speak. You should get a smart car.'

'Look at me,' James said, gesturing to his large frame. 'Look at the size of me. And Amy's six foot as well. This is a bloody smart car. For us.'

'Point taken,' Alan replied. 'But did it have to be pink?'

'It's not pink. It's cerise. Amy picked it specifically for the colour. It's very trendy.'

'It's not trendy. It looks like something a gay couple would take camping.'

'Fuck off. The bloke in the garage said it was a very masculine colour.'

'It's pink.' Muttered Alan under his breath.

'I'm sorry?' asked James.

'I said do you think...'

'Do I think what?'

'That this medium is the real deal?'

'Well she's not on TV, so she's got that going for her...'

'Yeah, I guess. By the way,' Alan prompted, changing the subject, 'where did you tell Amy you were going?'

Suppressing a snort, James said, 'I told her I was going to a gig, with you.'

'At two o'clock in the afternoon? And she bought that?'

'To be honest mate, I think she just wanted me out of the house. What did you tell Rosie?'

'She's working. I didn't tell her anything.'

'But you know she'll find out, mate. She always does. She's got some kind of sixth sense that woman.'

'Yeah,' Alan grinned. 'Perhaps I should buy a Ouija board and a couple of bottles of Chardonnay and let Rosie sort this out.'

'So you haven't told her then?'

'You *are* joking. *Rosie, listen, I think I am being haunted.* Yeah, she'll accept that. No questions asked.'

James laughed. 'Fair point, well argued. I think we're coming up to it now.'

James slowed and manoeuvred his car into a convenient parking space beside a row of large terraced three storey Victorian houses.

'This is a bit of alright,' Alan said, leaving the car and looking around at the grandly appointed houses. 'I could see myself living in one of these. It's all me.'

Turning his attention towards the road, a figure emerged from behind a tree immediately in front of him. It was Frankie.

'Sorry,' Frankie said, 'I had a bit of trouble getting back to you. This is a bit of alright,' he said looking up at the houses. 'I used to live in something like this once. It's all me.'

'CHRIST!' Alan shouted, grabbing at James's arm. 'It's him. He's standing there right in front of us,' Alan said, pointing to a tree.

'Where? I can't see him. All I can see is a tree,' whispered James, turning his head left and right, whilst simultaneously rubbing his now bruised arm. 'Why can't *I* see him?' James pouted, clearly put out that his friend could see something he himself could not.

'What's he doing?' Frankie asked, gesturing to James, who was now walking with arms held in front of him as though in a darkened room looking for the light switch.

'I have no idea,' said Alan, looking at his friend quizzically. 'I think he may be trying to find you.'

'But I'm right here.' Frankie replied.

'Yes, I know, but I don't think he can see you.'

'Well, that explains it. I thought he was just a bit slow,' Frankie said, looking James up and down. 'Are you sure he's not at least a little bit simple? I think they can do tests for that sort of thing.'

'Look,' Alan cut in, 'I'm not here to discuss my mate's intellect...'

'..Or lack of it...' Frankie added.

'...I'm here to talk to a medium,' Alan said, looking again at James, who had finally stopped wandering about and was now staring open mouthed at him.

'Why do you want to talk to a medium?' Frankie enquired.

'To talk to you of course.'

'But I'm right here...still,' said Frankie, opening his arms to convey this very fact.

'Yes, I know you're here now. But you keep disappearing, and I have a lot of questions I need to ask you.'

'Like what?' Frankie asked, keeping his arms outstretched.

'Like, what *are* you? I mean I know what you are. Or at least I think I do. But what I don't know is why? Why me? Why are you haunting me?'

'I wasn't aware I was haunting you...hang on, what's he staring at?' asked Frankie, angrily pointing again at James, still standing mouth agape.

Alan turned to look at his friend before turning back to Frankie. 'OK, he might be a *bit* slow.'

The words seemed to awaken James from his trance like state. 'Wait. What? Who's slow? Did he just call me slow? Did *you* just call me slow?'

163

'Sorry mate,' Alan replied, 'It's just difficult, what with him being invisible and stuff.'

'Who are you calling invisible?' said Frankie, indignantly. 'You can see me.'

'Oh, for f...*look,*' Alan pleaded, 'Can I just go to see this medium, to find out what the bloody hell's going on?'

Without waiting for James or Frankie, Alan strode toward the house, where he hoped to gain some answers.

James hurried to catch up to his friend. 'So, you really can see him?'

'..and talk to him,' Alan added.

'...so, what's the point of the medium, then?'

'It was your bloody idea.'

'Yes, but I'm a bit slow, remember?' James grinned at his friend.

Alan laughed. 'Yeah, I guess that's right. Look, we're here now,' he said, walking through the front gate.

'So, we're really doing this, then? I mean, can't you just ask him?' James said, gesturing to the vague area where he thought Frankie might be standing.

'Your weird friend is right,' Frankie said, dodging to the left of James's wildly flailing arms. 'You could just ask me.'

Alan turned from his friend to Frankie. 'Yes, but you could disappear at any time. I mean, it's happened before.'

'But I'm not planning to disappear. I just pop up. As it were. Unexpectedly like.'

Alan knocked on the door and turned to Frankie, 'But you really could be haunting me.'

'I think I would know if I was haunting someone.' Frankie said, rather put out.

'Well, are you haunting me?'

'I have absolutely no idea.'

'Well, that's helpful.'

'Hold up, I think I can hear someone coming,' James said, still slightly torn as to whether his friend was being haunted or whether he was having some kind of breakdown.

Alan turned to look at the approaching figure through the glass pane in the front door. 'Now, you, be on your best behaviour,' he said.

'I'm always on my best behaviour,' James pointed out helpfully.

'Not you, him!' Alan gesticulated to where Frankie had been standing, but where there was now nothing save for thin air and a depressingly fake gargoyle ornament by the wall.

'Oh, that's just brilliant. Just bloody brilliant.' Alan moaned as the front door opened.

*

The door opened to reveal a large man with long black hair tied into a pony tail, wearing a black suit at least one size too small for his frame, and a black shirt so tight a small triangle of exposed pale hairy flesh was visible above his waist.

'We're here to see Mrs Slocombe...' said James. 'The medium,' he added helpfully.

The man looked curiously at the two strangers in front of him. 'I'm afraid she's been unexpectedly called away. You can see me if you like.'

'She clearly didn't see that coming,' said James '...and you are..?'

'I'm Mr Marvon. The locum.'

'Marvellous,' said Alan, who had by now recovered from Frankie's latest disappearing act. Alan looked at James and grinned.

'I'm sorry?' queried the locum.

'Nothing. Sorry. A locum medium. Do you get much work?'

'Up and down. It's hard to tell when you're going to be busy.' Alan glanced at James, who shook his head grinning to himself. 'I'm sorry I didn't catch your names.'

'I'm Alan,' said Alan 'and this is The Cap...this is James,' he added, pointing at his friend.

'Well, hello Alan and...James. Would you like to come in for a session?' Marvon asked, opening the door wider to accommodate the two men.

The two friends entered the hallway and waited for Marvon to close the door.

'Thanks. So,' Alan asked, 'If you freelance, do you get the same ghosts following you about?'

'You know, like a harem,' James added.

Marvon frowned at the two men standing before him. They were clearly a pair of idiots on a wind up. He had encountered people like this before, full of derision and sarcasm. Well, he thought, money is money and I'll give them the full medium experience. Give them the fright of their lives, but only after they'd handed over the cash.

Marvon opened a door to their left, revealing an ordinary living room cluttered with books and DVDs. The walls were covered with exotic looking hangings that looked Asian but were actually bought from Camden market. Two slightly worn sofas were given extra life by two further purple throws that matched those on the wall.

'I'll go and make you chaps some tea. Please, take a seat.' Marvon closed the door leaving the two friends alone.

James relaxed into one of the sofas. 'There's no way he's a medium. XXL at least.'

Alan snorted a laugh. 'You can talk.' Gesturing at James's belly.

Ignoring his friend's comments about his expanding waistline, James added, 'It certainly *feels* like a medium's house. You know. Like you see on the telly.'

'I know. Just look at that picture. Is that Mrs Slocombe herself do you think?'

'If it is, she's been dead a long time.'

'Well, I guess she's in the right place. The eyes seem to follow you round the room.'

'There you go again, you're always thinking women are giving you the eye.'

'Yeah but this time I mean it...' Alan's thoughts were cut off as Frankie walked through the door and into the living room.

Although still unnerving, Alan was beginning to get used to Frankie's sudden appearances. 'He's here again,' Alan said to James before turning towards the door. 'What do you *want?*'

'I thought I would come and see what a medium is really like. You know. See if he can see me and stuff. He might be able to give me some answers.'

'Give *you* some answers? What about me? I'm the poor sod you're haunting.'

James stared at his friend who, for all the world looked like he was talking to a door. 'Are you talking to him now?'

'Seriously, is your friend an idiot?' Frankie asked Alan, nodding towards James.

'Look mate, he clearly can't see you, and I have no idea why I can see you. That's why we are here. To get some answers.'

The door opened, shielding Frankie from view. Marvon entered carrying a tray with a tea pot, three cups, saucers and a sugar bowl. 'OK. Help yourselves,' he said, setting the tray down precariously on a small table already overflowing with books and magazines. 'Who do you wish to speak to?' he said, looking at both men.

'It's me' said Alan. 'I...I...I want to speak to someone.'

'OK. Is it a relative?' Marvon enquired. 'I get a lot of those.'

'No, it's...it's a bit difficult to explain. He's an old man...'

'Oi, I'm not old!' Frankie interrupted from behind the door.

'Is he a friend?' asked Marvon, encouragingly.

'No!' said Alan and Frankie in unison.

'O...kay, then...' replied Marvon, surprised by the tone of Alan's response. 'Would you like to come into the séance room? Bring your tea with you if you like. Ghosts like tea.' he added, smiling.

'Actually, I prefer coffee, thanks,' Frankie mumbled from behind the door.

'Me too.' Alan replied.

Marvon looked quizzically at Alan whilst motioning him towards the séance room. 'Will...James be joining us?' he asked Alan, rather than speaking to James.

'No, ta,' James replied. 'I'll just sit here quietly. With the biscuits.'

Marvon nodded his acceptance, closing the living room door, glancing briefly at his biscuits and back to James.

The door closed, leaving James alone with the biscuits and a ghost he could not see.

'So, you're The Captain. Big bastard aren't you? You're not like any Captain I ever met. Most blokes your size were a little simple in my day. It's good to see nothing has changed.' Frankie stared as James put another biscuit in his mouth.

169

Oblivious to the ghostly taunts, James pulled out his phone and called Amy. 'Hi Ames. How you doing..?'

*

Marvon opened the door to the séance room. The curtains were shut tight with wall mounted spotlights providing scant illumination. Seven chairs surrounded a large circular table in the centre of the otherwise empty room.

'So, this is where the magic happens,' Alan said, pointing to the table.

'Magic? Are you taking the piss?'

'Sorry mate. That's not what I meant.'

'Well. OK. Please. Take a seat.'

The two men sat down at opposite ends of the table. Alan looked at Marvon for guidance and saw the man frowning. 'Is something wrong?' he asked.

'No. Yes. It's not right. I mean, this doesn't feel right. There's usually more people here. My vibrations are all wrong.'

'And you need good vibrations?' Alan grinned.

'Yes. Yes I do.'

'Boy, life can be a beach sometimes.'

Marvon frowned at his guest and stood up, leaving the room.

'Was it something I said?' As the door closed, Frankie emerged. 'Was that the medium? He looks like an extra, extra-large to me.'

Alan sighed. 'We've already done that one.'

'Well, I think he's a fake. I mean, surely he should be sensing my presence or whatever nonsense it is that they say.'

'Well, we'll find out soon enough. Are you sticking around?'

'If I can. I want to watch his Doris Stokes impersonation.'

'Doris who?'

'Before your time, son. Hang on, I think he's coming back. I need to hide.' Frankie said, looking round the room in a mild panic.

'If you think he's a fake, what do you need to hide for?'

'I'm not taking the chance. What if I get banished to the underworld or something? I saw The Exorcist. Bloody terrifying.' Frankie dived behind the curtains. Unfortunately the curtains stopped a few inches from the floor, leaving Frankie's feet exposed.

'I can still see your feet,' Alan laughed. 'And anyway, why don't you just disappear?'

Before Frankie could respond, the door opened and Marvon entered carrying two large plastic sacks. 'I'm sorry,' he said. 'Did you say something?'

'I just wondered where you'd disappeared to.'

'Nicely done,' Frankie said from behind the curtain.

'Thank you.' Alan replied.

Marvon frowned at Alan and began taking several items from the bags, placing them on the vacant chairs. At first

Alan thought they were some kind of spiritualist appliance, but on closer inspection he could see they were in fact a selection of dolls and stuffed toys. Even more bizarre, Marvon was naming them as he placed them on the seats; 'Little Ted. There you go. Big Ted, nice and comfy, hhmm? Humpty, there you go my fat little friend. Ah, Great Uncle Bulgaria. Such a wise old womble.'

Alan stared incredulously at the medium. 'Sorry mate, but what the fuck are you doing? I'm here for spiritual guidance, not a kid's tea party.'

'What? What's happening?' whispered Frankie nervously.

'Oh Christ, they're not going to be possessed are they?' said Alan, pointing at the range of vaguely familiar looking toys positioned around the table.

Frankie chanced a peak from behind the curtains and saw toys sitting in the previously empty chairs. 'Sod that, I'm not getting stuck in one of those bloody awful things. I might never get out. I'm not going to spend eternity being dragged around by a succession of sticky, smelly snotty nosed kids. I won't do it, do you hear me, fatso, I won't do it.'

Alan couldn't help but laugh at Frankie's rising panic. Misunderstanding the cause of Alan's amusement, Marvon said, 'This really is no laughing matter,' as he turned on a small CD player. Immediately the sound of pop music filled the room, causing Alan to laugh even harder.

'Sorry, wrong one,' said Marvon as he turned off the CD, replacing it with another disk. The sound changed to a haunting, folky melody that Alan presumed was made by a couple of deaf hippies with badly tuned lutes and too much time on their hands.

'This is nice,' Alan said. 'Is it in the charts?'

Marvon ignored the remark and relaxed into the only spare chair, opposite Alan. 'Now,' he said, 'shall we begin?'

'Yes let's,' Alan replied, sitting forward in his chair.

'Actually, I'm happy to wait a while,' whispered Frankie, peering out from behind the curtain.

Marvon frowned again, misinterpreting Alan's smile as sarcasm, then closed his eyes and held his hands palm up, index fingers lightly touching his thumbs. Marvon took three very deep breaths and whispered, 'The spirits are close. I can feel them. Is there anybody there?'

'He's behind you...' whispered Frankie from behind the curtain.

Suppressing a laugh, Alan feigned a cough. 'Sorry.'

Marvon slightly opened his right eye to stare at the man in front of him. He's clearly an idiot, but I'll get him, the thought to himself. Push the button hidden in his trousers at just the right time and all the toys would fall off the chairs. So, so easy. Yet so effective. It always got the same result, a frightened punter leaving with a sense that they really had been contacted by the dead. Works every time.

'I'm...I'm getting someone...it's a man. He says he is a relative. I'm sensing a close relative. Maybe a father...or grandfather..? I'm sorry I can't quite make it out yet. But he wants to talk to you. He is very insistent.'

Frankie whispered through the curtains. 'Ask him what the toys are for. Is he having some kind of spiritual tea party? Seriously, if Big Ted starts moving, I am going out through the square window.'

173

Alan suppressed another laugh. 'Can you be quiet, we're trying to concentrate here.'

Marvon opened his eyes. 'Who are you talking to?' he said, looking around the room.

'I think he's talking to me!' Frankie shouted to the medium. 'You know, the ghost in the room. Christ...'

'Sorry Mr Marvon. I thought I heard a voice,' Alan said, pointedly looking in Frankie's direction.

'Well, I doubt that very much. The spirits only speak through me,' Marvon replied rather smugly.

'He's rather smug for a charlatan, isn't he?' Frankie pointed out.

Closing his eyes again, Marvon relaxed back into position. 'I think I can feel someone coming through. The presence is very strong. It's definitely a man, and he's very close.'

'Yeah, it's almost like he's in the room with us!' Frankie muttered.

Marvon continued; 'Tell me, oh spirit, what is it you want to say to...to us..?'

'I want to tell you that I'm behind the curtain.'

Alan sniggered, causing Marvon to open his eyes once more. 'Really, if you are not going to take this seriously...I won't be able to focus and I will lose my connection and the spirits will leave us.'

'I'm not going anywhere,' Frankie said from behind the curtain.

'Ssshhh.......' Alan whispered at the curtains, trying desperately not to laugh.

Marvon looked towards where Alan had spoken. There was nothing there but the curtains. Oh shit, he thought to himself. Perhaps he's not an idiot at all. Perhaps he's crazy. That has to be it. And that other bloke...James..? He has to be this guy's carer. Bloody hell, he thought, how am I going to get out of this?

Marvon moved his finger away from the button in his trousers. The last thing he wanted to do is spook a crazy person with jumping teddy bears, he thought to himself. That's the quickest way to end up on the news. He'd just have to terminate the session as quickly as possible and get this madman out of the house.

'I can sense a presence by the curtains...but he is fading. Please, please, don't leave us,' Marvon implored, 'speak to us...'

'I am speaking to you, you old fraud,' said Frankie.

Alan placed his hands over his mouth to prevent further laughter, but he could not control himself any longer and collapsed into a fit of hysterics.

Right, that's it, thought Marvon, it's time to bring this to an end. 'I'm sorry,' he said, 'I can feel the energy has left the room. I will have to terminate the session.'

'But I wanted to ask which Christmas crackers you got your spiritualist's licence from,' said Frankie. 'I'll guess now I'll never know.'

'Come on, he's trying his best,' offered Alan in response.

Marvon had had enough of this. He needed this guy out of the house right now. He stood up and walked towards the curtains.

'Frankie, if you're going to disappear, I'd do it right now,' Alan shouted.

'What? Why? What's happening? I'm not spending eternity in a fluffy toy...'

At that precise moment, the curtains parted to reveal the overweight medium. 'Aarrrrgh!' said Frankie.

'Aarrrrgh!' replied Marvon, as he staggered backwards into the table, knocking over a couple chairs in the process.

Alan leapt from his chair 'What? What? Can you actually see him?'

'Of course I can fucking see him!' Frankie and Marvon shouted simultaneously.

'Bloody hell. It worked,' Alan laughed as the door opened.

'What's going on?' asked James nervously as he looked at the window and the overturned table and chairs. 'What's happened?'

Alan looked at Big Ted laying on the floor in front of him, and to the space where Frankie had stood before disappearing again. 'He went through the square window.'

'Well, that proves something,' James said.

'What?'

'He's not a fake,' James added, pointing to Marvon, who rushed past him and out through the door.

'What do we do now?' James asked.

'I've no idea. Marvon clearly saw him. But I get the impression it might have been a bit of a shock. I'm guessing he hasn't come across many ghosts before.'

'That must be a bit of a handicap for a medium.'

'I know. We'd better check to see if he's OK.'

The two friends wandered down the hallway towards the sound of whimpering. 'Are you OK in there?' asked Alan.

'Just...just go. There's...there's no charge. Just go.'

'OK. Well, thanks for your time,' Alan replied.

'Give my best to Mrs Slocombe,' added James helpfully.

'What did you say that for?' Alan asked as they headed towards the front door.

'Well, it's obvious, isn't it? We've just met Mrs Slocombe's pussy.'

It had been a terrible day. A truly terrible day. Alan had been called in to a meeting about some policy or other that he didn't understand and cared even less about. Everyone (except Alan) had an opinion which they wanted to share, and they worked on the basis that if they talked louder than anyone else, then their opinion was the correct one. If that wasn't bad enough, the meeting had dragged on in to the afternoon and there weren't even any sandwiches.

Alan accepted the argument for Government cutbacks. However, he drew the line at being less well fed than the Big Issue seller whose attentions he tried so hard to avoid every morning.

Walking home from the tube station, he considered calling into his favourite Indian restaurant for a takeaway. Rosie was due round later and she might be pleasantly surprised that he had gone to the trouble of getting something in, rather than his usual practice of not even considering food until she arrived.

Momentarily distracted by thoughts of curry, Alan almost didn't see the figure sitting on his front step. Elbows on his knees and chin resting on his palms, still wearing the green velvet jacket and frilly shirt.

Alan opened his gate, looked down and almost resignedly said, 'Will you please stop stalking me?'

'I'm not stalking you,' Frankie said defensively, 'I'm drawn to you.'

It had been two weeks since Alan and James had visited the medium. Following that experience, Alan had been free of Frankie's sudden appearances, and he hoped never to see him again.

'Have you had any idea of the trouble that you caused at Marvon's house?'

'Me?' Frankie exclaimed, slowly getting to his feet. 'You were trying to have me exorcised.'

'He was a medium. I told you I was trying to talk to you, which is very difficult when you keep disappearing.'

Frankie pushed his hands into his pockets. 'I'm here now. Let's talk.'

Alan suddenly became aware that to the casual onlooker he was standing on his path talking to himself. 'Right,' he said. 'You. Inside. Now.'

Alan walked past Frankie and up the single step to the front door. He paused momentarily and looked round.

'Why are you waiting for me to open the door? Why can't you just vanish in there?'

'Vanish in there?' Frankie repeated, 'What does that mean?'

'You know,' Alan groaned in despair. 'Disappear here and reappear in there. You've done it before. All the vanishing and appearing stuff.'

'I don't know. I really am very new to all this business. I'm very much a beginner.'

'OK,' Alan sighed, unlocking the front door. He stood back and allowed Frankie to enter ahead of him. 'After you,' he said sarcastically.

Frankie walked through the open door as Alan shook his head.

*

Frankie stood in the kitchen. 'You must remember this?' Alan asked, 'You were standing over there,' he pointed across the room, 'and I was standing here. You vanished, I fell over and spent the night in hospital.'

Frankie turned to face Alan. 'Can we get something clear here?' he said. 'I'm the one who's dead, I'm the one who has to get used to all the new stuff. It's easy for you, you've still got your life. I don't.'

'I'm so sorry,' Alan replied sarcastically, 'I really do apologise. I've forgotten everything that I was taught about welcoming the spirits of the dead into my home.'

Frankie remained silent. Alan opened a cupboard and looked for something to eat. Frankie leaned against the wall hands in pockets.

'Why don't you let me explain what's going on. At least as far as I understand it.'

Alan took a box of cereal and a bowl out of the cupboard. He went to the fridge and took out a bottle of milk. 'Go on then,' he said, tipping the cereal into the bowl and adding the milk. 'Can I get you anything? Cup of tea, sandwich?' after a pause he added, 'You can eat and drink. Can't you?'

Frankie frowned. 'I really have no idea, but I'm not hungry or thirsty at the moment.'

Alan sat at the table and began to eat his cereal. 'Go on then off you go.'

Frankie pulled a chair out from under the table and sat down. 'I'm dead,' he said.

'Yes, I think we've established that,' Alan replied.

'I died in 1982. I was on at the theatre, the Merton Palace Theatre. I died in my dressing room just after I had finished my act.'

Alan crunched on his cereal. 'I know,' he said. 'I looked you up after you appeared outside.'

'Looked me up?' said Frankie, quizzically. 'Where, at the library?'

Alan quickly realised that any explanation about the internet would take a while, so he decided not to answer. In any case, there was a strong possibility that Frankie could vanish before Alan could explain it, so instead he decided the easiest option was to not confuse matters. 'Yes. Of course. In the library. An old newspaper.'

Frankie looked interested. 'What did it say?'

'Very little actually. Pretty much what you just told me. You suffered a heart attack and died in your dressing room after delivering your act.'

Frankie pursed his lips and nodded. 'A heart attack! I thought as much.'

A thought suddenly occurred to Alan. 'Do you how long you've been dead?' he asked.

'I'm not sure. Sometimes I think I've been dead minutes, sometimes weeks. I don't know. It could be hours or even years I suppose.'

'It's 2015,' Alan said. 'You've been dead thirty three years.'

Alan wasn't sure but he thought that just for a moment Frankie had gone pale.

'Thirty three years. That makes me …. Let me think born 1919, it's 2015 that means I'm errrr,' he said, whilst counting his fingers.

'Ninety six years old,' Alan interrupted, 'but you don't look a day over sixty three, the age you were when you died.'

'Something else you looked up?' Frankie asked.

'No I just did the maths!'

Alan realised that the tables had turned. Despite being confronted by the ghost of a long dead comedian, it was he who was dealing with the situation a lot better than Frankie, who seemed to Alan shocked by what he had just found out.

'Why do you keep on appearing to me?' Alan asked. 'Are you appearing to anyone else?'

'I don't think so,' Frankie said appearing to have recovered his composure, 'It's only you. It's like I'm trying to make contact with you.'

'And the medium,' Alan said.

'Well yes the medium imbecile too I guess. But they don't really count. They're not normal are they?'

And this is such a normal situation, Alan thought sarcastically, before adding,

'Why me? Why have you homed in on me? I mean, I saw you at the theatre, twice, you appeared in here and then you were outside the medium's house a couple of weeks ago.'

'Oh, there's more than that. As I said I've been trying to get your attention for a while. I nearly did it when you were in the pub and I was standing outside here one night,' Frankie continued, 'each appearance seems to be getting longer and a bit more solid.'

Alan's mind ran through every weird strange experience that he had suffered recently. 'So, this has been going on for months...'

Frankie looked shocked again. 'Months?' he said.

'At least,' Alan answered. 'What, did you think it was the same day or something?'

'I don't know. I wasn't aware of time passing, at least not like it does when you're alive. I knew I was trying to make myself visible and every time I did, you were there. Yours was the only face I could see. It wasn't hard to work out that you were the person that I am meant to contact.'

Alan put his now empty bowl in the sink. 'I always thought ghosts were grey and hazy, holding their heads under their arms, or wailing under a sheet. You... you're touchable. You look solid, like a proper old man.'

'Oi!' Frankie snapped, 'that's enough of the "old man" thank you very much.'

'Sorry,' Alan said, 'I just meant that you look completely normal, like you've called in for a visit. Not like a ghost haunting someone.'

Frankie smiled. 'I suppose I am doing a haunting, I hadn't thought of it like that.'

'So, how does it work? Being a ghost that is.'

'To be honest, I'm not sure,' Frankie replied. It's not like I was met at the gates by St Peter who gave me a handy guide to the afterlife and...'

'You were a comedian in the 70s, what makes you think that you were going to heaven?' Alan interrupted, 'Everyone knows what it was like for your lot in those days.'

Ignoring Alan's comment Frankie continued, 'No tour, no meet the big guy, nothing like that. Just a lot of haziness and getting on with it.'

Alan scratched his head as he looked Frankie up and down. 'So you have no control over the vanishing, no influence, nothing?'

'I don't think so. Not at the moment. As I keep saying, it's all rather new to me.'

'So you can't just vanish and leave me alone?'

Frankie simply shrugged his shoulders.

'Great,' Alan said.

Frankie stood up and walked over to the worktop where Alan had made his cereal. His attention was drawn to the radio, its retro design catching Frankie's eye.

'I've got a theory,' he said, 'that it might be like radio waves.'

'What's like radio waves?' Alan asked. 'What are you talking about?'

Frankie returned to the table and sat back in a chair. He took a deep breath, not unlike some who was about to explain something very simple to someone very stupid. 'I served in the war, you know. I had to learn about radio waves.'

'You were in the war?' Alan said suddenly remembering the internet article. 'What did you do?'

'Do you want to know my theory or not?' Frankie snapped.

'OK, sorry, continue.'

'I think me as a...as a ghost,' he said, gathering his thoughts, 'is like a sort of radio wave that can be picked up by a receiver. That receiver would be you.'

Alan snorted. 'That's rubbish. It doesn't work like that.'

'And you know that do you?'

'Well no, but your version just sounds ridiculous,' Alan said defensively.

'Do you have any better explanations?'

'No,' Alan paused before continuing, 'Not at the moment.'

Alan stood up again and wandered over to the sink. He turned on the tap and started to rinse the bowl and cup he had been using. His normal practice was to save the washing up and do it one go at the end of the day. However, Rosie was fastidiously tidy and her imminent arrival was the trigger for him to at least make a token effort to wash up. He heard the sound of a chair scrape over the floor as Frankie stood up.

'So it looks like I'm stuck with you,' Frankie said.

Alan turned away from the sink towards him. 'You're stuck with me? I think you'll find that I'm stuck with you!'

Alan paused. Something was niggling him, something wasn't quite right.

'What's up?' Frankie asked, 'You're staring. You've gone all weird like you've seen a .....Well you know.'

Slowly, the cogs in Alan's brain whirred and engaged and the penny dropped. It had been falling since Alan and Frankie had entered the kitchen and now it had landed. 'You've gone real!' Alan said, staring at Frankie.

'I'm sorry, I've gone what? 'Frankie said, frowning.

'You're real. You're like a real person. You were sitting down at the table, you pulled a chair out to sit on it, and you pushed the chair back to stand up,' Alan said excitedly. He continued, 'What happens if I do this?'

Alan leaned towards Frankie and prodded him, his finger pressed into something remarkably like a human chest.

'Careful. That hurt.' Frankie cried out.

'The last time I did that, outside, I fell over. I went straight through you. Now you're solid.'

Frankie frowned, rubbing the spot where Alan had prodded him. 'I've got a dent there now. Why didn't you just pat my head or something?'

'Have you come back to life?' Alan asked.

'I don't know. It all feels the same to me,' Frankie said. 'Maybe you and I are tuned in properly now. Like the radio waves.'

'I still think that's rubbish, but you are definitely solid now,' Alan said. 'Can you still vanish?'

'I don't know. I keep telling you, I'm new to this. I can't seem to control anything.'

Alan looked at the large clock on the wall. 'You've got to go anyway,' he said, 'Rosie will be here soon.'

'Who's Rosie?' Frankie asked.

'My girlfriend and I don't want to explain to her about you.'

'Why not?' Frankie said, affronted. 'What's wrong with me?'

'She doesn't have the sort of brain that will accept you,' Alan said, 'There will be lots of questions that I can't answer and she will probably try to have you exorcised.'

Frankie put his hands up in surrender. 'She sounds lovely. Don't worry she probably won't be able to see me, anyway.'

'I can't take the chance. Go on just vanish!' Alan pleaded.

Ignoring Alan, Frankie walked over to the window and looked out. 'What does Rosie look like?' he asked.

'Brown Hair, about so high,' he said holding his hand out about chest height. 'Why?'

'Does she have a blue jacket?'

'I think so, why?'

'I think she's walking up your path!'

'Oh shit!' Alan said, beginning to panic. 'Right you,' he said, grabbing Frankie by the arm, 'come with me.'

Half dragging Frankie out of the kitchen, Alan opened the door directly opposite.

'Right. In here,' Alan said, opening the door to the bathroom and ushering Frankie inside. 'And try and vanish before she needs the toilet.'

Alan closed the door just as the front door opened. 'Hi,' Rosie called out.

Alan dashed back in to the kitchen and replied. 'Hello. You ok?'

Typically Rosie made her way into the kitchen without making a sound, and Alan was suddenly grateful for Frankie looking out of the window when he did.

Putting her bag on the table Rosie said, 'Are you OK? You look a bit flustered.'

'No, No I'm fine. All good. I've had a good day, how was yours?' Alan said, a bit too enthusiastically.

'It was OK. Are you sure you're OK?' Rosie asked, 'You're being a bit weird.'

Struggling to calm down, Alan was suddenly hit with a good idea. 'Are you hungry?' he asked, 'only I was thinking we could go for a curry.'

'That's a good idea. When do you want to go?'

'I was thinking that we could go now, before it gets too busy.'

Rosie frowned. 'It never gets busy in there, even on a Saturday they have to entice people with free poppadums.'

'I know, but I'm really hungry. Let's go now,' he said eagerly.

'OK,' Rosie said, 'if you're that hungry...'

Rosie wandered out of the kitchen. 'I'll just use the bathroom,' she said.

Before Alan could react he heard the door open and then click shut. He bounded across the hall to the bathroom door and stopped outside, half expecting Rosie to explode.

After a couple of minutes he heard the toilet flush. He stepped back and waited for the door to open.

'Have you been waiting outside all the time I've been in there?' Rosie said.

'No,' Alan lied. 'I realised I need to go myself, I only stood here when I heard the flush.'

Rosie eyed Alan up and down. She still thought he was being weird. 'You're being weird,' she said.

'No I'm not,' he insisted, 'I just need to use the toilet. You start walking, and I'll catch you up.'

'I'll wait in there,' Rosie said, pointing towards the kitchen. 'You do what you have to do and then we'll go.'

Alan waited for Rosie to enter the kitchen before opening the bathroom door, stepping inside, he shut and locked the door behind him.

'Frankie,' he whispered as he closed the door. It was a standard size bathroom, enough space for a bath, toilet and basin. A shower curtain was suspended from the ceiling and ran down the side of the bath. This was the only possible hiding place.

'Frankie,' Alan whispered again, and pulled back the shower curtain.

'I'm here,' Frankie whispered into Alan's ear.

'For fucks sake!' Alan span round. The sudden shock causing his heart to thump rapidly in his chest.

Frankie stood behind him. 'What?' he said.

'Will you please not do that?' Alan said, his voice no more than a croaky whisper.

'Sorry. I was standing behind the door when you opened it,' Frankie explained, 'keeping out of sight like you said.'

'What happened when Rosie was in here?' Alan croaked, not sure he wanted an answer.

'Nothing. I was standing behind the door, just like now. She shut the door and was right in front of me. She was staring at me, face to face but she didn't see me.'

'OK, that's good,' Alan whispered.

'Can I come out now?' Frankie asked, 'If she can't see me, I can just go and sit outside with you.'

'No you can't!' Alan snapped. 'You can go now and...' Alan stopped in mid-sentence, something suddenly occurred to him.

'You were in here with Rosie when she went to the toilet...' Alan stated this as a fact, rather than asking the question.

Frankie paused for a moment, 'Yes I suppose I was.'

'You did keep your eyes closed didn't you?' Alan asked, 'Don't tell me you watched her?'

Frankie looked past Alan at the wall. 'That's some decent tiling you have there, son. Did you get someone in, or do it yourself?'

'You didn't...' Alan groaned, his voice raising beyond a whisper. 'Please tell me you didn't.'

'She was in front of me,' Frankie protested, 'What was I supposed to do?'

'You're supposed not to look. You definitely can't stay now. You've seen Rosie on the toilet,' Alan argued, 'Even I haven't seen that,' he added as an afterthought.

'Haven't you? Why not.'

'I just haven't!' Alan said, 'and anyway, it's none of your business.'

Before either Alan or Frankie could say anything further they were interrupted by the sound of someone banging on the door. 'Alan!' Rosie called through the door, 'Are you OK?'

'Yes, nearly done, I'll be out in a sec...'

'...OK' Alan whispered, this time to Frankie, 'Rosie and I are going out and I want you gone by the time we get back.'

'Have you not heard anything that I've been saying?' Frankie said, 'It's not that easy.'

'Just try!'

'OK, son, I'll do my best, if not I'll hide under the bed.'

191

'No. Not the bed!' Alan said.

'Why, what's wrong with the bed?' Frankie asked.

'Do I have spell it out?' Alan replied.

'Oh that,' Frankie said, suddenly understanding exactly what Alan was insinuating.

'I wouldn't worry about that tonight. I've seen the underwear she's got on, and trust me she's not dressed to kill.'

'What are you talking about?' Alan said his voice rising again.

'Baggy white ones. All that says is that she's changing in the bathroom tonight and going straight to sleep.'

'Just go!' Alan hissed, hands rubbing the sides of his head.

Sitting at the kitchen table, Rosie heard the bathroom door open. 'So you're ready are you?' she asked.

'Sorry, yes good to go now,' Alan replied, standing in the doorway.

Grabbing her jacket off the back of a chair, Rosie wandered past Alan and down the hall.

Alan watched her go but before following her he quickly looked into the bathroom.

It was empty.

Chapter 23

Jayne checked her mobile for what seemed like the hundredth time that day. *Why are people so unreliable?* She thought to herself. Her musings were interrupted by the arrival of a tray being placed carefully on the table in front of her.

'Waiting for a call?' Alison asked as she sat down opposite Jayne.

Putting the mobile onto the table alongside the tray, Jayne said, 'Waiting, hoping but not really expecting. Why are people so unreliable?

'When you say people, you mean men, don't you?' Alison asked.

Jayne grinned. Pointing at the tray and its contents she said, 'What's this? I thought you were getting a couple of orange juices.'

'That's two multi-fruit smoothies, two oatmeal cookies and a couple of complimentary rice cakes,' Alison grinned. Jayne took one of the green coloured smoothies, peering into the glass she said, 'It doesn't move around much, does it?' Emphasising the point, she attempted to swirl the contents of her smoothie around with her straw. 'See, it's stagnant.'

'They're supposed to be very good for you,' Alison replied. 'The ideal post exercise refreshment!' Sensing that she wasn't convincing Jayne at all she added, 'And they're cheaper than the orange juice at the moment!'

'Well, that's one good argument for them,' Jayne laughed and took a slow mouthful of the drink. 'Vile,' she added, poking her tongue out a show of distaste.

'All this,' Alison said, gesturing at the food and drink on the table, 'is at a special introductory price.'

'It would have to be, otherwise no one would buy it!' Jayne said, before taking another mouthful. 'This should be the bar,' she continued. 'It's been a bar for the last two years and everyone was happy. You went to a class, had a session in the gym or went for a swim and then you went for a quick drink in the bar. It was simple and it was fun!'

'New owners, new ideas, I'm afraid.' Alison replied, trying to balance Jayne's views.

'It's a Health Spa now, not a Sports Centre,'' Jayne pointed out, 'and this is no longer a proper bar, it's a bloody juice bar.'

'Have an oatmeal cookie they're very...err...wholesome,' Alison said, pointing to the plate on the tray.

Taking another mouthful of the green gloop, Jayne noticed a red welt around Alison's wrist.

'That looks nasty,' she said. 'What did you do?'

Alison's face reddened and she pulled the sleeve of her fleece jacket down covering over her wrist.

'I caught my hand in the handle of a bag,' she said unconvincingly.

Before Jayne's suspicious police training could press the issue further, Alison changed the subject.

'So who are you expecting for a call from?''

'Someone I met on line. I thought they would have called by now. It's been a couple of days,' Jayne said, looking glumly into her smoothie.

'Still looking for Mr Right?' Alison asked.

Jayne laughed. 'Still looking for Mr That'll do.'

Alison picked up an oatmeal cookie and broke off a piece. 'Isn't there anyone at work?' she asked before popping it in her mouth.

Jayne pulled a face. 'No way. I spend all day with those people. There's no way I'm spending my social time with them as well.'

'But you must come into contact with other people all the time,' Alison asked. 'You know, normal people?'

'Criminals and people under stress. They're the ones that I meet on a daily basis. Do you want know what I had to deal with today?' Jayne asked.

'Go on, tell me,' Alison said, before adding, 'Do you want that last cookie?' pointing at the solitary oatmeal cookie left on the plate.

Jayne pushed the plate towards Alison. 'I'm not sure I wanted the first one!' she said and began.

'Today I had to deal with an idiot who had climbed onto the roof of a derelict old chapel to steal the lead, but ended up getting stuck on the roof. I had to phone the fire brigade to come and rescue him.'

'Not Mr Right material then?' Alison asked, keeping a straight face.

'Not even Mr That'll do material. He was a complete idiot.'

'So what was the story then?'

Jayne took a deep breath. 'So there's this old school. It's got a weird name,' Jayne paused for a moment, 'Buggerly Mount. It's closed down now and boarded up. Right on the edge of the site is the old school chapel. Matey had climbed over the hoardings with his bag of tools and then climbed up on to the roof of the chapel. A passer-by had seen him up there and called it in. When we got there we could see him half way up the roof hanging on for dear life.'

Alison giggled, and with a mouth full of oatmeal cookie asked, 'Did you have to go up and get him down?'

'No way was I going up there. As I said, I called the fire brigade and they got him down.'

'How did he end up stuck up on the roof? Surely the one thing that someone who steals lead from roofs knows is how to get down from a roof? It's a job skill.'

'Yeah, you'd have thought so, wouldn't you? Except, once he got up there his plans fell apart. The roof was, as, you'd expect, in a right old state. He was clambering over the tiles and managed to dislodge one. He could see into the roof space and there were apparently dozens of bats in there. He said he was so shocked he dropped his bag.' Jayne explained, shaking her head at the memory.

'So, he didn't demonstrate any of the qualities that you are looking for in Mr Right then? Alison asked.

'Not even remotely. Although he did prove to be a very lucky guy. We had to call out the key holder to let us on

196

to the site before the idiot could be arrested, and he refused to press charges. For some reason he had no interest in taking it any further.'

'Lucky guy.' Alison said.

Jayne looked at what remained of the food and drink that Alison had bought over from the bar. 'You enjoyed that then?' she asked.

Alison smiled. 'Not bad at all,' she said as she reached down into her bag and took out an envelope. 'The Twenty Sixth of next month,' she said. 'I'm having a party, a birthday party can you make it?'

'Yes, of course. I'd love to,' Jayne said.

'There's an invite in there,' Alison said, passing the envelope across the table. 'It's at the Old Grammarians Cricket Club. There's an invite for Rosie and her other half in there too.'

'Great. Thanks. I'll pass it on to her. So, dare I ask how old you will be?' Jayne said. 'I know you're not supposed to ask but, I'll need to get you a card with a badge.'

'I'll be Forty Five the day before the party.'

'Wow, you don't look it!' Jayne said.

Alison looked at her watch. 'Thank you, you're very kind. Anyway, time to make a move,' she said as she hoisted her sports bag onto the table. 'I've got school uniform to iron when I get home.'

'Not trained them to do it themselves yet?' Jayne asked.

'No, they're only seven and eleven, but I'm working on it.'

Jayne stood up and slung her bag over her shoulder. The bar was filling up now, the post work squash games having been played and the gym classes finished. Jayne looked at those entering the bar, smiling at some she recognised. No doubt she thought, in a few minutes they would be staring disappointedly into glasses of thick green gloop remembering the days of the proper bar and a few pints.

The two women parted in the car park. Alison sat in her Polo and watched as Jayne drove past in her Nissan Juke, flashing her lights goodbye. She started the car and as she released the handbrake she caught sight of the red welt around her wrist and smiled.

Chapter 24

Alan sensed, rather than saw movement to his left. He turned and saw a large envelope sliding onto his desk. He stared at the middle aged woman standing alongside him, thin narrow face, dark hair harshly tied back and wearing glasses that made her look more severe than she actually was.

'Sue,' he said, picking up the envelope. 'What's this?'

'It's Graham's birthday card. I did send an e-mail round letting everyone know it was coming,' she answered.

'You know I don't read e-mails, specifically any that have the word "Graham" in the subject line,' Alan paused. 'Anyway what do you want me to do with it?' he asked provocatively.

'Just sign the card Alan,' Sue said patiently. 'Then cross your name off the list and pass it on to someone who hasn't signed it. Do you think you can manage that?' she asked.

'No problem Sue, you know that you can rely on me!' He replied, turning back to face his computer screen, and tapping the keys on the keyboard.

'Sign the card Alan,' Sue said, before adding, 'and I'll have a fiver off you as well.'

Alan turned round, frowning. 'A fiver? What for? He asked.

'The present. It was in the e-mail I sent,' Sue said. 'The one that you didn't read.'

'Present?' he repeated, 'What present? Why does he get a present? I didn't get a present when it was my birthday. In fact I didn't even get a card.'

'It's a landmark birthday. We always get cards for people on special birthdays.'

Alan sighed as he opened the envelope, taking the card out. It was a typically large A4 sized birthday card, the size of it reflecting the number of people likely to sign it, rather than demonstrating how popular the recipient was.

Alan looked at the card which had a large "60" emblazoned across the front. 'Sixty, eh,' Alan muttered.

'Doesn't look it, does he?' Sue said. 'I don't think he looks a day over forty.'

'Yeah, I reckon he's got a picture of himself in his attic. I reckon it gets older whilst he stays the same age.'

'Alan,' Sue said reproachfully.

'Apparently,' Alan continued, 'he drinks the blood of a virgin every year on his birthday to retain his youthful looks.' Alan looked Sue up and down. 'You'd best go into hiding until he's satisfied.'

'Not funny Alan,' Sue replied. 'Please just sign the card.'

Detecting an edge to her voice, Alan relented. 'OK, leave it with me. I'll drop it back in about five minutes.'

As Sue turned to walk away, Alan called her back. 'Sue, one more thing,' he said.

'What?'

'What are you getting him as a present?' he asked.

'Amazon Vouchers I think,' Sue answered. 'Unless you can think of anything else?'

'If you get him Dignitas vouchers, I'll put a tenner in!'

Sue shook her head and, without saying a word, walked back to her desk.

Alan opened the card. A number of people had already signed it, wishing Graham "a very happy birthday" or telling him to "have a good day." Some had even asked "How old?" or suggested that he "doesn't do anything they wouldn't do." The usual collection of bland, insincere birthday messages from people who really didn't know the recipient. It was all so dull, he thought. Alan knew that Graham would quickly scan the card, only interested to see if anyone from a higher grade had signed it.

Alan quickly scribbled "Have a good day" on the card, and then changed pens. Finding the most prominent place in the card, Alan changed hands and carefully began to write "Happy Birthday You C..."

'What are you writing?' Sue's sudden reappearance at his side broke Alan's concentration.

'What now?' he said, annoyed at being caught out. 'I told you I would drop it back to you in five minutes.'

'I forgot the list of names of people who had signed the card,' Sue said, putting a sheet of paper on Alan's desk. 'What are you writing?' She asked again.

'Just Graham's birthday message.'

Looking over his shoulder, Sue read out loud, 'Happy Birthday You...' pausing she frowned, 'You C, what does that mean?'

'Let me finish it,' Alan said, and slid the card back in front him. Taking his pen he wrote the word "Champ."

'Happy Birthday You Champ' Sue read out, 'Is that right?'

Alan smiled smugly. 'Of course it is. Look at all the other messages. Boring happy birthday greetings showing no imagination whatsoever. I thought I'd make mine a bit more personal.'

Before Sue had a chance to think about what he had said, or indeed realise that his writing was different, he passed the card back to her. 'There you go, and here,' he said, taking something from his trouser pocket, 'is my fiver.'

'Thank you Alan,' Sue said, not quite believing that Alan had signed the card and parted with five pounds so easily.

Alan stood up. He was a good six inches taller than Sue even when, as now, she was wearing heels. 'I think I'll just pop out to lunch. See you later.' Without giving Sue an opportunity to reply, Alan slipped past her and made his way to the lifts.

*

Standing in the corridor waiting for the lift, Alan felt a hand on his shoulder. 'All right son?'

Looking round, Alan saw Frankie smiling at him. Still in the same green velvet jacket and frilly shirt. 'I was wondering when I would see you again,' Alan said.

'Why? Were you missing me?' Frankie asked, grinning.

'Desperately,' Alan said sarcastically. 'I was thinking only last night how I missed being haunted by the ghost of a long dead comedian.'

'Sarcasm,' Frankie said, 'is the lowest form of wit. It's always been the difference between a punter and the professional comedian.'

'Let me...' Alan stopped mid-sentence as two women he recognised from HR were approaching the lift. He grabbed Frankie by the arm and marched him back down the corridor and into the toilets. Pushing Frankie into a corner, Alan checked the cubicles to ensure they were all empty.

'What are you doing?' Frankie asked. Not receiving a reply, Frankie continued, 'Is this what you do? Lurk around in the toilets all day?'

Alan looked at him but did not reply.

'I could tell you some stories about some of the guys that I used to know back on the circuit. Some of their best work was done in toilets,' Frankie said before adding, 'When I was alive.'

Satisfied that the cubicles were empty and that they were alone Alan walked over to the basins. 'Look,' he said, 'No one else can see you. If I'm talking to you it looks to anyone watching that I'm talking to myself. I'll end up being sectioned.'

'Sectioned?' Frankie queried.

'People will think I'm mental.'

Frankie laughed.

'What?' Alan said irritably.

'Well it is a bit crazy isn't it?'

'What is?'

'Me and you here now. The dead comedian and the...' Frankie paused, and then asked, 'What is it you do?'

'I'm a civil servant,' Alan admitted.

'Me and you here now. The dead comedian and the civil servant.'

Frankie's words bounced round inside Alan's head. He had to admit that there was something farcical about the whole thing. Alan was proud of his ability to find the humour in any situation, and yet it hadn't dawned on him that he was living in a rich vein of comedy material.

Thinking he should set the record straight, Alan said, 'Actually, I'm a comedian too. I do stand up.'

Frankie frowned. 'I thought you said you were a Civil Servant?'

'Civil Servant by day, stand up by night,' Alan replied. 'It's hard work and the money's not great. Hence the day job.'

'So that's what you were doing on stage? We should really talk about this,' Frankie said, 'I could give you some pointers.'

'Thanks for the offer, but comedy has moved on since the days of casual sexism and racism. It's a much more sophisticated profession these days.'

'Sophisticated, you say?' Frankie snapped, 'I think I'll be the judge of that,' he paused before adding, 'and I was never racist.'

'Oh come on!' Alan replied. 'Your whole generation of comics thought that calling any black person Chalky was cutting edge comedy.'

'There were people like that, I grant you, but there were some decent guys on the circuit as well, and if you knew anything about comedy you'd know that.'

'Just calling it as I see it,' Alan said defensively.

'So when are you playing next?' Frankie asked, 'I'll come along, see this so called "sophisticated" comedy.'

'I've got a gig in a few days' time,' Alan said, 'but why do I need to tell you? Unless you've managed to learn how to control your spooky movements, there's no guarantee you'll be there.'

'I think you'll be surprised, I've been practising.'

'I'll believe that when I see it,' Alan said before correcting himself, 'or see you.'

Alan moved towards the door, 'Right,' he said, 'time for lunch.' Turning back, he noticed that Frankie had remained at the basins staring into the mirrors lining the wall behind the basins.

'What?' Alan said.

Frankie leaned forward peering into the mirror. 'This is the first time I've really looked at myself since I died,' scratching his nose he added, 'not bad for a ninety three year old, not bad at all.'

'Oh please,' Alan said and left the room.

*

Alan walked briskly along the pavement, swerving around slower moving pedestrians, Frankie a couple of steps behind. 'Will you please slow down,' Frankie shouted.

In response, Alan increased his pace, looking to put some distance between the two of them. Frankie again called out, 'I can't keep up with you!'

Alan slowed to normal walking pace. 'W...w...will you please slow down,' Frankie breathlessly asked again.

Alan slowed to a saunter, allowing Frankie to catch him up. 'Is this OK for you?'

'That's much better, thanks.' Frankie said, getting his breathing under control.

'Anyway, why the rush?' he asked.

'I'm at lunch,' Alan explained, 'I don't get long. I have to get out, get a sandwich, eat the sandwich and get back to work. I don't have time to wait for you while you dawdle along,' Alan paused, 'Are you limping?'

'Took a bullet during the war, it plays up sometimes,' Frankie said, patting his right leg.

'But you're dead,' Alan said, 'One of the plus points about being dead has to be that you no longer have to worry about all your old aches and pains.'

'You'd think so, wouldn't you' Frankie said.

Alan laughed. 'You really are a rubbish ghost.'

'And what are you basing this on? How many ghosts do you know? Anyway, where are you going for this sandwich?'

'In here,' Alan said, and led Frankie through the large glass doors of the supermarket.

'This is very nice,' Frankie said looking around. 'These places have changed a lot since my day.' Turning to Alan he said, 'Where's the Corned Beef?'

'I'm sorry, what?'

'The Corned Beef,' Frankie asked again, 'where do you think they keep it?'

Alan shrugged and under his breath he said 'I don't know. I'm not even sure you can get it anymore. Why do you want Corned Beef?'

'Or Spam,' Frankie added, 'I would have Spam if you can't find the Corned Beef.'

'Are you saying you can eat now?'

'No idea, but coming in here has reminded me about food.'

Hoping that no one was staring at him, Alan whispered into Frankie's ear, 'Just wait here. I won't be long.'

Alan went straight to the chiller unit and took a sandwich. On turning around, he could see Frankie standing exactly where he had left him, the other customers oblivious to his presence.

'Right let's go,' Alan said as he passed Frankie.

'What have you got there?' Frankie asked as Alan queued up at the checkout.

Alan turned the triangular package round in his hand. 'Tuna Mayonnaise,' he said. 'They don't do sandwiches with either Corned Beef or Spam.'

Hearing giggling, Alan turned around. Frankie had disappeared and in his place stood two school girls, the oldest of which could be no more than fifteen. She looked Alan up and down, put her head to one side and said, 'Mate, what's Corned Beef?'

The sign outside The Third Man public house announced that Thursday night was comedy night. It also said that it was Curry night on Mondays, Quiz night on Tuesdays and over 40's night on Fridays.

'So is it closed on Wednesdays?' James asked.

'I have no idea,' Alan replied as they stood at the bar.

'They are advertising something every night of the week except Wednesdays,' James said. 'I can't believe they have nothing happening on Wednesdays,' he paused before adding, 'I bet it's swinging, they couldn't advertise that outside, but I bet all the locals know.'

As he finished speaking, a couple walked up to the bar, both smartly dressed and looked to be in their mid-fifties. James turned his back to them and whispered to Alan, 'I think they're a day late.'

From the outside, The Third Man looked as if it had seen better days. The paintwork was peeling, two of the smaller windowpanes were cracked and one window was entirely covered with plywood. The blackboard that set out the packed weekly programme was bound to a lamppost by several lengths of chain, an obvious deterrent to the local sign thieves. The locals regarded The Third man as a place best avoided, except on Thursdays when it held comedy nights, as these were the only evenings the boisterous crowd were united in shouting at people on stage rather than each other.

'It's a bit of dump,' James said.

'It may not look much, but it's one of the most famous comedy pubs on the circuit,' Alan explained. 'I've been trying to play here for ages. I've been on a reserve list for six months.'

James looked around, shrugged and took a mouthful of beer.

'You didn't have to come,' Alan reminded him. 'I'm a big boy now and I'm even allowed out after ten o'clock.'

'I couldn't let you travel up to North London and play a new venue without some moral support. I'm just saying it's a bit of a dump.'

Alan had received a telephone call the previous week from the manager. One of the regular comics had landed a spot doing the warm up for a TV panel show and would not be available, and he had asked Alan if he was free to step in at short notice. Containing his excitement, Alan casually answered that he was indeed available and would look forward to it. What Alan didn't say was that he would crawl over broken glass for the opportunity to perform there, as he knew it was considered a stepping stone to bigger and greater things.

They had arrived at 8pm and Alan had had a brief chat with the manager. This being Alan's first time, he was due to open the show at 9pm. Looking at his watch, He realised there were just thirty minutes to go.

James asked his usual question. 'What are you doing tonight?'

'Sticking with what I know works,' Alan replied.

'Fat kid stuck in a flume?' James asked, grinning.

'Of course,' Alan grinned in response.

The pub had started to fill with people, and soon the comfortable space that Alan and James had found at the bar disappeared. Taking their glasses, they moved away from the bar and wandered over to a vacant table in the corner.

'I don't know why you never want to hang out in the Green Room,' said James.

Alan laughed. 'Mate, I really don't think this place has a Green Room. In my experience, "backstage" means changing in the disabled toilet.'

'Fair enough. So, have you seen him yet?' James asked between mouthfuls of beer.

'Who?'

'Frankie, obviously,' James replied. 'You said that he was going to come along, you know, watch you and give you some advice.'

'You don't really think he will be here do you?' Alan asked. 'I mean, he can't control what he's doing at the best of times, how he's going to manage to get himself across London?'

'He'll make the effort,' James said, looking over at the bar. 'After all, they serve spirits in here.'

Alan laughed. 'You're wasted mate. You should be writing jokes in Christmas crackers.'

Ignoring his friend's response, James finished his drink. 'Do you want another one?' he asked, pointing at Alan's half empty glass.

Alan shook his head. 'Better not. It never looks good if the comedian is drunker than the audience. Though sometimes that might be an advantage.'

'Just me then,' James said and made his way to the bar leaving Alan alone.

This suited Alan fine. He welcomed the opportunity to be on his own. He looked around the bar, taking in the atmosphere and tried to gauge the audience. Alan knew the problem with going on first was that there was no opportunity to assess who in the crowd was most likely to laugh and who was most likely to heckle.

Alan scanned the bar. He could see James waiting to be served. He appeared to be in conversation with the middle aged couple. Probably getting the low down on the swinging scene, he chuckled to himself. The rest of the prospective audience appeared to be fairly normal. No obvious idiots or drunks. So, most definitely, the fat kid was going to get stuck in the flume, and Alan would profess his attraction to a sexy cartoon rabbit.

*

The comedy took place in a room next to the bar, appropriately named the "Comedy Room."

'Does this mean,' James asked, 'that there's a swinging room too?'

Alan was concentrating on his routine and chose to ignore his friend's continuing chatter.

'Stands to reason doesn't it?' James continued. 'If they have a comedy room, they will have a swinging room. It's probably round the back,' he added with a smirk.

Alan looked around the room. It appeared slightly smaller than the bar, although he knew that it would comfortably take two hundred people. The stage was in the corner, diagonally opposite the door. Thick black drapes covered the walls, keeping the noise and more importantly, the atmosphere contained, within the room.

James hadn't finished sharing his views. 'You say this is the place to play,' he said. 'It doesn't look much to me.'

'Don't worry about how it looks,' Alan replied. 'It's the reputation this place has. Some of the greats have played here on their way to the top.'

James shrugged. 'Looks like the type of place you would play on the way down.'

Alan recognised several faces from the comedy circuit. He caught the eye of the manager, Tony Elson. Tony was a tall man with a mop of black curly hair and wearing a faded polo shirt which was straining to keep an expanding waistline under control. He nodded at Alan who turned to James. 'I'm off now, I'll see you later.' he said.

Alan made his way through the crowd towards Tony. James watched as the two men engaged in conversation, occasionally laughing.

Despite what their respective partners thought, James had no doubts that Alan could succeed at a career in comedy. He just needed that break. Maybe tonight would be that night. James scanned the room and noticed the audience was largely made up of men, which was good, he thought, as Alan's act could sometimes be perceived as a little *"mancentric."*

James was interrupted from his thoughts by the presence of Tony Elson stepping on to the stage to a round of applause. Tony welcomed the crowd to the "Third Man Comedy Night" and promised them that they were in for a good night, which generated another enthusiastic round of applause. Tony went on to address the audience for a further couple of minutes, cracking a couple of jokes and sharing banter with a pocket of the crowd.

Standing to one side of the stage, Alan was impressed by how at ease Tony appeared on the stage, getting laughs from the whole room. Alan considered this was inevitable if Tony were doing this same short act once a week, every week.

'Tonight' Tony said 'Our first act is a guy playing here for the first time. So let's give a warm Third Man welcome to Alan Rose...'

The crowd applauded as Alan stepped onto the stage, shaking Tony's hand as Tony walked off. Standing on the stage, Alan let the applause die down before launching himself into his routine;

'Thank you,' he said before continuing, 'This is my first time so be patient with me, and let's hope this lasts longer than the first time I said that.'

This was greeted by muted laughter. Alan quickly assessed where the noise was coming from, two or three little groups on either side of the room. Not ideal, he thought to himself, but a start.

As Alan scanned the first few rows of people he saw James standing at the back laughing, despite having heard that line every time Alan had played a new venue. Standing next to James was Frankie, grinning.

Alan noticed that Frankie had his own space, as if everyone had moved out of the way for him. Alan knew this wasn't possible because as far as he was aware, he was the only person who could see Frankie.

Suddenly Alan realised the room had gone quiet, waiting for him to continue. Alan knew that even a few seconds could seem like an eternity to an audience.

Thinking quickly, Alan said, 'I'd like to thank you all for coming out tonight, and I'd particularly like to thank my uncle Frankie for making the effort as he's been dead for thirty years.'

The awkward silence continued, but Alan pressed on regardless.

James, realising what his friend had just said, turned to his right. There was a decent space between him and the man standing next to him. Perhaps James thought, the space was large enough for someone to stand in. James realised that the complaints about the air conditioning may in fact have been down to Frankie's appearance. James gently moved his right arm out to see if he could feel anything, but all he felt was an icy chill.

*

'All I'm saying is that fat kids will eat anything. You could smear chocolate on a bar of soap and it would be in their mouths quicker than you can say parental neglect.'

Alan knew this part of his routine could sometimes divide a crowd, but tonight it seemed they were on his side.

'Look, we're all friends here.' Alan said, warming to the theme, prowling the small stage. 'I don't have a problem

215

with fat kids. Some of my best friends at school were fat. Well, I say best friends. What I actually mean by "friend" is someone who couldn't run as fast as I could when the mad kid with the wonky eye wanted to set fire to your hair.'

A mild splattering of laughter. Clearly the audience had attended a better class of school than he had. 'I'm guessing you guys attended a better class of school than I did. There probably aren't that many apprentice psychopaths in grammar schools. Unless you count those that end up as office sex pests and those destined to become politicians with a pathological hatred of the NHS. Of course, quite often they are one and the same.

'The thing is, I like fat kids. No, really, I do. They are the least discriminating people on the planet. Smother something in chocolate and a fat kid will eat it. I was worried that my girlfriend would discover how much porn I watched, so I dipped my laptop in a vat of melted chocolate and left it outside a primary school and let nature do the rest. To this day, my girlfriend has no idea of my old internet viewing habits. Although she did tell me once that she had x-rayed three large kids who had swallowed a variety of electrical hardware.'

Alan wasn't really sure about that bit, but it always made James laugh, so he figured it was worth keeping in for the time being. Frankie on the other hand, looked back at the stage blankly. Tough crowd, he thought to himself, before realising that Frankie wouldn't understand the reference to the internet.

The silence of the crowd brought Alan back to the present. 'Where was I?' he said, making it sound like part of the act. 'Oh yes. Fat kids. The thing is they will eat any old chocolate. It doesn't matter what it looks like, they just want to stuff it in their pudgy little mouths. But me...I'm like a woman. I want to be seduced by it. But sometimes...sometimes the chocolate isn't enough by itself. If you know what I mean..?'

Alan let that thought hang in the air for a moment. 'I'm going out on a limb here people. But I reckon the guys in the audience know exactly what I'm talking about. In the absence of any discernible differences in quality between some chocolate bars, you sometimes go for the advertising.

'Now, most guys will be swayed by the product that promises them the sexiest woman at the party. You know the sort. You're a bespectacled geek who no one talks to, but WHAM...you take out your bar of chocolate and suddenly all the girls at the party want to be with you.

'Not me. It's not that I look down on the one dimensional women who would sit on your knee for a bite of your chocolate bar, or the advertisers that suggest women are nothing more than vacuous shallow greedy trollops. No. It's just that I set my sights higher. I don't want the skank who is anyone's for a nibble on your confectionery. I want the sultry woman, the sensual woman, the woman of my dreams. What I want, ladies and gentlemen, is the Cadbury's Caramel Bunny.

'You know exactly what I mean,' Alan said, pointing to a laughing man in the front row. 'Well, sorry, mate, I saw her first. I mean, the Cadbury's Caramel Bunny. Now there's a woman. She has it all. Sexy voice, gorgeous big brown eyes, cute little pink neck bow. And she's just so...well...fluffy.' Alan mimed a squeezing motion with his hands to emphasise the point, drawing more laughs from the crowd.

'Look, all I'm saying is that I can't be the only one who has ever thought of grabbing hold of the Cadbury Caramel Bunny's ears, taking it from behind and riding it like a Harley Davidson. I'd mat its' fur up for it. *Dirty* little bunny.

'Ladies and gentlemen, you may now be thinking I am a little weird, and you may well be right, but think about it. If bunnies weren't sexy, Hugh Hefner would be nothing more than an office sex pest. OK, I guess, technically, he is a sex pest, but you see my point...'

*

Alan and James stayed until the end of the show, watching every act. Alan conceded that some were funnier than him, but encouragingly, some weren't. James however, was in no doubt that he was the star turn and offered him his usual motivational speech afterwards.

'You really nailed that. Did you see the manager? He loved that bit about the rabbit.'

Alan knew James was right. Tony had said to him afterwards that it brought back some very fond memories.

'You're too exclusive, 'Frankie said, appearing alongside Alan. 'Half the audience thought you were hilarious, but the other half just stared at you.'

'Yes, but I only heard the laughs,' Alan said sarcastically, making James' eyebrows raise as Alan now seemed to be talking to himself.

'Let me help you. I reckon with my input you could broaden your appeal,' Frankie offered.

Alan stood between James and Frankie as they both offered him advice, like the proverbial angel and devil on each shoulder. He looked to the sky and sighed.

Chapter 26

Alan sat on the edge of the bed watching Rosie place carefully folded clothes into a small overnight case.

'I'm just saying why do we have to go for the whole weekend? We'll run out of things to say to each other by Saturday night.'

Without stopping her packing Rosie countered, 'You said you were happy to come down with me to my parents for the weekend.'

'You never said it was for the weekend. You said it was just a visit.'

In all honesty, Alan couldn't remember what she had said. It was weeks ago that the subject had first been mentioned, and he had had a lot on his mind since then.

Rosie squeezed the two sides of the bag together and attempted to close the zip without any real success.

'You've got too much in that,' Alan said helpfully.

Taking her hands off the sides of the bag it slowly opened. 'You could help instead of standing there mocking me,' she said.

Alan reached over to the bag and took out a pair of jeans and two pairs of shoes.

'That'll be OK now,' he said as he easily zipped the bag closed.

Rosie stared at the small pile of clothes that had come out of her bag.

'You can put them in mine if you like,' he offered, pointing at a large sports bag which he had left in the middle of the floor.

Sighing, Rosie took the remaining clothes off of the bed and put them into Alan's sports bag.

'I don't know why you are so against spending the weekend at my parents. It's not like you have a busy weekend planned, and you have always got on with my mum.'

I would certainly like to get on with your mum, Alan thought to himself, but actually said, 'Your mum's great, it's your Dad that doesn't like me.'

'Of course he likes you. He was just disappointed that you didn't get that job after he arranged the interview for you. But he doesn't hate you,' Rosie insisted before adding, 'much...'

Alan laid back on the bed and looked at the ceiling. After they had been going out for a couple of years, Rosie had mentioned to her parents about Alan's constant moaning about his job. Attempting to help Alan and make Rosie's life happier, her father had made some calls and arranged for Alan to have an interview with a company in the city. Alan had been terrified at the prospect and had set out to fail the interview, something which he achieved in quite spectacular fashion. Alan always suspected that whilst everyone else thought he had just been unlucky, her father had known the truth - that Alan had deliberately failed the interview.

Rosie picked up the bags. 'I'm leaving in ten minutes, so I suggest that you hurry up if you're coming.'

*

Alan slammed down the boot on Rosie's small sporty Audi, both bags safely stowed away, before opening the passenger door and getting inside. He had never doubted that he would be going with Rosie, he just felt the need to re-establish his position on visiting. It wasn't just visiting Rosie's parents that he had an aversion to, it was visiting in general.

'I just think,' he said to Rosie as she navigated her way through the South London streets in the general direction of Sussex, 'that these days with e-mail, Facebook, Twitter and Skype, you can speak to people all over the world at any time. You don't have to physically visit them anymore, and you certainly don't have to drive for two hours to a village that still thinks Harold Macmillan is Prime Minister.'

Without taking her eyes off the road, Rosie replied, 'These are my parents you're talking about.'

Realising that he had just wandered out into the middle of a frozen lake, put on his favourite ice skates and began to skate in an area marked "Very Thin Ice" Alan backed off and changed the subject.

'What are the plans for tonight?' he asked.

'I'm not sure. Mum mentioned a meal in the village. Let's see shall we?'

Alan leaned forward and started searching for a radio station that was playing something he liked.

'I'll just find something worth listening to,' he said, adding, 'before we lose the signal and can only pick up War Time Radio.'

'You'll be happy then. You might find more modern material!' Rosie replied, grinning.

Alan slumped down in his seat and sulked.

*

Rosie had been talking for what seemed like hours. Alan nodded his agreement whenever Rosie had paused for breath.

'And don't forget next Saturday we have the party,' she said.

Alan's attention was drawn to the word *"party"* and he slipped back into the conversation. 'What Party?' he asked.

Rosie sighed. 'I've already told you, a friend of mine from the gym. She's having a birthday party next Saturday. Jayne's going.'

'Do I know her?' Alan asked.

'I don't think so. I know her from the gym.' Rosie repeated and then added by way of explanation, 'You

223

know the place that I go to a few times a week, get all hot and sweaty, and makes me fitter?'

'A gym...' Alan said in mock surprise, 'I thought you were working in a foundry.'

Ignoring him, Rosie continued, 'Alison – that's her name - it's her forty fifth, and her husbands booked out the Cricket Club.'

'Sounds like fun,' Alan said unenthusiastically.

'Can I come?'

The voice from behind startled him. Alan turned his head and saw Frankie sitting on the back seat.

'Oh for crying out loud!' Alan said in a voice that was just less than shouting.

'What!?' Rosie shouted back, concerned that they had forgotten something.

'That car behind us,' Alan said, desperately trying to find a rational reason for his outburst. 'It was really close.'

Rosie looked in the rear view mirror but see nothing to cause concern.

'You mean that old fiat panda? Its way back,' she said.

'He was really close a moment ago.'

'Whatever,' Rosie said and squeezed the accelerator gently, putting a little more space between herself and the car behind. 'Satisfied?' she asked.

'Can you move your seat forward a bit? Asked Frankie. 'Only there's hardly any space back here. How do you fit the kids in?'

Alan could hear Frankie fidgeting in his seat and then felt the bulge of Frankie's knees in his back. Reaching down he pulled up a lever and the seat eased forward.

'That's better thanks,' Frankie said, again readjusting his position.

Rosie watched out of the corner of her eye as Alan slid his seat forward until his knees were against the dashboard.

'What are you doing? She asked.

'I'm just more comfortable this way,' he replied.

Rosie shook her head, wondering if he was still suffering some after effects of his blow to the head.

'Where are we going?' Frankie asked.

Ignoring the question from the back seat, Alan looked out of the window. There were several bunches of flowers tied to railings at the side of the road.

'What are they there for?' he asked.

'This is an accident black spot,' Rosie answered. 'Someone must have died recently, those look really fresh.'

'Pullover,' Alan said, 'I'll get your mum some flowers.'

Rosie's colourful reply took Alan somewhat by surprise and although Alan couldn't see him, he could hear Frankie chuckling in the back.

*

Rosie's parents lived in a large detached house at the end of a cul-de-sac. She pulled into the driveway, showering gravel into the flowerbeds.

'Your dad will love that,' Alan grinned, looking at the roses.

Ignoring him, Rosie climbed out of the car. 'I'll go and find them,' she said.

Alan watched Rosie approach the front door and open it with a key she had taken out of her pocket. He turned to Frankie, having ignored his presence for the previous thirty minutes.

'You really pick your moments don't you?' he said.

'I'm really pleased to see you too,' Frankie replied sarcastically before asking, 'Where are we?'

'You my friend,' Alan said, 'have signed up for a weekend at Rosie's parents. A weekend in 1956.'

'Excellent. I remember 1956 like it was yesterday,' Frankie replied wistfully. 'In any case, I've been dead thirty odd years so it'll be good to have a weekend break.'

'Not this weekend break. This is going to be very dull. Imagine the quietest audience you've ever played. It'll be like that, but worse.' Alan grimaced.

'Well I don't know how long I'll be around for, so I may as well make the most of it. So get the door open and I can have a look around,' he said as he began to kick the back of Alan's seat.

'OK wait a second...' Alan said, '...and stop doing that.'

Alan opened his door and climbed out. He pulled down a lever and the back of his seat tipped forward. Frankie climbed out of the car, grumbling about how uncomfortable it was in the back seat.

'Not much room in there,' he said.

Before Alan could answer, the front door opened and Rosie stepped out, followed by her mother. Frankie grabbed Alan's arm.

'Who's that?' he asked. 'Is that your mother in law?'

Breaking away from Frankie's hold, Alan walked over to Rosie's mum.

'Alan, how are you?' she asked before giving him a hug.

'I'm good Cassie,' Alan said. 'You're looking well. Holiday tan?'

Cassie smiled. She was two or three inches shorter than Alan, roughly the same height as Rosie, and had short ash blonde hair - a tactic that Rosie said hid the grey.

'No Holiday,' she said, 'just working in the garden.'

'Well you're looking good on it,' Alan said with a smile.

'Do I get a hug?' Frankie asked.

Oblivious to Frankie's presence, Rosie turned to Alan. 'Can you get the bags? I've put the kettle on.'

Alan moved round to the back of the car and opened the boot. Frankie followed him round and said, 'She's a bit of a looker your mother in law.'

'She's not my mother in law,' Alan whispered. He thought for a moment, smiled and added, 'She is fit though.'

'You know that it's quite likely that your Rosie will turn out like her mum,' Frankie said, nudging Alan in his side.

'Yep, that's what I'm hoping!' Alan grinned.

Frankie laughed in response. 'Good luck with that.'

*

The house had a large farmhouse style kitchen, stone tiles on the floor, a large pine table in the middle of the room with six chairs arranged around it, and the obligatory Aga in the corner.

Cassie led Alan and Rosie into the kitchen. Alan put the bags onto the floor while Rosie made a beeline for a tabby cat which was curled up on one of the chairs.

'Hello Daisy,' she cooed, picking the animal up for a cuddle.

'Hey! A cat,' said Frankie, who followed everyone into the kitchen. 'Cats love me,' he said reaching to stroke the cat.

Daisy, who had been purring enthusiastically in Rosie's arms, began hissing and wriggling, before launching herself free from Rosie embrace and crashing through the cat flap.

'What did you do?' Rosie frowned, looking at suspiciously.

'Nothing,' Alan replied. 'You saw what happened, she took off before I could stroke her. Like he had seen a...' Alan let the sentence hang momentarily, slowly realising what he was about to say, before adding quietly, '...ghost.'

'Who saw a ghost?' A voice from behind Alan asked.

Alan turned to face Rosie's father. Michael was a tall man, taller even than Alan, with the bearing and poise of a man who had served for many years as an officer in the Army.

'Hi Dad,' Rosie said rushing over to greet her father.

'Hello Michael. How are you?' Alan asked, once Rosie and her father had finished hugging.

'I'm well thank you, Alan,' Michael replied, shaking Alan's hand with his customary iron grip. However hard he tried, Alan could never match the strength of the man's handshake.

'Daisy has just shot through the cat flap, like she saw a ghost,' Cassie explained to her husband while Alan tried to rub some life back into his crushed hand.

Ignoring Cassie's explanation, Michael continued talking to Alan. 'So, how's the civil service? Still enjoying it?' he said provocatively.

Biting his tongue, Alan replied, 'Well, it's still challenging.'

'Well keep working at it,' Michael said, 'you never know, you might get the hang of it eventually.'

Alan refused to take the bait. 'I doubt that Michael, I know my limits.'

Michael laughed, and out of the corner of his eye, Alan could see Rosie mouth the words *"thank you"* to him.

*

'Great lunch. Thanks mum,' Rosie said, leaning back in to her chair.

Alan and Rosie, Cassie and Michael were seated around the large table, having just enjoyed a lunch that Cassie had appeared to throw together with the minimum amount of fuss. It was the first meal in weeks that Alan had eaten which hadn't began with him staring into a half empty fridge hoping for inspiration.

'Yes, it was very nice. Thanks Cassie,' Alan added, and hoped that cooking was something else that Rosie would inherit from her mother.

'Rosie tells me that you had an accident a few weeks ago?' Cassie asked, looking at Alan's forehead.

'Yeah, nothing serious, though,' Alan said, 'I fell over and banged my head on the table on my way down. Bit silly really.'

'Of course it was serious,' Rosie contradicted him. 'You knocked yourself out.' Turning to Cassie she added, 'I had to take him to the hospital. They were very concerned.'

'You can't take a chance with head injuries,' Michael agreed.

'No harm done,' Alan said, trying to change the subject.

'Fortunately you hit your least vulnerable spot,' Frankie piped up from where he was leaning against the Aga. 'No sense, no feeling.'

Frankie had made several comments during the lunch, some Alan had found funny, some he had been irritated by, and on every occasion he had remained silent, trying to ignore the wit and wisdom of the dead comedian standing in the kitchen.

'How's the comedy going?' Cassie asked.

Surprised and flattered by Cassie's interest, Alan took full advantage of being able to talk about something he was interested in.

'It's not too bad, thanks, I've had a few bookings, and I've got a few more coming up in the next few weeks.'

Frankie started laughing again.

Turning back to Cassie, Alan asked, 'Do you remember a comedian from the Seventies. A guy by the name of Frankie Fortune?' he said, deliberately looking to where Frankie was standing.

Alan could see Frankie's face fall, no longer smirking, but now paying attention to the conversation.

'Not sure I do,' Cassie admitted. 'Why? Was he famous?'

'Not really. He appeared on a few shows, but generally he played low rent venues, working men's clubs, that kind of thing.'

'Hey!' Frankie called out, 'That's harsh. I'll have you know that I was fourth reserve for the 1969 Royal Variety Performance.'

Unimpressed by Frankie's attempt to prove his importance, Alan sat smugly back in his chair.

232

'Frankie Fortune you said?' Michael asked, deep in thought. Before Alan could answer, Michael continued, 'Actually the name does ring a bell. I think I saw him live in the early seventies.'

Michael suddenly had the complete and undivided attention of both Alan and Frankie.

'The trouble with all the seventies comedians was that they were all racist bigots,' Alan suggested.

'Not this again,' Frankie cried out, 'Give it a rest will you?'

Michael was rubbing his hand over his chin in thought. 'Actually,' he said, 'this one, Frankie, wasn't that bad. I think that's why we went to see him. He wasn't like the usual comedians, he was quite funny as I recall.'

'Now will you believe me?' Frankie called across the kitchen to Alan.

Cassie asked Rosie if she had been watching a TV programme that Alan had never heard of and the conversation changed again. Alan slumped in his chair and faded out of the conversation while Frankie stood opposite him grinning.

*

Alan stared up at the ceiling. There were no street lights outside to fill the room with a comforting glow. This was the countryside, and there were only stars and the moon to light the room at this time of the night.

He turned onto his right and looked at the digital alarm clock on the bedside table. It blinked 3.20 at him in bright green numbers. Alan rolled onto his back and continued to stare up at ceiling. It felt like he had been awake for ages, sleep being prevented by a combination of a full bladder and Frankie's snoring.

Frankie was asleep, slumped in a chair in the corner of the room head back, mouth open and making window rattling snoring sounds. At least he's not lying in bed with us, Alan thought to himself.

Alan had to concede that it hadn't been a bad night. They had spent the evening at the village pub, having a meal followed by a few drinks. Michael had even made an effort to get on with him, something that became a lot easier when he admitted to Alan's surprise that he had got his collection of LPs and 45s out of the loft and was actively looking to add to them. This was definitely something that Alan could identify with.

The conversation had turned to Jayne. As far as Alan could understand, whenever Rosie and Cassie got together, etiquette dictated that Cassie said how much she worried about her eldest daughter, and Rosie then spent the rest of the conversation assuring her mother that Jayne was fine and it was only a matter of time before she met Mr Right.

'Have you got any available friends?' Cassie had asked Alan.

'No, he hasn't,' Rosie had said, before Alan could open his mouth to reply.

'How about Ben?' Alan had said to Rosie.

'No way!' Rosie had replied.

'Why? What's wrong with him?' Cassie had asked.

'He's been arrested for kerb crawling. Twice...' Rosie explained to her mother.

'Jayne doesn't need to know that, he's not a bad bloke,' Alan said helpfully. 'He's just a bit lonely.'

'Yes, but Jayne was the one who arrested him. Both times!' Rosie said, shooting down Alan's attempt at match making.

Another round of Frankie's machine gun snoring brought Alan back to the present. His long dead companion had accompanied them to the pub, completing the fifteen minute walk with constant moaning about his aching legs. Frankie had then squeezed himself onto a stool and attempted to share it with Alan for the entire evening. Alan had spent the evening looking, to everybody else, like he was perching on the end of his stool for no apparent reason.

'Tell them that your piles are playing up,' Frankie had advised Alan. 'They'll understand.'

*

Frankie woke with a start. That was a bizarre nightmare, he thought. In his dream he was being throttled by a giant chicken, while simultaneously being tickled by its feathers. He wasn't sure what had woken him; the giant chicken, the being throttled or the feathers. Whatever the reason, it was very strange. Then he realised with a start, that he had been asleep. He was dead, surely he didn't need sleep, and if he did, what was the point of his dreaming?

Sitting up properly in the chair, he rubbed his face with his hands and looked over at the clock on the bedside table. The green glowing figures told him it was 6.45; nearly time to get up. Frankie briefly considered waking Alan and suggesting that they go for an early morning walk. It would give them chance to talk as they hadn't had many chances to speak alone since they arrived. Alan he assumed, was still concerned that people would think that he was going mad if he was seen talking to himself.

Before Frankie could decide on the best course of action, Rosie groaned in her sleep and turned over. She sighed, fidgeted and she turned over again.

Frankie leant back in the chair. He couldn't relax. The dream - however ridiculous it appeared to be - had disturbed him. Rosie stirred again, Frankie could see the mound of duvet moving around and Rosie's head poked out of the top. Sitting up in bed, she looked around the room, her eyes cast over the chair that Frankie was sitting in, not giving it a second glance. Turning to the still sleeping Alan she whispered, 'Are you awake?'

Alan responded by emitting occasional snores, answering her question. She gave it a few more seconds before trying again. 'Alan....Are you awake?'

Frankie continued to watch as Rosie refused to give up. Moving closer she whispered again. 'Alan...Alan...Alan...'

Armed with an idea, Frankie raised himself from his chair with a groan and padded over to Alan's side of the bed, where he could see that Alan was indeed fast asleep, with his back to Rosie. Frankie crouched down so that his face was inches away from Alan's. Frankie took a deep breath and bellowed, 'Alan. Wake Up!'

Alan jerked awake, his eyes sprang open and he sat bolt upright in bed. The sudden movement took Rosie by surprise and she shot back to her side of the bed.

'For God's sake,' he shouted, 'what are you playing at?'

Rosie stared back at him. 'I was just seeing if you were awake,' she explained.

'How?' Alan asked, his heart rate slowly returning to normal. 'By shouting in my ear?'

'I didn't shout in your ear,' Rosie protested. 'I whispered.'

'Well it sounded like you...' Alan paused, he could now see Frankie sitting in his chair looking innocently around.

Alan sighed, 'It doesn't matter.'

'Make your mind up,' Rosie said to him as she and turned her back to him fell promptly to sleep.

*

'This is the longest time that you've spent with me since your resurrection,' Alan said to Frankie as they sat on the patio in the large garden, both comfortable in garden chairs, a mug of tea for Alan on the table in front of them.

'I've got no idea why, but I'm not complaining. It's really nice here,' Frankie looked out at the manicured lawn and immaculate flower beds.

'Where did you live?' Alan asked, 'When you were alive I mean?'

'All over really. I travelled around a lot, touring. You know how it is.'

Not really, but where was home, family?'

Frankie paused before answering, 'On the south coast, not far from here, down Brighton way.'

'I know, I could pay it a visit, and you could come with me. You could see how things have changed.'

Frankie looked out across the garden. Changing the subject, he pointed at the pond at the end of the garden. 'Why,' he asked, 'are there some plastic birds round the edge of the pond?'

Alan looked to where Frankie pointed. He was right. Standing round the edge of the pond were several full sized plastic birds. 'I don't know, maybe they're like posh gnomes.'

'Talking to yourself Alan?' Michael said, suddenly approaching from the conservatory. 'Maybe that bang on the head caused more damage than you thought.'

Feeling himself flush, Alan replied, 'I was just wondering why you had the plastic birds around the edge of your pond.'

'They're supposed to be decoys,' Michael said.

Alan stared at him, inviting further explanation.

'The idea is that the real birds, herons for example, won't come down and take fish out of the pond because they'll see the plastic birds and think they are real.'

'Does it work?' Alan asked peering more closely at the plastic birds.

'We don't know, but we haven't lost as many fish since we bought them.'

Alan looked at Frankie and both men nodded in acceptance of the explanation.

'Anyway,' Michael said, 'I came out here to ask you if you wanted to see my record collection.'

Needing no further encouragement, Alan prised himself from the garden chair and followed Michael back in to the house.

*

Alan was impressed. Michael really had embraced the whole vinyl revival scene. The small box room at the top of the house was home to Michael's impressive collection. Records filled the shelves with several boxes stacked in the corner of the small room.

'This is a very impressive collection,' Alan said, browsing the shelves.

'I could never bear to throw them out once CDs took over, so I just kept them in the loft and a couple of years ago I started adding to them again. It's easy to get hold of them now,' Michael said his voice full of pride.

'There is something about vinyl isn't there?' Alan agreed, enjoying the opportunity to bond with Rosie's dad. 'The way that they feel, the smell, and the covers,' he added.

'I know, I loved the way that record shops used to smell,' Michael said, smiling at the memory. 'You don't get that now CDs are all wrapped in plastic.'

'I know, and downloads are making even CDs obsolete. It just isn't the same.' He took an album from the shelf and inhaled. 'That smell brings back so many memories,' Alan said.

Frankie was standing in the doorway watching the two men enthuse about records. 'You should get your Rosie a dress made of record vinyl. You'll like that.'

Without turning to look at Frankie, and forgetting that he and Frankie weren't alone, 'Rosie in a vinyl dress is an image that..." before realising that Michael was staring at him. Alan didn't even try to finish the sentence.

'Probably best that you don't finish that sentence Alan,' Michael said coldly. 'She is my daughter after all.'

*

The drive back that afternoon was a lot more peaceful than the drive down. Both Alan and Rosie were lost in their own thoughts whilst Frankie was again squeezed into the back seat looking out as the countryside slowly turned into towns. As they drove past a retail park, something caught his attention and brought a smile to his face. Tapping Alan on the shoulder he said, 'Fancy popping in there..?'

Looking out of the window, Alan saw the large retail warehouse and smiled. Rosie looked across at the retail park. 'What a funny name for a shop, "Vinyl World, I wonder what they sell?'

Chapter 27

Crozier read the article in the newspaper for a second time without commenting. He passed the paper across the desk to Alison, who picked it up and began to read.

'Have you helped out on this?' she asked Crozier.

'I have provided some consultancy services,' he answered, 'and I expect that my services will be required again throughout the process,' he concluded, a small smile on his face.

The headline read: **Shopping centre planned for High Street**

The half page article explained that a massive redevelopment of Merton High Street was planned. Contracts had been signed, and a number of properties, including the derelict 100 year old Merton Palace Theatre were to be demolished to make way for the ambitious project, the likes of which had never previously been seen in the town. A spokesman for the theatre's owners said that *'they were proud that from the ashes of such an iconic building would come the next leap forward in the town's future.'*

Alison finished reading the article and sat back in her chair. 'That's not going to go down well.'

'What isn't?' Crozier asked, puzzled.

'The theatre coming down. It's a very popular building. It has a lot of history attached to it,' she said.

'Come on, it's a horrible building. An eyesore,' Crozier said, trying to convince her. 'The shopping centre will bring people to spend money and will create jobs. The theatre needs hundreds of thousands of pounds spent on it, and even then it will only serve the needs of a tiny number of people.'

'You have no soul,' Alison said, mocking him.

'It makes no sense to keep it going,' Crozier argued. 'There's going to be a brand new shopping centre. There's nothing like it for miles, and all the locals have to do is put up with some building work and the loss of a derelict flea pit.'

'I'm just saying that there will be probably be some opposition for you to deal with.'

'They'll be too late. Preliminary contracts have been signed. Subject to formalities, it's going through,' Crozier said, and went back to the newspaper article.

'I still haven't had your response to my birthday party invite,' Alison said, changing the subject as she stood up.

Crozier looked up from the newspaper article and stared blankly at her.

'Are you coming?' she asked. 'I need to know for the catering.'

'Oh sorry,' he replied. 'We have something else on that night, one of my wife's aunts is having a get together and we can't get out of it.'

Crozier looked at Alison, unable to tell if she was disappointed or not. It was, he thought, impossible to tell what was going on behind her blue eyes.

'Never mind,' she said. 'If you do get out of it you can always come late. You're more than welcome.'

Alison turned to leave the room.

She's definitely disappointed he thought. 'Tell you what,' he said, 'I'll take you to lunch. A birthday lunch.'

Alison turned back to face him. 'That'll be really nice, thank you. We'll be bound to have a nice time,' she said with a smile.

*

James was sitting in his den when he heard the front door slam. It wasn't Amy's usual way of shutting the front door. It was, James considered, an early warning system that told him she wasn't happy.

He quickly assessed that it was either something he had done or something that had happened at school. On the balance of probabilities, he was likely to be blameless and, in order to distance himself from any potential crashing and slamming around down stairs, he slipped his headphones over his head, turned the music up another level and got on with marking exercise books.

Opening the first answer sheet, he looked briefly at the answers and his heart sank. He picked up a red pen and struck through all the answers with a big cross.

'How on earth can I find anything positive to add to this drivel? He said to himself out loud.

The music, which had been advising those in education to not hassle kids, suddenly went silent. He span round in his chair and saw Amy standing with her finger over the stop button.

'Hi Ames what's up?' he asked, as he slipped the headphones off his head.

244

'Have you seen the local paper?' She asked, waving a copy around in front of him.

'No, sorry I haven't. Anything interesting?' He asked, reaching out for the newspaper.

Snatching it back from him she said, 'They only want to pull the theatre down.'

James had seen Amy angry on many occasions, but he had rarely seen her so furious. He was however, experienced in his wife's mood swings and knew that his reaction would make the difference between her calming down and talking it through, or inflaming the situation so badly that it actually became his fault. He knew that his choice of words was vitally important.

'What theatre?' He asked.

'What do you mean *What Theatre?*' Amy shouted, letting James know in no uncertain terms that he had in fact chosen the wrong words.

'Sorry, but I'm not sure what theatre you are talking about,' he said, trying to placate his wife. 'There are lots of them.'

'The Merton Palace Theatre!' Amy exclaimed. 'We went to a fund raiser there, and I took the children there the other week.'

'Oh that theatre,' James replied. 'Why is it being pulled down?'

Amy waved the newspaper around again. 'They are building a bloody shopping centre in its place all in the guise of redeveloping the area.'

James reached out for the newspaper again, this time Amy passed it to him. She leaned against the door while he quickly read through the article.

He could see why she was so angry. 'I can see why you're so angry, he said in an effort to alleviate her mood.

'The children really loved their day there, they got so much out of it,' Amy said, her voice becoming calmer. 'It would be a tragedy if they never had the opportunity to go back there. It did wonders for their confidence.'

James leaned back in his chair, looking at the ceiling, a pose he often adopted when trying to convince people that he was deep in thought.

'I think,' he said in a considered tone, 'that this is going to need a strongly worded letter of complaint to the council.'

'What do you mean *a strongly worded letter of complaint?*' Amy answered, her voice becoming louder again.

'I think that a strongly worded letter objecting to the demolition of the theatre should be sent, explaining that the theatre has a place in the local community and that we would be very disappointed if the development was allowed to go ahead in its present form,' James explained patiently.

'You're actually serious aren't you?' Amy said in disbelief. 'You actually believe that these people...these *developers* will be so upset when they see your letter that *expresses disappointment* with their plans, that they will abandon them and write off the millions of pounds that they have resting on it.'

'Well, I think in the first instance it may get them thinking.'

'This is beyond "Mr Angry" letters. The only way to meet this threat is with some form of protest movement,' she said, frowning.

James's heart sank. Amy would protest against any idea, but particularly those that affected children. What concerned him was that he knew that he was going to get dragged into it whether he liked it or not. He sighed, 'Are you sure that is the best approach?' He asked.

'I don't think we have any choice,' she replied, moving some papers aside to sit on his desk. 'I'm sure that there will be lots of unhappy people who would be more than willing to protest about the loss of the theatre. I think we should coordinate with the Arts Council. They must have links with the theatre's owners.'

It had not gone unnoticed by James that Amy had said *"we"* and he felt his spirit deflate. 'You'll have to speak to Alan,' Amy said, looking at her husband.

'Why? What's he got to do with it?'

'He must know other comedians, people who want the theatre to be saved,' Amy explained.

'OK I'll call him,' James replied, knowing that Alan would be as enthusiastic as he was about getting involved with any protest.

*

From Sarah@theartspeople.co.uk

To Alanrose99@veryfunny.com

Hi.

I don't know if you've see the local news but apparently there are plans to demolish the Merton Palace Theatre and build a shopping centre. The owners seem happy to accept the cash and have the theatre demolished. We are clearly not going to take this lying down and are arranging a public meeting so some form of action can be organised.

I really hope you are able to join us, your contribution will be vital. Please e mail me to confirm that you'll be able to come along, and I'll let you know the date when it has been arranged.

Here's the link to the news story in case you haven't seen it.

Sarah XX

Alan read the e-mail twice. Despite the friendly greeting and the fact that it appeared to be addressed to him alone, he knew that this was a generic e-mail that had probably been sent to everyone in Sarah's address book. Although he didn't doubt that it was a worthy cause, he was far too busy with work and his stand-up career to help out, so he deleted it.

'Anything interesting?' 'Rosie said, suddenly appearing at his side and making him jump.

'Can you please stop creeping around like that,' Alan cried out, startled.

'Like what?' Rosie asked, sitting down next to him at the sofa.

'You're too quiet, you don't make any noise and it's unnerving.'

'I can't help that, I'm just a very quiet person,' Rosie replied indignantly.

'I'm getting you a collar with a bell on it. It will give me advance warning that you're close.' Alan briefly had a mental image of Rosie wearing a cat's collar, which he put to the back of his mind.

'You've been really strange since you banged your head,' Rosie said. 'I think you need a brain scan…don't worry I don't think they'll find anything,' she laughed at her own joke.

Choosing to ignore Rosie's uncharacteristic attempt at humour, Alan decided to come clean about the e-mail. 'I got an e-mail. Apparently the theatre is going to be pulled down and a shopping centre built in its place.'

'The Merton Palace Theatre?' Rosie asked.

'Yeah, the one we went to for the fund raiser.'

'That's a shame, it was a proper old theatre. I thought it was going to be refurbished.'

'That's what I thought too, but it looks like the owners have had a better offer.'

'I don't imagine that the Arts people will be very happy about that!' Rosie replied.

'No, they're not. There're looking to organise a protest group of sorts, that's what the e-mail was for, seeing who's prepared to sign up for the fight.'

'And you signed up I assume?' Rosie assumed.

'No way,' Alan said, astonished that Rosie could have reached such an assumption. 'It's great that they want to fight the plans, but I don't have the time to go to meetings and spend hours sitting around talking and not getting anything done.'

'I'm just surprised, that's all,' she replied. 'I would have thought that you would have wanted to protect an old venue like that.'

Alan sighed. 'Rosie, listen. There's going to be millions of pounds tied up in this deal and I can't see that a few placards and a dozen of us standing outside the town hall is going to change too many minds. I don't mind putting the effort in, but there has to be a chance of success. Otherwise what's the point?'

'It's a good job you weren't a suffragette, otherwise women would still be waiting for the vote,' Rosie said smiling.

*

Alan was slumped on the sofa, mobile phone pressed to his ear. 'I'm telling you mate, she's on a full one over this. Can you at least speak to some people at the Arts society or whatever it's called and see if they intend to organise a protest.' James had been talking for the last five minutes without giving Alan a chance to reply.

'Mate...mate...' Alan interrupted, 'can you stop a minute. Take a breath...'

'Sorry, but she's been chewing my ear off all evening.'

'Why is she so bothered about the theatre?' Alan asked. 'She didn't particularly like the comedy night.'

'She didn't like the comedy, but she loved the theatre, and took her class there for one of those learning through play workshop things they do. Apparently the kids loved it.'

'Sounds like she's taking it personally,' Alan grinned.

'She is mate, and that means I have to care too.'

'Doesn't she realise that you couldn't give a monkeys?'

'No of course not!' James replied, 'I'm not stupid.'

Alan knew only too well that James's wife was one of those people who failed to understand anyone who did not have the same social conscious that she had. That, coupled with her temper, could make her a passionate champion of a cause, and Alan appreciated that it was easier for his friend to play along than appear apathetic.

'Anyway,' Alan said, 'I've already received an e-mail from the Arts Council. They're organising a protest group, public meetings all that kind of stuff.'

'That's great, we'll join you at the meeting,' James sounded relieved that he wouldn't be alone.

'I'm not going. I don't want to get involved.'

'You are kidding me?' James said. 'You have to go, you're a performer. It's almost your duty to defend a theatre.'

'Sorry mate, I just think it's a waste of time. I told Rosie that there's been millions of pounds invested in this project and they're not going to be put off by a few placards and a gathering outside the town hall.'

'What am I going to tell Amy?' James asked.

'Tell her that I haven't heard anything. I'm sure she'll buy that.'

'This is Amy we're talking about. You know what she's like when she's got the bit between her teeth.'

Growing inpatient, Alan replied. 'Just tell her I haven't heard anything. It'll be fine.'

'Can't you tell her? 'James whined over the phone.

'Sorry mate, what was that?' Alan croaked into the phone. 'It's a terrible line,' he added before ending the call. He put the mobile down, grateful that it wasn't him having to tell Amy the news.

*

Clive Oneway looked out across the Thames from the balcony of his penthouse apartment. He always liked to give his guests some privacy to get dressed and leave without having to make unnecessary small talk. Clothes on and out the front door. Simple.

On the other side of the river, on the Embankment, he watched as the traffic moved slowly. To his far right he watched as a bus approached. He would watch it until it had passed him and disappeared out of his sight and then go back inside.

Oneway stepped back into the apartment sliding the glass door shut behind him, keeping the chilly evening air out. An attractive young woman was standing in the kitchen drinking a glass of water. She had shoulder length black hair and wore a short black dress, contrasting with the white gloss finish of the designer kitchen.

'I was thirsty,' she said in an Eastern European accent.

'That's fine,' he replied with a shrug. 'You must be thirsty after your exertions.'

He had hoped that in the ten minutes that he had been on the balcony, she would have dressed and left. However, she had got as far as dressing but no further than the kitchen. Oneway never asked personal questions. He knew their names, or at least the names that they gave him, but he knew no personal details. These women were of no interest to him.

Anna, if indeed that was her real name, finished her glass of water and Oneway gestured towards the tap. 'Go on have another. Or I could get you something stronger?'

'Vodka?' she asked.

'I was thinking of Bovril, but I do have Vodka if that's what you want,' he said, sniggering at his own joke.

'Sorry, not understand.' Anna said, frowning.

'Just a joke,' he explained, opening the vodka bottle and pouring her a drink.

Taking the glass from him, she wandered through to the adjacent room. 'What's this?' She asked.

Following her through to the living room, Oneway noticed her attention was drawn to a model building on the coffee table.

'I'm a developer, it's a model of my latest project,' he said proudly, by way of explanation. He leaned over and took the roof off the model, revealing several smaller units inside.

'It's a shopping mall,' he said. 'It's going to be the biggest in that part of London.'

'Will it make you lots of money?' She asked as she swirled the vodka round in the glass.

'That's the idea,' he replied, smugly.

Anna smiled in return and finished her drink. 'I must go now,' she said, 'but before I do, can you complete this?'

Suddenly confused, Oneway watched as Anna took an envelope from her bag and passed it to him.

'What's this?' He said, opening the envelope and taking out several sheets of A4 paper. Unfolding them he read the title. 'This is a customer satisfaction questionnaire!'

'Yes. Can you complete it please,' Anna asked politely. 'The agency would like feedback of your experience,' she added handing him a pen.

Lost for words, Oneway started reading through the questionnaire.

On a scale of 1-10 with 10 being very likely and 1 being very unlikely, would you recommend our service to a friend or family member?

Oneway looked at Anna, she was probably his Uncle Richard's type, and he circled the number 10.

On a scale of 1-10 with 10 being very likely and 1 being very unlikely, would you use our services again?

This was an easy one. He was a regular with the agency and even had an account, so he circled the number 10 again.

On a scale of 1-10 with 10 being exceptional and 1 being no more fun than laying on a sack of potatoes, how would you assess our employee today?

Oneway looked over at Anna. He smiled and circled the number 8.

He completed another seven questions and then put the questionnaire in an envelope, sealed it down and passed it back to Anna.

'Thank you,' she said, taking the envelope. 'I have this for you now,' she said as she passed him a small card. 'Is our new loyalty card,' she said proudly, 'and look, I have already stamped you for today.'

One side of the card was divided into equal sized squares. In the first square a smiley face had been stamped to indicate he had used the services. Unsure how else to respond, he simply said, 'Thank you.'

'When you have filled up your card you'll be entitled to a free fetish session,' Anna smiled.

'Something to look forward to then,' he replied, still surprised by the innovative methods used by modern escort agencies.

Anna put her coat on and made her way to the front door. 'I hope you have good luck with your shopping centre and make lots of money,' she smiled at him as she opened the door.

'No doubt about it,' he replied, and as the door closed he added, 'and heaven help anyone who tries to stop it.'

Chapter 28

As far as Alan was concerned the evening was his own. Rosie was working, there was football on the television, and he was waiting for his bumper curry meal for two to be delivered. He never found bumper meals for one to be nearly enough.

The doorbell rang and Alan checked his watch, thinking about leaving some positive feedback on line about promptness. He grabbed his wallet and made for the front door.

'Amy...hi' he said, as he opened the front door to find his best friends' wife standing on his doorstep. 'Rosie's working a night shift, I'm afraid. She'll be around tomorrow though.'

'Actually it's you I've come to see.'

Alan knew exactly what she wanted. There was no other reason she would come round on her own. The best he could do was deny everything and hope she couldn't see through the lie.

'Come on through,' he said, and stepped aside to allow her in to the hallway.

'Tea?' he offered, following her into the kitchen.

'Yes thanks,' she replied, taking a seat at the kitchen table.

Waiting for the kettle to boil, Alan asked, 'Is everything OK with James?'

'Oh, he's fine,' she replied. 'I need to speak to you about the theatre.'

Pouring boiling water into two mugs, Alan decided to go straight into denial mode.

'What theatre?' He asked.

'Oh come on Alan. I know you too well. You know all about the theatre and the plans to demolish it and build a shopping centre,' Amy frowned at him, 'So stop playing games.'

Putting the mug of tea down in front of her, Alan couldn't help notice her very short skirt and shapely legs. Clearly a tactic to divert his attention and weaken his resolve, he thought. Amy clearly underestimated him.

'Oh that. I read in the paper that it's going to be redeveloped and turned into a shopping centre,' he said.

Amy sat staring at him, saying nothing.

'A little shopping centre,' Alan added, feeling an obligation to fill the silence.

'Why aren't you joining the protest group?' Amy asked him, her frown deepening.

'Is there a protest organised?' Alan asked innocently.

'Alan!' Amy snapped, 'I know that you were sent details of the protest group so don't try to deny it.'

Alan sighed, clearly James had broken and sold him out. It must have been the legs.

'I only spoke to James yesterday, what did you do, water board him?'

Amy laughed. 'I think he would have lasted longer if I had just water boarded him. Instead I had to use my cunning female wiles,' she fluttered her eyelashes at him.

Alan glanced down at her legs again. 'You threatened to withhold sex didn't you?'

'To be fair, he held out for two whole hours before he cracked!'

'That's a sight I'm glad I missed!' Alan mused before adding, 'How did you know?'

Amy grinned. 'That's the thing. I didn't know for sure, but I thought it was likely that there would have been a protest of some sort, and considering your involvement with the Arts Council, you would have been at least told what was planned.'

'Very clever, Mrs Cook,' Alan conceded. 'But did you take into account the fact that I don't want to get involved?'

Before Amy could reply the doorbell rang. 'I'll be back,' he said and bounded off in search of his curry.

*

Amy watched as Alan shovelled the contents of his bumper meal for two onto his plate. 'Sure you don't want any?' he asked between mouthfuls.

'Look Alan,' Amy said impatiently, 'why won't you get involved in the protest? Isn't the theatre important to you?'

Alan looked up, wiping a piece of Naan bread around his plate. 'Not really', he admitted. 'I mean it's not like I didn't like the place, but people are spending a lot of money to build a shopping centre, and I don't think a few us standing outside the town hall with placards will make a difference,' he said.

'That's rubbish, you can't really believe that,' Amy snapped, starting to get frustrated. Everyone counts, everyone makes a difference.'

'Amy you're sounding like a motivational speaker,' Alan said, more interested in the remains of his meal. 'I'm sorry I'm not as interested as you are in saving the theatre, but that's just me, I'm afraid.'

Amy was clearly becoming frustrated by Alan's refusal to concede. 'Not even from a selfish point of view?'

'Sorry?' Alan mumbled through the last of his curry.

'I would have thought that it was in your interests to keep the theatre open. It must be a rare treat to play somewhere like that rather than the pubs and clubs.'

'There will always be venues to play,' Alan explained. 'Anyway, it's good to move around, play different places. It gets you known.'

Alan's bumper meal for two had been reduced to shards of poppadum and splatters of curry and rice. It resembled Amy's attempts to persuade Alan to help. It was a good idea at the time but ultimately had left both of them unsatisfied.

'If that was a bumper meal for two, I'm glad I didn't go for the meal for one. I'm still hungry. Do you want some toast?' he asked. 'I think I'm going to have toast now.'

Ignoring the offer of toast, Amy made a final plea for help. 'I think it wouldn't do your reputation any harm if

259

you were seen to be part of the protest. Can't you see that?'

Alan looked puzzled.

'Local Comedian Helps Save Theatre would make a good headline,' she suggested, appealing to his vanity.

Alan hadn't thought about it in those terms, and even though he knew that Amy didn't believe what she was saying, it was something worth thinking about.

'Look,' he said, 'let me give it some thought and see if I can really spare the time to get involved.'

'Because your life is so busy.' Amy said cynically.

'Exactly. It's OK for you teachers, finishing work at three o'clock each day. Some of us have to work until the sun goes down.'

Amy laughed. 'Still using the old ones then?'

'Do you want some toast?' He asked, looking up at the clock. 'Are you staying for the football, only it's nearly kick off.'

'That's a very generous offer,' Amy said sarcastically, 'but I think I will pass on the toast and anyway, I can be bored by the football at home.'

They both stood up and left the kitchen, walking through the hallway to the front door.

'Sorry I can't help you,' Alan said almost apologetically.

'Come on, admit it. You just can't be bothered.'

'Well there is that as well,' Alan said with a smirk.

Opening the front door Amy turned to Alan. 'Do you know that your flat is freezing? It's warmer outside.'

*

Making his way back into the kitchen, Alan could see the message light flashing on his mobile. Swiping the screen revealed a message from James;

AMY ON WAY TO SEE YOU. NOT HAPPY.

Alan quickly thumbed a reply.

SHE'S BEEN AND GONE. THANK YOU FOR HOLDING OUT FOR SO LONG.

One thing that Amy had been right about was that the temperature in the flat had been dropping considerably. He sighed, he hadn't noticed that increasing coldness and presumed it meant only one thing. He poked his round the corner and into the living room. 'How long have you been there?' He said to Frankie who was sitting in an armchair.

'You know I have no idea about time,' Frankie replied. 'I did see the attractive leggy woman leave. Does your Rosie know about her?'

'That's Amy, James's wife, she's a friend' Alan said, whilst hoping that was still the case.

'Don't you have any morals?' Frankie asked. 'You haven't stopped going on about me and the comedians of my era, and here you are with your best friend's wife.'

Alan wasn't going to get drawn into an argument with Frankie. 'Look, it's quite simple. Amy is a friend and she wants me to help her with something.

261

'That's all right then,' Frankie smirked.

Alan shrugged. 'Any idea how long you'll be staying around for this time?'

'What did she want your help with?' Frankie asked, ignoring Alan's attempt to goad him.

'She wants me to join a protest group to save a theatre from being demolished. It's a good cause, but I'm not really interested,' he admitted, sitting himself down on the sofa and turning the television on with the remote.

'What theatre?' Frankie asked.

'The Merton Palace Theatre,' Alan replied, flicking through the channels. On finding the football, he settled down to get his evening back on track.

'Did you ... sorry do you like football?' He asked Frankie, who had become strangely silent.

'Did you say The Merton Palace Theatre?' Frankie asked quietly.

'Yes, do you know it?'

Frankie's silence drew Alan's attention away from the screen. 'OK, what's up?'

'That's where I died, 'Frankie said quietly.

Of course. Alan realised at once. It wasn't that long since he'd sat in James's den and they been staggered to find that Frankie had died in the same theatre that Alan had recently performed in.

'I'm sorry,' Alan said, not entirely sure why he was apologising but feeling the need to say it anyway. 'I do remember, now you mention it.'

Frankie leaned forward in his chair. 'What are they doing with it?' He asked.

'Some developers have plans to pull down the theatre and the surrounding shops and put up a shopping centre.'

Frankie scratched the side of his head, deep in thought. 'And your friend Amy, she is opposing this?' Frankie asked.

'Not only Amy, there's the Arts Council as well. They want to save it too.'

'And you told her that you wouldn't help her. That you weren't really interested.'

'I don't really do protests. They never seem to achieve anything other than to give people the chance to have meetings and listen to the sound of their own voices,' Alan said whilst keeping one eye on the football.

'I can't believe you,' Frankie said. 'I would have thought that you of all people would have been the first to chain themselves to the railings as the bulldozers approached.'

Alan abandoned the football and gave Frankie his full attention. 'Not you as well!' he snapped. 'What is it with everyone? Why does everyone think that I should be fighting the fight, taking on the developers and the council; Rosie, James, Amy and now you as well.'

'Surely that tells you that you're wrong not to get involved?'

Alan was becoming frustrated. This was not turning out to be the night that he had planned. He was being pressurised by a dead comedian, a control freak in a short skirt and it now looked like he had missed a goal.

'Tell me why? Give me one good reason why I should get involved,' Alan demanded.

Frankie was on his feet now, standing in front of the Television. Alan waved him to one side. 'Can you move to one side I can't see.'

'I can give you two good reasons why you have to get involved,' Frankie said, stepping slightly to one side to give Alan the kind of view that would have had the warning *"Restricted View"* stamped on the ticket if he had actually been at the game.

'Firstly,' Frankie said, 'you are a performer. You have played at that theatre, and you owe it.'

'You can't owe a building,' Alan sneered. 'It's an object and you can't owe objects.'

'Secondly,' Frankie continued, it's a great place for you to play. It's a proper venue.'

'There's always going to be places to play, and you know it's good to move around, play different venues. It gets you known.'

'Thirdly...'

'Hold on, you said there were only two reasons, Alan said, still keeping one eye on the football.

'The other two were tasters, this is the important one,' Frankie said, not really answering Alan's question.

'Well, what is it?'

'I want you to do it for me,' Frankie said, pausing for effect. 'I can't help. I'm dead, remember.'

'I remember,' Alan replied, 'but why do you want the theatre saved?'

'It's my resting place. If it gets knocked down, it will be the equivalent of desecrating my grave.'

'But it's not your grave though, is it? You were buried somewhere else,' Alan pointed out. 'In a cemetery in your home town. Or were you stuffed and left in the museum of comedy with a label that says *"Here's Thingy."*

'Please Alan,' Frankie implored. 'I died there.'

'I know, I read the reviews.'

Frankie moved to one side, giving a clear view of the television. 'You see what's happened now?' Alan said, gesturing at the screen. 'I've missed the first half because of all this theatre nonsense.'

Frankie wandered over to the living room window. Looking out onto the street below he said, 'Of course, this might all be connected.'

Choosing Frankie over the panel of ex-professional footballers discussing a game he'd missed, Alan gave Frankie his full attention. 'What do you mean – connected?'

'Well,' Frankie turned to Alan, 'maybe it's not a coincidence that I'm here at this time.'

'Go on,' Alan encouraged.

'I'm here to save the theatre, obviously,' Frankie said before adding, 'with your help. I save the theatre and I go back to being dead.'

'We save the theatre and I'm no longer haunted by you?'

'Could be,' Frankie admitted. 'What do you say? You've nothing to lose. Take a chance or get stuck with me forever, popping up when you least expect it. You could be on toilet or in the middle of a quiet night in with young Rosie and there I am standing there grinning at you.'

'OK, OK, you've made your point,' Alan said, accepting defeat. 'I'll think about it.'

'Thank you,' Frankie replied and sat down next to Alan on the sofa. 'Now, how long until the second half?' he asked.

Chapter 29

David Crozier stood in the corner of the lift, avoiding eye contact with the five other occupants. He guessed without too much difficulty that they were on their way home, bags and coats giving the game away. Crozier on the other hand, had another hour or so before he would leave. He had spent the afternoon at a planning meeting, advising and assisting the planning committee in reaching decisions that he agreed with, and more importantly, could make him some extra money. He was keen to make sure these decisions went his way and were documented before he left for the day.

Leaving the lift on the first floor, he walked down the corridor to his office. He paused briefly outside his office door before moving swiftly to enter the next door along. Three desks occupied the small room, only one of which was occupied.

'You're back,' Alison announced.

'Nothing's getting past you today, is it?' Crozier replied uncharitably.

Used to Crozier's sarcasm, Alison asked, 'Well, how did it go?'

'Not too bad,' he said, while idly flicking through a wad of papers on her desk. 'Everything's approved except the application by the youth club to build a rifle range out the back.'

'That's a shame,' Alison said, 'they were looking forward to that.'

'I know. It's a pity,' Crozier agreed, 'and social services wonder why kids turn to crime.'

Alison logged off her computer and stood up to leave. 'I'm off now, but before I forget, this came for you,' she said, passing him a sealed A4 envelope. Crozier turned it over looking for a return address or some other clue as to the identity of the sender.

'Who's it from?' he asked.

'Sorry, no idea. It was brought up with the post earlier. Why don't you open it up?' Alison suggested helpfully.

'I wish I'd thought of that,' Crozier snapped as he tore the package open and pulled out the contents.

'Oh look, it's a comic,' Alison pointed out.

'I can see that, thank you,' Crozier said as he held out the comic for closer inspection. It was a Batman comic that was covered in a cellophane jacket and appeared to be in mint condition. Crozier looked inside the envelope, but there was no covering letter. He turned the comic over to reveal a yellow sticky note stuck on the cellophane. The note had two hand written words which simply said; *'Thank you.'*

Crozier smiled.

'I didn't know you were a comic geek,' said Alison, giggling at the front cover.

'I'm not,' Crozier replied, 'It's a present for my son. He's a Batman fan.'

'Aren't we all?' Alison replied, putting on her coat. 'I'll see you tomorrow,' she said, leaving the office without waiting for a response.

Crozier followed Alison out and in to his own office. He sat down and logged on to his own computer, and using the default search engine, entered the date and issue number of the comic in front of him.

The screen showed a digital version of the comic on his desk. Crozier squinted at the screen, at first disbelieving what he was being shown. Then he sat back and smiled. The comic was rare, extremely rare in fact. Collectors would pay in excess of £80,000 to get their hands on a mint condition copy of the comic he had been sent through first class mail.

Crozier mentally thanked Oneway for the gesture. This was typical of him, he thought, paying for his services in such a way that could never be traced. Crozier would have to take the comic to his safety deposit box at the bank in the morning, and keep an eye on its value. If it reached a certain figure, Crozier would contact the nerdy collector forums, saying he had found it in his attic.

Good old Batman, he thought.

Chapter 30

Sarah took the little flight of steps up to the stage and looked out across the scout hall at the rows of empty seats. Nav was at the back of the hall, having arranged the seats in rows of fifteen.

'How's it looking?' He shouted.

'All good thanks,' Sarah answered, stepping back onto the steps and leaving the stage. She met Nav at the end of row twelve.

'What do you think?' He asked. 'Too big a venue, too small a venue?'

Sarah looked round the hall again. 'If everyone turns up who said they would we will fill the place and it'll be standing room only.'

'Why didn't we just find a bigger venue then?' Nav asked.

'If two hundred and fifty people turn up and we fill a small venue like this,' Sarah said, waving her hand around the hall, 'and there are people standing round the sides, reporters can say the meeting was packed out, standing room only. If we had taken a bigger venue and two hundred and fifty people turn up, there's likely to be empty seats and reporters will say the meeting didn't attract a full house, despite the fact that we still had two hundred and fifty people in there.'

'So it's tactics,' Nav replied, wondering whether there would even be half of that figure.

'Definitely. We don't want them to think that we can't raise enough opposition.'

'And that's why we're in the scout hall.'

'That, and they were able to provide a space at short notice.'

'Excuse me...' A rich, plummy voice interrupted their conversation.

Sarah and Nav turned to face the voice. A tall elderly man dressed in a smart suit with, rather unusually for 21st Century South London, a cravat around his neck, was standing by the doors.

'Can I help you? 'Sarah asked, smiling.

'Is this the meeting to save the theatre?' he asked.

'Yes it is, or it will be in about...' Sarah checked her watch, 'fifteen minutes.'

'Excellent. I'll just get mother out of the car,' he said as he disappeared out of the door.

Sarah raised her eyebrows at Nav as they exchanged glances.

After a short while, the door reopened and the man reappeared, carrying a plastic carrier bag. He strode up to Sarah and Nav, reached into the bag and took out a small urn.

'Mother does so love a protest. I thought it right that she should be here.'

Sarah looked at Nav quizzically.

'When did she die?' Nav asked, looking for something to say to fill an embarrassing silence.

'1977,' the man said, 'But as I said, she loves a protest. She was a suffragette, you know. She marched shoulder to shoulder with Emily Pankhurst.' The man paused appearing to be lost in thought, 'Her death was so ironic.'

'Why?' Sarah asked. 'What happened?'

'She was run over by a bus outside Harrods,' the man said quietly.

'That's a shame,' Sarah said, not really seeing the irony.

'The bus was being driven by a woman.'

'Ah...' Sarah replied, seeing the irony.

The man coughed, clearing his throat. 'It was her last words that were so poignant.'

'What were they?' Nav asked, trying to keep his grin in check.

'Bloody women drivers...'

*

Alan stood in the small car park alongside Rosie's car. Frankie was leaning against it moaning. 'How do you fit into that thing?' he whined, 'There was more room in my bubble car.'

'Your *what?*' Alan asked.

'My bubble car,' Frankie answered, 'I had one in the sixties. They were very popular. You should look them up next time you're in the library.'

Alan nodded. He had been putting off explaining the internet to Frankie. He thought the concept of broadband might be too difficult to explain, so he continued to let Frankie think that Libraries were still the primary source of information.

'My legs are killing me,' Frankie moaned again. 'It's sitting in the back of that car. And all the time I spend on my feet these days.'

'No one asked you to come along tonight. You could have stayed behind and done some ghost stuff, you know, like levitating. That would rest your feet.'

'No chance. I wouldn't miss this for all the tea in China. I keep telling you, I have a vested interest.' Frankie eased himself down with a sigh onto the small wall that ran around the perimeter of the car park. 'That's better.'

They both watched as several cars, including a cerise SUV, pulled into the car park.

'Is the meeting in there?' Frankie asked, pointing at the scout hall at the other end of the car park.

'Yes, that's the scout hall,' Alan answered, more interested in watching James reverse the car between Rosie's Audi and a shopping trolley which had been abandoned in a parking bay of its own.

'That's definitely pink,' Alan muttered, turning to Frankie.

'Looks like Scooby Doo's Mystery Machine,' Frankie said.

'Strictly speaking, it wasn't Scooby Doo's Mystery Machine,' Alan pointed out. 'Didn't it belong to the scruffy looking guy?'

Frankie scratched the side of his nose. 'Are you sure?'

James made his way over to them, squeezing between the back of the Audi and the wall.

'Who owned the Mystery Machine van in Scooby Doo?' Alan asked him.

'Scooby Doo?'

'Told you,' Frankie said, rather smugly.

'No, don't be daft, Scooby Doo was the dog. Who actually owned it?' Alan asked again.

'It was either the scruffy guy or the poncey one in the white jumper,' James said, helpfully.

'He drove it, but did he own it?' Frankie asked.

Alan sat on the wall next to him. 'We'll need a DVLA search to sort this out.'

James looked at Alan sitting on the wall. 'Frankie?' he asked, pointing to Alan's left.

Alan gestured to his right, 'Frankie.'

'Evening big man,' Frankie said, offering his hand, then thinking better of it.

'He said hello,' Alan repeated for James's benefit.

'Evening Frankie, you OK?' James asked.

'Well, apart from being dead, I'm doing rather well, thank you' Frankie replied.

'He said he's fine.' Alan relayed, already tired of being an interpreter.

'That's good,' said James, and sat on the wall, allowing what he hoped was sufficient space for Frankie.

Rosie got out of her car, mobile phone in hand, and walked round to where she could see Alan and James sitting on the wall.

'What's up?' Alan asked, seeing the look on her face.

'That was mum,' she said, 'She took Daisy to the vets. Apparently she has chlamydia.'

'Who, your mum?' Alan asked, shocked at such news.

'No, of course not.'

'The vet has chlamydia,' James said, 'that must have been an interesting appointment.'

'For God's sake, no!' Rosie snapped, 'It's the cat. The cat has chlamydia.'

'Dirty little minx,' Frankie called out, chuckling.

'How the bloody hell does a cat get chlamydia?' Alan asked, not sure he wanted to know the answer.

'Dogging?' James offered, helpfully, making Frankie snort.

Ignoring James, Rosie said, 'Mum is really worried.'

Alan was saved from having to say something supportive by the arrival of Amy.

'Sorry I'm late,' she said apologetically, 'staff meeting over ran.'

'Rosie's mum's cat has chlamydia,' James said.

Amy turned to Rosie, 'Can cats get chlamydia?' she asked, clearly concerned.

'It would appear so,' Rosie said, regretting ever bringing the subject up in the first place.

'Shall we get in there now?' Alan said standing up.

The two couples made their way across the car park and into the scout hall.   Frankie followed behind, unseen, catching bits of a conversation about a cat with chlamydia and whether Scooby Doo would have had to undertake something called the written part of the driving test.

*

Alan stood at the end of the row, letting the others sit in the chairs, before taking the remaining seat.

'What about me, where can I sit?' Frankie stood at the end of the row looking down at Alan.

'What do you mean?' Alan replied, conscious that he had spoken out loud.

'I need to sit down. My legs are really playing up tonight. You'll have to budge up.'

James looked at Alan, apparently talking to himself and guessed that he was talking to Frankie. He turned to his left to face his friend, hoping that it would look like they were engaged in conversation.

'If you're not going to move up I'm going to have sit on your lap,' Frankie whined.

'Don't be ridiculous. You're not a child,' Alan hissed, hoping that Frankie would take this moment to disappear.

'OK then,' Frankie sulked and sat himself down on Alan's lap, blocking his view of the stage. Sighing, Alan peered round Frankie to get a better view.

Amy nudged Rosie and pointed down the row to where Alan appeared to holding his head at an angle. 'Is he OK?' She whispered.

Rosie shook her head.   'He's been acting weird since he hurt his head. I think I'll have to have him looked at.'

Laughing, Amy focused her attention toward the stage as a man climbed the steps to address the crowd, the hum of conversation dying away.

Alan found that by craning his neck further to his left he could see round Frankie and get a good view. The man on the stage introduced himself as Tim Baker, the Director of the Arts Council and, after thanking everyone for coming along, he went onto explain the importance of saving the theatre from the developers.

'This theatre,' he said, 'is not only an important part of the history of our community, but it continues to play a part in future of the community, with recent fund raising events raising money and interest in its refurbishment.'

By this stage Alan had already begun to lose interest in the proceedings. Frankie was fidgeting on his lap and the man on the stage was saying little to keep his attention. Alongside him, James was checking the sports news on his phone, an act that had brought disapproving looks from Amy, who would no doubt tell him off when they got home.

Tim invited contributions from the audience. Reacting to the silence that followed the invitation, Sarah left her seat on the front row and joined Tim on the stage. Introducing herself to the hall, she explained what the theatre meant to her, and asked for help in fighting the proposals. Her heartfelt plea provoked a number of raised hands. She pointed at someone Alan couldn't see from his position, and invited him to stand up. Alan heard the sound of a chair being scraped backwards as the man got to his feet.

The man turned around so that everyone could see his face. Unfortunately, as soon as Alan saw the man's face in full clown make up, he began to snigger. To his left he could see James struggling to keep a check on his emotions, and he was pretty sure that the strange noise coming from Frankie was giggling rather than snoring.

The clown man spoke. 'Ladies and Gentlemen, you can probably tell by my appearance that I am involved with the arts council,' he paused, to take off his red nose and blow his nose, 'I am part of the learning through clowning programme.'

Several of the sniggers turned into giggles. James decided to avoid the risk of a hernia and laughed loudly, which forced Alan into a fit of giggles.

'Please be QUIET!' Sarah shouted, breaking the spell of laughter that appeared to be taking over the meeting. The laughter and giggling subsided after a few seconds, with several of the audience wiping tears from their eyes.

'Thank you, Sarah,' the clown man said before continuing to speak to a now attentive audience. 'This is a very serious situation, and I come dressed as I do to show support to the arts council in their hour of need,' he paused again, 'As I drove here today do you know what I thought?' he asked.

'The wheels have fallen off my car!' someone from the back shouted, drawing laughter from the crowd.

Even clown man raised a smile, although to be fair, Alan thought, judging by the big red grin painted on his face, it would have been difficult to find anything that he couldn't raise a smile at.

'Other than that,' he said. 'I thought that every time we lose one of these magnificent old theatres, we lose a piece of our cultural soul. Are we prepared to let that happen?' He turned around, scanning the hall looking for agreement.

'No we're not!' Amy shouted. 'We're going to make a stand and fight.'

Heads turned to look in Amy's direction, and applauded. James sunk deeper into his seat while Alan looked in the opposite direction.

Sarah thanked the clown man for his contribution and asked for suggestions as to what form the protests should take.

The mime group offered to protest in the council chamber the day that the planning committee met to rubber stamp the deal. Alan shook his head in disappointment that nobody other than James and himself could see the irony in that.

'We will oppose these plans using the medium of mime,' they informed everyone.

Clown man rose to feet again, offering to chain his clown group to the railings outside the theatre.

'The problem I can see with that,' the leader of the mime group said, standing up and facing the clown, is that it will look like a chain gang of Ronald McDonalds.'

The hall once again descended into roars of laughter. From what Alan could see, only clown man and Rosie weren't laughing.

Frankie turned to Alan. 'This guy's not bad. You could pick up a few tips.'

Sarah again attempted to bring some control to the proceedings, wishing for all the world that she had a gavel. 'Can we focus on the big picture here,' she called out. 'We need to formulate an approach to the council and the developers that shows our strength and commitment to our opposition, and whilst individual approaches are encouraging, they will not have the effect of a larger better supported action.'

Clown man stood up again. 'I quite agree with Sarah,' he said. 'Clown Workshop will support any action that the arts council propose.'

'That'll make them feel a lot better about things,' the leader of the mime group shouted out from the back.

Alan nudged James and grinned.

Sarah brought the hall back under control.

'Does anyone else have any other questions or something to contribute?'

A hand shot up from the front of the hall. Sarah looked relived that it did not belong to a clown or a mime artist.

A quiet, almost meek female voice asked, 'What can we do? Everyone seems to be saying that it's a done deal, and the contracts have already been signed.'

There were murmurs of agreement from the audience. This was a question that had clearly been on people's minds.

Sarah looked at Tim who stood up and addressed the hall.

'I understand that, whilst contracts have been signed, there are a number of get out clauses written into these contracts. So I can tell you that we won't give up.' He took a deep breath and said in a louder voice, 'While there's a chance, we won't give up.'

Tim took his seat to a hearty round of applause. Sarah looked across at him and smiled.

Alan shifted in his seat trying to distribute Frankie's weight. 'Do you mind?' he said, taking advantage of the noise generated by the applause, 'You're uncomfortable now, and how come you're heavy? I thought you were supposed to be made of air. Can you move, I can't feel my legs?'

'Oh, for God's sake...' Frankie whined and moved from Alan's lap.

'Thank ....' Alan didn't have to finish the sentence as Frankie disappeared into thin air.

James nudged Alan. 'Has he gone?' he asked.

Alan nodded and turned his attention back to the stage where another question was being asked. 'I think we need more of a proactive presence. We need to be taking the fight to the council and to the developers now, not sitting around and laughing at the clowns and mime artists. We don't even know who the developers are.'

'Mr?' Sarah asked.

'Morris – The Residents Association.'

'Well Mr Morris,' Sarah said. 'First of all thank you for coming tonight. As far as we know the developers who are responsible for the development are the Oneway Property Development Company.'

Amy heard Sarah's reference to Oneway Property Development Company; it was a name that bounced around in her head ringing bells and sounding Klaxons. *It can't be,* she thought. *That creepy man from the theatre school trip. The one who sat with her and laughed at the children's play. The one who asked her out. Surely he's not the one behind the whole project?*

On the stage, Sarah continued to explain the developer's plans, while Amy continued to turn everything over in her head; *He must have known what he was planning when I met him - He was pretending to be a fan of the theatre just to see inside – The bastard!*

He had given her his business card and she was sure that she hadn't thrown it away. It was probably in her locker at the school with all the other notes that she had amassed from the theatre trip. She would check when she got back to the school tomorrow.

Amy was brought back into the room by shouting. James lent over and whispered into her ear. 'This is going to be brilliant.'

She looked across the hall in the direction that everyone else appeared to be staring. The clown was standing in the aisle between the rows directly in front of the man from the mime group. Amy could see that the mime artist was wearing a white T shirt with horizontal black lines across it and a slogan that said, *'Mime Artists Do It Quietly.'*

'I am sick and tired of you belittling everything I've said tonight,' the clown said angrily, adding, 'You talentless mute.'

The mime artist looked the clown straight in the face and mouthed, 'Fuck off.'

Those in the audience who saw the mime artist mouth the words began laughing, some even applauded, causing the mime man to take a bow. The majority of the audience were enjoying this more than the meeting itself.

'You talentless bastard,' the clown replied, and took off his curly red clown wig, causing a sharp intake of breath from several people in the hall, who knew the significance of the gesture.

According to the customs and tradition of clowns, the act of taking off the wig in front of an audience whilst otherwise in full clown costume was the precursor to an act of aggression or, as Alan heard someone behind him say; 'It's kicking off now.'

Unfortunately, as far as the clown was concerned, removing the red curly clown wig revealed his real hair to be a mass of tight ginger curls redder and even more ridiculous than the wig he had just removed.

The mime artist laughed out loud. Most of the audience joined in and began to applaud.

Alan turned to James and said, 'We can't just stand here.'

'You think we should get the girls out of the way?' James asked.

'No,' Alan said, shaking his head, 'I mean we can't see anything from here. We should get on the stage. We'll get a much better view from there.'

'Let's get out of here,' Alan said to Rosie with sufficient sincerity to convince her that it was in her best interests. Alan and James led Rosie and Amy past the rows of seats and up onto the stage.

In the centre of the hall, Tim was standing between the duelling wannabe circus acts, trying to calm the situation down. 'Can everyone just calm down?' he said sternly.

'He started it,' the mime artist whined and, in an effort to emphasise his position he mimed a gesture to the clown – a gesture universally known as the finger.

The clown launched himself aggressively at the mime artist, but got himself tangled up in his large red clown shoes, falling over before he reached his target, taking Tim to the ground with him.

On the stage, Alan joined in the applause while James laughed hysterically. Rosie grinned and Amy stared blankly at the scene unfolding in front of her.

As the Clown got back to his feet someone shouted, 'Leave him, Coco he's not worth it.'

The mime artist appeared to be miming running away on the spot, causing more laughter.

James had regained his composure and said to Alan, 'This is brilliant, I never knew protest meetings were such fun.'

'This is so disappointing,' Amy stomped her foot to emphasise the point. 'Don't these idiots know what is at stake?'

'It *is* quite funny.' Rosie said to her.

'We should have been making banners by now,' Amy replied, clearly disappointed.

Looking out into the hall, Alan could see a large number of people now circling the clown and the mime artist like a fight in a school playground.

'Fight, Fight, Fight.' James was saying under his breath until Amy nudged him in the ribs with a well-placed elbow.

Alan could see that Sarah was standing between the protagonists, trying to talk them both down. Unfortunately there was a hum of conversation going around the hall and he couldn't make out what she was saying. Eventually, she stopped gesturing with her hands and said something to each of them, and they both nodded in response.

'Looks like it's been calmed down,' Alan said, 'Let's get back to our seats,' and jumped off the stage leaving the others to follow him.

'I'm going to ask you both to leave...' Sarah said to the clown and the mime artist. 'Your behaviour is beyond reproach and is of no help whatsoever. If you still want to help you can e-mail me in the morning when you've both calmed down.'

The clown dusted himself down, put his wig back on and stomped out of the hall. A gesture which would have been more dramatic if his clown shoes hadn't been slapping on the floor like an excited seal waiting for fish.

As Alan made his way past Sarah, she grabbed his arm. 'Are you leaving?' she sounded disappointed. 'I think there are still some things that we should get through.'

'Of course we're staying,' Amy said on behalf of Alan, 'There's still lots to talk about,' and lead the others back to their chairs.

Several of the chairs had been knocked over in the melee. Alan righted his chair and heard the door scrape open, a voice shout across the hall; 'Sarah? They're at it again outside.'

Sarah groaned and made her way outside. Alan looked at James, raised his eyebrows and followed Sarah out into the car park.

Pushing open the doors and stepping outside, Alan could see the clown and the mime artist fighting on the small lawn at the front of the scout hall. 'Will you please stop NOW?' Sarah screamed.

'Great shout,' Amy whispered to James, 'That girl could be a teacher.'

Reacting to Sarah's ear piercing scream, the clown stopped hitting the mime artist and turned to look in her direction. The mime artist took full advantage of this and threw a punch which connected with the side of the clown's head, knocking him to the floor.

The door to the hall flew open and Tim bundled out, knocking Rosie aside. He stopped and looked on helpless as the clown staggered to his feet and threw the unsuspecting mime artist through the window and into the hall.

'No!' Sarah mouthed and ran over to the window. Peering through, she could see that by some miracle the mime artist did not appear to be injured. Although when he saw her looking at him, he mimed tears by rubbing both his eyes with balled up hands.

Sarah felt someone touch her arm, looking round she saw Alan. 'Come on, let's get out of here,' he said. 'Tim can deal with it now.'

The hall eventually emptied of people. Most were milling around in the car park laughing as they recounted the evening's events to each other and declaring it the best night out they'd had for ages.

Alan led Sarah over to where the others were waiting for them by their parked cars. 'Drink?' Amy suggested.

'I'm not sure,' Sarah said, 'I should really sit down and plan the next step.'

'You probably need a drink after that,' Alan laughed, throwing his weight behind Amy's suggestion.

Sarah shrugged, 'OK. I may as well get something out of the evening.'

*

'Well, that was a disaster.' Sarah said, leaning on the table with her head resting on her fist. The glass of wine in front of her was already half empty as Amy, sitting opposite her, was trying very hard to put a positive spin on the evening.

287

'It didn't go that badly. On the plus side, there were a lot of people there, all of whom want the same thing. Most people have probably forgotten about the scuffle and are now sitting at home trying to work out ways of saving the theatre.'

'I think they'll remember a clown throwing a mime artist through a window,' Sarah admitted.

James nodded, 'These things do tend to stick in the mind.'

'...And being so dedicated to his art he only complained afterwards in mime. You should be so proud of him,' Alan chipped in, smiling at the group.

'You're not helping.' Rosie glared at him.

'It's my own fault. I should have seen it coming.' Sarah admitted.

'How?' Alan asked.

'They fell out over a woman a few months ago. I thought it was settled.'

'I see,' said James, 'the age old problem; clown meets girl, girl meets mime artist. It all kicks off.'

'And you're not helping either...' Amy said to her husband.

'Of course, you know the really sad thing in all this..?' Alan said.

'What's that mate?' James asked.

'Well, if the girl was a magician's assistant, they could have sawn her in half.'

James burst into laughter.

'Bloody children.' Amy said, frowning at her husband.

'I'll get some more drinks,' Alan said trying to be helpful. 'Same again?'

Not waiting for an answer, he left the table, heading off to the bar, closely followed by James.

'What are we doing here?' Alan asked, looking around at the horrid glass and chrome décor.

'Well I couldn't take them to the *'Hoof.'* They'd hate that.'

'No, what I mean is, why are we here? Trying to make Sarah feel like there's still hope,' Alan explained to a confused looking James.

'You suggested it.'

'I know, but I thought we'd have a few drinks and a laugh about the evening. Instead your wife is stoking the fires of revolution.'

James laughed at that, as a cold draught blew across his shoulders.

'Chaps...' Frankie said, stepping into the space between Alan and James.

'Ghost in the room,' Alan announced.

'Is it the same day?' Frankie asked.

'It's the same hour,' Alan said, 'You've only been gone thirty minutes.'

'I don't suppose I missed anything?'

'Not really,' Alan said. 'Just a clown throwing a mime artist through a window.'

'Sounds like the after show party at the Royal Variety Performance,' Frankie laughed.

Both Alan and Frankie turned to look at James who was staring intently at Alan and the apparent gap beside him.

'What's up with him?' Frankie asked.

'What's up with you, mate. Why the face?' Alan asked his friend.

'I'm trying to work out what Frankie's saying by your answers,' he explained.

Alan exchanged looks with Frankie and passed the tray of drinks to James. 'Take these,' he said, 'I'll be over in a minute.'

As James made his way back to their table, Frankie asked Alan, 'So anything arranged? A protest march?'

Alan sighed, 'Nothing. We didn't get that far.'

Frankie shook his head, 'Looks like you're stuck with me, then son.'

Chapter 31

'Finger,' Rosie said.

'Sorry. What?' Alan replied puzzled.

'Put your finger there,' she said.

Alan grinned, 'I like it when you take the lead.'

Jayne giggled from the other side of the room, where she sat in an armchair reading a magazine.

'Put your finger here,' Rosie repeated this time gesturing at the two edges of wrapping paper that she wanted to join together.

Alan complied with Rosie's request and put his index finger where the edges of the wrapping paper over lapped. Rosie stuck a piece of sticky tape across the join. 'OK, done.'

'What is it?' he asked, looking at the neatly wrapped rectangular package in Rosie's hands.

'It's a picture frame,' Rosie explained.

'It's a nice one too. Silver.' Jayne added.

'People don't have picture frames anymore,' Alan pointed out. 'Everything's digital, pictures are kept on cameras, computers and phones. I suppose you could tell her it's a retro present.'

Rosie put the wrapped gift into a designer paper bag. 'It's a nice picture frame, not everyone carries their life around in their phone like you do.'

Alan sighed. 'So how old is she?' he asked.

'I told you, forty five.'

Forty five?' Alan paused, clearly in thought, before adding, 'Genesis!'

'What do you mean Genesis?' Rosie replied, exchanging puzzled looks with her sister.

Alan took a deep breath 'She's forty five, most of her friends will be the same age, mid-forties, early fifties.'

'Where are you going with this?' Rosie asked.

'Her husband's fifty one,' Jayne pointed out, not sure if that supported Alan's argument or shot it down in flames.

'That's even worse,' Alan said, frustrated that the sisters had not worked out where he was going with this,

'Anyone forty five or over was brought up on a diet of Genesis and Phil Collins, and that'll be the only music we'll hear tonight. Genesis when we get there, then a Phil Collins album thrown in for good measure, and when they want everyone to dance they'll put on a CD compilation of disco nonsense that they picked up for a fiver in a supermarket.'

'Shut up Alan,' Rosie snapped. 'They have a proper DJ.'

'Doesn't matter,' Alan replied. He was on a roll now, 'they've probably already asked him to play Genesis all night.'

'I quite like Genesis,' Jayne said.

'Enough said,' Alan smiled at her.

'Are you changing?' Rosie asked, changing the subject.

'Well, I'm probably a little less tolerant than I was five years ago, and I can't drink as much as I used to be able to.' Alan grinned at her.

Jayne giggled again.

'Your clothes, funny man, are you changing your clothes before we go?' Rosie asked.

Alan looked down at his jeans and lurid shirt. 'I have,' he said indignantly.

'Oh,' Rosie mumbled, 'that shirt...'

'What's wrong with it? It expresses my individuality. Anyway,' he continued, 'look at you two in your identikit party dresses.'

Rosie and Jayne looked at each other. They were both wearing similar black party dresses and similar high heels.

'You're just clones,' Alan mocked, 'I am an individual.'

'OK Mr Individual, can you phone us a cab?'

*

The sign on the gate welcomed visitors to the Old Grammarian Cricket Club. It told them to keep off the grass and asked them to follow the path to the club house. There were two balloons tied to the gate one said HAPPY BIRTHDAY the other had 45 written on it.

'I assume that this is the right place,' Alan grinned as he pushed the gate open and stepped onto the path.

'Let's take a chance,' Rosie said. 'It'll be a shame to turn back now, not since you made such an effort to dress for the occasion.'

'Give it a rest, it's all you've mentioned since we left home,' Alan moaned. 'I think deep down you wished you'd used more imagination in choosing something to wear.'

Behind him Rosie turned to Jayne. 'We should have left him in the cab and brought the cab driver with us, at least he was wearing a tie.'

Alan ignored Rosie's jibe, focusing instead on the club house, which stood at the end of the path directly in front of him. He paused at the door waiting for the others to catch him up.

'This is the right place,' he said pointing at the piece of A4 paper which had the words "Alison's Party" written across it in permanent marker pen and stuck to the door with a drawing pin. 'Ladies first,' he said, stepping aside.

'So kind,' Jayne grinned, pushing open the door and walking through.

Alan looked around the club house. There was a bar on one side and tables on the other, which although bare at the moment, would most likely be home to the food later in the evening. At the far side a DJ stood on a slightly raised platform behind several disco lights and two speakers. The floor was carpeted with the exception of a small square of polished wood directly in front of the DJ, which Alan assumed was the dance area, and made a mental note to avoid it at all costs.

Dozens of people were standing around talking in groups and pairs, the hum of conversation drowning out any other sounds in the room, but as Alan tuned the talking out he could hear Genesis pumping out from the speakers.

'Told you!' he told Rosie, smugly.

On the other side of the room, Alan could see an attractive blonde lady engaged in conversation with another couple. She looked in their direction and waved. Rosie and Jayne waved back and the blonde lady broke away from her friends and came over to them.

'Alison!' Rosie cried out, 'Happy birthday!' and presented her with the gift wrapped package and birthday card. Alison hugged both the sisters and then turned to Alan.

'You must be Alan,' she said, offering her hand.

'Happy birthday,' he said, shaking her hand.

'Thank you. Rosie tells me you're trying to be a comedian.'

Alan frowned at his girlfriend. 'Well, yes. Part time at the moment. When I can get the bookings.'

Alison listened intently, her big eyes staring up at him. 'You must be very brave, standing up in front of loads of people trying to make them laugh,' she said.

Alan laughed. 'Not at all. People either laugh or they don't.'

'Normally they don't!' Rosie interjected.

Alan laughed again, whilst making a mental note to bring that up when they had their next argument.

Alison turned to Rosie. 'Do you mind if I borrow him for a minute? I'd like him to meet my husband.'

'Please do, no rush to return him either!'

Alan put on a look of mock indignation and allowed Alison to take him by the arm and lead him away.

Watching Alison whisk Alan away, Jayne asked, 'what's all that about? Do you think she fancies him?'

'No chance. Not with that shirt!' Rosie said dismissively.

Jayne laughed. 'Drink?' she asked.

'Definitely. There's a free bar apparently,' Rosie pointed out and the two of them made their way through the crowd to the bar.

In the other direction, Alison skilfully manoeuvred Alan through the clusters of people who were standing together talking and drinking. She smiled at some, stopped briefly to welcome some to the party and exchanged pleasantries with others. She eventually came to a stop alongside two men who were deep in conversation standing in a corner. She touched one on the arm, who turned to face her. She propelled Alan forward.

'Alan, I'd like you to meet my husband Peter.'

'Pleased to meet you,' Alan said, offering Peter his hand. 'Nice party,' he added.

Peter stepped forward and shook Alan's hand. He was a couple of inches taller than Alan, several taller than his wife.

'Thanks for coming,' he said.

'Alans' a comedian,' Alison announced.

'A comedian, really?' Peter pursed his lips, suddenly very interested in Alan.

Not giving Alan an opportunity to answer for himself, Alison added, 'Yes he is.' She stepped back and added, 'I'll leave you two to talk. See you later,' before wandering back into the body of the room and starting another round of mingling.

*

Alan felt like he had been talking to Peter for hours. In truth it had been no more than ten minutes, which included Peter fetching him a drink. Now he stood, bottle of beer gradually warming in his hand while Peter told him all about the politics of a cricket club, and other interesting facts about cricket clubs.

'...and so that's why we need a comedian.' Peter's words jolted Alan out of his semi-comatose state.

'Err. Sorry Peter what was that?' Alan asked.

'Are you available to appear at the club Christmas party? I know it's several months away, but if you don't book early you don't get who you want,' Peter explained, oblivious to the fact that Alan had not listened to anything that he had said for the previous ten minutes.

Alan knew that he didn't have any bookings in December. He also knew that he had no bookings in November and only one so far in October. Probably best, Alan thought, though not to appear too keen though.

'Do you want to e-mail me all the details, I'll check my diary, see if I'm clear. If so I'll be happy to do it.'

Peter looked genuinely pleased. 'Thanks Alan. I'm really grateful,' he said. 'I'll get you a pen so you can give me your e-mail address...and another beer. It looks like that one is nearly finished.'

Alan watched as Peter wandered off to the bar, and as Alison had done, he smiled and greeted everyone he passed. Alan finished the last of his lukewarm beer and looked around the busy room. He could see Alison still circulating the room, spending a little time with all the guests, making it appear as though she was genuinely pleased they were there. She reminded him of a politician working the room, although she was significantly nicer and far more attractive than the politicians that he came across on a daily basis.

He could see Rosie and Jayne talking with a small group of people. Rosie appeared to be in conversation with a tall young looking man who appeared to have caught the attention of Jayne, although she was simply staring at him, while Rosie engaged him in conversation.

Peter returned from the bar and passed Alan a bottle of beer. 'How do you know Ali?' Peter asked.

Alan thanked Peter for the drink. 'She uses the same gym as my girlfriend Rosie and her sister Jayne.'

As Peter nodded, the lights dimmed and the background music was replaced by a louder, brasher dance beat. The lights the DJ had brought with him were clearly intended to be used at stadium rock concerts, and not at forty fifth birthday parties at the local cricket club. The lights began to rotate and flash, seemingly intent on blinding those who stepped too close.

Peter said something that Alan couldn't hear properly, so he just laughed politely. Peter, clearly pleased that a comedian had found his comment amusing, laughed too.

Alan felt the need to leave this strange scenario, where two grown men were just laughing at nothing in particular in the absence of conversation and told Peter for the third time that he was off to find Rosie. Peter laughed again as Alan slipped away.

Alan worked his way around the dance floor which was fast filling with middle aged women who had kicked their shoes off and were trying - and failing - to move in time to a dance beat. He could see Rosie and Jayne who were still in their small group on the far side of the room, and from the way they were laughing they didn't appear to be missing him at all.

Working his way towards them, Alan squeezed past a group of six who were talking and laughing loudly enough to ensure that they could be heard over the music. As he passed them, one particular peel of laughter caught his attention. He turned to see Frankie standing amongst the group, clearly enjoying himself.

Frankie waved at him. Alan instinctively waved back before realising what he had just done and walked back to the group containing Frankie. Once he was next to Frankie he whispered, 'Come with me,' into his ear and steered Frankie away from the group.

Without waiting for an answer, Alan led Frankie through the club house and out through the exit doors. Once outside he directed Frankie to an empty bench.

'What are you doing?' he asked.

'Mingling,' Frankie said, surprised that Alan couldn't see that for himself.

'Mingling!'

'Yes, mingling. Getting around, socialising. Meeting people.'

'But you can't mingle, you're dead. No one can see you.'

Frankie sighed. 'You're looking at this from the perspective of the living again.'

'Oh yes, sorry about that. Not sure why I would be doing that.'

'I am mingling, I am listening to what people are saying, looking at the way they are saying things, and laughing at their jokes, which in some cases are quite funny. It's something I always used to do,' Frankie explained. 'You never know when you will hear something which you can use in a routine. The fact that they can't see or hear me is actually an advantage, because they are saying things to each other that they wouldn't if they knew I was there.'

'How long have you been here?' Alan asked, staring at the apparition on the bench next to him.

'Same time as you. I followed you in through the door, then you were led away by the blonde, so I went and mingled.'

'She introduced me to her husband and he booked me for a gig,' Alan explained cheerfully.

'What, here?' Frankie waved his hand at the clubhouse.

'Yeah, at their Christmas party.'

'Christ, that should give you enough time to get some new material then,' Frankie grinned at him.

Before Alan had the opportunity to respond, the clubhouse door opened and Rosie stepped out. 'What are you doing out here on your own?' she asked.

'I'm not...' Alan stopped himself mid –sentence. 'It was really hot and loud in there, so I popped out here to finish my drink. I was just about to go back in.'

'Well recovered,' Frankie said.

'I was talking to Alison's husband. He asked me to do a gig at their Christmas party.'

'That's good, I suppose,' Rosie said. 'Are you coming back inside?'

Alan stood up and followed Rosie back into the clubhouse, closely followed by Frankie. 'Who were you talking to in there?' Alan asked.

'They're the people from the gym that we know. Jayne's got a thing about Tony the instructor.'

'Was that the twelve year old in a T-shirt several sizes too small?' Alan asked.

'I'd be quiet about fashion if I were you, and for the record he's at least sixteen!' Rosie said, turning to face Alan with a large grin.

Frankie put his hand on Alan's shoulder. 'Don't worry son, we all have to step aside for the youngsters eventually.'

*

Alan was drunk. Not falling over and not remembering a thing in the morning drunk, but drunk enough to know from experience that his head was going to hurt in the morning and that tomorrow was pretty much a write off.

On the plus side he thought, Jayne was worse, and even Rosie, who could normally be relied upon to act as the nominated sensible person had had enough to drink to join her gym friends on the dance floor.

Peter had twice told Alan how grateful he was that he was helping him out at the Christmas party, and had introduced him to a number of his friends as the comic who saved Christmas.

'So you see, I'm probably a bit of a hero round here now,' Alan explained to Frankie.

'Nothing less than a legend, I imagine,' Frankie replied, having had many years of dealing with drunk people while being the only one sober.

'I wouldn't be surprised if they renamed the ground after you,' Frankie suggested.

'You really think so?' Alan asked, trying to get his eyes to focus.

'Why wouldn't they?' Frankie said.

Alan took several seconds to think that through. 'The Alan Rose Ground,' he said. 'It has a nice ring to it.'

'That'll be the place,' Frankie said. 'Families will say that they're going down the Rose ground for the match.'

Alan took a long drink from his bottle, and after two attempts, placed it back down on the table.

'It's a shame that you can't drink. We could have got pissed together.' Alan paused. Frankie wasn't entirely sure if Alan had paused for effect, or had passed out. 'When was the last time you had a drink?' Alan suddenly asked.

'I can't remember,' Frankie replied honestly. 'At least thirty three years.'

'Thirty three years...' Alan repeated in a hushed tone. 'You must be gasping!'

My name is Frankie Fortune,' Frankie said, 'and I've been dry for thirty three years!' making them both chuckle.

Alan caught a movement out of the corner of his eye, as one of the chairs was pulled out. Alison sat down next to him, opposite Frankie. 'You must be very drunk,' she said to Alan. 'You're sat here talking to yourself.'

'She's in a worse state than you!' Frankie warned him.

'No,' Alan said in a hushed voice, making Alison lean to closer to hear what he was saying. 'I'm talking to my imaginary friend.'

Alison giggled. 'You are very funny,' she said and smiled sweetly at him.

'Have you had a nice party?' Alan asked.

Alison rested her head in the palm of her hand and leaned on the table, moving closer to him.

'Easy tiger,' Frankie called out from the other side of the table.

'I've had a brilliant time,' she said quietly. 'Really nice, and everyone has been so kind. Look at all the presents,'

303

Alison pointed vaguely to a table not too far from them where she had placed all the wrapped gifts. Alan couldn't help notice that they all appeared to be identical to the picture frame that Rosie had given her. *Another nail in the coffin of originality*, he thought and made a mental note to tell Rosie next time she mentioned his shirt.

'You are very popular,' Alan said, rather than point out that she would be needing lots of available shelf space to house all her new picture frames.

'Thank you,' she smiled and finished the remainder of wine from her glass.

As she moved, Alan's attention was drawn to a small brooch that was fixed to the front of her dress. 'That's nice,' he said. 'What is it?'

Alison looked down at her front and pulled the brooch up so she could see it clearly. 'It was a present, it's a bat,' she said, smiling at him again.

Alan could see the brooch was indeed vaguely bat shaped. He frowned, looking more closely. Yes, it was definitely a bat. 'Do you like bats then?' he asked.

'I love them. I think they're so cute. Some people get really into cats or dogs, but I love bats. I have little bat ornaments at home and bat pictures, anything I see that has a bat on it I normally pick up.'

Not sure how to respond, Alan simply nodded.

'And do you what's really funny about that?' she said.

'No, what's that?' Alan said, rather than give any of the possible dozen answers that he had thought of.

'My job,' she said simply. 'I work in the planning office of the council. My boss is a planning officer and if there are bats on site, they can't build on it. Because they're cute!' she looked at her brooch again.

'Did you hear that?' Frankie asked from across the table. 'Ask her to go over that again.'

Even without Frankie's prompting, Alan was aware of what Alison had said. 'So, if I wanted to knock down something and rebuild it into something different, I couldn't if there were bats in the building?' he asked.

'Yep. Bats or any other protected species I suppose,' Alison said. 'Funny isn't it? What with me loving bats.'

'Yes, very,' Alan replied, slowly thinking through a number of options.

In the background, the music had slowed down and Alison stood up putting her hand on Alan's shoulders. 'I should probably dance with my husband now,' she said, as she tottered off to the dancefloor.

Alan smiled at her. 'Thank you...for having such a great party.'

Alison smiled and staggered off to the dance floor.

Frankie moved over next to Alan. 'Are you sober enough to understand what she just said?' Frankie asked.

'I hope so, but if I'm not, you can remind me in the morning,' Alan said before resting his head on the table.

*

'What do you mean you've got a plan to save the theatre?' Rosie asked. 'You're drunk and in no fit state to do anything. Especially not come up with a plan to save the theatre.'

Rosie, Alan and Jayne were sitting on the back seat of a taxi on their way to Rosie's house. The motion of the taxi jumping over speed bumps was slowly rocking Alan to sleep, and he had no desire to have a conversation that could wait until morning.

Rosie dug him in the ribs. 'You can't tell us you have a plan to save the theatre and then fall asleep. Come on. Out with it.'

Alan recounted his conversation with Alison. 'So all I need are some bats or other rare species like a unicorn or a Panda and the theatre can be saved.'

Rosie waited until the taxi bounced over another speed bump before asking Alan, 'Where are you going to get bats from? It's not like they grow on trees.'

'I accept that part needs some work,' Alan conceded.

'I know where you can get some bats,' Jayne announced,

Rosie looked at her sister. 'I thought you were asleep.'

'No, I was resting my eyes,' Jayne said, rubbing her face with her hands to keep herself awake.

'Well, where can I get bats from?' Alan asked her.

'A few weeks ago I arrested a man who had climbed into a derelict school's grounds to steal lead from the old chapel roof. He said that when he looked into the roof it was full of bats,' Jayne explained.

'What school was that?' Alan asked.

'I can't remember.'

'Oh come on Jayne, how many old schools are on your patch?' Rosie asked her sister.

'Just the one, but I can't remember its name,' Jayne explained.

'Can you think about it, speak to your colleagues and get back to me?' Alan asked.

'Definitely. I'll do that tomorrow morning first thing,' Jayne offered.

Considering the state Jayne was in, Alan doubted that her idea of first thing in the morning was the same as his, to be fair, he thought, everyone would be having a lie in in the morning.

Jayne suddenly opened her eyes. 'It was called Buggerly Mount. The school was called Buggerly Mount, I remember now,' she said before slumping back into her seat.

'The Mount,' Alan smiled, 'who'd have thought it?'

'You know it?' Rosie asked.

'Certainly do. It was my old school. I went there with James,' Alan explained. 'All I have to do is break in, steal the bats, shove them in the theatre and wait for them to be found. What do you think of that?'

Alan's moment of self- belief was shattered by the sound of snoring from both sisters.

Chapter 32

Alan stood in middle of the room until Rosie asked him to move one side, as he was blocking her view of the television. On screen was a talent show that appeared to Alan to consist of everything but talent.

'I'd like to thank you all for coming tonight,' he said. He gripped his shirt lapels in the manner of a barrister addressing a court and looked around the room at his audience.

Rosie, Sarah and Amy sat on the sofa, Rosie with one eye on the television, Sarah listening intently to everything that Alan was saying, while Amy perched on the end, eagerly waiting for Alan to unveil his plan. She had been on tenterhooks since receiving his text that morning.

'What does he want?' She had asked James.

'I haven't a clue,' he had told her honestly. 'He was out at a party last night. He probably got drunk, stole something and needs an alibi.'

Jayne was slumped in an armchair half asleep, the effects of the night before not fully out of her system. She would occasionally doze off and wake suddenly with a start hoping that nobody had noticed. Frankie sat on the edge of the chair, amusing himself at Jayne's refusal to accept sleep.

James sat on one of the kitchen chairs that Alan had dragged through earlier that evening, after he realised how many people were coming. Watching Alan effect the pose of a barrister addressing the court made him think again that Alan may have done something wrong.

'So everyone, I suppose you're wondering why I have called you out here tonight on this wet and windy night,' Alan began.

Amy looked out of the window at the sunny warm evening and raised her eyebrows.

Alan continued, 'I've been considering a number of options, and together with information that has recently come to my attention, I can say that without a shadow of doubt that you...' Alan paused, enjoying the attention and looks of confusion that he was getting from everyone else. He moved back into the middle of the room so that the talent show was no longer getting Rosie's full attention or indeed occasional glances from the others.

Alan pointed at James '...YOU,' he repeated, 'murdered the housekeeper with a candlestick when she threatened to tell everyone of your affair.'

The room fell silent, looks of disbelief and contempt shot in Alan's direction. James stood and put his hands up. 'It's a fair cop,' he said.

'Constable Talbot,' Alan said turning to Jayne, 'take this man into custody.'

Jayne responded by gently snoring.

'Constable Talbot...WAKE UP!' Alan shouted.

Jayne woke with a start, much to Frankie's amusement. 'What? I'm, awake,' she said, though clearly hadn't been.

'Alan!' Rosie and Amy shouted simultaneously.

'Will you please get on with it?' Rosie pleaded.

Alan raised his hand, acknowledging the outburst. 'Sorry,' he said, 'I thought I'd lighten the mood before the serious stuff started.'

'Can we start the serious stuff now please?' Sarah asked quietly, 'The clock is ticking with the builders and if this isn't a serious idea I really should be meeting with the Arts Council to plan our next step.'

Alan nodded, acknowledging Sarah's request. 'OK,' he said 'let's get started...'

Rosie picked up the remote and turned the TV off, ready to pay attention.

'Last night,' Alan said, 'I was at a birthday party, a friend of Rosie's and Jayne's...'

'How old was she?' James asked interrupting him.

'Forty five,' Rosie answered. 'Why is that important?' she asked.

'I'm just setting the scene.' James replied. 'I find it easier to imagine forty five year olds at a party than eighteen year olds at a party.'

'I can lend you a DVD that'll help you visualise an eighteenth birthday party,' Alan offered.

'Is that the Tennis one?' replied James.

'Yep, Game, Set and ...'

Alan's reply was cut short by Amy's piercing shout; 'PLEASE! Will you please just get on with it?' Turning to James she said; 'It doesn't matter how old the people at the party were, so shut up unless you can say something constructive.' She then turned to Alan 'Can you just tell us why we're here without reference to your soft porn collection?'

Alan nodded apologetically before he was again interrupted by James.

'You weren't so dismissive of them when you wanted to borrow one for your hen night,' he grinned.

Alan winced, fearing Amy's reaction, but only noticed her stony faced glare at James. 'Rosie,' Alan said, 'can you make up the guest room for Captain Cook tonight.'

'Thanks mate.' James said sullenly.

'Anyway…getting back on track, we were at this party last night and the friend of Rosie's and Jayne's, who was forty five,' Alan paused, expecting a further interruption. When none came he continued. 'She had had a few…'

'To be fair,' Rosie interrupted, 'if you can't have a drink on your birthday, when can you?'

'Sorry,' Alan said, puzzled by Rosie's interruption, 'I'm not with you.'

'You were implying that she's a drunk.'

Alan shook his head. 'I wasn't, I was just saying that she may have had a drink or two last night.'

'Well, that's ok then,' Rosie said. 'Carry on.'

'I got drunk on VE day. Absolutely smashed…' Alan looked over at Frankie. 'Woke up the next morning stark bollock naked in a horse trough in the middle of a village just outside Paris. My privates really were on parade that morning.'

Alan snorted a laugh at the apparently empty seat before realising that everyone was staring at him. 'Sorry,' he said, momentarily distracted. 'Right where was I..? Oh yes. The party. So, the lady who was having the party, Alison, was a bit drunk...' He looked over at Rosie who nodded in confirmation. Alan continued, '...and she tells me that she works in the Council planning office, which is interesting because she has a thing about bats.'

'Bats?' James asked, nonplussed.

'Yes mate. Bats. Real bats, toy bats any bat related toy. She just loves bats.'

'Why's that interesting?' Sarah asked, scratching her head.

'Good question Sarah,' said Amy, supportively.

Alan smiled, 'Because, my friends, according to Alison, it turns out that bats, indeed, the very presence of bats can scupper building plans. They are a protected species.'

Alan paused waiting for a reaction.

'Are there bats in the theatre?' Amy asked looking at Sarah.

'It's unlikely.' Sarah said, 'If there were we would have found them by now.'

'So why are you telling us about bats?' James asked.

So many questions Alan thought, and at last a relevant one. 'Isn't it obvious? We put bats in the theatre. In the loft space.'

'Brilliant.' James said, 'One small point though. Where are you going to get bats from? It's not like they grow on trees.'

'I know exactly where we can get bats from.' Alan said smugly.

'Where?' Amy said, fast becoming inpatient with Alan's drawn out explanation of his plan.

Alan looked directly at James and said; 'The Mount.'

James's jaw dropped. 'The Mount. How do you know there are bats in The Mount?' He asked.

Jayne stuck her hand in the air like a child in a classroom. 'Because I arrested someone who was trying to steal lead from the roof of the chapel. He said he was scared off by the bats in the loft,' she said, pleased with herself.

Everyone looked at Jayne, who seemed to shrink slightly under the weight of attention focused on her.

'It's surprising,' she continued, 'It seemed such a silly thing at the time. I had no idea that bats were protected at all until I nicked the bloke.'

'I'm sorry, what's the Mount?' asked Sarah.

'Our old school. Buggerly Mount.' James answered, smiling at the memories.

Sarah looked disbelievingly at Amy.

'It's true.' Amy said, 'That was the name of their school. You really couldn't make it up.'

'Well, someone must've.' Sarah replied, 'It wasn't Kenneth Williams, was it?'

'I knew him,' Frankie replied, helpfully. 'Lovely fella. Do you know he tried to get me an audition for the Carry On films, but I had a row with the producer who said I wasn't famous enough. Bloody cheek.'

'So, anyway...' said Alan, loudly, to gain some order, '...all we have to do is break into the school, steal the bats and set them up in the theatre loft.' he said, reiterating his plan.

'But isn't that cruel?' Rosie said, 'Taking them from their home and making them live somewhere else?'

'Not at all.' Alan said, 'We'll put them into little boxes to move them, and hang the boxes in the theatre. It'll be like they're getting upgraded to business class.'

Alan looked around the room, expecting applause, or at least nods of agreement. However, everyone was looking at him open mouthed. Except Jayne, who was once again lightly snoring.

'You genius.' Amy said, 'That might just work.' She looked at Rosie, 'Can I hug him?'

'Be my guest.' Rosie said.

Amy squealed, bounded out of the sofa, took three steps and embraced Alan, her heels making her a couple of inches taller than him. On releasing him, she asked, 'So that's the plan. How's it going to work?'

'That's what we're going to sort out now,' Alan said, recovering his composure after Amy's show of affection.

'For a start we have Jayne,' Amy said helpfully, 'she'll know how to break into buildings.'

'You can count me out,' Jayne replied, having been woken up by Amy's earlier squeal of delight. 'It's more than my jobs worth. I'm not breaking into anything, and I'm not stealing an endangered species.'

'So, we'll put you down as a consultant.' Amy said.

'Whatever, but I'm not going anywhere near the school or the theatre.' Jayne replied.

Alan placed a pad of A4 paper on the table. Turning to James he asked, 'How much of the school can you remember?'

Taking a pen from the table, James began sketching out a plan of the school. 'These...' he said, pointing at two squares that he had sketched out, 'are where the craft rooms were. That was the nearest block to the chapel.'

Alan shook his head. 'That wasn't the craft rooms,' he said, 'that was where Mr Finley the first form fiddler had his classroom.'

'No, that was over there,' James said, gesturing at a point on the other side of the sketch. 'He had his classroom near the gym block so he could watch the first years' come back from cross-country running.'

Alan raised his eyebrows 'Are you sure?' he asked.

'Definitely, trust me' James said confidently.

Sitting on the sofa, Sarah turned to Amy and asked, 'Do they know what they're doing?'

Amy looked over at the two arguing friends. 'They may look like two immature adolescents let loose with the art box, but I'm afraid in the absence of anything better they are your best chance of success.'

Sarah slumped back into the sofa. 'God help us,' she mumbled.

'You've got to treat this like a military exercise,' Frankie said, peering over James' shoulder.

Alan looked at him across the table. 'How?' he whispered.

James looked up from his plan of the school, 'Frankie?' he mouthed.

Alan nodded. 'He says that we should be planning this like a military operation.'

'He's right.' James whispered, 'We can't go in without a plan.'

'Why not?' Alan whispered in reply, 'Isn't that US foreign policy?'

'OK everyone. Come and have a look at this,' Alan announced to the room, stepping back so that the others could see their work.

The plan of the school had been drawn across four sheets of A4 paper. Leaning over the table, Jayne said, 'That's the chapel isn't it?' Pointing at a square that James had written the word CHAPEL across.

'Yes. Is that how it looks now?' James asked.

Jayne scratched her head. 'Well there's a perimeter fence which has been put up by the developers who own the site. I wouldn't recommend climbing over the fence where that idiot did. You can be seen from the road.'

'So the best place to get into the school is ...?' Alan asked.

'There...' Jayne pointed at the drawing of the other side of the school grounds. 'That side of the school is next to the woods, if you climb over the fence there you can't be seen from the road.'

Frankie nodded in approval at Jayne's logic. 'She's smart this one. You need to keep her involved,' Frankie said to Alan.

Alan looked at Frankie and shrugged as Rosie said; 'Wait a minute. I've an idea,' and promptly left the room.

'An idea?' James asked Alan.

'Could be anything. Don't get your hopes up.' Alan answered.

Rosie came back into the room carrying a box of Monopoly.

'I told you not to get your hopes up.' Alan said to James.

Rosie looked at everyone staring at her, smiling back at them. 'Right, now you can show us the plan...' she said, while taking the Monopoly pieces out of the box and placing them on the table, '...using these.'

'OK, this is what we are going do...' Alan said, very aware that there were more eyes on the Monopoly pieces than on him. 'James, Amy and I will climb over the fence, here, by the woods.' He placed the Top Hat, Car and the Boot on the plan. 'We move through the school grounds as quietly and quickly as possible to the school chapel there.' Alan moved the three Monopoly pieces across the plan to where it said CHAPEL.

Looking at Rosie he said 'You drive the car, park up in the woods and wait for us, we may have to make a quick getaway.'

'Shouldn't I be the car then?' she asked.

'Sorry?' Alan said, a puzzled look on his face.

'Look,' she said, pointing at the three pieces on the Chapel. 'One of those is the car. That should be over here,' she picked up the car and placed it by the fence and woods. 'Because that's where I will be. Waiting in the car.'

Amy took the little Iron piece out of the box. 'We'll have to use this piece,' she said, and put it with the Top Hat and the Boot on the Chapel.

'I'm the Top Hat,' James announced.

'No, I'm the Top Hat,' Alan said, 'I'm always the Top Hat.'

'Then it's my turn.'

'We're not doing turns,' Alan said, 'It's my plan, and my Monopoly set. I'm the Top Hat.'

'I'll be the car then.' James said.

'No, you can't be the car,' Rosie responded, 'I'm going to be in an actual car so it makes sense that I'm the car. You should be the Boot.'

'I don't want to be the Boot.' James whined.

'Right!' Amy snapped, 'If you're going to act like children we can forget about the Monopoly pieces.' She swept the pieces into her hand and tipped them back in the box. 'Have you got Trivial Pursuit?' she asked Rosie.

'Yes, I think so. Yes.'

'Take the little wedge shaped pieces and use them – they're all the same shape and size. That should keep the children happy.'

'Can I be the brown one?' Alan asked.

'And they're cheeses, not wedges.' James added.

318

'They're wedges,' Amy said, irritated that James would question her description.

'Shall I get the box anyway?' Rosie asked.

Amy sighed, 'Please.'

As Rosie left the room, Amy turned both Alan and James. 'Do you think we could get this finished before one of us dies of old age?'

'One of us already has,' Frankie called out from the sofa.

Alan laughed. Fortunately for him, Rosie came back into the room with the box of trivial pursuit before Amy could ask him what he found so funny.

'Right, here you go,' she said and scooped out several of the plastic pieces placing them on the plan.

'OK,' Alan said. 'On the basis that these objects are neither cheese nor wedges and are only here to be used as representative of individuals,' he looked around, 'everyone happy with that?'

James nodded whilst everyone else stayed silent.

'Alan,' Sarah said, 'what do you want me to do?'

'Well you can come over here and sit on my lap!' Frankie offered from his position on the sofa.

Ignoring Frankie, Alan replied, 'Can you get us access to the theatre? We'll need to go straight there from the school once we have the bats.'

'I think so, yes. The Arts Council have a theatre liaison officer who can get a set of keys. He'll be glad to help.'

'Is that Nav?' Amy asked, 'I've met him, nice kid.'

'The boy from the meeting?' James asked.

'That's him.' Amy and Sarah said together.

'It'll be a late night. Does he have a curfew?' James asked.

'Good point, Alan said seriously, 'Sarah, speak to his mum check that he can stay up late.'

Amy shook her head, unamused by the inability of Alan and her husband to be serious for more than five minutes at a time.

'When are we going to do this?' Sarah asked. 'Unless I've missed something, you haven't mentioned when this is going to happen.'

'Good question.' Rosie said 'Well Alan...when?'

Everyone looked at Alan. 'As soon as possible,' he said. 'Tomorrow evening? Can everyone do tomorrow evening?'

The room was silent, the task in front of them suddenly seemed very real, tangible.

Amy broke the silence. 'Bring it on,' she said, 'It'll be like Mission Impossible.'

'I'm Tom Cruise then,' Alan said.

'No, you got to be the Top Hat. I'm Tom Cruise.' James said with a grin.

'Shut up you two,' Jayne snapped, now fully awake. 'What do you intend to do about the security?'

'What security?' Alan said.

'Why didn't you tell us about it earlier?' Rosie said finishing off Alan's sentence.

Alan heard Frankie groaning. 'Amateurs. Absolute amateurs. Wouldn't have lasted five minutes in the war.'

'I assumed that you knew that there would be a security guard. Every site has to have one,' Jayne explained.

James looked at Alan, Amy looked at Alan, Rosie looked at Alan, Sarah looked at Alan, Frankie had his head in his hands and Alan looked at Jayne.

'It's normal,' Jayne continued, 'It'll probably be an old guy, normally ex-police, who will spend most of the night dozing while listening to local radio phone–ins. He'll probably go for a walk around the site at some stage, but that'll be more likely to give his dog a chance to relieve itself.'

'He's got a dog?' James asked. 'No one said anything about a dog.'

'No one said anything about a guard.' Rosie added.

'Look, these guards don't want any trouble. They're just topping up their pensions. Keep quiet, don't draw attention to yourselves and you'll be fine.'

James turned to Alan mumbling, 'No one mentioned security guards with dogs.'

'Jayne said it'll be fine. She knows what she's talking about. She's our consultant after all,' Alan said attempting to reassure his friend.

'One more thing,' Rosie announced in a tone of voice that made Alan fear for his plan.

'What's that?' he said tentatively.

'How many bats do we need?' she asked. 'Surely we're going to need enough to make the theatre look like it's a proper home for them. If we only get a couple, what happens if they fly off before they're found? We'll be back to where we started.'

Alan didn't need to see anyone else's face to know that they were all nodding in agreement. In fact he would have nodded along with them if he hadn't suddenly realised that it was a very good question, and one he didn't know the answer to.

'Well..?' Amy said, disrupted his thought process. 'How many do we need?'

'I would say two dozen.' James offered, helpfully.

Grateful for the interruption, Alan trawled his memory of his conversation with Alison. Had she mentioned anything when they spoke the previous night?

'Why?' Amy asked, turning to her husband, 'Why are twenty four bats the optimum number for bat related mischief?'

'I think I saw it on a David Attenborough programme,' James said. 'I think.'

'You've just made that up haven't you?' Rosie sneered.

'How are we going to get twenty four bats out of the loft and into the theatre?' Sarah said, slowly wondering if she hadn't just wasted her evening.

'Ignore him,' Amy said to her, 'he hasn't a clue.'

Frankie moved alongside Alan. 'Kitchen,' he said. 'Now.'

Welcoming the opportunity to get away, Alan said 'I'll make some tea and we can have a think about it,' before slipping out of the room and following Frankie into the kitchen. He quietly closed the kitchen door behind him.

'Remember the herons?' Frankie said.

'What herons?' Alan asked, whilst filling the kettle at the sink.

'The herons in Rosie's parent's garden,' Frankie tried to explain, seeing Alan's confused face. 'Do you remember what Rosie's Dad told us? They had fake herons around their pond to scare off the normal herons.'

'OK, and this affects us ... *how?*'

'We'll do the same.' Frankie said, feeling frustrated that Alan was not seeing the obvious.

'I'm not sure that we can use fake herons disguised as bats,' Alan said. 'They're much bigger for a start.'

'Oh, for crying out loud. Have people got more stupid since I died?'

Alan stared back at Frankie, nonplussed.

'Listen, this is what we are going to do...' Frankie took a deep breath and began to explain his idea.

*

Alan stepped back into the living room carrying a tray of mugs. Putting the tray down on the table. 'OK, I've given it some thought, and this is what we are going to do. We take five or six bats. Not too many. Remember we have to put them into boxes and move them, so five or six is about right. We position them in the theatre, at the front of the loft nearest to the entrance. The rest of the loft we fill with fake bats, toy bats, plastic ones.'

'That's ridiculous. It'll never work,' Rosie said. 'It's madness.'

'It might work,' Sarah contradicted, 'if we make sure that there is limited lighting in the loft and that the bats are congregated around the entrance, then it will convince anyone looking in that the loft is full of bats.'

'And anyway,' Alan added, 'there only need be one bat who has set up home in the loft. Five or six is brilliant, but if it works it will look like there are dozens in there. Easily enough to derail the development.'

Standing unseen alongside Alan, Frankie said, 'Tell them the rest of it.'

'What we all have to do tomorrow is get out to the shops and get as many plastic toy bats as we can. I'll get the boxes to put the bats in. We meet back here at 10.00pm.'

Alan picked up a mug of tea from the table. 'Any questions?' he asked, taking a sip of his tea. Alan looked at the staring faces in front of him. 'I'll take that as a no then.' he said.

*

Rosie shut the door behind Amy, James and Sarah, who had taken them up on the offer of a lift. Jayne was asleep again and Alan resisted the urge to wake her up and tell her to use the spare bedroom.

'How do you think it went?' he asked Rosie as she came back into the living room.

'Mostly it was a disaster. You made most of it up as you went along, and as for the idea about using fake bats – where on Earth did you get that from?'

Alan looked around the room, but Frankie had vanished. 'I think I must have had some divine inspiration,' he said.

Chapter 33

Oneway looked across the studio. A diminutive woman with short black hair sat opposite him, her face partially obscured by a large microphone. On the wall behind her, a large sign read BBC Radio London.

The jaunty sounding jingle faded away and the woman began to speak into the microphone. 'Good afternoon, you are listening to the Local Affairs programme with me, Kelly Porter.'

She faded the jingle back up and let it come to its conclusion. 'I am joined this afternoon by Clive Oneway, managing director of Oneway Property Management – Good afternoon Clive.'

'Good Afternoon Kelly. Thanks for having me on the show.'

'You're welcome, Clive. I'm sure that you will forgive me if I say that despite you fast becoming one of the most influential people in London, most of our listeners will have never heard of you, and would certainly not recognise your face.'

Oneway laughed, 'I regard myself as one of many pioneers in shaping the future of not only London, but its outskirts too – I don't expect people to recognise me, in my line of work you only attract notoriety.'

Kelly looked down at some notes. 'Clive, your company, Oneway Property Management, is responsible for acquiring and developing many sites in London. You have been the leading figure behind several residential developments and more recently you are the driving force behind the planned 'Oneway To Shop – Shopping Mall in

South London, an ambitious project which has attracted much criticism from local residents and businesses due to the planned demolition of the Merton Palace Theatre.'

'Kelly...' Oneway said in the tone of a parent trying to convince a child of the existence of Santa Claus, 'The only opposition to the plan exists with the grumbles of a few members of the local arts group who believe that the theatre should be saved and that millions should be spent refurbishing it. Quite frankly I am at a loss to see any argument to keep it open. It's been empty and unused for most of the last thirty years. It has no historical importance, it's not a protected building, and it's not a church nor a place of worship.'

'So you refute any suggestion that you are...' Kelly looked down at her notes to quote; *ripping the heart out of the community*, as misplaced and inaccurate.'

Oneway was warming to this woman. 'If creating thousands of new jobs and attracting business to the area is ripping the heart out of the community, well then I'm afraid I must be guilty.'

Looking back at her notes Kelly added, 'Moving on, I'd like to talk to you about the Sun Setting Retirement Home.'

Oneway frowned. This wasn't on the agreed agenda. 'Please do,' he said suspiciously, leaning slightly forward in his chair in anticipation.

'Well, there have been allegations that you obtained planning permission to redevelop the site and moved the residents out and into alternative accommodation without consultation.'

Oneway smiled what he thought was his most charming smile. 'In the first instance, let me clarify that I simply own

327

the building. The home itself is run by a manager who has complete autonomy and in effect makes the decisions that affect the home and the guests on a daily basis.'

'So you're saying that it was the manager,' Kelly looked down at her notes again, 'Mr Wakefield, who took it upon himself to move the residents and sell the home. Perhaps we can get Mr Wakefield on the phone and ask him to address the allegations.'

Oneway thought of Wakefield. A spineless individual, but perfect for his needs. *"The puppet"* as he was known by one and all, had complete autonomy. That is, just so long as he agreed with everything that Oneway told him to do, had no original thoughts, and in the event that he did, he kept them to himself. Wakefield wasn't the brightest star in the sky, and allowing him to be interviewed would be a disaster.

'I think,' Oneway said, 'That in the circumstances, you should address any questions to me and I will do my best to answer them. Mr Wakefield and I have a very close working relationship and I would be aware of any decisions that he made that would affect the home.'

Kelly looked across the desk at him, 'So, are you able to respond to the allegations that you or Mr Wakefield obtained planning permission to redevelop the site and moved the residents out and into alternative accommodation without consultation.'

Oneway sighed, 'Well, of course that's going to be the sort of simplistic reaction that opponents to progress put forward.'

'So you deny the allegations?'

'It is true that permission was obtained to redevelop the site and erect several residential units, but this came about due to Government directives to build more affordable housing.'

'With prices ranging from £700,000 to £1m, there is a significant number of people who would not class that as affordable housing.'

'They are extremely affordable for the type of people who want to live there,' Oneway replied smugly.

Kelly frowned at the answer, looking at the papers in front of her. 'And what of the residents of the Sun Setting Retirement Home. It is alleged that you moved them to alternative accommodation without their consent or knowledge.'

'The residents were kept informed every step of the way. There was nothing that came as a surprise to them. They were moved to a comparable retirement complex which also had a beautiful view overlooking the river, and I froze the costs, none of the residents had to pay a penny more.'

'You moved them to another property that you owned overlooking the River Tyne.'

'Yes.'

'Three hundred miles away.'

'The distance was irrelevant. The residents had very few visitors. If anything I gave them a better view from their bedroom windows, plus it made no difference to the blind residents anyway.'

Kelly couldn't believe what she was hearing. 'And how would you respond to the allegation that they were moved without their consent or knowledge? We understand that the residents were simply transferred, thinking that they were going on a day trip. When they finally reached their destination they found that all their possessions had been already been moved and were in their new rooms waiting for them.'

'Kelly...' Oneway said, mustering as much sincerity was possible, 'A meeting was called and the residents were told that the home was closing. They were being given the choice of moving to the new home or being put out on the street. And let me tell you that those who bothered to turn up for the meeting were very much in favour of moving.'

'Can you tell us how many people were at that meeting?'

'Four.'

'Four?'

'Yes, four.'

'How many residents did you have at the time of the meeting?'

'Seventy four.'

'So the decision was based on the attendance of four out of seventy four residents?'

'Yes. To be fair everyone was invited, the other seventy chose not to attend.'

'So a fair cross section of the home?' Kelly asked sarcastically.

'I would regard it as one hundred per cent of the residents who were bothered to enough to attend.'

Kelly looked at a flashing light on her desk. 'Clive, we have a caller who would like to speak to you. Are you happy to take that call?'

'Always happy to talk to people Kelly, you know that.'

'Hello caller, you're through to Clive Oneway,' Kelly said to the mic, 'What's your name and what's your question?'

Silence.

'Hello caller. You're through to Clive Oneway. What's your question?' Kelly said again.

'Hello?' said a frail elderly female voice.

'Hello. You're through to Clive Oneway.'

'It's Mary here. Can I speak to Mr Oneway?'

Oneway rolled his eyes. 'Hello Mary, Clive here how can I help you?'

'Mr Oneway, I was a resident at the Sun Setting Retirement Home and I was moved to the new home and no one told me I was being moved.'

'Are you sure Mary? The manager at the home told me that all the residents were told of the meeting.'

'Was it the day that Countdown was on?'

'Sorry?'

'Did the meeting happen the day that Countdown was on? A Wednesday I think.'

'I have no idea. I could check with the manager. Is that important?'

'Well we all watch Countdown, you know. It's not the same since Richard Whitely passed away, but we all still watch it. No one would go to a meeting if it clashed with Countdown.'

'But do you like the new home Mary? I understand it's very nice.'

'No, it's horrible, it's always cold and raining.'

'So Clive, how do you respond to Mary's complaint?' Kelly asked.

'Well Kelly, I find that Mary is quite typical of the type of people that we have to deal with. She is ungrateful and selfish, she has no concept of the work that goes on to provide her with a comfortable room and hot meals every day. It's only a very strong sense of public spirit that keeps me in this business.'

'That, and I imagine a £1.3 Million turn over from the residential homes that you own,' Kelly suggested.

'Kelly, dear. You have to understand that there is more to providing residential homes than just serving tomato soup and turning the radiators on when Countdown is on. My staff have to listen to countless war stories and pick peas off the floor.'

'Mary how would you respond to that?'

'Well, he's a bit of a bastard really isn't he?'

'I'm sorry for the language listeners, though I wouldn't necessary disagree with you Mary. Thank you for your call.'

'Can I just ask Mr Oneway another question?' She asked.

'Of course you can, but please, try to watch your language. What's your question?'

'Mr Oneway, when are you coming up to see us next? It's been ages since I saw you.'

'I think I'm due up in a couple of months. I'm sure we can find time to talk then. But if you have anything urgent to say you can contact me through the manager, Mr Wakefield.'

'Thank you Mr Oneway.' Mary said and ended the call.

Kelly looked at Oneway. 'I have to say that despite the obvious problems that Mary has with you Clive, she does seem keen to stay in touch with you.'

'I suppose so,' Oneway said, 'but she is my mother.'

Alan leaned against the wall, staring out of the window. 'They're not here yet.'

'Will you please sit down and calm down.' Rosie said to her increasingly agitated boyfriend.

'It's nearly 10 o'clock, why aren't they here? Maybe they've lost interest.'

'They'll be here. There's no chance of Amy missing this is there?' Rosie tried to reassure him.

'I suppose not.' Alan conceded, and dropped down onto the sofa alongside Rosie.

'Are you nervous?'

'I just want to get on with it,' he said, 'too much hanging around.'

Rosie stood up and left the room. Alan sat back in the soft cushions and went over the plan again. Had he forgotten anything? Did everyone know what they were doing? Why was he in charge? Where was Frankie? Alan hadn't seen him since the previous evening. Now, when he wanted him here he was missing. Probably somewhere in ghost limbo or wherever it is dead people go on their day off, he thought.

'What do you think, black boots or white trainers?'

Alan looked up. Rosie was standing in front of him holding a white trainer in her left hand and a black boot in her right hand.

'The trainers are better for driving in, but they are white so they stand out a bit. The boots are black and will go with what I'm wearing, but they're not very good for driving in,' she explained.

Alan stared at her. In the event that he didn't plummet to his death from the loft of a condemned Chapel in approximately two hours, he would probably look back and find this moment funny. As it was, at this precise moment he was suffering a sense of humour failure.

'The trainers. You can drive in them and you're not actually getting out of the car,' he said, trying to sound calm.

'Right OK.' Rosie said and left the room.

Shaking his head, Alan sat back in the sofa just as the door-bell rang. He leapt out of the sofa and headed into the hall just as Rosie opened the door, letting Amy and James in. Both were carrying large cardboard boxes.

'Where do you want these?' James asked.

'Kitchen table,' Alan said, adding 'You guys OK?'

'Just want to get on with it.' James grinned.

'Amy?' Alan said, 'You OK?'

'I'm fine Alan,' she said, 'to be honest, I'm quite looking forward to it.'

Alan looked at James, shrugged, and followed them through to the kitchen. There were four cardboard boxes on the table. Rosie, James and Amy stood around the table looking into them. Amy was dressed all in black, looking very much the image of a cat burglar, while James was dressed in patterned green army fatigues.

'Why are you dressed like that?' Alan asked him.

'Camouflage,' he replied. 'You said that we should dress so as not to stand out.'

Alan mentally recalculated their odds of survival down to zero. 'Yes, if we were in the jungle,' Alan snapped. 'We're going to a 1980s Comprehensive School. I meant dark clothes like this...' he gestured to his black jeans and sweat shirt.

'We're going through the woods. This is camouflage for the woods,' James explained, posing as though for a camera.

'And then we're going into a school. Did you bring a school uniform to change into?'

'Alan, will you please calm down,' Rosie said, putting her hand on his shoulder. 'I'm sorry James, he's getting a bit nervy.'

'It's OK,' James mumbled and turned back to the cardboard boxes.

Amy delved into one of the boxes. 'I have these,' she said, and dropped several rubber bats onto the table. 'Twenty in total. I got them from a joke shop. They were left over from last Halloween.'

Alan nodded his approval. 'Well done.'

'I'm surprised that they had any left,' Rosie said.

'Apparently fallen celebrities from the 1970s masks were the thing last year,' Amy explained, with a grimace.

'My shop didn't have any, but I did get these,' James said, removing several Pterodactyl models from another box.

'What!' Alan exclaimed, 'Are these?'

'Pterodactyls. I told you, the shop that I tried didn't have any bats but in the dark there isn't much difference between bats and pterodactyls.'

'Except that pterodactyls are three times as large. In any case it's supposed to be endangered species mate, not extinct ones. I don't think that the cast of Jurassic Park are going to be much help.' Alan felt his mood deteriorating again.

'Put them at the back of the loft. In the dark no one will tell the difference,' a voice said from behind Alan. A quick glance over his shoulder told him that Frankie was back, and he felt oddly reassured.

'They can go at the back of the loft. In the dark I suppose they could be mistaken for bats,' Alan conceded.

Frankie looked around the table. 'Which one of you is delivering the Milk Tray?' he asked.

Under normal circumstances, Alan would have liked nothing better than to discuss the ridiculous TV commercials of his youth, and the logistics of delivering chocolates to the love of your life by breaking in to her house. However this was not one of those days.

'In this box we have some more bats,' Rosie knocked on the side of another of the boxes.

'And in this one,' Alan reached into the remaining cardboard box and took out what appeared to be a bird house, 'we have bat boxes. There's another seven in there.'

James reached out and picked it up, weighing it in his hand. 'They're quite solid aren't they? The bats should be secure in them.'

Rosie scratched her chin thoughtfully. 'So the live bats go into the bat boxes. What about the fake bats? How are you going to get them to sit on the rafters? They won't grip on,' she said before adding, 'they're fake.'

'Duct Tape.' James said, taking three rolls out of the large pocket of his camouflage jacket and placing them on the table. 'That should do the trick.'

'Duck Tape? 'Rosie repeated, 'Will that work on bats?' she asked.

Frankie put his hand on Alan's shoulder. 'Son, you're surrounded by idiots.'

Alan groaned inwardly and found himself agreeing with his ghostly friend.

'Where's Sarah?' Amy asked.

'She's already at the theatre. I'm going to call once we're on our way. She'll have the door open,' Alan said while checking his watch.

'Its 10.15,' he said. 'Time to get moving.'

'I'll just use your toilet,' Amy said. 'I don't want to get caught short,' and moved towards the hall.

'Good Idea, I'll come with you.' Rosie said, following Amy out of the door.

'Think I'll use it as well,' James said. 'I'm not sure I can remember where they are in the school if I need them,' and followed the two women.

Alan turned to Frankie, 'Do you need to use the toilet too?' he asked.

'Think I'll pass. Haven't had the need since I started this whole haunting thing. Not quite sure what will happen if I try and go.'

'Let's put off that unpleasant exercise until we get tonight's little adventure out of the way shall we?'

Frankie leaned back against the wall and looked up at the ceiling. 'Reminds me of the war. The wait before a mission.'

'The tension?'

'No, the visits to the toilet,' Frankie smiled, clearly enjoying his memories. 'Word of advice; never follow a paratrooper into the toilet when he's waiting to go on a mission. Not unless you have your gas mask.'

Alan smiled. 'Sounds like following James into the toilet.'

Both men fell into silence, different thoughts running through their heads. Frankie's taking him back seventy years while Alan's took him forward seventy minutes.

'Right, that's me done,' James said as he came back into the room. 'Glad I went actually, feeling a lot better now.'

'Thank you James,' Alan said, wrinkling his nose. 'Can we make a move now?'

James picked up one of the boxes from the table.

'Where are the girls?' Alan asked. 'They should have been back by now.'

'They're in your bedroom, talking.'

'Oh, for god's sake…' Alan muttered and set off for the bedroom. As he approached he heard Rosie's voice.

339

'Alan thinks the trainers, as they're easier to drive in. But the boots really go with the jeans.'

Walking in the bedroom, he could see Rosie with a white trainer in her left hand and a black boot in her right hand.

'It's difficult,' Amy said. 'If it were me I'd go with the boots.'

'Can we PLEASE get a move on?' Alan pleaded with them.

Both Rosie and Amy looked at him as if he'd just burst into the women's shower room and asked for help jump starting his car.

'Give us a couple of minutes will you?' Rosie said. 'We're just sorting something out.'

Alan turned and left the bedroom. He was used to being ignored in favour of shoes.

'Right let's get these boxes down to the car,' he said as he stormed back into the kitchen.

Sensing Alan's mood, James silently picked up two of the boxes and made his way towards the front door.

*

Alan, James and Amy stood on the pavement alongside Rosie's car. Rosie stood on the other side of the car by the driver's door, wearing a pair of black trainers. Alan had noticed the change of footwear but had wisely kept silent on the subject.

'Why can't we use my car?' Rosie said indignantly.

'It's a sports coupe,' James pointed out. 'We won't all fit in. Certainly not with all the boxes.'

Rosie walked round to the back of the car and opened the boot. 'Look, it has a boot. We can put the boxes in there.'

Alan took one of the boxes and put it in the boot. Unfortunately the box was clearly too big for the boot to close properly.

'Ahh...' Rosie said, understanding.

'Yes, ahh,' Alan replied.

'It was your plan,' Rosie said helpfully. 'What now?'

'We'll use our car,' Amy offered. 'It's bigger.'

They all looked across at the brightly coloured SUV parked on the other side of the road.

'We're supposed to be discreet. You can't get any less discreet than a pink tank.' Alan pointed out.

'It's Cerise!' Amy said firmly.

'Nice colour,' Rosie said. 'Shall we put the boxes in the boot?'

Not waiting for an answer, Alan and James picked up the boxes and placed them safely in the boot of the SUV.

Alan and Rosie climbed into the back of the car while Amy and James argued outside over whose turn it was to drive. Frankie sat between Alan and Rosie, causing Rosie to comment on how cold it was in the back.

James climbed into the driver's seat, having clearly won the argument. 'OK, time to move out,' he announced, starting the engine. 'No standing on the upstairs deck and no distracting the driver when the bus is in motion.'

Alan was just about to respond to James' announcement when Rosie cried out, 'Stop. I've forgotten something.'

Alan looked across at her. 'What?'

'Wait a second,' she said and got out of the car. They watched her run back to the flat and up the path.

'What's she forgotten?' Amy asked, turning round to Alan.

'I've no idea,' he replied. 'But if she changes shoes again I'll hang her up with the bats.'

Rosie opened the door and climbed back into the SUV. Alan peeked down at her feet. Mercifully, she was still wearing the black trainers.

'OK, we can go now,' she said.

'What was that about?' Alan asked.

'I'd forgotten to record Room 101.'

Amy turned round again. 'I love that show.'

Alan looked at Frankie who simply shook his head.

*

The late hour meant the traffic was light, and the journey took a little over thirty minutes. Everyone tried making small talk, but nerves ultimately got the better of them and they slipped back into silence.

'Is this the first time that you've been back to your old school?' Frankie asked.

Alan had been looking out of the window, but turned to answer Frankie's question in such a way that it wouldn't appear that he was talking to himself.

'I haven't been back to The Mount since I left all those years ago.'

'Me neither.' James said.

'Didn't you ever have a reunion?' Amy asked.

'It was never worth it. Most of the kids are either in prison or dead,' Alan said. 'Come to think of it, most of the teachers are either in prison or dead,' he added

'In fact, one of the teachers is in prison because he killed one of the pupils,' James added.

'Christ. Really?' Rosie exclaimed, looking at Alan for clarification.

'Oh yeah. Mr Clarke went crazy with a T- square. Bludgeoned a fifth year to death,' Alan explained.

'Best Harvest Festival we ever had...' James added, smiling at the memory.

Amy looked at her husband. 'Are you winding us up?' she asked.

'Of course not.' James said indignantly. 'Tell them Alan.'

'It's true,' Alan insisted. 'Would we wind you up over something like that?'

Alan relaxed in his seat, staring at the back of James' head, which was moving gently up and down as he silently laughed at the memory of the Harvest Festival Massacre.

*

James slowed the SUV as he approached the woods. On his left was a grass verge, and a further ten metres beyond the verge the tree line began.

'There's a track up here on the left,' he said to no one in particular.

Frankie looked at the woods. 'Nice and dark. That'll help.'

James saw the track he wanted and slowly turned off the road, the SUV bumping over the rutted surface. 'Four wheel drive,' he said proudly. 'This is what it's made for.'

'What was it made pink for? Travelling round the countryside with a talking dog catching caretakers in masks?' Frankie asked, innocently. Alan stifled a giggle.

The track opened out into a clearing. James parked on the edge, in the shelter of the trees and out of the moonlight.

Alan opened his door and got out, followed by Frankie. He went round to the boot and took out the cardboard box containing the bat boxes. 'We'll need these and our backpacks. Everything else can wait until we get the theatre.'

James, Amy and Rosie stood in the clearing. They looked across at Alan as he walked round the SUV carrying the box.

'What do you think?' Amy said looking straight ahead.

They were staring at a fence made of corrugated sheet metal. It stretched both left and right from where they stood, curving with the tree line.

'It must wrap around the perimeter of the school site,' Alan said.

Amy and James walked up to the fence.

'It's just over six feet. Look,' James said as he stood on tip toes, his head just clearing the top of the fence.

'Can you see anything?' Alan asked.

'No, not a thing.' James answered, looking round.

'I thought you could see over,' Amy said.

'Yes, I can. But it's dark. Can't see a thing,' James replied, surprised that they hadn't realised the obvious.

'Still think we can climb over?' asked Rosie.

'Shouldn't be a problem.' James said and walked over to the SUV.

Everyone looked at each other for guidance while James started rummaging through the boot, occasionally swearing as he searched.

'That's normal when he's looking for something,' Amy said. 'Just ignore him.'

Alan stood with his hands in his pockets, Frankie standing alongside began to complain. 'You knew you had to climb over the fence. Surely you brought something with you?'

Alan smiled at him. 'Have faith.'

'Pardon?' said Rosie.

'I said have faith. In James. He knows what he's doing...sometimes.'

James appeared in front them, carrying something under his arm. 'Here we go. One roll up ladder. Available in all good mountaineering shops.'

'Told you.' Alan smiled at Rosie and followed James over to the fence.

'Right,' said James, 'all we have to do is fix the top of the ladder to the top of the   fence and we climb over. Simples.'

James let the ladder unroll, picking up the end nearest him and using two hooks, curved it over the top of the fence.

'The mountains must have shrunk since my day,' Frankie said. 'That rope ladder can only be eight feet long.'

Ignoring Frankie, Alan looked around. 'Where are the girls?' he asked.

'We're over here.' He heard Rosie call out. 'There's a loose bit of fence over here. We can probably pull it away and get through the gap.'

'No need,' Alan pointed to where James was standing. 'We have our very own ladder here,' he stepped back to show off James's handiwork.

'Who's going over first?' Amy asked.

'Let's draw lots,' said James.

'You're going over first, mate,' Alan laughed at James. 'If you've bought a cheap one from the market you should be the one to test it. And if it breaks, we'll know you got sold a pup.'

'Happy to,' James grinned in return. 'The lady in the shop said that they have never had anyone come back and complain that one of these babies had ever let them down.'

'I suppose that would be quite difficult when you're laying at the bottom of a ravine smashed into little pieces.' Frankie pointed out.

Alan saw the logic in Frankie's argument, but thought it best not to mention this to James until they had successfully traversed the fence. 'Right,' he said. 'Rosie...in the car. Call me if the police or anyone turns up and you have to leave. Otherwise just wait.'

'And pray.' Frankie added.

James passed Rosie the key. 'The radio is tuned to Radio 1, if you want something to listen to while you're waiting.'

'Keep it quiet though,' Alan said. 'You don't want to draw attention to yourself.'

'I'm sitting in a pink car in the middle of the woods in the middle of the night,' Rosie frowned. 'I think it's too late to worry about that.'

Rosie walked over to the SUV and climbed into the driver's seat. Once inside she gave the others a wave and settled in for the wait.

'Time for us to go over now,' Amy said, nervously.

Alan picked up the cardboard box. 'You go over and I'll pass this to you,' he said to James.

James stood in front of the fence and gave the ladder a tug. 'That feels OK,' he said. 'Shall I go now?'

'Yes, now please,' Alan said.

'So now then?' James repeated.

'Get over that fence you wuss,' Amy hissed, giving him a push in the back at the same time.

James took a grip on both sides of the ladder and began the climb. With each step up he gained more confidence and with a few seconds he had reached the top. He looked out over the school.

'Can you see anything?' Alan asked from below.

'No, too dark,' he replied, 'I'll just ...'

James never got a chance to finish the sentence. As a result of a combination of his weight, and falling standards in the construction industry, the corrugated fence panel that James was climbing broke away from its adjacent panels and fell forward. The panel hit the ground with James clinging to the top, making a whooshing sound as it pushed the air out from underneath it.

Alan and Amy looked at each other and walked through the gap that the fallen panel had created. Alan stopped as he walked past the prone figure of James. 'Laying down on the job again, Cook!'

On the other side of the site to where James was successfully breaking into the school by falling through a metal fence, Roy and Donald sat in their Portakabin and prepared for another night at work.

'Here you are Donald,' Roy said as he placed a cup of tea in front of his colleague.

'Thank you,' Donald replied. 'Any biscuits on the go?'

Roy walked back over to the side of the Portakabin which had been designated the kitchen - by virtue of it having a plug socket and a table to rest a kettle on – and collected a packet of biscuits, passing them to Donald.

'Hobnobs,' he said.

'That's grand, thank you,' Donald said excitedly and set about trying to open the packet.

Roy and Donald were the security presence that Omega Security provided as part of their contract with Oneway Property Services. They ensured that from 8pm to 8am seven days a week, the Buggerly Mount School site was safe from thieves, kids looking for a place to party and what they both referred to as "wrong uns."

Like several of Omega Securities, operatives both Roy and Donald had been police officers before retiring. Unlike Omega Securities other retired police officers, they had retired some twenty five years earlier, and were both in their late seventies. Employed as part of an initiative that facilitated older people back in to the work force, Roy and Donald were trusted with the Buggerly Mount School site on the reasonable assumption that the place was condemned, had nothing worth stealing, and that only an idiot would try to break in.

Donald sat at the table studying a crossword, a cup of tea with two Hobnobs resting on the saucer to his right. 'Mmm,' he muttered, while scratching his head with a pen.

'Tricky one?' asked Roy as he poured tea from his saucer back into his cup.

'Three letters...' Donald said. 'To wink briefly.'

Roy closed his eyes and leaned back into his chair, apparently deep in thought.

'Fluttered?' Roy said his eyes springing open.

'Three letters!' Donald repeated.

'Oh, you never said.'

Donald ignored him and went back to the crossword.

Finishing his tea, Roy looked across at his colleague. 'Looks like another quiet one,' he said.

Donald put his pen down, looking up from the crossword. 'Roy,' he said patiently, 'we've been working here for three weeks and out of those twenty one nights how many would you say have been eventful?'

Roy closed his eyes, clearly deep in thought. 'Well,' he said opening his eyes. 'There was that night that we ran out of milk, so I'd say that we've probably had twenty quiet nights.'

Donald dunked his biscuit in his tea and watched as half of it dropped into his cup.

'So you'd have to agree that it is most likely that tonight will be a quiet one?' he said, whilst dredging the bottom of his cup with a tea spoon.

'Let's not get complacent. It only takes a minute for us to lose concentration and they're in!' Roy swept his arm across the room to emphasise the point.

Donald looked up from his dredging efforts. 'The only things worth stealing on this site are in here,' he said, waving his arm around the portakabin. And we'd have to be having a massive loss of concentration not to notice someone coming in here and filling a bag marked Swag with all the biscuits from our tin.'

Roy chuckled. 'It's that thinking that cost you the chance of making DCI.'

Donald had given up dredging his tea and was now spooning biscuit sediment into his mouth. 'Nearly time for the midnight inspection,' he said, changing the subject.

Roy looked up at the clock, which he thought was the only thing worth stealing in the portakabin. 'Plenty of time yet,' he replied, still in the mood for a chat. 'I looked up the history of this school on the internet, it was very interesting.'

Pushing his tea to one side, Donald went back to his crossword. He was still baffled by the clue "to wink briefly," he looked over at his colleague. 'What's interesting about it?' he asked.

'It was opened in 1973 by the Secretary of State for education at the time. You'll never guess who. Only Margaret bloody Thatcher!' Roy said, not giving Donald the option to guess at all.

'Nothing unusual about that. I suppose opening schools would have been one of her jobs.'

'There should have been a plaque,' Roy said. 'You know, those ones that say such and such opened this building on whatever date.'

'So, what about it?' Donald asked.

'Well I reckon it would be worth something now. That would be a reason to break in,' Roy explained.

'Why it would be worth anything?'

'Thatcher memorabilia goes for quite a high sum on the internet, there's dealers and everything!'

Donald shook his head. This conversation was becoming painful. 'If there had been a plaque, it would have been taken away when the school closed. The place was gutted and nothing was left behind.'

'I'll have a look round when I do the inspection.' Roy looked up at the clock. 'It'll be time soon.'

Donald looked back at his crossword, the outstanding clue jumping out of the page at him. His concentration was broken by a grumbling sound from under the table followed by the smell of rotting cabbage.

'Cliff!' Donald winced at the smell.

Roy looked under the table, a couple of old rheumy eyes stared back at him. 'I think it's time for Cliff's walk,' he said, wafting the air in front of his nose.

Donald stood up and opened the door. 'That's a bad one,' he admitted, fanning the door.

Roy stood and fixed a lead to Cliff's collar, leading the limping dog through the door. Donald stood aside, allowing them past and out through the portakabin.

Cliff was an old mongrel dog. No one was quite sure how old he was. Roy, who had been a police dog handler, couldn't remember if Cliff was there before he started. There was some suggestion that Cliff's grandfather was one of the two dogs that Noah had taken onto the ark.

Parked immediately outside the Portakabin was a Mobility scooter. Roy picked up Cliff and put him on the platform behind the seat. Appreciative that their employees were no longer in the prime of life, Omega Security had presented their more experienced guards with a mobility scooter to assist them with their inspections. The Interceptor MK 2 was the security specific mobility scooter which had been adapted to meet the needs of the elderly security guard. It had LED intruder beam headlights, an additional cup holder, and an improved top speed of 8mph.

Roy switched the engine on and pulled slowly away. Cliff was sitting on the rear platform, one eye open. The improved headlight illuminated the way and Roy soon had the interceptor up to 5mph. He liked to hold a couple of mph back, in case of emergencies, although more importantly, Cliff had been known to slide off his platform at higher speeds.

Donald walked alongside the Interceptor as it trundled between the two blocks of the derelict school, pausing occasionally to allow it to catch him up.

'If there was a plaque, it would be at the school entrance,' Roy said.

'We would have seen it by now,' Donald replied, pointing his own torch over the cracked window panes. 'We walk past the entrance every night.'

'It won't do any harm to have proper look though, will it?' Roy asked.

'OK, we'll have a look.' Donald conceded, pausing to allow the interceptor to catch him up again.

*

Amy followed her husband and Alan as they moved silently along the edge of the playground. They were keeping in the shadows and out of the moonlight. Once they reached the buildings, they moved forward, keeping low under the windows. Approaching the corner of the building, Alan stopped and turned to James.

'We cross the covered way and follow the outside of B Block all the way round,' he whispered.

'Let's go through the block, the doors are open,' James replied, pointing across the covered way. 'We can work our way through the block. The chapel is on the other side.'

Amy squeezed up behind them. 'Come on,' she whispered. 'We're a bit exposed here.'

'What do you think?' James asked, looking at Alan.

'Go for it,' he answered, and they set off across the covered way. Alan slipped through the door, followed by Amy and a few seconds later James followed them in.

'You're coming to the gym with me!' Amy grinned at James as he leaned against the wall getting his breath back.

Alan looked down the dark corridor.

'Bring back memories?' Amy asked, standing at his shoulder.

'Too many to talk about now,' he said and they moved off down the corridor.

Eighteen years after they had left, Alan and James had finally returned to Buggerly Mount.

*

Roy stopped the Interceptor underneath the covered way between the two blocks. He pointed at the double doors leading to Block 2. 'If there's a plaque, it will be in there. That was generally regarded as the main school entrance.'

'Are you sure?' Donald asked. 'Surely the main entrance would be in Block 1.'

Roy shook his head, causing the Interceptor to rock slowly from side to side.

'They put the admin offices in Block 2, so that was considered the main entrance.'

Donald walked over to the entrance and shone his torch through the cracked glass doors. 'I can't see anything, either inside or out here by the doors.'

'We'll have a look inside,' Roy said, moving the Interceptor up to the doors. 'I don't think they're locked,' he added, giving them a push with his front wheel. The doors slowly opened, scraping on the ground beneath them.

Donald walked into the school and pointed his torch at the walls, the beam highlighting the chipped paint work, but not revealing a plaque, or any sign a plaque had ever been there. 'Still nothing,' he said.

Roy sighed. 'We've got to do the inspection so let's have a look round. Maybe they put it somewhere else, like in the staffroom.'

Donald moved to one side and waved Roy and the Interceptor through. 'Mad old fool,' he said under his breath as he followed his colleague down the corridor.

*

Alan gripped James's forearm tightly, stopping him in his tracks. 'Look!' he hissed.

James and Amy looked down to where Alan pointed. A beam of light was shining out of a class room some thirty feet ahead of them.

'Back!' James ordered, and they began moving quietly back the way they had come.

'In here.' Alan whispered, pushing open a set of double doors to his left. James followed Amy through, pausing to gently close the doors behind them.

Amy and Alan switched on their torches, illuminating their surroundings. Amy had been expecting a classroom. Instead she was surprised to be standing in a large hall with a stage at the far end. 'What is this place?' she asked, looking around.

'Drama Hall,' James said, switching on his own torch. 'Did you remember it was here, or was this just luck?' he asked Alan.

'Bit of both,' Alan confessed. 'It was only when we were outside that it came back to me.'

'In the nick of time,' Amy grinned. 'So what did you use this for?' she added, moving her torch beam all over the stage.

Alan looked at James and raised his eyebrows. 'Drama, mainly,' he said, 'the school had a drama hall and thought it would be a good idea to have drama classes in here. It was a bit big for Woodwork.'

Amy shook her head and walked over to the stage, shining her torch over the remainder of the hall. She could see Alan and James in whispered conversation on the other side of the hall.

'Is Frankie here?' James asked.

'I haven't seen him since we came through the fence. It's a pain because I was hoping that he would act as a scout and warn us of any potential trouble.'

James shook his head. 'That's the trouble with dead people, they're so unreliable.'

'What's this?' Amy called out from the stage.

Alan and James joined her on the stage as she pointed her torch at a small door to the side.

'That is the special secret stage door,' James said.

'It leads through to the class room on the other side of the hall,' Alan added.

'When the school put on plays, the kids would change in the class room and enter the stage through the special secret door,' James said, completing Amy's introduction to the Buggerly Mount drama hall.

'Can't we use it to get out of here without going down that corridor?' Amy asked.

Alan and James exchanged looks. 'Good thinking Mrs Cook,' James grinned at his wife and opened the small door.

*

'Everything looks OK.' Donald gave the doors a cursory glance. 'Just the north side to view and we can go back.'

'So a quiet one then. I thought so,' Roy answered. 'That gives us a bit more time to look for the plaque.'

'I'm not wandering around the school looking at the walls for some old plaque. I keep telling you, there is nothing of value here, there hasn't been for donkeys years.'

Roy opened his mouth to argue but Cliff chose that exact moment to bark. This was not a bark to indicate the presence of intruders, but a sign that he needed to move his bowels.

'OK Cliff, I'll take you outside,' Roy muttered, turning round to talk to the geriatric hound on the platform behind him. 'Donald, I'll take him outside onto the playground. I'll see you there.'

Donald watched as the Interceptor pulled away, reaching its maximum speed of 8mph it took a corner slightly too fast, and Cliff slid from the vehicle landing on the ground with a yelp before emitting a particularly noxious bowel movement.

'Sorry Cliff,' Roy gasped, while putting the flatulent dog back on his platform.

*

Alan, James and Amy froze. 'Did you hear that?' Amy asked.

'That was definitely a dog,' James replied.

Alan left the stage and crept over to the double doors. He pressed his ear against them, listening for any noise. He heard a yelp and a voice, though he couldn't make out what was being said. He jogged back to James and Amy who were still standing on the edge of the stage.

'Time to go,' he whispered. 'You're right. That was a dog and I heard a voice too. Probably a guard.'

'Exit stage door left?' James asked.

'Definitely!' Alan agreed, turning his torch on again and ducking down into the passage way.

The light from the three torches illuminated the dark tunnel, highlighting to Alan that it had not been used for quite some time.

'It's filthy. I've got cobwebs in my hair!' Amy whispered, brushing her hair.

359

'Sorry, if I'd known we were coming this way I would have got a cleaner in,' Alan whispered in response.

'Just get a move on,' she replied, crouching lower as she passed under a light fitting.

Alan stopped as he reached a door. Dropping to his knees, he placed his hand on the door knob and pushed. 'It won't open. It's stuck,' Alan hissed, pushing harder.

'What do you mean stuck?' James hissed in return.

'It won't open. It's stuck.'

James sighed. 'No one's used that door for years, it's probably warped in the frame. We'll never get through.'

Amy leaned across Alan, grabbed the door knob and pulled it. The door swung open. 'Just get through will you, you pair of idiots,' she said, giving Alan a push and followed him out of the passageway and into the classroom.

'It looks like all the others we've seen,' she said, brushing herself down and shaking spiders out of her hair.

'They were all gutted. There's nothing left.' Alan swept his arm across the room.

'Except this,' James replied emerging from the passage way carrying a slightly damp and dusty cardboard box which he then dumped onto the floor at his feet.

Alan looked at the box. 'That might be because it's a box of junk in a secret passage that hasn't seen the light of day in years.'

'Look, it's full of stuff,' James began rummaging through the assorted items, not in the least put off by Alan's lack of interest.

Alan turned away and joined Amy at the door of the classroom. Like every other room they had seen, it was stripped bare except for the cardboard box.

'How's it looking?' Alan asked Amy.

'Quiet,' she replied. 'The guards must be on the other side.'

'Let's get going then,' Alan ushered them forward.

'Hang on, take a look at this.'

Alan and Amy turned to see James holding what appeared to a flat square metal plate.

'Do you know what this is?' James asked.

'Looks like a flat metal plate. Bring it home and I'll give you your tea on it.'

'No, no. Look what it says on it,' he passed the plate to Alan.

'It says that on the 3rd September 1973, Buggerly Mount School was opened by the Secretary of State for Education and Science, Margaret Thatcher.' Alan read out loud.

'I never knew Margaret Thatcher opened our school,' James said.

'It's certainly a surprise,' Amy replied.

'Why's that?' Alan asked.

'Because once she became Prime Minister she closed everything down!' Amy grinned, before taking the plaque from Alan and dumping it back in the box

'Now can we go and find some bats?'

*

Amy looked up at the chapel, hands on hips. Like many places of worship, the stone structure managed to look imposing yet welcoming at the same time. It must be at least seventy feet high, and almost as long, Amy thought. The building was fringed by columns that reached up to form turrets, with two further turreted columns flanking the huge wooden doors. Arched windows gave the building an almost gothic feel.

'Blimey, what an amazing building,' she gasped. 'James, I can't believe this was part of your school. You always said it was a bit of a tip. But this...' she said, moving her arm from left to right '...is just amazing. It's no wonder so many people turned to religion.'

'To be fair, these doors did have at least one religious moment,' James said, turning towards his wife. 'Alan, do you remember that time Delroy got nailed to these doors after metalwork class?'

Alan laughed. 'Christ, yeah, I remember that.'

'Hang on,' Amy interrupted, someone got nailed to the chapel doors? Like...like a *crucifixion?'*

'Yes...no, well, sort of. Only his clothes were nailed to the doors. Of course, Delroy was still in them at the time. So he just kind of, well, hung there.'

'It took a team of firemen to get him down,' Alan giggled.

'What on earth would possess someone to nail a child to a door?' Amy asked incredulously.

'I think Delroy passed comment on the state of Jimmy's nunchucks,' James said. 'Personally, I thought they looked rather good. But even if I didn't, I wasn't going to tell Jimmy that. The kid was crazy.'

'Yeah,' Alan agreed, 'Do you remember when he...'

'Look, can we just get on with this?' Amy hissed. 'My backpack isn't getting any lighter, but the bloody sky will be soon if you two idiots don't stop reminiscing about your bloody school days.'

'She has a point, son,' Frankie added, suddenly appearing next to Alan.

'OK, then, let's get cracking. Did anyone remember to bring the key?' Alan asked, pushing on the doors, before turning round to James and Amy. 'Only it might be difficult without it.'

Amy stared at Alan open mouthed, 'Oh, for Christ's sake, are you seriously telling me we didn't think about how to open the chapel door? I give up.'

'Sorry Ames, he's only pulling your leg. The key is usually kept under a plant pot,' James said, edging towards the large potted plant situated by the right hand side of the chapel doors.

'You've got to be kidding me...' huffed Amy, becoming increasingly agitated. She moved towards the identical potted plant situated to the left of the chapel doors and only then looked up into Alan's smiling face as he gently pushed the doors open.

'The doors were never locked when it was in use, I didn't think for a minute the owners had the intelligence to lock them now. Seems I was right. I guess the custodian thinks even the local hooligans would have more sense than to rob a chapel.'

'Or nick some bats,' James added. 'Ladies first,' he said, beckoning his wife toward the open doors.

'Idiots.' Amy huffed again as she entered into darkness. Turning on her mini headlight torch she looked around the inside of the building. 'Wow,' she said, 'this place is incredible.'

Amy's headlight cast meagre light on rows of wooden benches set along the sides of the chapel. Along the walls, imposing statues of Jesus and, Amy assumed, various Saints stood benignly, sunken within sculpted arches as if looking down upon those who would be seated. Walking down the aisle, Amy turned from the walls to look straight ahead where several small steps led up to an altar, pulpit, and beyond, a large cross.

'Just, beautiful,' she said looking up towards the ceiling. 'I take it the bats are up there somewhere? How are we going to find them?'

'I know roughly where they are,' Alan said, walking towards where Amy now stood. 'There's a set of stairs that lead to the first floor, and off of that a small attic space. I bunked off a few times in there,' he smiled, pointing upwards. 'The last place anyone would look.'

'Especially the school chaplain. He spent most of his time making excuses to get into the changing rooms,' James added. 'We'd better get moving, or else Rosie will be wondering where we are.'

'Oh, don't worry about her, she's probably having a great time relaxing and listening to music,' Alan said as he moved off towards the stairs, followed by James and Amy. Frankie was nowhere to be seen. Probably not a bad thing, Alan thought. The place is spooky enough in the dark as it is, without having a real ghost groaning on about his arthritic hip.

Reaching the top of the stairs, Alan said in a hushed voice, 'This way,' as he led his friends past more seats to their right towards another, smaller set of stairs which led up to a door. He thought momentarily of doing the key joke again, but acknowledged he had just got lucky with the chapel doors. Mentally keeping his fingers firmly crossed, he turned the door handle. The door was stiff, but unlocked. It opened slowly with a discerning creak that made Alan think of every Hammer Horror film he'd ever seen. Putting that to the back of his mind, he walked inside.

The attic space hadn't changed much since his school days. OK, it was a lot more dusty and smelled like a toilet in an old people's home, but in essence, it felt exactly the same. Except for the ghost standing in front of him looking up at the rafters.

'I can see a few things moving up there, but I can't see if they are bats,' Frankie said, peering intently at the rafters six feet above him.

'Can you see anything?' asked Amy, who, along with James had followed Alan into the room.

'I'm not sure. I think so. There's movement, for sure.' The torches of the three friends bobbed along the attic ceiling, looking for evidence of movement. 'I need a closer look,' Alan said. 'We might have to turn off our torches so as not to scare them.'

'Then how the bloody hell are we going to see anything?' asked Amy.

'It's a full moon. There's probably enough moonlight coming in through those,' Frankie suggested, motioning to the windows.

'I think there should be enough moonlight coming through the windows,' Alan said triumphantly.

'Mate, that's brilliant,' said James. 'Think of that all on your own, did you?'

'Well, there's no one else here, is there?' Alan grinned, carefully not looking towards Frankie, who was shaking his head.

The friends turned off their torches, momentarily leaving them in complete darkness. After a few seconds, their eyes adjusted to the gloom, assisted by the light of the moon seeping through the thin arched windows.

'That's better,' Amy said. 'Great idea, Alan.'

'Oh, I'm full of great ideas, Amy,' Alan said.

'You're full of something, son,' added Frankie, for Alan's ears alone.

Ignoring the ghostly abuse, Alan peered again at the rafters. Sure enough there was some movement. 'I can see movement,' he said. 'OK, guys, let's get prepared. James, get the boxes ready. Amy, can you take the towels out of the backpacks?'

James and Amy did as they were told. 'What are these?' said Amy, taking out a pair of rubber pterodactyls. 'We won't need these until we get to the theatre.'

'I put them in just in case,' James said.

'Just in case what?'

366

'Just in case we needed them. Obviously.'

Amy stared at her husband. Sometimes she wondered whether James was the full ticket. Other times she knew he wasn't.

'Can we stop arguing and get on with it?' Alan said as he pulled two small tables together to make a platform. He climbed slowly on to the uneven tables, a combination of his weight and poor carpentry made the structure wobble as he tried to get some balance.

Standing up to his full height, Alan's head almost reached the rafters. He could clearly see movement all around him, and for a moment thought of a science fiction film he had seen where aliens were crawling along the walls.

Ignoring his overly active imagination, Alan leaned close to where the movement was coming from. Sure enough there were bats. Lots of bats. Perhaps thirty or so. And they clearly were not happy at having an intruder in their house.

'What can you see?' whispered James.

'Why are you whispering?' asked Amy.

'Don't bats see by hearing?' whispered James again.

'See by hearing? I take it you mean echo location,' said Amy, shaking her head.

'That's what I said, echo location.' James grinned.

Alan looked down at his bickering best friends. 'Can you two stop bickering and pass me up some of the towels?'

Amy placed two small towels into Alan's hands. 'Is that enough, do you think?'

'Thanks,' he said, taking the towels. 'I'm going to have to play it by ear.'

'Like a bat, then,' said James, helpfully.

'You're not helping, James,' Amy admonished her husband.

'What?' James laughed, opening his arms wide in a gesture of mock confusion.

Ignoring his friends once again, Alan opened one of the small towels and gingerly approached the mass of increasingly agitated bats, all the while trying to maintain his balance on the uneven tables. OK, he thought to himself, how do I do this? He really didn't want to hurt any of the creatures, but he knew he had no choice but to take some of them from their home. What if I separate families? Do bats care about such things he wondered? Aside from half an hour's worth of internet browsing, Alan's only knowledge of bats came from watching Batman films. Unsurprisingly, he could think of nothing in those films which helped him now. However, thinking of Batman led Alan to think of Cat Woman. He tried to shake the image of Halle Berry in a PVC outfit before he embarrassed himself. I don't want to give the bats anywhere else to hang from, he thought to himself, and tried focussing on the task in front of him.

'What are you waiting for?' Amy said.

'I don't know which ones to get,' Alan whispered, not wanting to agitate the bats any further. 'I could end up taking babies from their mothers.'

'Oh God, I hadn't thought of that. James, we can't break up families. That's just cruel. We can't do this,' Amy said, visibly upset.

'Mate,' James whispered up to Alan. 'How many are there?'

'I dunno, about twenty or thirty I guess, why?'

'I think we might have to take them all.'

'What? There's no way I am going to be able to catch them all.'

'It's all or nothing,' Amy said, now almost in tears. 'We can't be taking children from their parents.'

Frankie, who had decided to take a back seat in the proceedings, began humming to himself. The noise seemed to agitate the bats, which did nothing for Alan's disposition, but it did give him an idea.

'Hang on, guys, I think I have an idea,' Alan said, looking at Frankie. 'What I need is a distraction. No, a diversion. I need some kind of sound that will make the bats fly in a certain direction,' he added, hoping Frankie would understand his meaning. Unfortunately, Frankie seemed to be in his own little world, humming, nodding his head and tapping his feet to his own imaginary rhythm.

'What sort of distraction?' Amy whispered.

One that I can't tell you about, Alan thought to himself. To James he said; 'Mate, can you walk about five steps to your left and wave your warms about?'

'What good is that going to do? I thought we needed noise?' Asked Amy.

'James, trust me, just do it...' Alan said, nodding sideways to where Frankie stood, still oblivious to current events.

'Ah, I understand,' James winked at his friend and crab walked the suggested distance. 'This OK?' he asked.

'Perfect. Now, wave your arms.'

James did as he was told, feeling slightly stupid under Amy's puzzled gaze. 'Is it working?' he asked.

'No, he's...sorry, *they're* not paying any attention. Perhaps if you turn round..?'

'Will do.' James turned his back to Alan and faced the wall, waving his arms up and down. 'Any luck?'

'No. Nothing. Try coughing.'

James coughed once quietly, then again several more times, disguising Frankie's name in between coughs.

'What's this idiot doing?' Frankie said, looking past James to where Alan was perched precariously on two tables.

'OK, James,' Alan said, more for Frankie's benefit than James's, 'What I need is a little help. I'm going to start picking the bats up, but there may be one or two left over that I'll need your help with.'

'No problem,' Frankie and James said in unison.

This isn't going to end well, Alan thought to himself. Turning back to the bat infested rafters, Alan reached out and gently smothered the nearest bat with a towel. 'Sorry little fella. I'm not going to hurt you. You're going to a nice new place where...'

Alan didn't have a chance to finish the sentence as his smothering of the bat caused the remaining bats to jitter and fly between beams.

370

'Fuck sake,' Alan hissed, as several bats flew around his head. Taking a deep breath to steel himself, Alan focused on the bat contained within the towel. He turned and bent down, presenting the towel to James. 'Here you go. Open the towel and place the bat slowly and gently into the box. Then close the lid.'

James took the towel from his friend and gently placed the bat into the box, closing the small door to keep the creature trapped inside. 'OK, good start. Let's do this.'

Alan turned and faced the rafters once more. Some of the bats had started to flit about the roof, but Alan ignored them and selected a bat that had not moved. One at a time, he thought to himself, as again he enveloped a bat with a towel.

'You're doing a fine job, there, son.' Frankie said.

'Thanks. But I need to focus.'

'What did you say?' asked Amy.

'Nothing. I just need to focus,' Alan replied, making a mental note to be careful in responding to Frankie.

The friends soon got in to a rhythm; Alan would surround a perched bat with a towel, then give them in turn to James and Amy, who would gently place them into the boxes.

'Do we have enough boxes?' Amy asked. 'I don't want to leave any behind.'

'I reckon we'll be fine,' Alan replied as he reached up and picked another bat from the wooden beam. 'There's not many left,' he said, handing another bat engulfed towel to James.

James took the towel but as he did so, the bat began to wriggle free, flying away in panic.

'Shit,' James hissed. 'Little sod got away.'

'Christ sake James, be more careful,' Amy said to her husband.

Amy was prevented from saying anything further as the freed bat seemed to galvanise its friends still in the rafters. The remaining bats began to fly around the roof, unwilling to participate any further in this bizarre human game.

'James, hand me a towel,' said Alan, reaching his hand down to his friend.

James however was more interested in the frenzied activity on the ceiling and wasn't paying full attention to Alan's request. He picked up the nearest object and placed it in his friends' hand.

Alan looked down at the rubber pterodactyl, then back at his friend. 'What the fuck is this?'

'Sorry?' James replied. 'What is what?'

'This. It's a bloody plastic toy.'

Momentarily distracted by his friend's foolishness, Alan wobbled slightly on the tables. As he tried to regain his balance, several bats flew past his head. One momentarily catching itself in Alan's hair, causing him to shriek and wave the rubber pterodactyl at the flying creatures. Which only seemed to irritate them further.

'See, I told you they would come in handy,' said James smugly.

'Alan!' Amy shouted. 'Don't you dare hurt those bats.'

'I'm more worried about these bats hurting me!'

'Oh, for God's sake, you can be such a baby.'

'She has a point, there, son,' added Frankie.

'And you can fuck off as well!'

'Mate, don't talk to Amy like that. She's only trying to help,' James glowered at his friend.

'Thank you James,' Amy smiled at him.

'I wasn't talking to her...Oh, for Christ sake, let's just get on with it,' Alan said, reaching for a bat that was clearly exhausted from all the flying about. 'Here, James, take this one, but be careful this time.'

Alan stood looking into the darkened beams for any bats that had ceased flying. He moved towards where three bats hung close together and wrapped the nearest one in a towel. 'Frankie,' he whispered, 'I think I'm going to need your help with these last few.'

'We are helping,' Amy said.

'Sorry Amy, I was talking to myself,' Alan said, placing a towel around another bat.

'OK son. What do you need?' Frankie said, suddenly standing on the tables beside him.

'I need you to herd these last few bats into one place,' Alan whispered as quietly as he could, hoping Amy would not overhear.

'I'm not a sheepdog. I don't know that I can herd anything anywhere.'

'Can you at least give it a try?'

'I'll give it a go. Seeing as you were so nice to me before.'

'Sorry about that.'

Below them Amy turned to James. 'Is he talking to himself? Rosie mentioned she'd caught him talking to himself a couple of times after he banged his head.'

'I think he's just trying to work out how to get the last bats to settle down,' James replied, knowing that his friend was once again having a conversation he would never be part of.

'Well, I think he should go back to the hospital. He could have brain damage.'

James grinned 'Yeah, but how would we tell?'

Amy laughed. 'Fair point.'

Above them, something appeared to be happening.

'OK,' Frankie said, 'Let's try this,' and began singing the theme from the Batman TV show.

Despite himself, Alan couldn't help but chuckle. The remaining bats flew in zig zag patterns, clearly agitated by the ghostly wail. They can definitely hear it, Alan thought to himself, as Frankie repeated the tune a second time.

'I'm not sure it's working. Maybe I should try a different song. One they might have heard of. Perhaps they might like some Meatloaf,' and he began to bellow.

Perhaps it was the song. Perhaps it was because they were tired. Perhaps it was a combination of both, but Frankie's insane caterwauling seemed to have the desired effect, and the remaining bats settled back on the rafters.

'Look,' Amy pointed, 'They seem to be settling own again. Well done Alan.'

'Thank you,' he replied, handing her an exhausted bat swamped in a small towel. 'We're nearly done.'

'Thank Christ for that,' James said as he held out his hands waiting for his own little bat towel.

Alan covered the last bat in a towel and handed it to his friend. 'That's the lot, guys. It's time to get moving.'

Amy placed the towels and rubber pterodactyl back into her rucksack and picked up two of the boxes. Alan and James picked up the remaining boxes and made their way down the stairs. Letting Amy go on ahead James asked, 'What happened up there?'

'You wouldn't believe it if I told you.'

'Go on,' James urged.

'Well,' said Alan slowly. 'For a singer, Frankie makes a great comedian.'

'I heard that son,' Frankie laughed as they made their way out of the chapel.

Alan turned around to smile at Frankie, but he had disappeared.

Chapter 36

Rosie tapped another of the pre-set radio station buttons on the SUV's dash board. She went from a late night radio show which encouraged listeners to request songs which brought back dark memories to a non-stop country music extravaganza.

'For god's sake, isn't there anything worth listening to at this hour?' she said to no one in particular.

She looked at her mobile, there were no missed calls and no text messages. She chewed her lip, a habit she had developed as a child when anxious. Should she call? What if they were trying to keep quiet and avoiding being caught by guards? A ringing mobile would give them away.

Rosie sighed, feeling helpless, while on the radio a country and western singer was warbling on about fidelity.

Looking in the rear view mirror, she saw a car emerge into the clearing from the same single lane track they had used earlier that evening. It drove slowly, bumping over the uneven ground before coming to a stop on the other side of the clearing.

Rosie watched as the headlights blinked off. A man emerged from the vehicle and made his way over to her. The man looked to be in his late thirties and not particularly menacing. His mop of untidy brown hair giving Rosie more the impression of a lost child than a grown man. Rosie thought the man was unlikely to be a security guard, but, she thought, who else would be out here at this time of night?

Rosie had a cover story worked out in the event of being discovered by security guards. She had decided she would play the role of an upset girlfriend who had driven to this spot to give herself time to think. As she assembled her cover story in her mind, the man tapped on the window.

She lowered the window a few inches. 'Hello can I help you?'

'Good evening,' the man replied. 'Nice evening for it, isn't it?'

Rosie looked at the clock on the dashboard.

'Well it's more night than evening, but it is quite a pleasant night.'

The man looked around nervously. 'I understand that this is the place...' he said, smiling, glancing into her eyes.

'I'm sorry, what?' Rosie answered, more confused than nervous as to his sudden appearance. 'What do you mean *this is the place?*'

'The place, you know. The. Place. I was told to be here at eleven o'clock.'

Rosie was suddenly struck with a thought. *What if this is a friend of Alan's who had been asked to lend a hand? It would be typical of him to forget to tell anyone.*

'Do you mind if I just ring a friend?' Rosie picked up her mobile.

The man s face broke into a huge grin. 'Of course, not at all. In fact I'd be delighted,' he grinned at her again.

Rosie scrolled through her mobile for Alan's number.

'I'm quite nervous actually,' the man said, shuffling his feet. 'This is my first time.'

Rosie looked up at the man. 'It's the first time for us too. We don't normally make a habit of this kind of thing.'

'The blind leading the blind!' The man said with a smile.

Rosie looked at her mobile. She still wasn't sure about calling Alan. If he was trying to be quiet, then her calling him would give him away.

The man interrupted Rosie's thoughts. 'I suppose we'll be using your car, it's much bigger than mine.'

Rosie laughed. 'It's funny, I originally thought I could take my car, but it's much smaller than this one, and I couldn't get all the equipment in.'

The man stared at her open mouthed. 'You really have thought of everything.'

Looking over at the other car, Rosie replied. 'Your car's not too small. It looks like the same size as my car, and I've had two in the back on more than one occasion.'

The man grinned again.

Rosie opened the door and stepped out of the SUV.

'I like the colour,' he said. 'Pink. It's an unusual colour for a car.'

'It's Cerise actually,' Rosie replied.

'Of course it is. It must be the moonlight making it look pink,' the man said, eager to agree with her.

Rosie wandered over to the gap in the fence and looked across the open space towards the school some distance away. *Where are they?* She thought to herself, beginning to worry. However, she was calmed by her the fact that she hadn't heard sirens or barking dogs, which reassured her they hadn't been caught.

'Looking for your friend?' The man asked, appearing at her side.

'Shouldn't be too long now,' she replied.

'It's no problem,' he said. 'I'm happy to wait.'

Rosie looked back at the SUV. 'Listen,' she said. 'When my friend gets here, we may be pressed for time, so can you go right round the back and just do what I tell you?'

'Oh god yes,' he muttered.

This guy was becoming a little weird, she thought. She'd quiz Alan later about who he was and where he came from.

'If you're going to need anything from your car, I suggest that you get it now,' Rosie suggested.

The man nodded. 'Yes, I'll go and get them from the glove compartment,' he said, jogging off across the clearing to his car.

'Rosie!' A cry rang out from behind her, and as she turned she saw Amy running through the break in the fence. 'We got them!' Amy explained breathlessly. 'The others are coming, get the car ready.'

The man watched Amy run up to Rosie through his windscreen. *This night was getting better and better*, he thought to himself.

Amy slipped off her back pack and made her way round to the back of the SUV. Rosie went back to the break in the fence. She could see two figures running towards her. Strictly speaking she could see one figure running towards her, the other appeared to walking briskly. She could hear Alan calling out.

'Come on, faster!' Alan shouted.

'You try running with a rucksack full of bat boxes strapped to your back!' James shouted in response.

Rosie smiled. Even in the most unusual circumstances their relationship remained constant.

The man got out of his car and began to walk back to the SUV. Suddenly he saw two figures, clearly both men, emerging from the break in the fence, making their way to the pink car.

The man stopped, curious as to what was going on. He watched as the two men took off their back packs and put them into the back of the SUV. They then climbed in and the vehicle turned and accelerated away back down the track. He stared in disappointment as his fantasies went with the SUV.

Amy drove the SUV up the track as fast as she felt she could under the circumstances. The vehicle bumped up and down over the rutted ground, bouncing the occupants around inside.

'Do you think your friend will follow us?' Rosie said to Alan.

'Sorry,' he said. 'What friend?'

'The man that you asked along to help us. I was talking to him while you were in the school.'

380

'I have no idea what you're talking about,' Alan said.

'That can't have been one of Alan's friends,' James added.

'Why not?' said Rosie.

Because every friend he has in the world is in this car now!'

Alan laughed. 'Just drive will you.'

*

Donald poured over the crossword again. That one clue was still eluding him. He scratched his head again, took a mouthful of tea and sighed.

'Still no joy?' Roy asked.

'No, nothing. I'll leave it for another five minutes. You never know, it might come to me later.'

Under the table Cliff groaned in his sleep.

'Shall we have another look for the plaque tomorrow?' Roy asked.

'I don't think so, Roy,' Donald replied. 'It really is a waste of time. There isn't a plaque, is there?'

'I suppose you're right,' Roy conceded.

Donald turned back to the crossword and read the clue again. *To wink briefly.* He picked up his pen and wrote BAT in the squares provided.

Chapter 37

Amy pulled the SUV into a vacant parking space adjacent to the run down theatre.

'Sorry guys, I think this is as close as we're going to get.'

'No worries,' said Alan, cheerfully, 'once we've released the bats, we can have a go at finding a solution to the parking round here. It's ridiculous.'

'That's not a bad idea,' James agreed. 'Maybe we can kidnap a few traffic wardens.'

'That'll never work, mate. No one is going to pay a ransom for those bloody parasites.'

'Fair point, well argued!' James agreed.

'Can we just get on with it please?' Rosie huffed, glaring at Alan. 'We've still got work to do,' she added as she unbuckled her seat belt and opened her door.

The friends followed suit as Rosie opened the boot and began handing out the rucksacks and bat boxes.

'Thanks Rosie,' James said as he turned the hood up on his hoodie and began an exaggerated walk slightly on tip toe, leaving everyone else behind.

'James, what on earth are you doing?' Amy asked incredulously, whilst rushing to catch him up.

'I'm trying to sneak up to the door without making a sound.'

'You realise you are talking to me, right?'

'Oh. Yeah. Sorry Ames. It just seemed like the right thing to do.'

Amy sighed and shook her head, wondering if her husband would ever actually grow up, but realising almost immediately that his immaturity was one of the reasons she loved him. OK, when he was with Alan she sometimes felt like their teacher, trying to get them to concentrate in class. But at other times, such as right now, helping her make sure the bats came to no harm, she realised just what a wonderful man he was.

'Where are Alan and Rosie?' James asked his wife as they approached the theatre.

'They're just behind us, I think Rosie had trouble locking our boot.'

'We're here!' James whispered into the closed theatre door just as Alan and Rosie arrived.

The door opened slightly and a female voice asked, 'Who is it?'

'Batman!' whispered James into the tiny space, '...and Robin,' he added as an afterthought, looking at Alan as the door widened to let them in.

'Why do I get to be Robin?' Alan whined.

'Shush!' Rosie hissed at him as she adjusted the boxes in her hands.

As soon as everyone was inside, Sarah shut the door. 'This is quite exciting, isn't it?' she said. 'Are the bats in those boxes, then?'

'Yep, and they're surprisingly heavy,' Rosie said, moving into the main foyer.

'How exciting!' Sarah exclaimed again. 'Can I have a look?'

'Better not,' Alan said, 'we don't want them getting out before we're ready. Is that Nav over there?'

'Yes, go on in and get ready.'

Walking through the foyer, they passed several posters advertising the 24 hour comedy marathon.

'I can't see your name on that, mate,' James grinned at Alan.

'I know. Gutted. I am thinking of changing my name to "Special Guests." At least I'll get mentioned on a billboard or two.'

'Or, "Doors open at 7pm". That might work.'

Amy turned to Rosie, 'Don't you just love them?'

'Sometimes,' she replied. 'Other times I'd like to get them tested.'

'You wouldn't want to do that. I don't think they could pass a blood test.'

'Oi, I do the jokes,' said Alan, pretending to be affronted.

'Sort of,' replied James.

'See what I mean,' Rosie grinned at Amy as they all followed Nav up the stairs to the circle seating.

Nav opened a set of double doors, gesturing the friends into the circle level foyer. Once everyone was through, he took a set of keys from his pocket. 'This way,' he said, and walked through an open doorway. 'It's just through here, up another flight of stairs.'

'I hope you know where you're going?' James asked. 'Only I've had lots of problems with Sat Navs in the past!'

Nav turned around and grimaced, while Amy punched her husband on his arm.

The friends followed Nav up another small set of carpeted stairs, through a corridor with several doors to the right. Finding the right key, Nav walked towards the final door. He inserted the key into the lock, but the pressure of his hand pushed the door gently open.

'He should have done the key gag,' James said to Alan as they walked through the doors and up a set of circular stairs where yet another door awaited.

'He can do it now,' Alan said, nodding at what he hoped was the final door.

Nav didn't bother with the keys this time, instead he pushed on the door. Finding it locked, he frowned and reached back into his pocket for the set of keys.

'Told you,' Alan said, triumphantly, as Nav used the keys to open the door.

'Here we are…' Nav said, beckoning the friends up the final few steps into the loft.

'Bloody hell,' said Alan, looking up towards the rafters some thirty feet above his head. 'How are we going to get them up there?'

'I thought we just let the things go. Let them find their own way.' Rosie replied.

'I was thinking more of the Pterodactyls,' Alan said, nodding towards his backpack.

'Let's worry about them later. Let's just get the bats out and settled first,' Rosie said, placing the bird boxes at her feet.

'OK,' Alan agreed, looking around the attic for a raised platform. To his left he saw a row of six dusty filing cabinets. 'Let's place the boxes on those,' he said pointing towards the cabinets.

'Who puts a filing cabinet in an attic?' asked Amy.

'Perhaps the writers of Hong Kong Phooey needed a place to store their unused scripts,' Alan replied.

'Or it might be Hong Kong Phooey himself, stuck in the cabinet. I guess Spot the Cat is dead..?' James asked.

'What the bloody hell are you two idiots talking about?' Rosie asked, as she placed her boxes on top of the filing cabinets.

'Hong Kong Phooey? Greatest TV show ever. Cartoon Dog? Crime fighting secret agent?' Alan looked at Rosie.

'Incompetent secret agent. Needed his cat, Spot to get him out of trouble every week,' added James. 'It's certainly up there with Wacky Races.'

'Oh God. How could I forget Wacky Races? Do you remember the episode when...?'

'Can we get on with this please?' Rosie hissed at Alan. 'Anyway, why are you watching cartoons at your age?'

'Actually, Rosie, they were before my time. But classic TV is classic TV. You wouldn't frown upon someone listening to The Beatles. So why is TV different?'

'Because, *Alan*,' Rosie raised her voice, 'because its children's TV. And you are supposed to be a grown up.

Now start acting like one and help me get these bats out of these boxes.'

'Yes, Miss...' Alan whispered quietly, whilst James grinned.

'And don't you look so pleased with yourself,' Amy said, 'you are just as bad, if not worse.'

'What did I do?' James asked innocently.

'You encourage him. Now stop it and be serious.'

'Yes, Miss...' James whispered as Alan grinned in response.

'Children!' Rosie and Amy said simultaneously.

Once the boxes were placed on the filing cabinets, James asked, 'OK. So what do we do now? Do we just open the doors and let them find their own way out or do we shake them out?'

'James!' shouted Amy and Rosie again in unison.

'We will not be shaking these poor creatures anywhere,' Amy frowned at her husband. 'It is bad enough that we have moved them from their home. I will not allow them to be hurt.'

OK, Ames, calm down,' James said defensively. 'I just thought I'd ask. I mean, I don't want to hurt the things. But I also want to make sure they stay here and don't fly off back to the school chapel.'

'Well, that's OK, then,' Amy replied. 'Are all the doors facing the same way? Yes, good, let's open them up and wait for the bats to find their own way out.'

Rosie and Amy opened the small doors that held the bats and stood back in anticipation. Nothing.

'Maybe we should shake them after all,' Alan said.

'Wait a minute, will you?' Rosie glowered at Alan.

For a few moments nothing happened then, as James bent to look towards the nearest box, a small pair of black wings emerged, followed by the rest of the body as the first tiny bat crawled its way out of the box and took flight.

Within a few seconds another bat emerged, followed by yet another. Within a few seconds all the trapped bats had found their way from their prison and were flying around the theatre roof.

'Job done,' James grinned.

'Isn't it beautiful?' Amy agreed, staring at the circling bats.

'The job isn't done, mate,' said Alan. 'I've still got to stick these Pterodactyls up there somehow.'

'Do we still have to do that? If the bats settle here, then there's no need for any subterfuge,' James said to his friend.

'I reckon we should do it anyway. It sends a message,' Alan replied.

'What sort of message will half a dozen duct taped pterodactyls send then mate?'

'It will let the planners know someone was on to them. And that we won't take this lying down.'

Rosie and Amy looked at their respective partners then at each other. 'Sometimes,' Rosie said, 'sometimes I forget how lovely Alan can be.'

'I know what you mean,' Amy said, looking at her husband. 'I wonder if you can buy Hong Kong Phooey on DVD?'

'I think we should have a look,' agreed Rosie.

'And Wacky Racers,' Amy added.

'It's Wacky *Races*. Anyway, listen guys,' Alan said to his friends, 'Don't hang about for me...'

Rosie shook her head. 'Such a child...'

'...I'll figure out where to stick these rubber whatnots and catch up with you in a bit.'

James sniggered at a perceived joke and ushered the friends out of the attic. 'I'll see you in a bit, mate.'

'Yep. Won't be long,' Alan replied, taking the Pterodactyls and duct tape from his rucksack.

*

Alan made his way down the stairs, pleased with his handiwork. He hoped someone would see the funny side. Perhaps not, he thought. Developers were notoriously ruthless, placing money over humanity, history and heritage. Still, he thought to himself, at least we've given them a fight.

Alan paused as he reached the ground floor. Something was bothering him. A slight chill found its way between his shoulders and made him turn one hundred and eighty degrees away from the exit towards the theatre stalls.

He opened the double doors and walked down the slight incline of the aisle between rows of empty red seats. The tingling sensation became more intense the closer he got to the stage. Alan had almost reached the short flight of stairs leading up to the stage when he realised this was where Frankie had made his final live appearance.

Taking a deep breath, Alan walked slowly up the stairs and on to the stage itself. He looked out onto the empty expanse in front of him, a strange feeling somewhere between euphoria and melancholy rising from the depths of his soul. With an odd sense of certainty he knew where he had to go. He walked slowly from the stage, down another short flight of steps to the corridor, where he knew the dressing rooms were situated.

The tingling at the back of his neck intensified as Alan made his way slowly along the corridor. He stopped suddenly at a sound very much like a huge sigh, coming from a partially open doorway. Alan glanced inside the room. Inside he could see Frankie standing with his back facing the door, shoulders gently shaking. Christ, Alan thought, he's in tears. Who knew ghosts could cry?

Alan stood for a moment at the door, not knowing whether to enter or to quietly leave. He had no desire to intrude on Frankie's thoughts, even if that was exactly what Frankie had been doing to him for weeks.

Before he could make a decision, Frankie's shoulders ceased their movement and Alan heard another shuddering sigh. Feeling so much like a voyeur, Alan turned to leave.

'Don't go...' Frankie said, his voice sounding broken.

'I...I...I'm sorry, Frankie, I don't want to be in the way.'

'Don't be daft, son. You're not in the way,' Frankie said, composing himself before turning towards Alan who was still standing uncomfortably at the door. 'This is where it happened.'

'Where what...oh, *shit*, sorry, I didn't realise.'

'No reason you should, son. Thing is, I felt great when I came off the stage. I really felt like I had gone down well. It was a bit of a tough crowd. Full of alternative types. But I got them laughing,' he smiled at the memory. 'Most of them, anyway. There were a few that didn't get it. Probably wanted some anti Thatcher hooligan to shout and swear at them. Not sure that was ever me.'

'The thing is, I probably hated her more than anyone in the audience. But I just wanted to tell jokes. It's the only thing I've ever really been good at. Well, that and getting shot at during the war.'

'Me, too. The jokes, that is. Not the shooting thing.'

'I know, son. You know, you remind me of me when I was younger. Just not as good looking.'

'Yeah, whatever,' Alan smiled.

'It's all over now, though, isn't it? I mean. Life. Death. This...' Frankie spread his arms wide. 'This whole thing. You never really think about death when you're alive. I guess it's your mind's way of coping with the inevitability of it. But when you're dead and you get a second chance.

391

You just want to grab it with both hands and never let go. But when you're close to losing it all again. It just seems so...so...' he struggled for the words, 'So fucking unfair.' Frankie wiped a tear from his eye. 'I mean. Why me? Why did I come back? I am sure there are better people than me that deserved this chance. Why was I so lucky?' he paused for a moment, breath coming in shakes, before composing himself. 'Sorry son, you don't need me being old and stupid. Let's get out of here. Anyway, this place smells of roast chicken.'

'Listen, Frankie, whatever happens, we know we've done some good here tonight. That's all we can do as people. Try to make a difference.'

Alan and Frankie walked in silence out of the theatre to where Rosie stood, hugging herself against the cold, deep in conversation with Sarah and Nav. 'Where have you been?' she asked.

'Sorry, Rosie, I got distracted.'

'Why am I not surprised?'

'Look after that one, son. She's worth hanging on to,' said Frankie as he disappeared.

'Yeah, I know,' Alan said, turning to his friend who was nowhere to be seen.

'Who are you talking to?' Rosie asked, eyebrows arched.

Alan turned to his girlfriend. 'No one. Come on, let's get out of here. This place is giving me the creeps.'

Oneway could see Crozier through the windscreen of his car, pacing up and down on the pavement outside the Merton Palace Theatre. He slowed and without indicating pulled up onto the pavement narrowly missing a pedestrian.

Crozier walked over to meet him at the car. 'You can't park there.'

'I practically own the ground that you're standing on. I can park wherever I like,' Oneway replied arrogantly as he locked the car with the remote key.

Crozier shrugged. 'You'd better come with me,' he said and started walking back to the theatre's main entrance.

'You said it was urgent on the phone. So what's the problem?' Oneway asked, following Crozier to the Theatre's large double front doors.

Crozier stopped and turned. 'I had a call, well the planning department had a call, from the theatre staff. They said simply that there had been a development and could the council send someone as quickly as possible.'

Crozier began banging on the Theatre's large wooden door. 'Any ideas what they might want?' he asked.

Oneway shook his head. 'Not a clue,' he replied and joined Crozier in banging on the door.

The theatre doors swung open. Nav stood in the open doorway. 'Hello. Yes? 'Can I help you?' he asked.

'I'm from the council,' Crozier said. 'You called the planning office and asked for someone to come out here as soon as possible. Well, here I am.'

Whilst Nav didn't recognise Crozier he recognised Oneway straight away. It wasn't that long ago that Nav had showed him around the theatre when he had told them he was looking to make a donation to the "Save the Theatre Fund." *Well*, Nav thought, *now it's time we paid you back for your deceit. Let's see how you like it.*

Nav stepped aside to let Crozier and Oneway through. 'Do you gentlemen have any ID on you?' he asked politely.

'Why?' Crozier said.

'Souvenir hunters. You'd be surprised how many people want a bit of the theatre before it's pulled down. A piece of history I suppose.'

'I own the bloody building. As far as I'm concerned it's one great big souvenir,' Oneway said and passed his business card to Nav.

'OK Mr Oneway, thank you,' Nav said, looking at the name on the card, 'and if you'd like to confirm you mother's maiden name I can let you through,'

Oneway growled something that Nav couldn't quite make out.

'Just a joke Mr Oneway. Relax, just a bit of theatre humour.'

Crozier showed his council issued identification to Nav, who gave it a casual glance.

'What's the problem?' Crozier asked. 'Why the summons?'

Nav looked at both men. 'I suppose it's easier if I show you. Can you follow me?' he said, and set off through the foyer towards the stairs.

Nav bounded up the stairs two at a time, making no effort to explain where he was leading them.

'Where are we going?' Oneway gasped as he followed Nav up several flights of stairs.

'Just up this way,' Nav replied, continuing his rapid ascent of the stairs.

Oneway and Crozier exchanged looks and continued to climb, though more slowly now.

Nav finally came to a halt at the top of a flight of stairs. A shut door in front of them. Oneway vaguely remembered this from his recent tour,

'This, gentlemen is the loft space,' Nav explained. 'I think you should see what we have here.' He pushed a key into the lock and opened the door, stepping aside so that both Oneway and Crozier could see into the room.

'What am I looking at?' Crozier asked squinting into the darkness.

'There's no lights in there I'm afraid, but I have this though,' Nav said brandishing a torch.

Oneway snatched it away from him, switched it on and pointed it into the room. The torch beam picked out joists, beams cobwebs and nothing else.

'There's nothing there,' Oneway said. 'This is a waste of time.'

'No!' Crozier shouted, putting his hand on Oneway's arm. 'Look at the corner again.'

Oneway pointed the torch into the corner of the loft. A beam of light cut through the darkness and picked out an object on a beam, which began to move.

'What's that?' Crozier asked.

Taking the torch back, Nav played the light around the room for a second or two before he paused and focused the shaft of light on one of the higher level beams.

'Look there,' he said, dropping his voice to a whisper, enjoying the moment.

Oneway and Crozier focused their attention on the illuminated area. 'Is that a...' Crozier started to say before being interrupted by Nav.

'Yes, it's a bat,' he whispered, 'and look at this...'

Nav moved the torch beam along the joists and wooden beams pausing as he passed the figures of several sleeping bats.

'Are they all bats?' Crozier asked, a cold sensation beginning to creep across his shoulders.

'How many?' Oneway asked sharply, not giving Nav an opportunity to answer the earlier question.

'They appear to be bats, but I'm not sure how many I'm afraid,' he said. 'I don't want to disturb them by trying to count them. In any case it's not safe.'

'It's strange', Crozier said, regaining some of his composure, 'but some of them look like rubber to me.'

Nav clicked the torch off and quietly closed the attic door.

'What are you going to do about this?' Oneway said to Nav.

'Well,' Nav replied in his most condescending voice, 'I have already made a call and the BIFFER man will be here as soon as possible.'

Oneway frowned. 'I can't see how he can help, you haven't even got ramps.'

Nav threw a puzzled look at Crozier.

'BIFFER, The Bat Institute For Further Environmental Research,' Crozier explained to Oneway. 'This is bad news. Bad news indeed.'

Oneway sighed and leaned against the wall. 'I don't care who you call. You can call these BIFFERs in, you can call in the child catcher from Chitty Chitty Bang Bang for all I care,' he shouted, 'I want these flying mice out of here now, or they can get squashed while I knock the place down on top of them.'

Nav looked at Crozier. 'Can I leave it to you to explain things to your friend?'

Crozier nodded and turned to Oneway while Nav wandered back down the stairs, a huge grin on his face. At the bottom of the stairs he turned out of sight and waited, listening intently to the conversation between the two men.

'You need to understand, Clive this is important.'

'It's going to slow things down, I know. I suppose I'll have to offer to pay to have them re-housed.'

'No, it's not as simple as that, these aren't people. You can't just move them on,' Crozier explained as though to a child, 'Depending on what they find, it may mean other solutions will be considered in the first instance.'

'What do you mean?'

'I mean, you can't throw money at this to make it go away. You know what public opinion is like when you involve something like small defenceless creatures.'

'Defenceless!' Oneway exclaimed, 'haven't people seen Dracula!'

Ignoring him, Crozier continued. 'The council will be under pressure to review its planning permission in the light of this new information.'

'What? You can't turn it down!' Oneway shouted. 'It's gone too far.'

'It'll be out of my hands,' Crozier said. 'I think you should put in a proposal to drop the theatre out of your plans. You may wish to consider issuing a statement to the effect that in view of your commitment to the welfare of wildlife and endangered species, you are going to amend the plans to allow the theatre to continue and the bats to flourish. And you keep the moral high ground.'

'Moral high ground? Coming from you? You aren't serious?'

'Completely.'

'There's absolutely no chance of that!' Oneway seethed. 'Too much work has gone into this project already for me to just walk away.'

'You may have no choice. Do you want to speak to the BIFFER man?' Crozier offered.

'I will pull this place down even if I have to do it with my bare hands, brick by brick!' Oneway screamed, spittle flying from his mouth.

Crozier shook his head. 'You're not thinking this through properly, Clive.'

'Can you blame me? The rug is being pulled from under my feet, all the effort and work will be for nothing. I smell a rat.'

Crozier thought about pointing out that it was bats, rather than rats that had likely scuppered the deal. However, he decided to keep quiet considering the look on Oneway's face.

'I'll leave the site derelict. It can stay fallow.' Oneway said.

Crozier noticed a small tick in the corner of Oneway's eye. 'Can concrete be left fallow?' he asked.

'This one can. I'll leave it ten years. It'll be an eyesore, and the council will be begging me to build something in its place.'

'Clive I want this project to succeed as much as you do, but my gut reaction is that the council will have no choice but to pull the plug.'

Oneway looked at Crozier like he had just spoke a foreign language and shook his head. 'NO!' he screamed again. 'This simply will succeed!'

Crozier rubbed his head. 'Why don't you speak to the BIFFER man?' he suggested again.

Oneway leaned back and slowly began thumping the back of his head against the wall, reminding Crozier of a child who had failed to get his own way.

'So what do you say, Clive?' Crozier said. 'Time for a rethink?'

Oneway took a deep breath. 'I've got to speak to my lawyers,' he shouted as he stormed off down the stairs.

Nav, tucked away around the corner at the bottom of the staircase, had heard a lot of what Crozier and Oneway had discussed. He was waiting for them to leave so that he could call Sarah and bring her up to date. Hearing footsteps on the stairs, he sneaked off back to the foyer before he was seen.

Crozier stood outside the loft. He knew that he would have to report back to the council who, in the circumstances, were unlikely to allow the development to continue. His thoughts turned back to the bats themselves. There was, he had to concede, something about the way that the bats had slept upside down that he found oddly appealing.

His thoughts were interrupted by Nav running up the stairs. 'You'd better come down quickly,' he said.

'Why what's happened?' Crozier asked.

'It's your friend. He's just hit the BIFFER man!'

Chapter 39

It took two days. Two days of intense negotiations, bribes and a fair bit of wheedling for David Crozier to extricate himself, the council and Clive Oneway from the collapse of the deal.

The council, as Crozier had anticipated, did not want any negative publicity and amended the planning permission, which resulted in the Merton Palace Theatre no longer forming part of the 'Oneway to Shop' Shopping Mall.

A short statement was released by the Planning Department which simply reported that following meetings between the developers, the council and other interested parties, plans for the 'Oneway to Shop' Shopping Mall were suspended pending review.

*

Rosie's Audi pulled into the car park of "The Weary Traveller" and slipped into one of the few empty parking spaces.

'I think you should be the guest of honour,' Rosie grinned at Alan. 'If it hadn't been for your idea, they'd still be writing to the local papers and moaning about how unfair it all is.'

'They can't mention what we did. If it got out that we actually stole bats and moved them into the theatre, we could be in a lot of trouble, and there's no telling where the bats would end up.'

Rosie reached across and touched his hand. 'Well I'm very proud of you.'

Alan, unnerved by Rosie's uncharacteristic show of affection, opened his door and got out of the car. Sarah had telephoned him earlier that afternoon and gave him the news that the theatre had been saved, and invited him, James, Amy and Rosie to a few celebratory drinks that evening at the oddly named "Weary Traveller."

'This really is a last minute thing isn't it?' Rosie said, appearing at his side and pointing at the sign over the pub door.

A banner which had the slogan 'SAVE THE MERTON PALACE THEATRE' had been hurriedly amended to read 'we SAVEd THE MERTON PALACE THEATRE. The alterations having been made in black marker pen.

'Last minute parties are normally the best ones,' Alan chuckled, already mentally deciding that he wouldn't be turning up for work the next day.

He opened the door for Rosie to walk through, and as he turned to follow her, Frankie barged in front of him. 'Thank you!' he said.

Alan let the door close in front of them. 'We did it, Frankie, we saved the theatre.'

Frankie smiled. 'Yes, you really did, and they might have gotten away with it if it hadn't been for you pesky kids.'

Alan laughed. 'This is the celebration party.'

'I know.'

'How?' Alan asked, puzzled. 'I haven't seen you for two days.'

Frankie nodded towards the partially handwritten sign above the door.

'Oh yeah, right.' Alan nodded and opened the door for them both to join the party.

*

Entering the busy pub, Alan spied Rosie who, despite being only a minute or so in front of him, was already tucked into a corner and deep in conversation with a serious looking Amy. Alan had no wish to spend what should be a light hearted fun evening in a serious conversation so he turned his attention to the other side of the bar where James was entertaining a small group of people.

Working his way across the bar, he saw Sarah out of the corner of his eye. She smiled and waved at him. He smiled back at her as he joined James's group, not surprised to see that Frankie was already there.

'What's happening?' Alan asked.

James turned to him. 'Hello mate,' he said, introducing him to his new friends; Bev Johnson, Robin Hurst and Tim Baker, who Alan remembered from the public protest meeting. 'Tim is the Chairman of the Arts council,' James said.

Tim offered his hand to Alan. 'Sarah has told us what you did. We're all extremely grateful.'

Alan shook the offered hand, unsure how much Sarah had told him. 'It was the least we could do.'

James however had abandoned discretion and gave them a full account of the process of removing bats and placing them in the theatre. His account differed from that remembered by both Alan and Frankie, who spent the duration of James's account exchanging puzzled looks and raising their eyebrows as James recounted his own courageous exploits.

After hearing how James had hung from the Chapel roof with a bat in each hand, Bev, Robin and Tim made their excuses and set off to mingle.

'You pillock!' Alan turned to James after they were out of ear shot.

'What did I say?'

'The whole bat thing is supposed to be a secret. No one is supposed to know what we did,' Alan attempted to explain without losing his temper.

'You heard them,' James whined, 'Sarah had already told them.'

'We don't know that she told them everything. It would have been better to keep quiet.'

Frankie looked at James. 'I think it would be kinder to have him shot!'

'What's up with Amy?' Alan asked James, attempting to change the subject. 'She's talking to Rosie. It looks quite intense.'

James looked over to where Rosie seemed to be placating Amy and shook his head. 'No idea mate. She's been in a funny mood for a couple of hours, actually since you called with the news.'

'You'd better go and find out, 'Alan suggested. 'Let me know if it's anything I've done and I'll steer clear of her for a bit.'

'Will do.' James drained his bottle and placed it on the table. 'I'll be back,' he said and wandered off to see his wife.

Finishing his drink, Alan turned to Frankie and, hoping that no one could see him apparently talking to himself, he asked, 'Does it feel different? I mean, now we have saved the theatre, I take it you will be going soon?'

Frankie scratched his chin. 'To be honest, I don't actually feel any different. In any case, we've only just found out that the theatre is safe.'

'It'll be weird without you,' Alan admitted. 'I've got used to you popping up at the worst possible moment.'

Frankie opened his mouth to reply, but was drowned out by the howl of feedback and a voice attempting to talk over it.

'Testing, testing...' Tim was standing in the corner. Someone had kindly put a crate on the floor, and he stepped onto it giving him a very slight height advantage over everyone there.

He thanked everyone for their efforts, and whilst not specifically mentioning Alan by name, made a reference to those who climbed new heights in their commitment to keep the theatre open. Everyone listened politely and applauded warmly when Tim finished his speech, and he proposed a toast to the future of the Merton Palace Theatre.

By this time, James had made his way over to Amy and Rosie, stopping at the bar on route to purchase a round of drinks. 'There you go,' he said handing, them both bottles of beer. 'Everyone OK?'

'It's just not right!' Amy said.

'What isn't?' James asked.

'This whole situation. It's just wrong.'

'I'm not with you. I can't see what your problem is. The theatre's been saved. We saved it.' He took a gulp from his bottle as if toasting himself. 'You'll get to take your kids there, and probably more often now with all the publicity surrounding it.'

'You're not seeing the big picture James,' Rosie said. 'The developer appears to have come out of this as the hero.'

James laughed. 'I was talking to Nav earlier, apparently the developer,' he paused trying to recall the name, '...Oneway, laid out the BIFFER man. Really good punch by all accounts.'

'What?' Amy snapped, 'Is the BIFFER man?'

James laughed again. 'Sorry Ames, the BIFFER man was the representative from the Bat Institute For Further

406

Environmental Research. He was sent along to examine the bats that had been *'found'* in the loft. Oneway laid him out with one punch. Didn't even bother waiting around for the man's opinion.'

'Blimey, what happened?'

'Well, to be caught like that he probably didn't have his guard up. Surprise punch I'd say,' James grinned.

'No, what happened after he was punched?'

'Well, according to Nav, the planning man from the council was also there and he sorted things out and made the peace. He told the BIFFER man that there were bats in the loft and that the council would be reviewing the planning position.'

'Did he inspect the bats at all?' Rosie asked.

'According to Nav, once the BIFFER man felt better, he was taken up to the loft by the man from the council, and he had a look around.'

'I assume that there were no problems then?'

'The BIFFER man had double vision, to go with his glass jaw. He probably thought he was seeing twice as many bats as were actually there. Turned out rather well in the end, I'd say.'

Amy sighed. 'You still don't see it do you?'

'See what?' James asked.

'The developer. He has come out of this a hero. He planned to redevelop the theatre and its surrounding area, pulling down numerous properties. He had no interest in anything other than his own bank balance, despite the wishes of the local community...'

'How has he come out of this a hero? – I'm still not with you.' James interrupted.

'It's going to be reported that because of his concern over environmental issues he chose to amend and downsize his plans and that he is contributing to a bat charity.'

'How do you know all this?' James asked.

'Sarah told me as soon as we got in here.'

James nodded, understanding. 'Oh well, at least the theatre is safe. That's the main thing.''

'Aren't you bothered that he has got away with this? Aren't you bothered by all the heartache and stress he caused?'

'Not really,' James admitted. 'He's probably a fair few quid out of pocket, and that'll probably hurt him more than it would a normal person.'

Rosie looked away and considered offering James her spare room for the night.

'I can't believe you sometimes,' Amy said, exasperated.

'Give it a rest Ames, he said, tiring of the conversation. 'We played our part. We achieved something massive, mainly because of your enthusiasm. Now just chill out and relax a bit.'

'I'm going to get some drinks,' Rosie interrupted. 'Same again?' Without waiting for an answer she made for the bar, leaving the bickering couple alone.

*

Alan was standing in the very corner of the room. Sarah stood in front of him, positioned so that she had his complete attention. 'You know we couldn't have done any of this without you,' she said.

'To be fair it was a team effort. James, Amy and Rosie all helped.'

'Yes, them as well,' she said, although without the same level of sincerity. 'But it was your idea.'

Alan's cheeks reddened at the compliment.

'That's your trouble,' she said. 'You're too modest.'

'I don't think I am.'

'Oh you are, but you just can't see it. It's like your stand-up routines. They're really funny, you can make people laugh, but you need to push yourself onto a bigger platform.'

'How do you suggest I go about that?' Alan asked. 'It's not easy, and I have a day job. I can't travel too far during the week as I have to get up and be bored shitless for eight hours.'

'I said to you before, once the theatre gets going it's going to need a regular comedian. I was thinking of putting your name forward for the job, and with the goodwill that you've built up with the arts council, I reckon it would be yours to lose.'

Alan had received promises of work several times before. He'd been given promises in the past, names of people who may have regular slots and even once a guy who thought Alan would make an excellent warm up man for a TV panel show. None of these had ever worked out and so he was deeply cynical about Sarah's suggestion.

'I'm deeply cynical about this,' he told her, explaining about his previous experiences.

'The difference between then and now is that this time I'm involved, and I'm making you a promise. So what do you say?'

Alan wasn't sure if it was her big brown eyes, the promise of regular work or the beer, but in any case, he didn't feel he could say no. 'How could I say no?'

'Brilliant!' Sarah squeaked, clapping her hands together rapidly. 'Wait here,' she grinned excitedly and headed to the bar.

Alan watched her leave, turning slightly to see Frankie on his left. 'Did you catch any of that?' he asked.

'All of it,' Frankie said stepping closer. 'This is a golden opportunity for you. You've got somebody on your side who is in the business, she likes your work, and I don't know if you've noticed but she seems quite keen on you. It's a no brainer. Though if you want my advice, I'd keep her away from Rosie for a bit.'

'I'll bear that in mind,' Alan replied just as Sarah reappeared holding two glasses and a bottle of Champagne.

'Left over from the toast,' she said. 'And I've thought of something else we can toast too.'

'Isn't it a bit premature to be assuming that I have the theatre gig? Shouldn't there be an official announcement first?' Alan asked.

'No, No, it's not that, it's something else.' She handed him a glass of champagne.

Alan frowned in confusion. 'What?'

'Well, I've made quite a few contacts doing this job over the last few years and it's about time I started using them to my advantage. I've been thinking of setting myself up as an agent for a while and I've decided now is the time.'

'Sounds like a great idea,' Alan said supportively.

'I'm glad you think so, because I was going to ask if you would like to be my first client!'

'Now that's an offer that I can hardly refuse,' he said as he and Sarah clinked glasses.

Sarah gave him a big smile and held her hand out. 'Have we got a deal then?'

'Deal!' he said shaking her hand just as James appeared with Rosie and Amy close behind.

'What's going on here?' James asked, grinning at his friend.

Alan turned to face everyone. 'I have myself an agent!' he said proudly and pointed at Sarah.

'Well done mate,' James said. 'This could be the start of something massive.'

'I hope it goes better than the last time he said that!' Amy announced, causing an outburst of laughter.

'Sounds like I should be signing you up as well!' Sarah chuckled.

'So what have you got planned for him?' James asked.

'Well, we will have to sit down and talk about it, but I really do think he should get out of his comfort zone and start doing gigs further afield. There are plenty of venues outside London that he should be doing.'

James nodded in agreement. 'I've always said that he should be out there a bit more. What about the Edinburgh festival?'

'It's certainly something that he should be aiming for,' Sarah agreed.

Alan took a step back and watched his best friend arrange his life with his newly appointed agent, wondering just what he had let himself in for.

'She's very pretty isn't she?' Rosie whispered in his ear.

Alan felt himself redden, remembering Frankie's words from earlier. 'Who is?' Alan asked unconvincingly.

'Sarah. She is very pretty. That could be an asset for an agent.'

'Is she? I hadn't really noticed,' Alan replied, satisfied that he had successfully deflected Rosie's question away.

'I'm not stupid,' Rosie said. 'Anyway, I think you should speak to Amy, she's not happy about the way things have turned out.'

Alan looked towards where Amy was standing with Sarah and James as they continued to organise his life, although she didn't appear to contributing. Faced with listening to Rosie's barely disguised barbs, he took the opportunity to speak to Amy.

'How's it going?' he asked her.

'It's OK. I'm just frustrated that the developer appears to have got away with it, and is going to be made out to be some kind of saviour.'

'I know what you mean,' he said, although in all honesty Alan didn't know what she meant at all. He only understood one thing, and that was that he was asked to help save the theatre, and he did. The fact that his

413

aspiring comedy career had received a boost was an unexpected and much welcome bonus.

'Well I hope he's getting a hard time from his other half. I hope she's giving him hell over this,' Alan said, offering a line of his own logic to placate her.

Amy nodded in response to Alan's thinly disguised attempt to alleviate the situation, his words ringing in her ears over and over again. She smiled to herself as she began to formulate a plan. *Oneway was not going to get away with this*, she thought to herself, *not if I've got anything to do with it.*

'Alan, you're right. Let's hope that's what's happening, and thanks for backing me up on this.'

Alan looked over to where Frankie was leaning against the wall, on the fringes of their group. He raised his champagne glass to Frankie in salute. Frankie smiled at him and then vanished. He turned back to Amy. 'It was a pleasure.'

*

David Crozier finished writing his report, checked it again, pressed save on his computer before switching it off. He had spent the last two days tidying up the mess surrounding the theatre, a mess made worse by Clive Oneway and his loss of self-control.

He had met with council leaders, planning officers, the man from BIFFER and finally Clive Oneway, and worked out a solution that appeared to suit everyone, although typically, Oneway took more convincing than the others. But fortunately the presence of a recently assaulted man from BIFFER persuaded Oneway to accede to Crozier's proposal.

Crozier stood up from his desk and walked over to the large metal cabinet in the corner of the room. Opening the door he looked inside. Hanging upside down, reminiscent of a sleeping bat, was Alison, her big eyes staring back at him, or more specifically back at his knees. He stepped back and looked her up and down.

'Ready to come out?' he asked, and reached down to release the gag.

Alison shook her head. 'Another five minutes?' she asked.

Crozier slid the gag back into place and closed the door.

'That woman's completely batty,' he said and went back to his desk.

Chapter 40

Clive Oneway checked his reflection in the bathroom mirror before walking down the hallway to open his front door. He had been expecting her, she had buzzed through a minute or so earlier and he had released the door letting her into the building.

Amy stood outside Oneway's apartment waiting for him to open the door. Since she had made the call she hadn't thought of anything else, like a teenager on a first date. Amy however hadn't been a teenager for fourteen years and this certainly didn't qualify as a date.

Oneway looked through the peep hole and was pleased that she was as attractive he remembered. Smiling to himself, he opened the door. 'Come in,' he said, with an exaggerated sweep of his hand. 'Did you find he place OK?'

'No problem at all. Not that I could miss it, it's a lovely building. You must have a fantastic view.'

'I'll show you later, he said, taking her damp coat. 'Is it raining?'

'Just starting. Apparently we're in for a storm later.'

Oneway's capacity for small talk and pleasantries was limited, so he offered her a drink and gestured her towards the living room.

The flat and its decoration didn't surprise Amy at all. This was the penthouse suite of an exclusive block of apartments overlooking the River Thames. She expected the designer furniture, minimalistic decoration and the 50 inch TV on the wall. She put her bag on the floor and wandered out to the kitchen where Oneway was opening a bottle of wine and emptying what looked like Twiglets into a bowl.

'Wine?'

'Just a small one please, I'm driving,' Amy said whilst looking around the designer kitchen.

Oneway paid no attention and almost filled the large glass, handing it to her. 'I have to admit I was surprised to hear from you. It's been a while since we met.'

'To be honest,' Amy paused to take a sip of her wine, 'I wasn't going to, but I got to hear about your involvement with the theatre and then putting your plans on ice so that you could save some bats. I thought that was a lovely thing to do.'

Oneway smiled as Amy continued, 'I was really impressed that you were prepared to compromise your project on an environmental issue, so I thought I'd make contact and take you up on your offer of a drink.'

'Some things are more important that projects and profits,' he answered smugly.

Amy forced a smile in return over the top of her wine glass, the contents of which were disappearing quicker than she had anticipated.

Oneway gestured that she go through to the living room. He followed her through, dropping himself into one of the large leather sofas.

417

'Can I offer you something to eat?' he asked. 'We could go out. There's a lovely Italian not far from here.'

Amy had no intention of joining him for dinner, but decided to play along. 'Maybe later. It's an amazing place you have here,' she said, looking around the room.

Oneway put his glass on the glass coffee table situated between the two sofas. 'It was only finished a couple of years ago. I had my eye on the land for several years before it became available. The homeless shelter that was here before burnt down one night and I made a bid for the land.'

'That's terrible. Was anyone hurt?'

'No it was OK. There was no big issue about it,' he grinned.

Amy ignored what she presumed was his attempt at a joke. 'What did the homeless people do, where did they go?'

He shrugged. 'I never asked. It was summer, so in a way they were quite lucky. They could sleep on a park bench.'

Amy bristled at his lack of empathy and felt herself losing her temper so she changed the subject. 'Did you design this yourself? She gestured around the apartment.

Oblivious to the fact that he had already irritated her he said, 'Yes, I designed the penthouse apartment and kept it for myself.'

'Well it's certainly very nice.'

'Do you live far from here?' he asked, eyeing her wine glass.

'Out towards the theatre,' she replied, being deliberately vague and not wishing to give him any more information about herself than was necessary

'I suppose this must all be quite luxurious compared to what you must be able to afford on a teacher's salary.'

Amy felt her anger rising again and tried to let his comment wash over her. 'How about showing me the view then?'

Oneway grinned, thinking she was being seduced by his apartment. He walked to the sliding glass doors which dominated one side of the room, sliding them open and inviting Amy onto the balcony.

It was more of a patio than a balcony, with room enough for a garden table, chairs and a large sun umbrella. Amy walked to the edge and looked out over the River Thames. The view was breath taking, especially at night, with so many lights illuminating the river. Despite herself Amy could not help but be impressed.

At the base of the building, large spotlights shone powerful beams which illuminated the buildings' façade, without encroaching into the apartments themselves. Amy was reminded of the lights at a concert she had attended in Hyde Park, although if anything, these looked more expensive.

'This is amazing,' she said.

Oneway gradually leaned in next to her, casually leaning against the waist height guard rail. 'So you like it, then?'

'Definitely, I've never seen London like this before.'

Oneway gently touched her on the arm. 'Come on, let's go back inside. We're getting wet. Another drink or would you prefer something to eat?' he asked when they were back inside.

'Just coffee please,' Amy replied, following him out to the kitchen. Leaning against the fridge she asked, 'You must have taken a hell of a loss having to amend your shopping centre plans at such short notice.'

He pushed a button on his expensive coffee machine and it slowly began to fill two cups. He turned to Amy with a sly grin. 'Between you and me,' he said. 'The council offered me a deal.'

'Oh, what deal was that?' Amy asked innocently, despite having a very good idea what he was going to say.

'They basically told me that if I backed out this time, I'd pretty much get a free pass to do whatever I like with my next development.'

'Anything?'

Well, not anything. 'No churches they said, which is a shame as there's one I had my eye on which I reckon would make a great spa retreat.'

'Seriously?' You would turn a church into a spa retreat?'

'Or a bowling alley,' he replied passing Amy a cup of coffee.

'Is there nothing that you wouldn't demolish or rebuild?'

'No. Nothing at all, 'he said without a second thought. 'If I think I can make money on it, I'll tear it down. Old or new it doesn't matter to me.'

'And that's why you would have pulled the theatre down? Just for the money?

'I would have pulled that building down without a moment's thought. It is an absolute eyesore. It served no purpose and was simply eating money. Pulling it down would have improved the area immeasurably.'

Amy leaned forward in her sofa. 'Did you know that you wanted to pull it down when we met there that time?'

'Of course I did. I was just having a look around, seeing where we could put a Tie Rack,' he laughed.

'Why didn't you mention it?'

'You never asked!'

'I'm sorry I forgot to ask such an obvious question. I must remember to make that a priority next time I meet someone new. *Are you going to flatten the building we're standing in?* Christ.'

He spread his arms in a conciliatory fashion. 'I'm sorry, it slipped my mind. I was too preoccupied with how attractive you were.'

He was expecting her to warm to the compliment. Unfortunately Amy didn't really respond to flattery at the best of times and she wasn't going to accept it from someone she had already decided was a nasty, despicable excuse for a human being.

'So as we sat there and watched the children playing and enjoying themselves, it never occurred to you that you should perhaps mention that you were going to pull the place down?'

'Nope. Not once. Why should I?' He drained his coffee.

Amy shook her head angrily. 'You just don't get it do you?'

'Sorry, not sure what you mean?'

Amy sighed. 'Developers. You just don't appreciate what's around you. You're only interested in making money. You don't care that you are destroying beautiful buildings all over the country and replacing them with soulless identikit flats that no normal person can afford. It's obscene.'

'Oh for God's sake woman give it a rest,' he shouted. 'I invited you here because you are normally what I would consider to be a very attractive woman. I thought we could have a few drinks, eat some Twiglets and possibly grab a bite to eat. Then I might have allowed you to sleep with me, but to be honest you've really turned me off.'

He stuffed a handful of Twiglets into his mouth, crunching sullenly.

Amy simply stared back at him, her eyes narrowing at his lack of compassion. And what on earth had he said about *allowing* her to sleep with him? As *if*.

Finishing his Twiglets, he continued. 'It's your type of people that really hold this country back. You are the wrong type of leaves on the train track of progression,' he sat back, pleased with that, and made a mental note to use it again.

'What do you mean *'your type?'* Amy sneered at him.

'Lefty arty types with a misplaced romantic notion that all the world's problems can be solved by an understanding of poetry and plays that were written five hundred years ago instead of hard work. People like you stand in the way of genuine progress.'

Oneway desperately wished that someone else was there to give him a round of applause, but in the absence of anyone else he grabbed another handful of Twiglets.

'You're impossible!' Amy slammed her hand down on the sofa.

'To be honest, dear, we're both wasting our time. I don't why you're still here and to be honest if I'd known you were like this I wouldn't have given you my card. I'm going outside, and while I'm taking in the view you may as well go,' he shouted as he got up and opened the patio doors, stepping outside and shutting the doors behind him.

Before Amy could react, the door opened and he stomped back inside soaking wet.

'It's chucking it down out there,' he said, taking a rain coat from a hat stand. 'You still here?'

Amy sat in her chair, silently seething. This was not how she planned it at all. She had intended to give him an earful and hopefully make him understand just what he had done wrong. Instead Oneway had shouted at her, and had the final word before stomping off, which was exactly what she had planned to do.

'I'm not having this,' she said to the empty room. Picking up her bag she followed Oneway onto the balcony. As she did so she was hit by a gale force wind and driving rain which stung her eyes, momentarily blinding her. Within a matter of seconds she was soaked to the skin, her flimsy jacket offering no protection whatsoever. She could see Oneway leaning against the guard rail, looking out at the city. She walked closer to him and called out, 'I suppose you think you're clever?'

He turned to face her. 'What don't you get about the end of the evening? Go home, there's really nothing more to say.'

The howling wind and driving rain made it difficult for Amy to hear him and she found herself shouting despite their close proximity. 'There's plenty more to say, and you have plenty to listen to. Whether you like it or not!'

Oneway turned back to his view. 'Please. Just go home.'

'I know you didn't back out of the deal as a matter of conscience. I know that you were persuaded to pull out because the council got cold feet after they found the bats, and then you hit a defenceless man.'

Oneway turned back to her, irritated by her persistence and accuracy of her statement. 'I'm really struggling to understand you,' he shouted over the wind. 'What has it got to do with you anyway? You're a teacher, that's all. It's not like you're important.'

'You were there. You saw how much it meant to the children, how much they were getting out of it, but it didn't even register with you. You have no idea how important it is to children like them to have that kind of opportunity.' Amy wiped rain out of her eyes and stared at Oneway before continuing, 'Were you bullied at school is that it?'

Oneway felt a nerve above his eye twitch. He had heard enough. 'Do you know what?' he shouted without waiting for an answer, 'I really couldn't give a toss about whether a collection of half–wit simpleton kids had a good time or not. I would have willingly knocked the place down with the kids in it. I would have built a shopping centre and got rich on the profits. The only reason I didn't was because none of those idiot surveyors had noticed there were bats in the loft.'

Oneway turned away from Amy and looked back out across the river. 'So why don't you go back to the special school, sit all the mongs down and explain that they can go back to their stupid theatre whenever they like. But don't forget to make sure that they are sitting on the rubber sheet when you tell them, because no doubt they'll piss themselves with excitement.'

Amy tensed. She didn't think she hated anyone quite so much as she hated Clive Oneway at that moment. Shaking from a combination of the driving rain, wind and rage Amy opened her bag.

'How could you say that about children, you horrid little man. But here's the thing, whatever you say, we beat you. We took you on and we beat you,' she said triumphantly.

'What do you mean?' he sneered. 'How could you beat me?'

Amy reached into her bag and took out two rubber bats. 'We put them there. We put the bats in the theatre and called the Council.' Amy threw the bats to the ground at his feet.

Bending down to look at the toys at his feet, Oneway asked, 'Are these pterodactyls?'

Amy reached into her bag again and removed another handful of bats which she threw directly at him. The rubber toys bounced off of his chest and splashed onto the ground.

Oneway instinctively turned away, putting his hand in front of his face to protect himself from the rubber projectiles, as another barrage of bats landed on him.

In the torrential rain he didn't see the bat under his foot. As he stepped onto it, a combination of the rain, the rubber bat and the surface of the balcony caused him to slip forward. Amy watched in slow motion as Oneway's hand missed the guard rail and he fell from the balcony.

She stood frozen for several seconds before shaking herself free of the paralysis that had gripped her. She tentatively peered over the edge of the balcony and looked down.

Oneway lay over the lens of one of the giant spotlights. His large raincoat covering his body, rearranged to look, Amy thought distractedly, very much like a bat.

'Look, all I'm saying is that I can't be the only one who has ever thought of grabbing hold of the Cadbury Caramel Bunny's ears, taking it from behind and riding it like a Harley Davidson. I'd mat its' fur up for it. Dirty little bunny.

'Ladies and gentlemen, you may now be thinking I am a little weird, but think about it, if bunnies weren't sexy, Hugh Hefner would be nothing more than an office sex pest. OK, I guess, technically, he *is* a sex pest, but you see my point...'

'I feel like I may have lost some of the room here,' he laughed as he placed his right hand over his eyes to peer into the audience. 'Well, those that haven't left already.'

'Look,' he added, 'an image of bunny ears is symbolic of adult entertainment. You see bunny ears...' Alan mimicked the universal sign of bunny ears, like quotation marks, '...and you know you're in for a good time. OK, probably not as good as a weekend when the wife's visiting her parents and you are on your own with pizza, beer and a fist full of computer games, but a good time nonetheless.

'Oh, and by the way, gents, don't think our partners don't know what we're up to when they are away. Of course they do. It's why they give us a list of pointless tasks to be completed by their return. Take the rubbish out, fix the lock on the bathroom door, run a hoover through the place. It's never *slob around the place all day playing computer games and then fuck off to the pub with your mates in the evening.* It's just cruelty. In fact, Oxfam have made an advert about the plight of men left alone for the weekend.

'This is Mark. Mark is thirty years old. Mark is alone. If he could, Mark would like to tell you something. Mark would like to tell you that it is not OK to expect him to dust the flat when the footballs' on. Mark would tell you that it's not OK to fix the garden roof when there's a video of the skateboarding cat championships that just needs to be seen. If he could, Mark would tell you that all he wants to do is mess about with his mates and sink a few beers. But he can't. Why? Because you've selfishly fucked off to your parents for the weekend and expect him to do a little bit of tidying up while you're away.'

'Here's a little tip, gents. Get a cleaner...She'll never know.

'Yep. That always separates the room...' Alan smirked. 'But anyway, where was I? Oh yes. Sexy bunnies. You see bunny ears on a door of a club and you know what you are going to get. But it's not just sweaty bankers snorting their bonuses off a Ukrainian prostitutes' arse in a strip club that get off on bunnies. No. Ladies, you are implicit in this as well. Don't believe me..? Well then, explain to me the Rampant Rabbit.'

'Yes, gents, the dirty little secret your missus hasn't told you is she has a battery operated toy of her own that gives her more pleasure than you ever could.'

Listen, I don't want to give you the impression that I am some kind of misogynist. I'm not. Really. I love women. I do. My girlfriend's a woman. That's one of my favourite things about her. That and her innate ability to find fault in everything I do and say.'

'Fuck off, sexist..!'

Alan looked towards the middle of the room, where he thought the heckle had come from. A group of women, probably on a hen night, were getting louder and louder, oblivious the disruption they were causing to everyone else's night out.

'I see my girlfriend is in tonight,' he quipped.

'You wish!' shouted the girl in response.

'Actually, my fairy Godmother granted me three wishes this morning. But I think she misunderstood. I wanted a friend *with* benefits, not a friend *on* benefits.'

Alan's riposte received a welcome round of applause and a small cheer, but the heckler clearly was not phased into being quiet. 'Yeah, so what were your other two wishes?'

'That you fuck off and die.' At this the audience laughed and cheered, the biggest and best reaction Alan had had all night. Thankfully the heckler remained silent, her friends visibly urging her to keep her mouth shut.

'Sorry, where was I..? Oh yes. Women's toys. You see, bloke's toys are computer consuls, MP3 players. You know, practical stuff. Stuff that's useful around the house.

In a few years' time we will have robots to help women with the housework. Who will be responsible for these technological breakthroughs? That's right. Men. Men who want the latest gadgets. Men who push the boundaries of science by demanding affordable drones so that we can sneak a peek at our sexy neighbours as they sunbathe topless. It is men who are driving technology forwards. We are doing it for you, ladies. And you're welcome.

'But let's turn it round a little bit, shall we? Let's talk about women's toys. Let's see, there's the...' Alan mimed thinking hard, thumb and forefinger on chin. 'Let me see, there's...no I'm not sure a washing machine counts...There's nothing. Really nothing. The only toys women have are sex toys. Why is that?'

Alan half expected the rowdy hen party heckler to voice her opinion, but it seemed she was now more interested in her bottle of cheap Pinot Grigio than hurling abuse. Alan considered trying to wind her up some more, but decided to just finish the routine and get to the bar.

'Guys, perhaps we just have to accept we aren't enough to keep our women happy. All the nice things we do, like not forgetting birthdays and anniversaries, putting the rubbish out on only the third time of asking, it's just not enough. Women need something more. Something secret. Something with batteries.

'Ultimately, men's toys are visible, they're out in the open, available for all to see. Women's toys are hidden. Secret. Something to be ashamed of. And it's only right. You see, when men play games, their kids can join in. What man hasn't been slaughtered by a twelve year old boy on Football Manager? Then claimed his controls weren't working properly.

'But I just can't see little Alfie playing choo choo with a twelve inch black rubber dildo. Though I guess if he does, he'll end up playing with real dolls in a psychologist's office throughout his teens.

'What am I trying to say? Well, I guess women, and, to a lesser extent, men, have to take responsibility when their kids stay indoors all day playing and eat nothing but junk food. Because if you're not careful, one day it will be you explaining to a fireman just how your fat kid got stuck in a flume at the water park. Ladies and gentlemen...goodnight...'

*

Alan stood alone at the bar watching the female comedian on stage completely own the crowd. The more the audience laughed, the more depressed Alan became.

'She's better than you are.'

Alan didn't need to turn round to know that Frankie now stood beside him.

'Yeah, I know.' Alan agreed, running his hand through his hair. 'I feel as though I need to get back out there and do it all again. But funnier.'

'I know what you mean. Many's the time I came off stage thinking I needed to go back out and explain myself.' Frankie replied, seemingly lost in thought.

'So, how did you overcome it?'

'I'm not sure I did really, I just focused on the next gig.'

'I'm beginning to wonder if I'll ever make it.'

'Look, Alan, take my advice. If you really want to succeed in this business, you are going to have to work at it. And work hard. Give up your job and follow your dreams.'

'But Rosie will kill me.'

'Then I guess we could spend even more time together.'

'Great. Thanks. That's just what I need.'

'No, seriously. You have something. I've seen you do this routine a couple of times now. It's actually quite good...'

'...thanks...'

'It's just that, well, sometimes, it comes across as a little, well, *sexist*.'

Alan laughed, 'That's rich coming from someone who was around during the mother in law jokes.'

'I know, but did you meet my mother in law? Terrible woman. Seriously, if you had actually listened to my act, you would know that I always stayed away from the crappy sexist and racist gags that everyone else was doing. In fact, I was beginning to earn a few quid on the alternative comedy circuit when I had my heart attack.'

'Yeah, you mentioned that the other week at the theatre. Sorry. I had no idea.'

'That's OK, son, I don't think the alternative crowd were taking me that seriously anyway. Which was kind of the point.' Frankie grinned to himself at the memory. 'Listen,' he continued, 'I've been thinking. What would you say to getting a little help on your routine?'

'I'm sorry, I don't really want a writing partner. If nothing else, it would cost money.'

'No, son, that's not what I meant. I meant me. I reckon I could give you a few tips. And I won't need paying.'

'I don't know. It seems like cheating.'

'Who's going to know? And in any case, lots of people have a ghost writer.'

'I cannot believe you just said that,' Alan laughed. 'If that is as good as it gets, I may as well quit now.'

'Come on, son,' said Frankie, turning towards the bar. 'It's your round...'

'Sorry, Frankie, what do you want?' Alan asked, reaching into his pocket for his wallet before realising his error.

'Christ, son, I think you need all the help you can get.'

'Hang on, what are you still doing here?'

'Well, I was talking to you…'

'…No, that's not what I meant. I mean, the theatre has been saved.'

'I know, son. I was there, remember.'

'No, no, listen. You, *we,* thought that once the theatre was saved you would just disappear.'

'Charming. But I know what you mean,' said Frankie, staring down at his outstretched arms as though seeing them for the first time.

'But you're still here.'

'Obviously,' said Frankie, turning his hands up and down lost in thought.

'So, if you're not here because of the theatre, then why are you here..?'

'I don't know son. I really don't know.'

The End.

Acknowledgements

Thanks to Kit Foster at Kitfosterdesign.com for the brilliant cover and Robert Chute for the invaluable advice. We genuinely appreciate it.

And to Lucy and Dave for fresh eyes and endless encouragement.

And finally.

No bats were harmed in the writing of this book.